CONTENTS

INTRODUCTION

The Triumph of Artifice

Oscar Wilde's short run of success with his brilliant social comedies was one of the most remarkable episodes in literary history. In a span of just three years, from 1892 to 1895, Wilde established himself, alongside George Bernard Shaw, as the premier playwright of England. Then, just as quickly and brilliantly as he had ascended, Wilde plunged into obscurity. After three scandalous trials centering on the issue of Wilde's homosexuality, *The Importance of Being Earnest* and *An Ideal Husband* were shut down in the middle of their lucrative runs, and Wilde's career as a playwright was over. His writing was obscured by prurient rumor, homophobia, and hypocritical shock and condemnation.

It took decades for Wilde's work to reemerge as worthy of study. When it did, his readers found that the plays that had delighted Wilde's contemporary audiences had a doubled life on the page. What seemed on the surface to be merely ridiculous situations and nonsensical paradoxes designed to get a laugh revealed themselves to be subtle experiments in social critique and philosophy. Wilde's plays move expertly from the subject of faith in marriage to political power to motherhood and back to romance, desire, and identity. When scholars have returned to Wilde's life to mine its fascinating contradictions for insight into the quicksilver genius of the plays, they have found parables of identity, codes of gay life, and commentary on truth and art. Looking at *Salomé,* the only play presented in this volume that was banned from production in England, they found further evidence of Wilde's bold imagination, complexity, and tolerance for endless paradox.

For more than one hundred years, Wilde's comedies have retained their fresh laughter and their delicate grace, and Hollywood, whose worship of style and glamour could have been invented by Wilde himself, turns out new productions of them on a regular basis. *Salomé*'s weird sensuality and chilling perversity still shock and enthrall theatergoers in an age when it sometimes seems there are no taboos left. Wilde's epigrams, which have turned ever more from nonsense to truth as the years have progressed, are regularly quoted (and misquoted) by those who have no idea that they were written by Wilde, let alone which play they come from. To enter the world of these plays is to be lifted into Wilde's strange and surprising world and to realize how thoroughly his sensibility has become our own.

Life and Work of Oscar Wilde

Oscar Fingal O'Flahertie Wills Wilde was born on October 16, 1854, to the Irish nationalist and writer Speranza Wilde and eye-and-ear doctor William Wilde. Young Oscar did exceptionally well at school, earning scholarships and taking high honors at both Trinity College Dublin and Oxford. While at Oxford, he met his teacher and mentor, Walter Pater, and became an enthusiastic follower of the aesthetic movement Pater championed.

After graduating from Oxford in 1874, Wilde moved to London. He quickly gained notoriety for his sharp wit and flamboyant style of dress—he was especially famous for wearing a dyed-green carnation, a French symbol of decadence and homosexuality, in his lapel. In addition to writing plays and criticism, Wilde traveled in London's most brilliant social circles, becoming a local celebrity. When he traveled to America to speak on aestheticism in 1882, he thrilled audiences from New York City socialites to western miners. By the time he returned to London, he was a transatlantic sensation.

In the early 1880s, Wilde was regularly publishing plays and poems, but they were received badly. It wasn't until the late 1880s and early 1890s that he published some of his best-loved works, including *The Happy Prince and Other Tales* (1888), as well as a number of influential critical volumes, including *Intentions* (1891) and *The Soul of Man under Socialism* (1891).

Wilde married Constance Lloyd in 1884. They had two sons, Cyril (1885) and Vyvyan (1886). Wilde had been married only two years when he met Robert Ross, who claimed to have initiated him into physical homosexuality. Whether or not he did, Ross became a close and loyal friend to Wilde and later was his literary executor.

In 1891, the thirty-seven-year-old Wilde was captivated by handsome, spoiled, twenty-year-old playboy Lord Alfred "Bosie" Douglas and began the major affair of his life, one whose volatility soon would endanger him. The same year, Wilde's greatly expanded version of the "Dorian Gray" story was published as the novel *The Picture of Dorian Gray.* Dorian's sensual life caused enormous controversy—almost as much as Wilde's life itself. Together, Dorian and Bosie spelled disaster for Wilde.

Wilde's relationship with Douglas infuriated the latter's father, the Marquess of Queensberry. When Queensberry left a card for Wilde at his club, addressed to "Oscar Wilde, Somdomite [*sic*]," Wilde foolishly sued for libel. He lost, and Queensberry retaliated by instituting proceedings against Wilde for homosexuality. Waving aside opportunities to flee England, Wilde stood two trials. The first ended without a verdict. At the end of the second trial, Wilde was convicted and sentenced to two years in prison. Because Queensberry forced him into bankruptcy, all his possessions were auctioned. Tragically, Wilde's downfall came at the height of his career. *An Ideal Husband* and *The Importance of Being Earnest* had been playing to full houses in London.

Although he was allowed only one sheet of paper at a time while in prison, Wilde managed to compose *De Profundis,* a chronicle of his spiritual quest. During his years in prison, his mother died, and his wife, Constance, moved abroad and took the name of Holland for herself and their sons. After her death in 1898, Wilde was denied access to his sons. When he had served his sentence, a greatly weakened Wilde moved to Paris and took the name Sebastian Melmoth, after the protaganist of *Melmoth the Wanderer,* a novel about a man who sells his soul to the devil, written by Wilde's relative Reverend Charles Maturin. In the final years of his life, Wilde wrote little besides "The Ballad of Reading Gaol," which he signed only as "C.3.3," the number of his cell. Wilde died in a hotel room, either of syphilis or of complications from an ear infection and meningitis, in Paris on November 30, 1900.

Historical and Literary Context

The late Victorian era

Wilde's life and work belong to the late Victorian era, a period marked by both genteel country house parties and growing political unrest. The complicated tangle of political matters known as the "Irish Question" was particularly urgent. Home Rule, the idea that the Irish could and should rule themselves, was one of the great controversies of the day. The great wave of the Industrial Revolution had swelled England's cities with underpaid, exploited workers who lived in teeming slums. Karl Marx and Friedrich Engels had published their famous works—*The Communist Manifesto* and *Capital*—and the question of the laborer and his role in society was fiercely debated, especially as some workers gained the vote and the labor movement became an important force in politics. The "New Woman" was growing increasingly vocal in her demands for freedom, education, political power, and clothes that allowed her to move and breathe easily while she campaigned for equality. Abroad, the great British Empire, ever more important to the "luster of the crown" in the popular imagination, drifted in and out of crisis.

Fin de siècle, Decadence, and Symbolism

In addition to being a part of this tumultuous era, Wilde's plays also responded to the mood special to the 1890s, or the *fin de siècle* ("end of the century"), as it was known in France. Exhausted by nearly a century of cultural, economic, political, technological, and religious change, Victorians on the brink of the century's turn affected a jaded weariness and searched out fresh sensations and spectacles to relieve their ennui. In France, the *fin de siècle* expressed itself in the Decadence movement, which sought beauty in that which mainstream society rejected as gruesome, immoral, and perverse, and in the experiments of the Symbolist poets and playwrights, who rejected the tenets of Realism and sought instead to provide a link to the inexpressible. Rather than emphasizing meaning and plot, the

Symbolists experimented with patterns of color, sound, and synesthesia. The experimental, color-coded lyricism of *Salomé* owes much to the Symbolists—Wilde conceived of the play while in Paris and originally wrote it in French. The father of the Decadence movement was Symbolist poet Charles Baudelaire, author of *Les fleurs du mal (The Flowers of Evil*, 1857), which provided the Symbolists with their pattern. Joris-Karl Huysmans's 1884 novel *A rebours (Against the Grain)*, referred to as "the little yellow book," was a virtual textbook for Decadence and profoundly influenced Wilde. Other poets associated with the Decadence movement include Arthur Rimbaud, Paul Verlaine, and Stéphane Mallarmé.

Aestheticism

While Decadence reigned in France, Aestheticism flourished in England. Wilde's teacher and friend at Oxford, Walter Pater, was regarded as the founder of the movement. In *Studies in the History of the Renaissance* (1873), Pater had explored in intimate, seductive detail the pleasures of a life devoted to the appreciation of beauty and had called for his readers to fan the "hard, gem-like flame" of self-fulfillment through a devotion to their senses. In the context of a Victorian culture devoted to efficiency, the bottom line, and the suppression of sensuality in all its forms, this was a radical idea. Pitting themselves directly against the moralizing sentimentality of didactic Victorian art and literature (such as the "three volume novels" mentioned in *The Importance of Being Earnest*), the Aestheticists argued that art's role was not to be moral or useful or to teach "lessons" but to be an object of beauty that transcended humans and human questions. The Aestheticists strove to make their lives works of art, an idea typified by Wilde's devotion to the artful dress and speech of the dandy.

"Well-made plays" and the new social realism

In the mid-Victorian age, the theater had fallen into disrepute and had been replaced by that enchanting new literary genre, the novel. But by the late Victorian age, the respectable middle class had been wooed back to the theater by pleasant entertainments such as Gilbert and Sullivan's musicals and the "well-made plays" patterned after French playwright Eugene Scribe's template. These fashionable, lavishly produced, technically adroit, but insubstantial comedies and melodramas were the Hollywood films of their day. They provided thrills, chills, spills, and happy endings (or a good, moral cry). Although these works often dabbled in immorality—adultery was a common subject—transgressors were always punished, villains and heroes were easily identified, and the more dangerous subjects were set safely in ancient history. In the early 1890s, the new Social Realism of Norwegian playwright Henrik Ibsen arrived to baffle and scandalize the fans of well-made plays with thrillingly intense examinations of the dark side of middle-class life. Wilde admired Ibsen's daring critique, but, like the Symbolists, he rejected the tenets of Realism, choosing instead to subvert the well-made plays to his own end in the same ways in which his dandies subvert their social worlds without ever leaving them.

CHRONOLOGY OF OSCAR WILDE'S LIFE AND WORK

1854: Oscar Fingal O'Flahertie Wills Wilde is born in Dublin on October 16.

1871: Wilde studies Classics at Trinity College Dublin on scholarship.

1874: He wins a scholarship to Magdalen College, Oxford, where he studies Greek and Classics. He meets teachers John Ruskin and Walter Pater.

1877: Wilde reviews the Grosvenor Gallery, his first published prose and criticism.

1878: He wins the Newdigate Prize for Poetry for "Ravenna."

1880: *Vera*, a play, is published and badly received.

1881: Wilde self-publishes *Poems*, which is badly received.

1882: He goes to America on a wildly successful lecture tour.

1883: *The Duchess of Padua* is not successful.

1884: Wilde marries Constance Lloyd.

1885: Son Cyril is born.

1886: Son Vyvyan is born. Wilde meets Robert Ross.

1887: Wilde becomes editor of *The Lady's World* for two years.

1888: *The Happy Prince and Other Tales* is published.

1890: "The Picture of Dorian Gray" is published as a story in *Lippincott's Monthly Magazine;* controversy ensues.

1891: The revised version of "Dorian Gray" is released as a book. Wilde meets Lord Alfred "Bosie" Douglas. He publishes *Intentions, Lord Arthur's Savile Crime and Other Stories, The Soul of Man under Socialism,* and *A House of Pomegranates.* In November and December, he writes *Salomé.*

1892: *Salomé* is banned from the British stage, and *Lady Windermere's Fan* is produced to critical and general acclaim.

1893: *A Woman of No Importance* is produced successfully.

1894: An English translation of *Salomé* by Lord Alfred Douglas is published, with censored drawings by Aubrey Beardsley.

1895: The hits *The Importance of Being Earnest* and *An Ideal Husband* are produced. Wilde stands trial for homosexuality. The first trial ends without a verdict. After a second trial, on May 25, he is convicted and sentenced to two years in prison. Both plays are shut down in spite of their huge financial success.

1896: Wilde's mother dies.

1897: Wilde composes *De Profundis* in prison. In May, he is released, adopts the name Sebastian Melmoth, and moves to France.

1898: Wilde publishes "The Ballad of Reading Gaol" under the name "C.3.3.," the number of his cell. Constance Wilde dies.

1900: Ill, penniless, and exiled, Wilde converts to Catholicism on his deathbed and dies in Paris on November 30.

HISTORICAL CONTEXT OF
The Importance of Being Earnest and Other Plays

1837: Queen Victoria is crowned.

1853: France outlaws cross-dressing.

1854: Arthur Rimbaud is born.

1855: Walt Whitman publishes the first edition of *Leaves of Grass*.

1859: Charles Darwin publishes *On the Origin of Species*.

1861: The death penalty is abolished as a punishment for sodomy in England.

1865: *The Fortnightly Review* is founded by Anthony Trollope and others. William Butler Yeats is born.

1868–69: The Spanish Revolution; Queen Isabela abdicates.

1869: André Gide is born.

1870: The Second Industrial Revolution begins. Isaac Butt introduces Home Rule in Dublin, proposing that the Irish rule themselves.

1872: Théophile Gautier dies.

1873: Walter Pater's *Studies in the History of the Renaissance* is published.

1882: Henry James's *The Portrait of a Lady* is published.

1883: The Orient Express makes its first run.

1885–98: Height of French Symbolism and artistic Decadence movements.

1885–1940: Irish Literary Renaissance.

1885: The Criminal Law Amendment Act, calling for two years' imprisonment for any male convicted of "gross indecency," is passed in England.

1888: In the Whitechapel area of London, Jack the Ripper kills several prostitutes.

1894: *The Yellow Book*, a magazine of aesthetic arts and literature, is founded by Aubrey Beardsley, Henry Harland, and John Lane.

1895: The Aesthetic movement is widely considered to end with Wilde's trial.

1967: England decriminalizes sodomy.

THE IMPORTANCE OF
BEING EARNEST

THE PERSONS OF THE PLAY

JOHN WORTHING, J.P. — Wants to go to country
ALGERNON MONCRIEFF
REV. CANON CHASUBLE, D.D.
MR. GRIBSBY, Solicitor
MERRIMAN, Butler
LANE, Manservant
MOULTON, Gardener
LADY BRACKNELL
HON. GWENDOLEN FAIRFAX
CECILY CARDEW
MISS PRISM, Governess

Act One

SCENE: *Morning-room in Algernon's flat in Half-Moon Street,*[1] *London, W.* TIME: *The present. The room is luxuriously and artistically furnished. The sound of a piano is heard in the adjoining room.*

> LANE *is arranging afternoon tea on the table, and after the music has ceased,* ALGERNON *enters.*

ALGERNON: Did you hear what I was playing, Lane?

LANE: I didn't think it polite to listen, sir.

ALGERNON: I'm sorry for that, for your sake. I don't play accurately—any one can play accurately—but I play with wonderful expression. As far as the piano is concerned, sentiment is my forte. I keep science for Life.

LANE: Yes, sir.

ALGERNON: And, speaking of the science of Life, have you got the cucumber sandwiches cut for Lady Bracknell?

LANE: Yes, sir.

ALGERNON: Ahem! Where are they?

LANE: Here, sir. (*Shows plate.*)

ALGERNON: *(inspects them, takes two, and sits down on the sofa):* Oh! . . . by the way, Lane, I see from your book that on Thursday night, when Lord Shoreman and Mr. Worthing were dining with me, eight bottles of champagne are entered as having been consumed.

LANE: Yes, sir; eight bottles and a pint.

ALGERNON: Why is it that at a bachelor's establishment the servants invariably drink the champagne? I ask merely for information.

LANE: I attribute it to the superior quality of the wine, sir. I have often observed that in married households the champagne is rarely of a first-rate brand.

ALGERNON: Good heavens! Is marriage so demoralising as that?

LANE: I believe it *is* a very pleasant state, sir. I have had very little experience of it myself up to the present. I have only been married once. That was in consequence of a misunderstanding between myself and a young person.

ALGERNON *(languidly):* I don't know that I am much interested in your family life, Lane.

LANE: No, sir; it is not a very interesting subject. I never think of it myself.

ALGERNON: Very natural, I am sure. That will do, Lane, thank you.

LANE: Thank you, sir. (LANE *moves to go out.*)

ALGERNON: Ah! . . . just give me another cucumber sandwich.

LANE: Yes, sir. *(Returns and hands plate.)*

LANE *goes out.*

ALGERNON: Lane's views on marriage seem somewhat lax. Really, if the lower orders don't set us a good example, what on earth is the use of them? They seem, as a class, to have absolutely no sense of moral responsibility.

Enter LANE.

LANE: Mr. Ernest Worthing.

Enter JACK. LANE *goes out.*

ALGERNON: How are you, my dear Ernest? What brings you up to town?

JACK: Oh, pleasure, pleasure! What else should bring one anywhere? Eating as usual. I see, Algy!

ALGERNON *(stiffly)*: I believe it is customary in good society to take some slight refreshment at five o'clock. Where have you been since last Thursday?

JACK *(sitting down on the sofa)*: Oh! in the country.

ALGERNON: What on earth do you do there?

JACK *(pulling off his gloves)*: When one is in town one amuses oneself. When one is in the country one amuses other people. It is excessively boring.

ALGERNON: And who are the people you amuse?

JACK *(airily)*: Oh, neighbours, neighbours.

ALGERNON: Got nice neighbours in your part of Shropshire?[2]

JACK: Perfectly horrid! Never speak to one of them.

ALGERNON: How immensely you must amuse them! *(Goes over and takes sandwich.)* By the way, Shropshire is your county, is it not?

JACK: Eh? Shropshire? Yes, of course. Hallo! Why all these cups? Why cucumber sandwiches? Why such reckless extravagance in one so young? Who is coming to tea?

ALGERNON: Oh! merely Aunt Augusta and Gwendolen.

JACK: How perfectly delightful!

ALGERNON: Yes, that is all very well; but I am afraid Aunt Augusta won't quite approve of your being here.

JACK: May I ask why?

ALGERNON: My dear fellow, the way you flirt with Gwendolen is perfectly disgraceful. It is almost as bad as the way Gwendolen flirts with you.

JACK: I am in love with Gwendolen. I have come up to town expressly to propose to her.

ALGERNON: I thought you had come up for pleasure? . . . I call that business.

JACK: How utterly unromantic you are!

ALGERNON: I really don't see anything romantic in proposing. It is very romantic to be in love. But there is nothing romantic about a definite proposal. Why, one may be accepted. One usually is, I believe. Then the excitement is all over. The very essence of romance is uncertainty. If ever I get married, I'll certainly try to forget the fact.

JACK: I have no doubt about that, dear Algy. The Divorce Court was specially invented for people whose memories are so curiously constituted.

ALGERNON: Oh! there is no use speculating on that subject. Divorces are made in heaven—(JACK *puts out his hand to take a sandwich.* ALGERNON *at once interferes.*) Please don't touch the cucumber sandwiches. They are ordered specially for Aunt Augusta. *(Takes one and eats it.)*

JACK: Well, you have been eating them all the time.

ALGERNON: That is quite a different matter. She is my aunt. *(Takes plate from below.)* Have some bread and butter. The bread and butter is for Gwendolen. Gwendolen is devoted to bread and butter.

JACK *(advancing to table and helping himself)*: And very good bread and butter it is too.

ALGERNON: Well, my dear fellow, you need not eat as if you were going to eat it all. You behave as if you were married to her already. You are not married to her already, and I don't think you ever will be.

JACK: Why on earth do you say that?

ALGERNON: Well, in the first place girls never marry the men they flirt with. Girls don't think it right.

JACK: Oh, that is nonsense!

ALGERNON: It isn't. It is a great truth. It accounts for the extraordinary number of bachelors that one sees all over the place. In the second place, I don't give my consent.

JACK: Your consent! What utter nonsense you talk!

ALGERNON: My dear fellow, Gwendolen is my first cousin. And before I allow you to marry her, you will have to clear up the whole question of Cecily.

JACK: Cecily! What on earth do you mean? (ALGERNON *goes to the bell and rings it. Then returns to tea table and eats another sandwich.*) What do you mean, Algy, by Cecily! I don't know any one of the name of Cecily . . . as far as I remember.

Enter LANE.

ALGERNON: Bring me that cigarette case Mr. Worthing left in the smoking-room the last time he dined here.

LANE: Yes, sir.

LANE *goes out.*

JACK: Do you mean to say you have had my cigarette case all this time? I wish to goodness you had let me know. I have been writing frantic letters to Scotland Yard[3] about it. I was very nearly offering a large reward.

ALGERNON: Well, I wish you would offer one. I happen to be more than usually hard up.

JACK: There is no good offering a large reward now that the thing is found.

Enter LANE *with the cigarette case on a salver.* ALGERNON *takes it at once.* LANE *goes out.*

ALGERNON: I think that is rather mean of you, Ernest, I must say. (*Opens case and examines it.*) However, it makes no matter, for, now that I look at the inscription inside, I find that the thing isn't yours after all.

JACK: Of course it's mine. *(Moving to him.)* You have seen me with it a hundred times, and you have no right whatsoever to read what is written inside. It is a very ungentlemanly thing to read a private cigarette case.

ALGERNON: Oh! it is absurd to have a hard and fast rule about what one should read and what one shouldn't. One should read everything. More than half of modern culture depends on what one shouldn't read.

JACK: I am quite aware of the fact, and I don't propose to discuss modern culture. It isn't the sort of thing one should talk of in private. I simply want my cigarette case back.

ALGERNON: Yes; but this isn't your cigarette case. This cigarette case is a present from some one of the name of Cecily, and you said you didn't know any one of that name.

JACK: Well, if you want to know, Cecily happens to be my aunt.

ALGERNON: Your aunt!

JACK: Yes. Charming old lady she is, too. Lives at Tunbridge Wells.[4] Just give it back to me, Algy.

ALGERNON *(retreating to back of sofa)*: But why does she call herself little Cecily if she is your aunt and lives at Tunbridge Wells? *(Reading.)* "From little Cecily with her fondest love."

JACK *(moving to sofa and kneeling upon it)*: My dear fellow, what on earth is there in that? Some aunts are tall, some aunts are not tall. That is a matter that surely an aunt may be allowed to decide for herself. You seem to think that every aunt should be exactly like your aunt! That is absurd! For Heaven's sake give me back my cigarette case. *(Follows ALGERNON round the room.)*

ALGERNON: Yes. But why does your aunt call you her uncle? "From little Cecily, with her fondest love to her dear Uncle Jack." There is no objection, I admit, to an aunt being a small aunt, but why an aunt, no matter what her size may be, should call her own nephew her uncle, I can't quite make out. Besides, your name isn't Jack at all; it is Ernest.

JACK: It isn't Ernest; it's Jack.

ALGERNON: You have always told me it was Ernest. I have introduced you to every one as Ernest. You answer to the name of Ernest. You look as if your name was Ernest. You are the most earnest-looking person I ever saw in my life. It is perfectly absurd your saying that your name isn't Ernest. It's on your cards. Here is one of them. *(Taking it from case.)* "Mr. Ernest Worthing, B.4, The Albany, W." I'll keep this as a proof that your name is Ernest if ever you attempt to deny it to me, or to Gwendolen, or to any one else. *(Puts the card in his pocket.)*

JACK: Well, my name is Ernest in town and Jack in the country, and the cigarette case was given to me in the country.

ALGERNON: Yes, but that does not account for the fact that your small Aunt Cecily, who lives at Tunbridge Wells, calls you her dear Uncle. Come, old boy, you had much better have the thing out at once.

JACK: My dear Algy, you talk exactly as if you were a dentist. It is very vulgar to talk like a dentist when one isn't a dentist. It produces a false impression.

ALGERNON: Well, that is exactly what dentists always do. Now, go on! Tell me the whole thing. I may mention that I have always suspected you of being a confirmed and secret Bunburyist; and I am quite sure of it now.

JACK: Bunburyist? What on earth do you mean by a Bunburyist?

ALGERNON: I'll reveal to you the meaning of that incomparable expression as soon as you are kind enough to inform me why you are Ernest in town and Jack in the country.

JACK: Well, produce my cigarette case first.

ALGERNON: Here it is. *(Hands cigarette case.)* Now produce your explanation, and pray make it improbable. *(Sits on sofa.)*

JACK: My dear fellow, there is nothing improbable about my explanation at all. In fact, it's perfectly ordinary. Old Mr. Thomas Cardew, who adopted me when I was a little boy, under rather peculiar circumstances, and left me all the money I possess, made me in his will guardian to his grand-daughter, Miss Cecily Cardew. Cecily, who addresses me as her uncle from motives of respect that you could not possibly appreciate, lives at my place in the country under the charge of her admirable governess, Miss Prism.

ALGERNON: Where is that place in the country, by the way?

JACK: That is nothing to you, dear boy. You are not going to be invited. . . . I may tell you candidly that the place is not in Shropshire.

ALGERNON: I suspected that, my dear fellow! I have Bunburyed all over Shropshire on two separate occasions. Now, go on. Why are you Ernest in town and Jack in the country?

JACK: My dear Algy, I don't know whether you will be able to understand my real motives. You are hardly serious enough. When one is placed in the position of guardian, one has to adopt a very high moral tone on all subjects. It's one's duty to do so. And as a high moral tone can hardly be said to conduce very much to either one's health or one's happiness if carried to excess, in order to get up to town I have always pretended to have a younger brother of the name of Ernest, who lives in the Albany,⁵ and gets into the most dreadful scrapes. That, my dear Algy, is the whole truth pure and simple.

ALGERNON: The truth is rarely pure and never simple.

Modern life would be very tedious if it were either, and modern literature a complete impossibility!

JACK: That wouldn't be at all a bad thing.

ALGERNON: Literary criticism is not your forte, my dear fellow. Don't try it. You should leave that to people who haven't been at a University. They do it so well in the daily papers. What you really are is a Bunburyist. I was quite right in saying you were a Bunburyist. You are one of the most advanced Bunburyists I know.

JACK: What on earth do you mean?

ALGERNON: You have invented a very useful younger brother called Ernest, in order that you may be able to come up to town as often as you like. I have invented an invaluable permanent invalid called Bunbury, in order that I may be able to go down into the country whenever I choose.

JACK: What nonsense.

ALGERNON: It isn't nonsense. Bunbury is perfectly invaluable. If it wasn't for Bunbury's extraordinary bad health, for instance, I wouldn't be able to dine with you at the Savoy[6] to-night, for I have been really engaged to Aunt Augusta for more than a week.

JACK: I haven't asked you to dine with me anywhere to-night.

ALGERNON: I know. You are absurdly careless about sending out invitations. It is very foolish of you. Nothing annoys people so much as not receiving invitations.

JACK: Well, I can't dine at the Savoy. I owe them about £700. They are always getting judgments and things against me. They bother my life out.

ALGERNON: Why on earth don't you pay them? You have got heaps of money.

JACK: Yes, but Ernest hasn't, and I must keep up Ernest's reputation. Ernest is one of those chaps who never pays a bill. He gets writted about once a week.

ALGERNON: Well, let us dine at Willis's.

JACK: You had much better dine with your Aunt Augusta.

ALGERNON: I haven't the smallest intention of doing any-thing of the kind. To begin with, I dined there on Mon-day, and once a week is quite enough to dine with one's own relations. In the second place, whenever I do dine there I am always treated as a member of the family, and sent down[7] with either no woman at all, or two. In the third place, I know perfectly well whom she will place me next to, to-night. She will place me next Mary Far-quhar, who always flirts with her own husband across the dinner-table. That is not very pleasant. Indeed, it is not even decent . . . and that sort of thing is enormously on the increase. The amount of women in London who flirt with their own husbands is perfectly scandalous. It looks so bad. It is simply washing one's clean linen in public. Besides, now that I know you to be a confirmed Bun-buryist I naturally want to talk to you about Bunburying. I want to tell you the rules.

JACK: I'm not a Bunburyist at all. If Gwendolen accepts me, I am going to kill my brother, indeed I think I'll kill him in any case. Cecily is a little too much interested in him. She is always asking me to forgive him, and that sort of thing. It is rather a bore. So I am going to get rid of Ernest. And I strongly advise you to do the same with Mr. . . . with your invalid friend who has the absurd name.

ALGERNON: Nothing will induce me to part with Bunbury, and if you ever get married, which seems to me ex-tremely problematic, you will be very glad to know Bun-bury. A man who marries without knowing Bunbury has a very tedious time of it.

JACK: That is nonsense. If I marry a charming girl like Gwendolen, and she is the only girl I ever saw in my life that I would marry, I certainly won't want to know Bun-bury.

ALGERNON: Then your wife will. You don't seem to realise, that in married life three is company and two is none.

JACK (*sententiously*): That, my dear young friend, is the theory that the corrupt French Drama[8] has been propounding for the last fifty years.

ALGERNON: Yes; and that the happy English home has proved in half the time.

JACK: For heaven's sake, don't try to be cynical. It's perfectly easy to be cynical.

ALGERNON: My dear fellow, it isn't easy to be anything nowadays. There's such a lot of beastly competition about. (*The sound of an electric bell is heard.*) Ah! that must be Aunt Augusta. Only relatives, or creditors, ever ring in that Wagnerian manner.[9] Now, if I get her out of the way for ten minutes, so that you can have an opportunity for proposing to Gwendolen, may I dine with you tonight at Willis's?

JACK: I suppose so, if you want to.

ALGERNON: Yes, but you must be serious about it. I hate people who are not serious about meals. It is so shallow of them.

Enter LANE.

LANE: Lady Bracknell and Miss Fairfax.

ALGERNON *goes forward to meet them. Enter* LADY BRACKNELL *and* GWENDOLEN.

LADY BRACKNELL: Good-afternoon, dear Algernon, I hope you are behaving very well.

ALGERNON: I'm feeling very well, Aunt Augusta.

LADY BRACKNELL: That's not quite the same thing. In fact the two things rarely go together. (*Sees* JACK *and bows to him with icy coldness.*)

ALGERNON (*to* GWENDOLEN): Dear me, you are smart!

GWENDOLEN: I am always smart! Am I not, Mr. Worthing?

JACK: You're quite perfect, Miss Fairfax.

GWENDOLEN: Oh! I hope I am not that. It would leave no room for developments, and I intend to develop in many directions. (GWENDOLEN *and* JACK *sit down together in the corner.*)

LADY BRACKNELL: I'm sorry if we are a little late, Algernon, but I was obliged to call on dear Lady Harbury. I hadn't been there since her poor husband's death. I never saw a woman so altered; she looks quite twenty years younger. And now I'll have a cup of tea, and one of those nice cucumber sandwiches you promised me.

ALGERNON: Certainly, Aunt Augusta. *(Goes over to tea table.)*

LADY BRACKNELL: Won't you come and sit here, Gwendolen?

GWENDOLEN: Thanks, mamma, I'm quite comfortable where I am.

ALGERNON *(picking up empty plate in horror)*: Good heavens! Lane! Why are there no cucumber sandwiches? I ordered them specially.

LANE *(gravely)*: There were no cucumbers in the market this morning, sir. I went down twice.

ALGERNON: No cucumbers!

LANE: No, sir. Not even for ready money.[10]

ALGERNON: That will do, Lane, thank you.

LANE: Thank you, sir. *(Goes out.)*

ALGERNON: I am greatly distressed, Aunt Augusta, about there being no cucumbers, not even for ready money.

LADY BRACKNELL: It really makes no matter, Algernon. I had some crumpets with Lady Harbury, who seems to me to be living entirely for pleasure now.

ALGERNON: I hear her hair has turned quite gold from grief.

LADY BRACKNELL: It certainly has changed its colour. From what cause I, of course, cannot say. (ALGERNON *crosses and hands tea.*) Thank you. I've quite a treat for you to-night, Algernon. I am going to send you down with Mary Farquhar. She is such a nice woman, and so attentive to her husband. It's delightful to watch them.

ALGERNON: I am afraid, Aunt Augusta, I shall have to give up the pleasure of dining with you to-night after all.

LADY BRACKNELL (*frowning*): I hope not, Algernon. It would put my table completely out. Your uncle would have to dine upstairs. Fortunately he is accustomed to that.

ALGERNON: It is a great bore, and, I need hardly say, a terrible disappointment to me, but the fact is I have just had a telegram to say that my poor friend Bunbury is very ill again. (*Exchanges glances with* JACK.) They seem to think I should be with him.

LADY BRACKNELL: It is very strange. This Mr. Bunbury seems to suffer from curiously bad health.

ALGERNON: Yes; poor Bunbury is a dreadful invalid.

LADY BRACKNELL: Well, I must say, Algernon, that I think it is high time that Mr. Bunbury made up his mind whether he was going to live or to die. This shilly-shallying with the question is absurd. Nor do I in any way approve of the modern sympathy with invalids. I consider it morbid. Illness of any kind is hardly a thing to be encouraged in others. Health is the primary duty of life. I am always telling that to your poor uncle, but he never seems to take much notice . . . as far as any improvement in his ailment goes. Well, Algernon, of course if you are obliged to be beside the bedside of Mr. Bunbury, I have nothing more to say. But I would be much obliged if you would ask Mr. Bunbury, from me, to be kind enough not to have a relapse on Saturday, for I rely on you to arrange my music for me. It is my last reception, and one wants something that will encourage conversation, particularly at the end of the season[11] when every one has practically said whatever they had to say, which, in most cases, was probably not much.

ALGERNON: I'll speak to Bunbury, Aunt Augusta, if he is still conscious, and I think I can promise you he'll be all right by Saturday. Of course the music is a great difficulty. You see, if one plays good music, people don't listen, and if one plays bad music people don't talk. But I'll run over the programme I've drawn out, if you will kindly come into the next room for a moment.

LADY BRACKNELL: Thank you, Algernon. It is very thoughtful of you. (*Rising and following* ALGERNON.) I'm sure the programme will be delightful, after a few expurgations. French songs I cannot possibly allow. People always seem to think that they are improper, and either look shocked, which is vulgar, or laugh, which is worse. But German sounds a thoroughly respectable language, and indeed, I believe is so. Gwendolen, you will accompany me.

GWENDOLEN: Certainly, mamma.

LADY BRACKNELL *and* ALGERNON *go into the music-room,* GWENDOLEN *remains behind.*

JACK: Charming day it has been, Miss Fairfax.

GWENDOLEN: Pray don't talk to me about the weather, Mr. Worthing. Whenever people talk to me about the weather, I always feel quite certain that they mean something else. And that makes me so nervous.

JACK: I do mean something else.

GWENDOLEN: I thought so. In fact, I am never wrong.

JACK: And I would like to be allowed to take advantage of Lady Bracknell's temporary absence . . .

GWENDOLEN: I would certainly advise you to do so. Mamma has a way of coming back suddenly into a room that I have often had to speak to her about.

JACK (*nervously*): Miss Fairfax, ever since I met you I have admired you more than any girl . . . I have ever met since . . . I met you.

GWENDOLEN: Yes, I am quite well aware of the fact. And I often wish that in public, at any rate, you had been more demonstrative. For me you have always had an irresistible fascination. Even before I met you I was far from indifferent to you. (JACK *looks at her in amazement.*) We live, as I hope you know, Mr. Worthing, in an age of ideals. The fact is constantly mentioned in the more expensive monthly magazines, and has now reached the provincial pulpits, I am told; and my ideal has always been to love some one of the name of Ernest. There is something in that name that inspires absolute confidence. The moment Algernon first mentioned to me that he had a friend called Ernest, I knew I was destined to love you. The name, fortunately for my peace of mind, is, as far as my own experience goes, extremely rare.

JACK: You really love me, Gwendolen?

GWENDOLEN: Passionately!

JACK: Darling! You don't know how happy you've made me.

GWENDOLEN: My own Ernest! (*They embrace.*)

JACK: But you don't really mean to say that you couldn't love me if my name wasn't Ernest?

GWENDOLEN: But your name is Ernest.

JACK: Yes, I know it is. But supposing it was something else? Do you mean to say you couldn't love me then?

GWENDOLEN (*glibly*): Ah! that is clearly a metaphysical speculation, and like most metaphysical speculations has very little reference at all to the actual facts of real life, as we know them.

JACK: Personally, darling, to speak quite candidly, I don't much care about the name of Ernest. . . . I don't think the name suits me at all.

GWENDOLEN: It suits you perfectly. It is a divine name. It has a music of its own. It produces vibrations.

JACK: Well, really, Gwendolen, I must say that I think there are lots of other much nicer names. I think Jack, for instance, a charming name.

GWENDOLEN: Jack? . . . No, there is very little music in the name Jack, if any at all, indeed. It does not thrill. It produces absolutely no vibrations. . . . I have known several Jacks, and they all, without exception, were more than usually plain. Besides, Jack is a notorious domesticity for John! And I pity any woman who is married to a man called John. She would have a very tedious life with him. She would probably never be allowed to know the entrancing pleasure of a single moment's solitude. The only really safe name is Ernest.

JACK: Gwendolen, I must get christened at once—I mean we must get married at once. There is no time to be lost.

GWENDOLEN: Married, Mr. Worthing?

JACK *(astounded)*: Well . . . surely. You know that I love you, and you led me to believe, Miss Fairfax, that you were not absolutely indifferent to me.

GWENDOLEN: I adore you. But you haven't proposed to me yet. Nothing has been said at all about marriage. The subject has not even been touched on.

JACK: Well . . . may I propose to you now?

GWENDOLEN: I think it would be an admirable opportunity. And to spare you any possible disappointment, Mr. Worthing, I think it only fair to tell you quite frankly beforehand that I am fully determined to accept you.

JACK: Gwendolen!

GWENDOLEN: Yes, Mr. Worthing, what have you got to say to me?

JACK: You know what I have got to say to you.

GWENDOLEN: Yes, but you don't say it.

JACK: Gwendolen, will you marry me? *(Goes on his knees.)*

GWENDOLEN: Of course I will, darling. How long you have

been about it! I am afraid you have had very little experience in how to propose.

JACK: My own one, I have never loved anyone in the world but you.

GWENDOLEN: Yes, but men often propose for practice. I know my brother Gerald does. All my girl-friends tell me so. What wonderfully blue eyes you have, Ernest! They are quite, quite blue. I hope you will always look at me just like that, especially when there are other people present.

Enter LADY BRACKNELL.

LADY BRACKNELL: Mr. Worthing! Rise, sir, from this semi-recumbent posture. It is most indecorous.

GWENDOLEN: Mamma! *(He tries to rise; she restrains him.)* I must beg you to retire. This is no place for you. Besides, Mr. Worthing has not quite finished yet.

LADY BRACKNELL: Finished what, may I ask?

GWENDOLEN: I am engaged to Mr. Worthing, mamma. *(They rise together.)*

LADY BRACKNELL: Pardon me, you are not engaged to any one. When you do become engaged to some one, I, or your father, should his health permit him, will inform you of the fact. An engagement should come on a young girl as a surprise, pleasant or unpleasant, as the case may be. It is hardly a matter that she could be allowed to arrange for herself. . . . And now I have a few questions to put to you, Mr. Worthing!

JACK: I shall be charmed to reply to any questions, Lady Bracknell.

GWENDOLEN: You mean if you know the answers to them. Mamma's questions are sometimes peculiarly inquisitorial.

LADY BRACKNELL: I intend to make them very inquisitorial. And while I am making these inquiries, you, Gwendolen, will wait for me below in the carriage.

GWENDOLEN (*reproachfully*): Mamma!

LADY BRACKNELL: In the carriage, Gwendolen!

> GWENDOLEN *goes to the door. She and* JACK *blow kisses to each other behind* LADY BRACKNELL's *back.*
>
>   LADY BRACKNELL *looks vaguely about as if she could not understand what the noise was. Finally turns round.*

Gwendolen, the carriage!

GWENDOLEN: Yes, mamma. (*Goes out, looking back at* JACK.)

LADY BRACKNELL (*sitting down*): You can take a seat, Mr. Worthing.

Looks in her pocket for note-book and pencil.

JACK: Thank you, Lady Bracknell, I prefer standing.

LADY BRACKNELL (*pencil and note-book in hand*): I feel bound to tell you that you are not down on my list of eligible young men, although I have the same list as the dear Duchess of Bolton has. We work together, in fact. However, I am quite ready to enter your name, should your answers be what a really affectionate mother requires. Do you smoke?

JACK: Well, yes, I must admit I smoke.

LADY BRACKNELL: I am glad to hear it. A man should always have an occupation of some kind. There are far too many idle men in London as it is. How old are you?

JACK: Twenty-nine.

LADY BRACKNELL: A very good age to be married at. I have always been of opinion that a man who desires to get married should know either everything or nothing. Which do you know?

JACK (*after some hesitation*): I know nothing, Lady Bracknell.

LADY BRACKNELL: I am pleased to hear it. I do not approve

of anything that tampers with natural ignorance. Ignorance is like a delicate exotic fruit; touch it and the bloom is gone. The whole theory of modern education is radically unsound. Fortunately in England, at any rate, education produces no effect whatsoever. If it did, it would prove a serious danger to the upper classes, and probably lead to acts of violence in Grosvenor Square. What is your income?

JACK: Between seven and eight thousand a year.

LADY BRACKNELL (*makes a note in her book*): In land, or in investments?

JACK: In investments, chiefly.

LADY BRACKNELL: That is satisfactory. What between the duties expected of one during one's lifetime, and the duties exacted[12] from one after one's death, land has ceased to be either a profit or a pleasure. It gives one position, and prevents one from keeping it up. That's all that can be said about land.

JACK: I have a country house with some land, of course, attached to it, about fifteen hundred acres, I believe; but I don't depend on that for my real income. In fact, as far as I can make out, the poachers are the only people who make anything out of it.

LADY BRACKNELL: A country house! How many bedrooms? Well, that point can be cleared up afterwards. You have a town house, I hope? A girl with a simple, unspoiled nature, like Gwendolen, could hardly be expected to reside in the country.

JACK: Well, I own a house in Belgrave Square,[13] but it is let by the year to Lady Bloxham. Of course, I can get it back whenever I like, at six months' notice.

LADY BRACKNELL: Lady Bloxham? I don't know her.

JACK: Oh, she goes about very little. She is a lady considerably advanced in years.

LADY BRACKNELL: Ah, nowadays that is no guarantee of

respectability of character. What number in Belgrave Square?

JACK: 149.

LADY BRACKNELL *(shaking her head)*: The unfashionable side. I thought there was something. However, that could easily be altered.

JACK: Do you mean the fashion, or the side?

LADY BRACKNELL *(sternly)*: Both, if necessary, I presume. What are your politics?

JACK: Well, I am afraid I really have none. I am a Liberal Unionist.[14]

LADY BRACKNELL: Oh, they count as Tories. They dine with us. Or come in the evening at any rate. You have, of course, no sympathy of any kind with the Radical Party?

JACK: Oh! I don't want to put the asses against the classes, if that is what you mean, Lady Bracknell.

LADY BRACKNELL: That is exactly what I do mean . . . ahem! . . . Are your parents living?

JACK: I have lost both my parents.

LADY BRACKNELL: Both? . . . To lose one parent may be regarded as a misfortune . . . to lose both seems like carelessness. Who was your father? He was evidently a man of some wealth. Was he born in what the Radical papers call the purple of commerce, or did he rise from the ranks of the aristocracy?

JACK: I am afraid I really don't know. The fact is, Lady Bracknell, I said I had lost my parents. It would be nearer the truth to say that my parents seemed to have lost me. . . . I don't actually know who I am by birth. I was . . . well, I was found.

LADY BRACKNELL: Found!

JACK: The late Mr. Thomas Cardew, an old gentleman of a very charitable and kindly disposition, found me, and gave me the name of Worthing, because he happened to have a first-class ticket for Worthing in his pocket at the time. Worthing is a place in Sussex. It is a seaside resort.

LADY BRACKNELL: Where did the charitable gentleman who had a first-class ticket for this seaside resort find you?

JACK *(gravely)*: In a hand-bag.

LADY BRACKNELL: A hand-bag?

JACK *(very seriously)*: Yes, Lady Bracknell. I was in a hand-bag—a somewhat large, black leather hand-bag, with handles to it—an ordinary hand-bag in fact.

LADY BRACKNELL: In what locality did this Mr. James, or Thomas, Cardew come across this ordinary hand-bag?

JACK: In the cloak-room at Victoria Station.[15] It was given to him in mistake for his own.

LADY BRACKNELL: The cloak-room at Victoria Station?

JACK: Yes. The Brighton line.

LADY BRACKNELL: The line is immaterial. Mr. Worthing, I confess I feel somewhat bewildered by what you have just told me. To be born, or at any rate bred, in a hand-bag, whether it had handles or not, seems to me to display a contempt for the ordinary decencies of family life that reminds one of the worst excesses of the French Revolution.[16] And I presume you know what that unfortunate movement led to? As for the particular locality in which the hand-bag was found, a cloak-room at a railway station might serve to conceal a social indiscretion—has probably, indeed, been used for that purpose before now—but it could hardly be regarded as an assured basis for a recognised position in good society.

JACK: May I ask you then what you would advise me to do? I need hardly say I would do anything in the world to ensure Gwendolen's happiness.

LADY BRACKNELL: I would strongly advise you, Mr. Worthing, to try and acquire some relations as soon as possi-

ble, and to make a definite effort to produce at any rate
one parent, of either sex, before the season is quite over.

JACK: Well, I don't see how I could possibly manage to do
that. I can produce the hand-bag at any moment. It is in
my dressing-room at home. I really think that should satisfy you, Lady Bracknell.

LADY BRACKNELL: Me, sir! What has it to do with me? You
can hardly imagine that I and Lord Bracknell would
dream of allowing our only daughter—a girl brought up
with the utmost care—to marry into a cloak-room, and
form an alliance with a parcel. (JACK *starts indignantly.*)
Kindly open the door for me sir. You will of course understand that for the future there is to be no communication of any kind between you and Miss Fairfax.

LADY BRACKNELL *sweeps out in majestic indignation.*
ALGERNON, *from the other room, strikes up the Wed-
ding March.* JACK *looks perfectly furious, and goes to the
door.*

JACK: For goodness' sake don't play that ghastly tune, Algy!
How idiotic you are!

The music stops and ALGERNON *enters cheerily.*

ALGERNON: Didn't it go off all right, old boy? You don't
mean to say Gwendolen refused you? I know it is a way
she has. She is always refusing people. I think it is most
ill-natured of her.

JACK: Oh, Gwendolen is as right as a trivet. As far as she is
concerned, we are engaged. Her mother is perfectly unbearable. Never met such a Gorgon.[17] . . . I don't really
know what a Gorgon is like, but I am quite sure that
Lady Bracknell is one. In any case, she is a monster,
without being a myth, which is rather unfair. . . . I beg
your pardon, Algy, I suppose I shouldn't talk about your
own aunt in that way before you.

ALGERNON: My dear boy, I love hearing my relations abused. It is the only thing that makes me put up with them at all. Relations are simply a tedious pack of people, who haven't got the remotest knowledge of how to live, nor the smallest instinct about when to die.

JACK: Ah! I haven't got any relations. Don't know anything about relations.

ALGERNON: You are a lucky fellow. Relations never lend one any money, and won't give one credit, even for genius. They are a sort of aggravated form of the public.

JACK: And after all, what does it matter whether a man ever had a father and mother or not? Mothers, of course, are all right. They pay a chap's bills and don't bother him. But fathers bother a chap and never pay his bills. I don't know a single chap at the club who speaks to his father.

ALGERNON: Yes! Fathers are certainly not popular just at present. (*Takes up the evening newspaper.*)

JACK: Popular! I bet you anything you like that there is not a single chap, of all the chaps that you and I know, who would be seen walking down St. James' Street with his own father. (*A pause.*) Anything in the papers?

ALGERNON (*still reading*): Nothing.

JACK: What a comfort.

ALGERNON: There is never anything in the papers, as far as I can see.

JACK: I think there is usually a great deal too much in them. They are always bothering one about people one doesn't know, one has never met, and one doesn't care twopence about. Brutes!

ALGERNON: I think people one hasn't met are charming. I'm very much interested at present in a girl I have never met; very much interested indeed.

JACK: Oh, that is nonsense!

ALGERNON: It isn't!

JACK: Well, I won't argue about the matter. You always want to argue about things.

ALGERNON: That is exactly what things were originally made for.

JACK: Upon my word, if I thought that, I'd shoot myself. . . . (*A pause.*) You don't think there is any chance of Gwendolen becoming like her mother in about a hundred and fifty years, do you, Algy?

ALGERNON: All women become like their mothers. That is their tragedy. No man does. That's his.

JACK: Is that clever?

ALGERNON: It is perfectly phrased! And quite as true as any observation in civilised life should be.

JACK: I am sick to death of cleverness. Everybody is clever nowadays. You can't go anywhere without meeting clever people. The thing has become an absolute public nuisance. I wish to goodness we had a few fools left.

ALGERNON: We have.

JACK: I should extremely like to meet them. What do they talk about?

ALGERNON: The fools? Oh! about the clever people of course.

JACK: What fools.

ALGERNON: By the way, did you tell Gwendolen the truth about your being Ernest in town, and Jack in the country?

JACK (*in a very patronising manner*): My dear fellow, the truth isn't quite the sort of thing one tells to a nice, sweet, refined girl. What extraordinary ideas you have about the way to behave to a woman!

ALGERNON: The only way to behave to a woman is to make love to her, if she is pretty, and to some one else, if she is plain.

JACK: Oh, that is nonsense.

ALGERNON: What about the young lady whose guardian

you are! Miss Cardew? What about your brother? What about the profligate Ernest?

JACK: Oh! Cecily is all right. Before the end of the week I shall have got rid of my brother . . . I think I'll probably kill him in Paris.

ALGERNON: Why Paris?

JACK: Oh! Less trouble: no nonsense about a funeral and that sort of thing—yes, I'll kill him in Paris. . . . Apoplexy will do perfectly well. Lots of people die of apoplexy, quite suddenly, don't they?

ALGERNON: Yes, but it's hereditary, my dear fellow. It's a sort of thing that runs in families.

JACK: Good heavens! Then I certainly won't choose that. What can I say?

ALGERNON: Oh! Say influenza.

JACK: Oh, no! that wouldn't sound probable at all. Far too many people have had it.

ALGERNON: Oh well! Say anything you choose. Say a severe chill. That's all right.

JACK: You are sure a severe chill isn't hereditary, or anything dreadful of that kind?

ALGERNON: Of course it isn't.

JACK: Very well then. That is settled.

ALGERNON: But I thought you said that . . . Miss Cardew was a little too much interested in your poor brother Ernest? Won't she feel his loss a good deal?

JACK: Oh! that is all right. Cecily is not a silly romantic girl, I am glad to say. She has got a capital appetite, goes long walks, and pays no attention at all to her lessons.

ALGERNON: I would rather like to see Cecily.

JACK: I will take very good care you never do. And you are not to speak of her as Cecily.

ALGERNON: Ah! I believe she is plain. Yes: I know perfectly well what she is like. She is one of those dull, intellectual girls one meets all over the place. Girls who have got large minds and large feet. I am sure she is more than usually plain, and I expect she is about thirty-nine, and looks it.

JACK: She happens to be excessively pretty, and she is only just eighteen.

ALGERNON: Have you told Gwendolen yet that you have an excessively pretty ward who is only just eighteen?

JACK: Oh! one doesn't blurt these things out to people. Life is a question of tact. One leads up to the thing gradually. Cecily and Gwendolen are perfectly certain to be extremely great friends. I'll bet you anything you like that half an hour after they have met, they will be calling each other sister.

ALGERNON: Women only do that when they have called each other a lot of other things first. Now, my dear boy, if we want to get a good table at Willis's, we really must go and dress. Do you know it is nearly seven?

JACK (irritably): Oh! it always is nearly seven.

ALGERNON: Well, I'm hungry.

JACK: I never knew you when you weren't. . . . However, all right. I'll go round to the Albany and meet you at Willis's at eight. You can call for me on your way, if you like.

ALGERNON: What shall we do after dinner? Go to a theatre?

JACK: Oh, no! I loathe listening.

ALGERNON: Well, let us go to the Club?

JACK: Oh, no! I hate talking.

ALGERNON: Well, we might trot round to the Empire[18] at ten?

JACK: Oh, no! I can't bear looking at things. It is so silly.

ALGERNON: Well, what shall we do?

JACK: Nothing!

ALGERNON: It is awfully hard work doing nothing. However, I don't mind hard work where there is no definite object of any kind . . .

Enter LANE.

LANE: Miss Fairfax.

Enter GWENDOLEN. LANE *goes out.*

ALGERNON: Gwendolen, upon my word!

GWENDOLEN: Algy, kindly turn your back. I have something very particular to say to Mr. Worthing. As it is somewhat of a private matter, you will of course listen.

ALGERNON: Really, Gwendolen, I don't think I can allow this at all.

GWENDOLEN: Algy, you always adopt a strictly immoral attitude towards life. You are not quite old enough to do that. (ALGERNON *retires to the fireplace.*)

JACK: My own darling.

GWENDOLEN: Ernest, we may never be married. From the expression on mamma's face I fear we never shall. Few parents nowadays pay any regard to what their children say to them. The old-fashioned respect for the young is fast dying out. Whatever influence I ever had over mamma, I lost at the age of three. But although she may prevent us from becoming man and wife, and I may marry some one else, and marry often, nothing that she can possibly do can alter my eternal devotion to you.

JACK: Dear Gwendolen!

GWENDOLEN: The story of your romantic origin, as related to me by mamma, with unpleasing comments, has naturally stirred the deeper fibres of my nature. Your Christian name has an irresistible fascination. The simplicity of your character makes you exquisitely incomprehensible to me. Your town address at the Albany I have. What is your address in the country?

JACK: The Manor House, Woolton, Hertfordshire.

ALGERNON, *who has been carefully listening, smiles to*

himself, and writes the address on his shirt-cuff. Then picks up the Railway Guide.

GWENDOLEN: There is a good postal service, I suppose? It may be necessary to do something desperate. That, of course, will require serious consideration. I will communicate with you daily.

JACK: My own one!

GWENDOLEN: How long do you remain in town?

JACK: Till Monday.

GWENDOLEN: Good! Algy, you may turn round now.

ALGERNON: Thanks, I've turned round already.

GWENDOLEN: You may also ring the bell.

JACK: You will let me see you to your carriage, my own darling?

GWENDOLEN: Certainly.

JACK (*to* LANE, *who now enters*): I will see Miss Fairfax out.

LANE: Yes, sir.

JACK *and* GWENDOLEN *go off.*

    LANE *presents several letters on a salver to* ALGERNON. *It is to be surmised that they are bills, as* ALGERNON, *after looking at the envelopes, tears them up.*

ALGERNON: A glass of sherry, Lane.

LANE: Yes, sir.

ALGERNON: To-morrow, Lane, I'm going Bunburying.

LANE: Yes, sir.

ALGERNON: I shall probably not be back till Monday. You can put up my dress clothes, my smoking jacket, and all the Bunbury suits . . .

LANE: Yes, sir. (*Handing sherry.*)

ALGERNON: I hope to-morrow will be a fine day, Lane.

LANE: It never is, sir.

ALGERNON: Lane, you're a perfect pessimist.

LANE: I do my best to give satisfaction, sir.

Enter JACK. LANE *goes off.*

JACK: There's a sensible, intellectual girl! the only girl I ever cared for in my life. (ALGERNON *is laughing immoderately.*) What on earth are you so amused at?

ALGERNON: Oh, I'm a little anxious about poor Bunbury, that is all.

JACK: If you don't take care, your friend Bunbury will get you into a serious scrape some day.

ALGERNON: I love scrapes. They are the only things that are never serious.

JACK: Oh, that's nonsense, Algy. You never talk anything but nonsense.

ALGERNON: Nobody ever does.

JACK *looks indignantly at him and leaves the room.* ALGERNON *lights a cigarette, reads his shirt-cuff, and smiles.*

Act Drop

Act Two

SCENE: *Garden at the Manor House, Woolton. A flight of grey stone steps leads up to the house. The garden, an old-fashioned one, full of roses. Time of year, July. Basket chairs, and a table covered with books, are set under a large yew-tree.*

MISS PRISM *discovered seated at the table.* CECILY *is at the back watering flowers.*

MISS PRISM (*calling*): Cecily, Cecily! Surely such a utilitarian occupation as the watering of flowers is rather Moulton's duty than yours? Especially at a moment when intellectual pleasures await you. Your German grammar is on the table. Pray open it at page fifteen. We will repeat yesterday's lesson.

CECILY: Oh! I wish you would give Moulton the German lesson instead of me. Moulton!

MOULTON (*looking out from behind a hedge, with a broad grin on his face*): Eh, Miss Cecily?

CECILY: Wouldn't you like to know German, Moulton?

German is the language talked by people who live in Germany.

MOULTON (*shaking his head*): I don't hold with them furrin tongues, miss. (*Bowing to* MISS PRISM.) No offence to you, ma'am. (*Disappears behind hedge.*)

MISS PRISM: Cecily, this will never do. Pray open your Schiller[1] at once.

CECILY (*coming over very slowly*): But I don't like German. It isn't at all a becoming language. I know perfectly well that I look quite plain after my German lesson.

MISS PRISM: Child, you know how anxious your guardian is that you should improve yourself in every way. He laid particular stress on your German, as he was leaving for town yesterday. Indeed, he always lays stress on your German when he is leaving for town.

CECILY: Dear Uncle Jack is so very serious! Sometimes he is so serious that I think he cannot be quite well.

MISS PRISM (*drawing herself up*): Your guardian enjoys the best of health, and his gravity of demeanour is especially to be commended in one so comparatively young as he is. I know no one who has a higher sense of duty and responsibility.

CECILY: I suppose that is why he often looks a little bored when we three are together.

MISS PRISM: Cecily! I am surprised at you. Mr. Worthing has many troubles in his life. Idle merriment and triviality would be out of place in his conversation. You must remember his constant anxiety about that unfortunate young man his brother.

CECILY: I wish Uncle Jack would allow that unfortunate young man, his brother, to come down here sometimes. We might have a good influence over him, Miss Prism. I am sure you certainly would. You know German, and geology, and things of that kind influence a man very much.

CECILY *begins to write in her diary.*

MISS PRISM (*shaking her head*): I do not think that even I
could produce any effect on a character that according
to his own brother's admission is irretrievably weak and
vacillating. Indeed I am not sure that I would desire to
reclaim him. I am not in favour of this modern mania for
turning bad people into good people at a moment's notice. As a man sows so let him reap.

CECILY: But men don't sew, Miss Prism. . . . And if they
did, I don't see why they should be punished for it.
There is a great deal too much punishment in the world.
German is a punishment, certainly, and there is far too
much German. You told me yourself yesterday that Germany was over-populated.

MISS PRISM: That is no reason why you should be writing
your diary instead of translating "William Tell." You must
put away your diary, Cecily. I really don't see why you
should keep a diary at all.

CECILY: I keep a diary in order to enter the wonderful secrets of my life. If I didn't write them down, I should
probably forget all about them.

MISS PRISM: Memory, my dear Cecily, is the diary that we all
carry about with us.

CECILY: Yes, but it usually chronicles the things that have
never happened, and couldn't possibly have happened. I
believe that Memory is responsible for nearly all the
three-volume novels that Mudie sends us.[2]

MISS PRISM: Do not speak slightingly of the three-volume
novel, Cecily. I wrote one myself in earlier days.

CECILY: Did you really, Miss Prism? How wonderfully
clever you are! I hope it did not end happily? I don't like
novels that end happily. They depress me so much.

MISS PRISM: The good ended happily, and the bad unhap-
pily. That is what Fiction means.

CECILY: I suppose so. But it seems very unfair. And was your novel ever published?

MISS PRISM: Alas! no. The manuscript unfortunately was abandoned. (CECILY *starts*.) I use the word in the sense of lost or mislaid. To your work, child, these speculations are profitless.

CECILY (*smiling*): But I see Dr. Chasuble[3] coming up through the garden.

MISS PRISM (*rising and advancing*): Dr. Chasuble! This is indeed a pleasure.

Enter CANON CHASUBLE.

CHASUBLE: And how are we this morning? Miss Prism, you are, I trust, well?

CECILY: Miss Prism has just been complaining of a slight headache. I think it would do her so much good to have a short stroll with you in the Park, Dr. Chasuble.

MISS PRISM: Cecily, I have not mentioned anything about a headache.

CECILY: No, dear Miss Prism, I know that, but I felt instinctively that you had a headache. Indeed I was thinking about that, and not about my German lesson, when the Rector came in.

CHASUBLE: I hope, Cecily, you are not inattentive.

CECILY: Oh, I am afraid I am.

CHASUBLE: That is strange. Were I fortunate enough to be Miss Prism's pupil, I would hang upon her lips. (MISS PRISM *glares*.) I spoke metaphorically. My metaphor was drawn from bees. Ahem! Mr. Worthing, I suppose, has not returned from town yet?

MISS PRISM: We do not expect him till Monday afternoon.

CHASUBLE: Ah yes, he usually likes to spend his Sunday in London. He is not one of those whose sole aim is enjoyment, as, by all accounts, that unfortunate young man his brother seems to be. But I must not disturb Egeria and her pupil any longer.

MISS PRISM: Egeria? My name is Lætitia, Doctor.

CHASUBLE (*bowing*): A classical allusion merely, drawn from the Pagan authors. I shall see you both no doubt at Evensong?

MISS PRISM: I think, dear Doctor, I will have a stroll with you. I find I have a headache after all, and a walk might do it good.

CHASUBLE: With pleasure, Miss Prism, with pleasure. We might go as far as the schools and back.

MISS PRISM: That would be delightful. Cecily, you will read your Political Economy in my absence. The chapter on the Fall of the Rupee[4] you may omit. It is somewhat too sensational for a young girl. Even these metallic problems have their melodramatic side.

CHASUBLE: Reading Political Economy, Cecily? It is wonderful how girls are educated nowadays. I suppose you know all about relations between Capital and Labour?

CECILY: I am afraid I am not learned at all. All I know is about the relations between Capital and Idleness—and that is merely from observation. So I don't suppose it is true.

MISS PRISM: Cecily, that sounds like Socialism! And I suppose you know where Socialism leads to?

CECILY: Oh, yes! That leads to Rational Dress,[5] Miss Prism. And I suppose that when a woman is dressed rationally, she is treated rationally. She certainly deserves to be.

CHASUBLE: A wilful lamb! Dear child!

MISS PRISM (*smiling*): A sad trouble sometimes.

CHASUBLE: I envy you such tribulation.

Goes down the garden with MISS PRISM.

CECILY (*picks up books and throws them back on table*): Horrid Political Economy! Horrid Geography! Horrid, horrid German!

Enter MERRIMAN *with a card on a salver.*

MERRIMAN: Mr. Ernest Worthing has just driven over from the station. He has brought his luggage with him.

CECILY *(takes the card and reads it)*: "Mr. Ernest Worthing, B.4, The Albany, W." Uncle Jack's brother! Did you tell him Mr. Worthing was in town?

MERRIMAN: Yes, Miss. He seemed very much disappointed. I mentioned that you and Miss Prism were in the garden. He said he was anxious to speak to you privately for a moment.

CECILY *(to herself)*: I don't think Miss Prism would like my being alone with him. So I had better send for him at once, before she comes in. *(To* MERRIMAN.*)* Ask Mr. Ernest Worthing to come here. I suppose you had better talk to the housekeeper about a room for him.

MERRIMAN: I have already sent his luggage up to the Blue Room, Miss: next to Mr. Worthing's own room.

CECILY: Oh! That is all right.

MERRIMAN *goes off.*

I have never met any really wicked person before. I feel rather frightened. I am so afraid he will look just like everyone else.

Enter ALGERNON, *very gay and debonair.*

He does!

ALGERNON *(raising his hat)*: You are my little cousin Cecily, I'm sure.

CECILY: You are under some strange mistake. I am not little. In fact, I believe I am more than usually tall for my age. *(ALGERNON is rather taken aback.)* But I am your cousin Cecily. You, I see from your card, are Uncle Jack's brother, my cousin Ernest, my wicked cousin Ernest.

ALGERNON: Oh! I am not really wicked at all, cousin Cecily. You musn't think that I am wicked.

CECILY: If you are not, then you have certainly been deceiving us all in a very inexcusable manner. You have made Uncle Jack believe that you are very bad. I hope you have not been leading a double life, pretending to be wicked and being really good all the time. That would be hypocrisy.

ALGERNON (looks at her in amazement): Oh! Of course I have been rather reckless.

CECILY: I am glad to hear it.

ALGERNON: In fact, now you mention the subject, I have been very bad in my own small way.

CECILY: I don't think you should be so proud of that, though I am sure it must have been very pleasant.

ALGERNON: It is much pleasanter being here with you.

CECILY: I can't understand how you are here at all. Uncle Jack telegraphed to you yesterday at the Albany that he would see you for the last time at six o'clock. He lets me read all the telegrams he sends you. I know some of them by heart.

ALGERNON: The fact is I didn't get the telegram till it was too late. Then I missed him at the Club, and the Hall Porter said he thought he had come down here. So, of course, I followed as I knew he wanted to see me.

CECILY: He won't be back till Monday afternoon.

ALGERNON: That is a great disappointment. I am obliged to go up by the first train on Monday morning. I have a business appointment that I am anxious . . . to miss!

CECILY: Couldn't you miss it anywhere but in London?

ALGERNON: No: the appointment is in London.

CECILY: Well, I know, of course, how important it is not to keep a business engagement, if one wants to retain any sense of the beauty of life, but still I think you had better wait till Uncle Jack arrives. I know he wants to speak to you about your emigrating.

ALGERNON: About my what?

CECILY: Your emigrating. He has gone up to buy your outfit.

ALGERNON: I certainly wouldn't let Jack buy my outfit. He has no taste in neckties at all.

CECILY: I don't think you will require neckties. Uncle Jack is sending you to Australia.

ALGERNON: Australia! I'd sooner die.

CECILY: Well, he said at dinner on Wednesday night, that you would have to choose between this world, the next world, and Australia.

ALGERNON: Oh, well! The accounts I have received of Australia and the next world, are not particularly encouraging. This world is good enough for me, cousin Cecily.

CECILY: Yes, but are you good enough for it?

ALGERNON: I'm afraid I'm not that. That is why I want you to reform me. You might make that your mission, if you don't mind, cousin Cecily.

CECILY: How dare you suggest that I have a mission?

ALGERNON: I beg your pardon: but I thought that every woman had a mission of some kind, nowadays.

CECILY: Every female has! No woman. Besides, I have no time to reform you this afternoon.

ALGERNON: Well, would you mind my reforming myself this afternoon?

CECILY: It is rather Quixotic of you. But I think you should try.

ALGERNON: I will. I feel better already.

CECILY: You are looking a little worse.

ALGERNON: That is because I am hungry.

CECILY: How thoughtless of me. I should have remembered that when one is going to lead an entirely new life, one requires regular and wholesome meals. Miss Prism and I lunch at two, off some roast mutton.

ALGERNON: I fear that would be too rich for me.

CECILY: Uncle Jack, whose health has been sadly undermined by the late hours you keep in town, has been ordered by his London doctor to have pâté de foie gras sandwiches and 1889 champagne[6] at twelve. I don't know if such invalid fare would suit you.

ALGERNON: Oh! I will be quite content with '89 champagne.

CECILY: I am glad to see you have such simple tastes. This is the dining-room.

ALGERNON: Thank you. Might I have a buttonhole first? I never have any appetite unless I have a buttonhole first.

CECILY: A Maréchal Niel?[7] (*Picks up scissors.*)

ALGERNON: No, I'd sooner have a pink rose.

CECILY: Why? (*Cuts a flower.*)

ALGERNON: Because you are like a pink rose, Cousin Cecily.

CECILY: I don't think it can be right for you to talk to me like that. Miss Prism never says such things to me.

ALGERNON: Then Miss Prism is a short-sighted old lady. (CECILY *puts the rose in his buttonhole.*) You are the prettiest girl I ever saw.

CECILY: Miss Prism says that all good looks are a snare.

ALGERNON: They are a snare that every sensible man would like to be caught in.

CECILY: Oh, I don't think I would care to catch a sensible man. I shouldn't know what to talk to him about.

They pass into the house. MISS PRISM *and* DR. CHASUBLE *return.*

MISS PRISM: You are too much alone, dear Dr. Chasuble. You should get married. A misanthrope I can understand—a womanthrope, never!

CHASUBLE *(with a scholar's shudder)*: Believe me, I do not deserve so neologistic a phrase. The precept as well as the practice of the Primitive Church[8] was distinctly against matrimony.

MISS PRISM *(sententiously)*: That is obviously the reason why the Primitive Church has not lasted up to the present day. And you do not seem to realise, dear Doctor, that by persistently remaining single, a man converts himself into a permanent public temptation. Men should be more careful; this very celibacy leads weaker vessels astray.

CHASUBLE: But is a man not equally attractive when married?

MISS PRISM: No married man is ever attractive except to his wife.

CHASUBLE: And often, I've been told, not even to her.

MISS PRISM: That depends on the intellectual sympathies of the woman. Maturity can always be depended on. Ripeness can be trusted. Young women are green. (DR CHASUBLE *starts.*) I spoke horticulturally. My metaphor was drawn from fruit. But where is Cecily?

CHASUBLE: Perhaps she followed us to the schools.

Enter JACK slowly from the back of the garden. He is dressed in the deepest mourning, with crêpe hatband and black gloves.

MISS PRISM: Mr. Worthing!

CHASUBLE: Mr. Worthing?

MISS PRISM: This is indeed a surprise. We did not look for you till Monday afternoon.

JACK *(shakes MISS PRISM's hand in a tragic manner)*: I have returned sooner than I expected. Dr. Chasuble, I hope you are well?

CHASUBLE: Dear Mr. Worthing, I trust this garb of woe does not betoken some terrible calamity?

JACK: My brother.

MISS PRISM: More shameful debts and extravagance?

CHASUBLE: Still leading his life of pleasure?

JACK (*shaking his head*): Dead!

CHASUBLE: Your brother Ernest dead?

JACK: Quite dead.

MISS PRISM: What a lesson for him! I trust he will profit by it.

CHASUBLE: Death is the inheritance of us all, Miss Prism. Nor should we look on it as a special judgment, but rather as a general providence. Life were incomplete without it . . . Mr. Worthing, I offer you my sincere condolence. You have at least the consolation of knowing that you were always the most generous and forgiving of brothers.

JACK: Poor Ernest! He had many faults, but it is a sad, sad blow.

CHASUBLE: Very sad indeed. Were you with him at the end?

JACK: No. He died abroad; in Paris, in fact. I had a telegram last night from the manager of the Grand Hotel.

CHASUBLE: Was the cause of death mentioned?

JACK: A severe chill, it seems.

MISS PRISM: As a man sows, so shall he reap.

CHASUBLE (*raising his hand*): Charity, dear Miss Prism, charity! None of us are perfect. I myself am peculiarly susceptible to draughts. Will the interment take place here?

JACK: No. He seems to have expressed a desire to be buried in Paris.

CHASUBLE: In Paris![9] (*Shakes his head.*) I fear that hardly points to any very serious state of mind at the last. You would no doubt wish me to make some slight allusion to this tragic domestic affliction next Sunday. (JACK *presses his hand convulsively.*) My sermon on the meaning of the manna in the wilderness can be adapted to almost any occasion, joyful, or, as in the present case, distressing. *(All sigh.)* I have preached it at harvest celebrations, christenings, confirmations, on days of humiliation and festal days. The last time I delivered it was in the Cathedral, as a charity sermon on behalf of the Society for the Prevention of Discontent among the Upper Orders. The Bishop, who was present, was much struck by some of the analogies I drew.

JACK: Ah! that reminds me, you mentioned christenings, I think, Dr. Chasuble? I suppose you know how to christen all right? (DR. CHASUBLE *looks astounded.*) I mean, of course, you are continually christening, aren't you?

MISS PRISM: It is, I regret to say, one of the Rector's most constant duties in this parish. I have often spoken to the poorer classes on the subject. But they don't seem to know what thrift is.

CHASUBLE: The Church rejects no babe, Miss Prism. In every child, there is the making of a saint. But is there any particular infant in whom you are interested, Mr. Worthing? Your brother was, I believe, unmarried, was he not?

JACK: Oh yes.

MISS PRISM *(bitterly)*: People who live entirely for pleasure usually are.

JACK: But it is not for any child, dear Doctor. I am very fond of children. No! the fact is, I would like to be christened myself, this afternoon, if you have nothing better to do.

CHASUBLE: But surely, Mr. Worthing, you have been christened already?

JACK: I don't remember anything about it.

CHASUBLE: But have you any grave doubts on the subject?

JACK: I have the very gravest doubts. There are circumstances, unnecessary to mention at present, connected with my birth and early life that make me think I was a good deal neglected. I certainly wasn't properly looked after, at any rate. Of course I don't know if the thing would bother you in any way, or if you think I am a little too old now.

CHASUBLE: Oh! I am not by any means a bigoted Paedobaptist.[10] The sprinkling and, indeed, the immersion of adults was a common practice of the Primitive Church.

JACK: Immersion! You don't mean to say that . . .

CHASUBLE: You need have no apprehensions. Sprinkling is all that is necessary, or indeed I think advisable. Our weather is so changeable. At what hour would you wish the ceremony performed?

JACK: Oh, I might trot round about five if that would suit you.

CHASUBLE: Perfectly, perfectly! In fact, I have two similar ceremonies to perform at that time. A case of twins that occurred recently in one of the outlying cottages on your own estate. Poor Jenkins the carter, a most hard-working man.

JACK: Oh! I don't see much fun in being christened along with other babies. It would be childish. Would half-past five do?

CHASUBLE: Admirably! Admirably! (*Takes out watch.*) And now, dear Mr. Worthing, I will not intrude any longer into a house of sorrow. I would merely beg you not to be too much bowed down by grief. What seem to us bitter trials are often blessings in disguise.

MISS PRISM: This seems to me a blessing of an extremely obvious kind.

Enter CECILY *from the house.*

CECILY: Uncle Jack! Oh, I am pleased to see you back. But what horrid clothes you have got on! Do go and change them.

MISS PRISM: Cecily!

CHASUBLE: My child! my child!

CECILY goes towards JACK; he kisses her brow in a melancholy manner.

CECILY: What is the matter, Uncle Jack? Do look happy! You look as if you had toothache, and I have got such a surprise for you. Who do you think is in the dining-room? Your brother!

JACK: Who?

CECILY: Your brother Ernest. He arrived about half an hour ago.

JACK: What nonsense! I haven't got a brother.

CECILY: Oh, don't say that. However badly he may have behaved to you in the past he is still your brother. You couldn't be so heartless as to disown him. I'll tell him to come out. And you will shake hands with him, won't you, Uncle Jack? *(Runs back into the house.)*

CHASUBLE: These are very joyful tidings. That telegram from Paris seems to have been a somewhat heartless jest by one who wished to play upon your feelings.

MISS PRISM: After we had all been resigned to his loss, his sudden return seems to me peculiarly distressing.

JACK: My brother is in the dining-room? I don't know what it all means. I think it is perfectly absurd.

Enter ALGERNON and CECILY hand in hand. They come slowly up to JACK

JACK: Good heavens! *(Motions ALGERNON away.)*

ALGERNON: Brother John, I have come down from town to tell you that I am very sorry for all the trouble I have given you, and that I intend to lead a better life in the future. *(JACK glares at him and does not take his hand.)*

CHASUBLE *(to MISS PRISM)*: There is good in that young man. He seems to be sincerely repentant.

MISS PRISM: These sudden conversions do not please me. They belong to Dissent. They savour of the laxity of the Nonconformist.[11]

CECILY: Uncle Jack, you are not going to refuse your own brother's hand?

JACK: Nothing will induce me to take his hand. I think his coming down here disgraceful. He knows perfectly well why.

CHASUBLE: Young man, you have had a very narrow escape of your life. I hope it will be a warning to you. We were mourning your demise when you entered.

ALGERNON: Yes, I see Jack has got a new suit of clothes. They don't fit him properly. His necktie is wrong.

CECILY: Uncle Jack, do be nice. There is some good in everyone. Ernest has just been telling me about his poor invalid friend Mr. Bunbury whom he goes to visit so often. And surely there must be some good in one who is kind to an invalid, and leaves the pleasures of London to sit by a bed of pain.

JACK: Oh! he has been talking about Bunbury has he?

CECILY: Yes, he has told me all about poor Mr. Bunbury, and his terrible state of health.

JACK: Bunbury! Well, I won't have him talk to you about Bunbury or about anything else. It is enough to drive one perfectly frantic.

CHASUBLE: Mr. Worthing, your brother has been unexpectedly restored to you by the mysterious dispensations of providence, who seems to desire your reconciliation. And indeed it is good for brothers to dwell together in amity.

ALGERNON: Of course I admit that the faults were all on my side. But I must say that I think that Brother John's coldness to me is peculiarly painful. I expected a warmer welcome, especially considering it is the first time I have come here.

CECILY: Uncle Jack, if you don't shake hands with Ernest I will never forgive you.

JACK: Never forgive me?

CECILY: Never, never, never!

JACK: I suppose I must then. (*Shakes hands and glares.*) You young scoundrel! You must get out of this place as soon as possible. I don't allow any Bunburying here.

CHASUBLE: It's pleasant, is it not, to see so perfect a reconciliation? You have done a beautiful action to-day, dear child.

MISS PRISM: We must not be premature in our judgments.

Enter MERRIMAN.

MERRIMAN: I have put Mr. Ernest's things in the room next to yours, sir. I suppose that is all right?

JACK: What?

MERRIMAN: Mr. Ernest's luggage, sir. I have unpacked it and put it in the room next to your own.

JACK: His luggage?

MERRIMAN: Yes, sir. Three portmanteaus,[12] a dressing case, two hat-boxes, and a large luncheon-basket.

ALGERNON: I am afraid I can't stay more than a week this time.

MERRIMAN (*to* ALGERNON): I beg your pardon, sir, there is an elderly gentleman wishes to see you. He has just come in a cab from the station. (*Hands card on salver.*)

ALGERNON: To see me?

MERRIMAN: Yes, sir.

ALGERNON (*reads card*): Parker and Gribsby, Solicitors. I don't know anything about them. Who are they?

JACK (*takes card*): Parker and Gribsby. I wonder who they can be. I expect, Ernest, they have come about some business for your friend Bunbury. Perhaps Bunbury wants to make his will and wishes you to be executor. (*To* MERRIMAN.) Show the gentleman in at once.

MERRIMAN: Very good, sir.

MERRIMAN goes out.

JACK: I hope, Ernest, that I may rely on the statement you made to me last week when I finally settled all your bills for you. I hope you have no outstanding accounts of any kind.

ALGERNON: I haven't any debts at all, dear Jack. Thanks to your generosity I don't owe a penny, except for a few neckties, I believe.

JACK: I am sincerely glad to hear it.

Enter MERRIMAN.

MERRIMAN: Mr. Gribsby.

MERRIMAN goes out. Enter GRIBSBY.

GRIBSBY (*to* DR. CHASUBLE): Mr. Ernest Worthing?
MISS PRISM: This is Mr. Ernest Worthing.
GRIBSBY: Mr. Ernest Worthing?
ALGERNON: Yes.
GRIBSBY: Of B.4, The Albany?
ALGERNON: Yes, that is my address.
GRIBSBY: I am very sorry, sir, but we have a writ of attachment for twenty days against you at the suit of the Savoy Hotel Co. Limited for £762 14*s*. 2*d*.[13]
ALGERNON: Against me?
GRIBSBY: Yes, sir.
ALGERNON: What perfect nonsense! I never dine at the Savoy at my own expense. I always dine at Willis's. It is far more expensive. I don't owe a penny to the Savoy.
GRIBSBY: The writ is marked as having been served on you personally at The Albany on May the 27th. Judgment was given in default against you on the fifth of June. Since then we have written to you no less than fifteen times, without receiving any reply. In the interest of our

clients we had no option but to obtain an order for committal of your person.

ALGERNON: Committal! What on earth do you mean by committal? I haven't the smallest intention of going away. I am staying here for a week. I am staying with my brother. If you imagine I am going up to town the moment I arrive you are extremely mistaken.

GRIBSBY: I am merely a Solicitor myself. I do not employ personal violence of any kind. The Officer of the Court, whose function it is to seize the person of the debtor, is waiting in the fly[14] outside. He has considerable experience in these matters. That is why we always employ him. But no doubt you will prefer to pay the bill.

ALGERNON: Pay it? How on earth am I going to do that? You don't suppose I have got any money? How perfectly silly you are. No gentleman ever has any money.

GRIBSBY: My experience is that it is usually relations who pay.

ALGERNON: Jack, you really must settle this bill.

JACK: Kindly allow me to see the particular items, Mr. Gribsby . . . (turns over immense folio) . . . £762 14s. 2d. since last October. I am bound to say I never saw such reckless extravagance in all my life. (Hands it to DR. CHASUBLE.)

MISS PRISM: £762 for eating! There can be little good in any young man who eats so much, and so often.

CHASUBLE: We are far away from Wordsworth's[15] plain living and high thinking.

JACK: Now, Dr. Chasuble, do you consider that I am in any way called upon to pay this monstrous account for my brother?

CHASUBLE: I am bound to say that I do not think so. It would be encouraging his profligacy.

MISS PRISM: As a man sows, so let him reap. This proposed

incarceration might be most salutary. It is to be regretted that it is only for twenty days.

JACK: I am quite of your opinion.

ALGERNON: My dear fellow, how ridiculous you are! You know perfectly well that the bill is really yours.

JACK: Mine?

ALGERNON: Yes, you know it is.

CHASUBLE: Mr. Worthing, if this is a jest, it is out of place.

MISS PRISM: It is gross effrontery. Just what I expected from him.

CECILY: And it is ingratitude. I didn't expect that.

JACK: Never mind what he says. This is the way he always goes on. You mean now to say that you are not Ernest Worthing, residing at B.4., The Albany. I wonder, as you are at it, that you don't deny being my brother at all. Why don't you?

ALGERNON: Oh! I am not going to do that, my dear fellow. It would be absurd. Of course I'm your brother. And that is why you should pay this bill for me.

JACK: I will tell you quite candidly that I have not the smallest intention of doing anything of the kind. Dr. Chasuble, the worthy Rector of this parish, and Miss Prism, in whose admirable and sound judgment I place great reliance, are both of the opinion that incarceration would do you a great deal of good. And I think so, too.

GRIBSBY (*pulls out watch*): I am sorry to disturb this pleasant family meeting, but time presses. We have to be at Holloway[16] not later than four o'clock; otherwise it is difficult to obtain admission. The rules are very strict.

ALGERNON: Holloway!

GRIBSBY: It is at Holloway that detentions of this character take place always.

ALGERNON: Well, I really am not going to be imprisoned in the suburbs for having dined in the West End.

GRIBSBY: The bill is for suppers, not for dinners.

ALGERNON: I really don't care. All I say is that I am not going to be imprisoned in the suburbs.

GRIBSBY: The surroundings I admit are middle class; but the gaol itself is fashionable and well-aired; and there are ample opportunities of taking exercise at certain stated hours of the day. In the case of a medical certificate, which is always easy to obtain, the hours can be extended.

ALGERNON: Exercise! Good God! No gentleman ever takes exercise. You don't seem to understand what a gentleman is.

GRIBSBY: I have met so many of them, sir, that I am afraid I don't. There are the most curious varieties of them. The result of cultivation, no doubt. Will you kindly come now, sir, if it will not be inconvenient to you.

ALGERNON (appealingly): Jack!

MISS PRISM: Pray be firm, Mr. Worthing.

CHASUBLE: This is an occasion on which any weakness would be out of place. It would be a form of self-deception.

JACK: I am quite firm, and I don't know what weakness or deception of any kind is.

CECILY: Uncle Jack! I think you have a little money of mine, haven't you? Let me pay this bill. I wouldn't like your own brother to be in prison.

JACK: Oh! I couldn't possibly let you pay it, Cecily. That would be absurd.

CECILY: Then you will, won't you? I think you would be sorry if you thought your own brother was shut up. Of course, I am quite disappointed with him.

JACK: You won't speak to him again, Cecily, will you?

CECILY: Certainly not, unless, of course, he speaks to me first. It would be very rude not to answer him.

JACK: Well, I'll take care he doesn't speak to you. I'll take care he doesn't speak to anybody in this house. The man should be cut. Mr. Gribsby . . .

GRIBSBY: Yes, sr.

JACK: I'll pay this bill for my brother. It is the last bill I shall ever pay for him, too. How much is it?

GRIBSBY: £762 14*s*. 2*d*. Ah! The cab will be five-and-ninepence extra: hired for the convenience of the client.

JACK: All right.

MISS PRISM: I must say that I think such generosity quite foolish.

CHASUBLE (*with a wave of the hand*): The heart has its wisdom as well as the head, Miss Prism.

JACK: Payable to Parker and Gribsby, I suppose?

GRIBSBY: Yes, sir. Kindly don't cross the cheque. Thank you. (*To* DR. CHASUBLE.) Good day. (DR. CHASUBLE *bows coldly.*) Good day. (MISS PRISM *bows coldly.*) (*To* ALGERNON.) I hope I shall have the pleasure of meeting you again.

ALGERNON: I sincerely hope not. What ideas you have of the sort of society a gentleman wants to mix in. No gentleman ever wants to know a Solicitor who wants to imprison one in the suburbs.

GRIBSBY: Quite so, quite so.

ALGERNON: By the way, Gribsby: Gribsby, you are not to go back to the station in that cab. That is my cab. It was taken for my convenience. You have got to walk to the station. And a very good thing, too. Solicitors don't walk nearly enough. I don't know any Solicitor who takes sufficient exercise. As a rule they sit in stuffy offices all day long neglecting their business.

JACK: You can take the cab, Mr. Gribsby.

GRIBSBY: Thank you, sir.

GRIBSBY *goes out*.

CECILY: The day is getting very sultry, isn't it, Dr. Chasuble?

CHASUBLE: There is thunder in the air.

MISS PRISM: The atmosphere requires to be cleared.

CHASUBLE: Have you read "The Times" this morning, Mr. Worthing? There is a very interesting article on the growth of religious feeling among the laity.

JACK: I am keeping it for after dinner.

Enter MERRIMAN.

MERRIMAN: Luncheon is on the table, sir.

ALGERNON: Ah! That is good news. I am excessively hungry.

CECILY (*interposing*): But you have lunched already.

JACK: Lunched already?

CECILY: Yes, Uncle Jack. He had some pâté de foie gras sandwiches, and a small bottle of that champagne that your doctor ordered for you.

JACK: My '89 champagne!

CECILY: Yes. I thought you would like him to have the same one as yourself.

JACK: Oh! Well, if he has lunched once, he can't be expected to lunch twice. It would be absurd.

MISS PRISM: To partake of two luncheons in one day would not be liberty. It would be licence.

CHASUBLE: Even the pagan philosophers condemned excess in eating. Aristotle speaks of it with severity. He uses the same terms about it as he does about usury.

JACK: Doctor, will you escort the ladies into luncheon?

CHASUBLE: With pleasure.

He goes into the house with MISS PRISM *and* CECILY.

JACK: Your Bunburying has not been a great success after all, Algy. I don't think it is a good day for Bunburying, myself.

ALGERNON: Oh! There are ups and downs in Bunburying,

just as there are in everything else. I'd be all right if you would let me have some lunch. The main thing is that I have seen Cecily and she is a darling.

JACK: You are not to talk of Miss Cardew like that. I don't like it.

ALGERNON: Well, I don't like your clothes. You look perfectly ridiculous in them. Why on earth don't you go up and change? It is perfectly childish to be in deep mourning for a man who is actually staying for a whole week with you in your house as a guest. I call it grotesque.

JACK: You are certainly not staying with me for a whole week as a guest or anything else. You have got to leave . . . by the four-five train.

ALGERNON: I certainly won't leave you so long as you are in mourning. It would be most unfriendly. If I were in mourning you would stay with me, I suppose. I should think it very unkind if you didn't.

JACK: Well, will you go if I change my clothes?

ALGERNON: Yes, if you are not too long. I never saw anybody take so long to dress, and with such little result.

JACK: Well, at any rate, that is better than being always overdressed as you are.

ALGERNON: If I am occasionally a little over-dressed, I make up for it by being always immensely over-educated.

JACK: Your vanity is ridiculous, your conduct an outrage, and your presence in my garden utterly absurd. However, you have got to catch the four-five, and I hope you will have a pleasant journey back to town. This Bunburying, as you call it, has not been a great success for you. (*Goes into the house.*)

ALGERNON: I think it has been a great success. I'm in love with Cecily, and that is everything. It is all very well, but one can't Bunbury when one is hungry. I think I'll join them at lunch. (*Goes towards door.*)

Enter CECILY.

CECILY: I promised Uncle Jack that I wouldn't speak to you again, unless you asked me a question. I can't understand why you don't ask me a question of some kind. I am afraid you are not quite so intellectual as I thought you were at first.

ALGERNON: Cecily, mayn't I come in to lunch?

CECILY: I wonder you can look me in the face after your conduct.

ALGERNON: I love looking you in the face.

CECILY: But why did you try to put your horrid bill on poor Uncle Jack? I think that was inexcusable of you.

ALGERNON: I know it was; but the fact is I have a most wretched memory. I quite forgot I owed the Savoy £762 14s. 2d.

CECILY: Well, I admit I am glad to hear that you have a bad memory. Good memories are not a quality that women admire much in men.

ALGERNON: Cecily, I am fearfully hungry.

CECILY: I can't understand your being so hungry, considering all you have had to eat since last October.

ALGERNON: Oh! Those suppers were for poor Bunbury. Late suppers are the only things his doctor allows him to eat.

CECILY: Well, I don't wonder then that Mr. Bunbury is always so ill, if he eats suppers for six or eight people every night of the week.

ALGERNON: That is what I always tell him. But he seems to think his doctors know best. He's perfectly silly about doctors.

CECILY: Of course I don't want you to starve, so I have told the butler to send you out some lunch.

ALGERNON: Cecily, what a perfect angel you are! May I not see you again before I go?

CECILY: Miss Prism and I will be here after lunch. I always have my afternoon lessons under the yew-tree.

ALGERNON: Can't you invent something to get Miss Prism out of the way?

CECILY: Do you mean invent a falsehood?

ALGERNON: Oh! Not a falsehood, of course. Simply something that is not quite true, but should be.

CECILY: I am afraid I couldn't possibly do that. I shouldn't know how. People never think of cultivating a young girl's imagination. It is the great defect of modern education. Of course, if you happened to mention that dear Dr. Chasuble was waiting somewhere to see Miss Prism, she would certainly go to meet him. She never likes to keep him waiting. And she has so few opportunities of doing so.

ALGERNON: What a capital suggestion!

CECILY: I didn't suggest anything, Cousin Ernest. Nothing would induce me to deceive Miss Prism in the smallest detail. I merely pointed out that if you adopted a certain line of conduct, a certain result would follow.

ALGERNON: Of course. I beg your pardon, Cousin Cecily. Then I shall come here at half-past three. I have something very serious to say to you.

CECILY: Serious?

ALGERNON: Yes: very serious.

CECILY: In that case I think we had better meet in the house. I don't like talking seriously in the open air. It looks so artificial.

ALGERNON: Then where shall we meet?

Enter JACK.

JACK: The dog-cart is at the door. You have got to go. Your place is by Bunbury. (*Sees* CECILY.) Cecily! Don't you think, Cecily, that you had better return to Miss Prism and Dr. Chasuble?

CECILY: Yes, Uncle Jack. Good-bye, Cousin Ernest. I am afraid I shan't see you again, as I shall be doing my lessons with Miss Prism in the drawing-room at half-past three.

ALGERNON: Good-bye, Cousin Cecily. You have been very kind to me.

CECILY *goes out.*

JACK: Now look here, Algy. You have got to go, and the sooner you go the better. Bunbury is extremely ill, and your place is by his side.

ALGERNON: I can't go at the present moment. I must first just have my second lunch. And you will be pleased to hear that Bunbury is very much better.

JACK: Well, you will have to go at three-fifty, at any rate. I ordered your things to be packed and the dog-cart[17] to come round.

Act Drop

ACT THREE

The drawing-room at the Manor House. CECILY *and* MISS
PRISM *discovered; each writing at a separate table.*

MISS PRISM: Cecily! (CECILY *makes no answer.*) Cecily! You
are again making entries in your diary. I think I have had
occasion more than once to speak to you about that morbid habit of yours.

CECILY: I am merely, as I always do, taking you for my example, Miss Prism.

MISS PRISM: When one has thoroughly mastered the principles of Bimetallism[1] one has the right to lead an intro-
spective life. Hardly before. I must beg you to return to
your Political Economy.

CECILY: In one moment, dear Miss Prism. The fact is I have
only chronicled the events of to-day up till two-fifteen,
and it was at two-thirty that the fearful catastrophe occurred.

MISS PRISM: Pardon me, Cecily, it was exactly at two-forty-
five that Dr. Chasuble mentioned the very painful views
held by the Primitive Church on Marriage.

CECILY: I was not referring to Dr. Chasuble at all. I was alluding to the tragic exposure of poor Mr. Ernest Worthing.

MISS PRISM: I highly disapprove of Mr. Ernest Worthing. He is a thoroughly bad young man.

CECILY: I fear he must be. It is the only explanation I can find of his strange attractiveness.

MISS PRISM (rising): Cecily, let me entreat of you not to be led away by whatever superficial qualities this unfortunate young man may possess.

CECILY: Ah! Believe me, dear Miss Prism, it is only the superficial qualities that last. Man's deeper nature is soon found out.

MISS PRISM: Child! I do not know where you get such ideas. They are certainly not to be found in any of the improving books that I have procured for you.

CECILY: Are there ever any ideas in improving books? I fear not. I get my ideas . . . in the garden.

MISS PRISM: Then you should certainly not be so much in the open air. The fact is, you have fallen lately, Cecily, into a bad habit of thinking for yourself. You should give it up. It is not quite womanly . . . Men don't like it.

Enter ALGERNON.

Mr. Worthing, I thought, I may say I was in hopes that you had already returned to town.

ALGERNON: My departure will not long be delayed. I have come to bid you good-bye, Miss Cardew. I am informed that a dog-cart has been already ordered for me. I have no option but to go back again into the cold world.

CECILY: I hardly know, Mr. Worthing, what you can mean by using such an expression. The day, even for the month of July, is unusually warm.

MISS PRISM: Profligacy is apt to dull the senses.

ALGERNON: No doubt. I am far from defending the weather. I think however that it is only my duty to mention to you, Miss Prism, that Dr. Chasuble is expecting you in the vestry.

MISS PRISM: In the vestry! That sounds serious. It can hardly be for any trivial purpose that the Rector selects for an interview a place of such peculiarly solemn associations. I do not think that it would be right to keep him waiting, Cecily?

CECILY: It would be very, very wrong. The vestry is, I am told, excessively damp.

MISS PRISM: True! I had not thought of that, and Dr. Chasuble is sadly rheumatic. Mr. Worthing, we shall probably not meet again. You will allow me, I trust, to express a sincere hope that you will now turn over a new leaf in life.

ALGERNON: I have already begun an entire volume, Miss Prism.

MISS PRISM: I am delighted to hear it. (*Puts on a large unbecoming hat.*) And do not forget that there is always hope even for the most depraved. Do not be idle, Cecily.

CECILY: I have no intention of being idle. I realise only too strongly that I have a great deal of serious work before me.

MISS PRISM: Ah! that is quite as it should be, dear.

MISS PRISM goes out.

ALGERNON: This parting, Miss Cardew, is very painful.

CECILY: It is always painful to part from people whom one has known for a very brief space of time. The absence of old friends one can endure with equanimity. But even a momentary separation from anyone to whom one has just been introduced is almost unbearable.

ALGERNON: Thank you.

Enter MERRIMAN.

MERRIMAN: The dog-cart is at the door, sir.

ALGERNON *looks appealingly at* CECILY.

CECILY: It can wait, Merriman, for five minutes.
MERRIMAN: Yes, Miss.

Exit MERRIMAN.

ALGERNON: I hope, Cecily, I shall not offend you if I state quite frankly and openly that you seem to me to be in every way the visible personification of absolute perfection.

CECILY: I think your frankness does you great credit, Ernest. If you will allow me, I will copy your remarks into my diary. *(Goes over to table and begins writing in diary.)*

ALGERNON: Do you really keep a diary? I'd give anything to look at it. May I?

CECILY: Oh, no. *(Puts her hand over it.)* You see, it is simply a very young girl's record of her own thoughts and impressions, and consequently meant for publication. When it appears in volume form[2] I hope you will order a copy. But pray, Ernest, don't stop. I delight in taking down from dictation. I have reached "absolute perfection." You can go on. I am quite ready for more.

ALGERNON *(somewhat taken aback)*: Ahem! Ahem!

CECILY: Oh, don't cough, Ernest. When one is dictating one should speak fluently and not cough. Besides, I don't know how to spell a cough. (W*rites as* ALGERNON *speaks.*)

ALGERNON *(speaking very rapidly)*: Miss Cardew, ever since half-past twelve this afternoon, when I first looked upon your wonderful and incomparable beauty, I have not merely been your abject slave and servant, but, soaring upon the pinions of a possibly monstrous ambition, I have dared to love you wildly, passionately, devotedly, hopelessly.

CECILY (*laying down her pen*): Oh! please say that all over again. You speak far too fast and far too indistinctly. Kindly say it all over again.

ALGERNON: Miss Cardew, ever since you were half-past twelve—I mean ever since it was half-past twelve, this afternoon, when I first looked upon your wonderful and incomparable beauty . . .

CECILY: Yes, I have got that, all right.

ALGERNON (*stammering*): I—I—

    CECILY *lays down her pen and looks reproachfully at him. (Desperately.)* I have not merely been your abject slave and servant, but, soaring on the pinions of a possibly monstrous ambition, I have dared to love you wildly, passionately, devotedly, hopelessly. (*Takes out his watch and looks at it.*)

CECILY (*after writing for some time, looks up*): I have not taken down "hopelessly." It doesn't seem to make much sense, does it? (*A slight pause.*)

ALGERNON (*starting back*): Cecily!

CECILY: Is that the beginning of an entirely new paragraph? Or should it be followed by a note of admiration?

ALGERNON (*rapidly and romantically*): It is the beginning of an entirely new existence for me, and it shall be followed by such notes of admiration that my whole life shall be a subtle and sustained symphony of Love, Praise and Adoration combined.

CECILY: Oh, I don't think that makes any sense at all. The fact is that men should never try to dictate to women. They never know how to do it, and when they do do it, they always say something particularly foolish.

ALGERNON: I don't care whether what I say is foolish or not. All that I know is that I love you, Cecily. I love you, I want you. I can't live without you, Cecily! You know I love you. Will you marry me? Will you be my wife? (*Rushes over to her and puts his hand on hers.*)

CECILY (*rising*): Oh, you have made me make a blot! And yours is the only real proposal I have ever had in all my life. I should like to have entered it neatly.

Enter MERRIMAN.

MERRIMAN: The dog-cart is waiting, sir.

ALGERNON: Tell it to come round next week at the same hour.

MERRIMAN (*looks at* CECILY *who makes no sign*): Yes, sir.

CECILY: Uncle Jack would be very much annoyed if he knew you were staying on till next week, at the same hour.

ALGERNON: Oh! I don't care about Jack! I don't care for anybody in the whole world but you. I love you. Cecily! you will marry me, won't you?

CECILY: You silly boy! Of course. Why, we have been engaged for the last three months.

ALGERNON: For the last three months?

CECILY: Three months all but a few days. (*Looks at diary, turns over page.*) Yes; it will be exactly three months on Thursday.

ALGERNON: I didn't know.

CECILY: Very few people nowadays ever realise the position in which they are placed. The age is, as Miss Prism often says, a thoughtless one.

ALGERNON: But how did we become engaged?

CECILY: Well, ever since dear Uncle Jack first confessed to us that he had a younger brother who was very wicked and bad, you of course have formed the chief topic of conversation between myself and Miss Prism. And of course a man who is much talked about is always very attractive. One feels there must be something in him, after all. I dare say it was foolish of me, but I fell in love with you, Ernest.

ALGERNON: Darling! And when was the engagement actually settled?

CECILY: On the 14th of February last.[3] Worn out by your entire ignorance of my existence, I determined to end the matter one way or the other, and after a long struggle with myself I accepted you one evening in the garden. The next day I bought this little ring in your name. You see I always wear it, Ernest, and though it shows that you are sadly extravagant, still I have long ago forgiven you for that. Here in this drawer are all the little presents I have given you from time to time, neatly numbered and labelled. This is the pearl necklace you gave me on my birthday. And this is the box in which I keep all your letters. (*Opens box and produces letters tied up with blue ribbon.*)

ALGERNON: My letters! But my own sweet Cecily, I have never written you any letters.

CECILY: You need hardly remind me of that, Ernest. I remember it only too well. I grew tired of asking the postman every morning if he had a London letter for me. My health began to give way under the strain and anxiety. So I wrote your letters for you, and had them posted to me in the village by my maid. I wrote always three times a week and sometimes oftener.

ALGERNON: Oh, do let me read them, Cecily.

CECILY: Oh, I couldn't possibly. They would make you far too conceited. The three you wrote me after I had broken off the engagement are so beautiful and so badly spelt that even now I can hardly read them without crying a little.

ALGERNON: But was our engagement ever broken off?

CECILY: Of course it was. On the 22nd of last March. You can see the entry if you like. (*Shows diary.*) "Today I broke off my engagement with Ernest. I feel it is better to do so. The weather still continues charming."

ALGERNON: But why on earth did you break it off? What had I done? I had done nothing at all. Cecily, I am very much hurt indeed to hear you broke it off. Particularly when the weather was so charming.

CECILY: Men seem to forget very easily. I should have thought you would have remembered the violent letter you wrote to me because I danced with Lord Kelso at the county ball.

ALGERNON: But I did take it all back, Cecily, didn't I?

CECILY: Of course you did. Otherwise I wouldn't have forgiven you or accepted this little gold bangle with the turquoise and diamond heart, that you sent me the next day. *(Shows bangle.)*

ALGERNON: Did I give you this, Cecily? It's very pretty, isn't it?

CECILY: Yes. You have wonderfully good taste, Ernest. I have always said that of you. It's the excuse I've always given for your leading such a bad life.

ALGERNON: My own one! So we have been engaged for three months, Cecily!

CECILY: Yes; how the time has flown, hasn't it?

ALGERNON: I don't think so. I have found the days very long and very dreary without you.

CECILY: You dear romantic boy . . . *(Puts her fingers through his hair.)* I hope your hair curls naturally. Does it?

ALGERNON: Yes darling, with a little help from others.

CECILY: I am so glad.

ALGERNON: You'll never break off our engagement again, Cecily?

CECILY: I don't think that I could break it off now that I have actually met you. Besides, of course, there is the question of your name.

ALGERNON: Yes, of course. *(Nervously.)*

CECILY: You must not laugh at me, darling, but it had always been a girlish dream of mine to love some one whose name was Ernest.

ALGERNON *rises*, CECILY *also*.

There is something in that name that seems to inspire absolute confidence. I pity any poor married woman whose husband is not called Ernest.

ALGERNON: But, my dear child, do you mean to say you could not love me if I had some other name?

CECILY: But what name?

ALGERNON: Oh, any name you like—Algernon—for instance . . .

CECILY: But I don't like the name of Algernon.

ALGERNON: Well, my own dear, sweet, loving little darling, I really can't see why you should object to the name of Algernon. It is not at all a bad name. In fact, it is rather an aristocratic name. Half of the chaps who get into the Bankruptcy Court are called Algernon. But seriously, Cecily—*(moving to her)*—if my name was Algy, couldn't you love me?

CECILY *(rising)*: I might respect you, Ernest, I might admire your character, but I fear that I should not be able to give you my undivided attention.

ALGERNON: Ahem! Cecily! *(Picking up hat.)* Your Rector here is, I suppose, thoroughly experienced in the practice of all the rites and ceremonials of the Church?

CECILY: Oh, yes. Dr. Chasuble is a most learned man. He has never written a single book, so you can imagine how much he knows.

ALGERNON: I must see him at once on a most important christening—I mean on most important business.

CECILY: Oh!

ALGERNON: I shan't be away more than half an hour.

CECILY: Considering that we have been engaged since February the 14th, and that I only met you to-day for the first time, I think it is rather hard that you should leave me for so long a period as half an hour. Couldn't you make it twenty minutes?

ALGERNON: I'll be back in no time. (*Kisses her and rushes out.*)

CECILY: What an impetuous boy he is! I like his hair so much. I must enter his proposal in my diary.

Enter MERRIMAN.

MERRIMAN: A Miss Fairfax has just called to see Mr. Worthing. On very important business, Miss Fairfax states.

CECILY: Isn't Mr. Worthing in his library?

MERRIMAN: Mr. Worthing went over in the direction of the Rectory some time ago.

CECILY: Pray ask the lady to come in here; Mr. Worthing is sure to be back soon. And you can bring tea.

MERRIMAN: Yes, Miss. (*Goes out.*)

CECILY: Miss Fairfax! I suppose one of the many good elderly women who are associated with Uncle Jack in some of his Philanthropic work in London. I don't quite like women who are interested in Philanthropic work. I think it is so forward of them.

Enter MERRIMAN.

MERRIMAN: Miss Fairfax.

Enter GWENDOLEN. *Exit* MERRIMAN.

CECILY (*advancing to meet her*): Pray let me introduce myself to you. My name is Cecily Cardew.

GWENDOLEN: Cecily Cardew? (*Moving to her and shaking hands.*) What a very sweet name! Something tells me that we are going to be great friends. I like you already more than I can say. My first impressions of people are never wrong.

CECILY: How nice of you to like me so much after we have

known each other such a comparatively short time. Pray sit down.

GWENDOLEN *(still standing up)*: I may call you Cecily, may I not?

CECILY: With pleasure!

GWENDOLEN: And you will always call me Gwendolen, won't you?

CECILY: If you wish.

GWENDOLEN: Then that is all quite settled, is it not?

CECILY: I hope so.

A pause. They both sit down together.

GWENDOLEN: Perhaps this might be a favourable opportunity for my mentioning who I am. My father is Lord Bracknell. You have never heard of papa, I suppose?

CECILY: I don't think so.

GWENDOLEN: Outside the family circle, papa, I am glad to say, is entirely unknown. I think that is quite as it should be. The home seems to me to be the proper sphere for the man. And certainly once a man begins to neglect his domestic duties he becomes painfully effeminate, does he not? And I don't like that. It makes men so very attractive. Cecily, mamma, whose views on education are remarkably strict, has brought me up to be extremely short-sighted; it is part of her system; so do you mind my looking at you through my glasses?

CECILY: Oh! not at all, Gwendolen. I am very fond of being looked at.

GWENDOLEN *(after examining* CECILY *carefully through a lorgnette)*: You are here on a short visit, I suppose.

CECILY: Oh no! I live here.

GWENDOLEN *(severely)*: Really? Your mother, no doubt, or some female relative of advanced years, resides here also?

CECILY: Oh no! I have no mother, nor, in fact, any relations.

GWENDOLEN: Indeed?

CECILY: My dear guardian, with the assistance of Miss Prism, has the arduous task of looking after me.

GWENDOLEN: Your guardian?

CECILY: Yes, I am Mr. Worthing's ward.

GWENDOLEN: Oh! It is strange he never mentioned to me that he had a ward. How secretive of him! He grows more interesting hourly. I am not sure, however, that the news inspires me with feelings of unmixed delight. *(Rising and going to her.)* I am very fond of you, Cecily; I have liked you ever since I met you! But I am bound to state that now that I know that you are Mr. Worthing's ward, I cannot help expressing a wish you were—well, just a little older than you seem to be—and not quite so very alluring in appearance. In fact, if I may speak candidly—

CECILY: Pray do! I think that whenever one has anything unpleasant to say, one should always be quite candid.

GWENDOLEN: Well, to speak with perfect candour, Cecily, I wish that you were fully forty-two, and more than unusually plain for your age. Ernest has a strong upright nature. He is the very soul of truth and honour. Disloyalty would be as impossible to him as deception. But even men of the noblest possible moral character are extremely susceptible to the influence of the physical charms of others. Modern, no less than Ancient History, supplies us with many most painful examples of what I refer to. If it were not so, indeed, History would be quite unreadable.

CECILY: I beg your pardon, Gwendolen, did you say Ernest?

GWENDOLEN: Yes.

CECILY: Oh, but it is not Mr. Ernest Worthing who is my guardian. It is his brother—his elder brother.

GWENDOLEN *(sitting down again)*: Ernest never mentioned to me that he had a brother.

CECILY: I am sorry to say they have not been on good terms for a long time.

GWENDOLEN: Ah! that accounts for it. And now that I think of it I have never heard any man mention his brother. The subject seems distasteful to most men. Cecily, you have lifted a load from my mind. I was growing almost anxious. It would have been terrible if any cloud had come across a friendship like ours, would it not? Of course you are quite, quite sure that it is not Mr. Ernest Worthing who is your guardian?

CECILY: Quite sure. *(A pause.)* In fact, I am going to be his.

GWENDOLEN *(inquiringly)*: I beg your pardon?

CECILY *(rather shy and confidingly)*: Dearest Gwendolen, there is no reason why I should make a secret of it to you. Our little county newspaper is sure to chronicle the fact next week. Mr. Ernest Worthing and I are engaged to be married.

GWENDOLEN *(quite politely, rising)*: My darling Cecily, I think there must be some slight error. Mr. Ernest Worthing is engaged to me. The announcement will appear in the "Morning Post" on Saturday at the latest.

CECILY *(very politely, rising)*: I am afraid you must be under some misconception. Ernest proposed to me exactly ten minutes ago. *(Shows diary.)*

GWENDOLEN *(examines diary through her lorgnette carefully)*: It is certainly very curious, for he asked me to be his wife yesterday afternoon at 5.30. If you would care to verify the incident, pray do so. *(Produces diary of her own.)* I never travel without my diary. One should always have something sensational to read in the train. I am so sorry, dear Cecily, if it is any disappointment to you, but I am afraid I have the prior claim.

CECILY: It would distress me more than I can tell you, dear Gwendolen, if it caused you any mental or physical anguish, but I feel bound to point out that since

Ernest proposed to you he clearly has changed his mind.

GWENDOLEN *(meditatively)*: If the poor fellow has been entrapped into any foolish promise I shall consider it my duty to rescue him at once, and with a firm hand.

CECILY *(thoughtfully and sadly)*: Whatever unfortunate entanglement my dear boy may have got into, I will never reproach him with it after we are married.

GWENDOLEN: Do you allude to me, Miss Cardew, as an entanglement? You are presumptuous. On an occasion of this kind it becomes more than a moral duty to speak one's mind. It becomes a pleasure.

CECILY: Do you suggest, Miss Fairfax, that I entrapped Ernest into an engagement? How dare you? This is no time for wearing the shallow mask of manners. When I see a spade I call it a spade.

GWENDOLEN *(satirically)*: I am glad to say that I have never seen a spade. It is obvious that our social spheres have been widely different.

Enter MERRIMAN, *followed by the footman. He carries a salver, table cloth, and plate stand.* CECILY *is about to retort. The presence of the servants exercises a restraining influence, under which both girls chafe.*

MERRIMAN: Shall I lay tea here as usual, Miss?

CECILY *(sternly, in a calm voice)*: Yes, as usual.

MERRIMAN *begins to clear table and lay cloth. A long pause.* CECILY *and* GWENDOLEN *glare at each other.*

GWENDOLEN: Are there many interesting walks in the vicinity, Miss Cardew?

CECILY: Oh! yes! a great many. From the top of one of the hills quite close one can see five counties.

GWENDOLEN: Five counties! I don't think I should like that; I hate crowds.

CECILY (*sweetly*): I suppose that is why you live in town?

GWENDOLEN *bites her lip, and beats her foot nervously with her parasol.*

GWENDOLEN (*looking round*): Quite a charming room this is of yours, Miss Cardew.

CECILY: So glad you like it, Miss Fairfax.

GWENDOLEN: I had no idea there was anything approaching good taste in the more remote country districts. It is quite a surprise to me.

CECILY: I am afraid you judge of the country from what one sees in town. I believe most London houses are extremely vulgar.

GWENDOLEN: I suppose they do dazzle the rural mind. Personally I cannot understand how anybody manages to exist in the country—if anybody who is anybody does. The country always bores me to death.

CECILY: Ah! This is what the newspapers call agricultural depression, is it not? I believe the aristocracy are suffering very much from it just at present. It is almost an epidemic amongst them, I have been told. May I offer you some tea, Miss Fairfax?

GWENDOLEN (*with elaborate politeness*): Thank you. (*Aside.*) Detestable girl! But I require tea!

CECILY (*sweetly*): Sugar?

GWENDOLEN (*superciliously*): No, thank you. Sugar is not fashionable any more.

CECILY *looks angrily at her, takes up the tongs and puts four lumps of sugar into the cup.*

CECILY (*severely*): Cake or bread and butter?

GWENDOLEN (*in a bored manner*): Bread and butter, please. Cake is rarely seen at the best houses nowadays.

CECILY (*cuts a very large slice of cake and puts it on the tray*): Hand that to Miss Fairfax.

MERRIMAN *does so, and goes out with footman.* GWEN-
DOLEN *drinks the tea and makes a grimace. Puts down
cup at once, reaches out her hand to the bread and butter, looks at it, and finds it is cake. Rises in indignation.*

GWENDOLEN: You have filled my tea with lumps of sugar,
and though I asked most distinctly for bread and butter,
you have given me cake. I am known for the gentleness
of my disposition, and the extraordinary sweetness of my
nature, but I warn you, Miss Cardew, you may go too far.

CECILY (*rising*): To save my poor, innocent, trusting boy
from the machinations of any other girl there are no
lengths to which I would not go.

GWENDOLEN: From the moment I saw you I distrusted
you. I felt that you were false and deceitful. I am never
deceived in such matters. My first impressions of people
are invariably right.

CECILY: It seems to me, Miss Fairfax, that I am trespassing
on your valuable time. No doubt you have many other
calls of a similar character to make in the neighbourhood.

Enter JACK

GWENDOLEN (*catching sight of him*): Ernest! My own
Ernest!

JACK: Gwendolen! Darling! (*Offers to kiss her.*)

GWENDOLEN (*drawing back*): A moment! May I ask if you
are engaged to be married to this young lady? (*Points to
CECILY.*)

JACK (*laughing*): To dear little Cecily! Of course not! What
could have put such an idea into your pretty little
head?

GWENDOLYN: Thank you. You may! (*Offers her cheek.*)

CECILY (*very sweetly*): I knew there must be some misunderstanding, Miss Fairfax. The gentleman whose arm is

at present round your waist is my guardian, Mr. John Worthing.

GWENDOLEN: I beg your pardon?

CECILY: This is Uncle Jack.

GWENDOLEN (*receding*): Jack! Oh!

Enter ALGERNON.

CECILY: Here is Ernest.

ALGERNON (*goes over to* CECILY *without noticing anyone else*): My love. (*Offers to kiss her.*)

CECILY (*drawing back*): A moment, Ernest! May I ask you—are you engaged to be married to this young lady?

ALGERNON (*looking round*): To what young lady? Good heavens! Gwendolen!

CECILY: Yes! to good heavens, Gwendolen, I mean to Gwendolen.

ALGERNON (*laughing*): Of course not! What could have put such an idea into your pretty little head?

CECILY: Thank you. (*Presenting her cheek to be kissed.*) You may. (ALGERNON *kisses her.*)

GWENDOLEN: I felt there was some slight error, Miss Cardew. The gentleman who is now embracing you is my cousin, Mr. Algernon Moncrieff.

CECILY (*breaking away from* ALGERNON): Algernon Moncrieff! Oh!

The two girls move towards each other and put their arms round each other's waists as if for protection.

CECILY: Are you called Algernon?

ALGERNON: I cannot deny it.

CECILY: Oh!

GWENDOLEN: Is your name really John?

JACK (*standing rather proudly*): I could deny it if I liked. I could deny anything if I liked. But my name certainly is John. It has been John for years.

CECILY (*to* GWENDOLEN): A gross deception has been practised on both of us.

GWENDOLEN: My poor wounded Cecily!

CECILY: My sweet wronged Gwendolen!

GWENDOLEN (*slowly and seriously*): You will call me sister, will you not?

They embrace. JACK *and* ALGERNON *groan and walk up and down.*

CECILY (*rather brightly*): There is just one question I would like to be allowed to ask my guardian.

GWENDOLEN: An admirable idea! Mr. Worthing, there is just one question I would like to be permitted to put to you. Where is your brother Ernest? We are both engaged to be married to your brother Ernest, so it is a matter of some importance to us to know where your brother Ernest is at present.

JACK (*slowly and hesitatingly*): Gwendolen—Cecily—it is very painful for me to be forced to speak the truth. It is the first time in my life that I have ever been reduced to such a painful position, and I am really quite inexperienced in doing anything of the kind. However, I will tell you quite frankly that I have no brother Ernest. I have no brother at all. I never had a brother in my life, and I certainly have not the smallest intention of ever having one in the future.

CECILY (*surprised*): No brother at all?

JACK (*cheerily*): None!

GWENDOLEN (*severely*): Had you never a brother of any kind?

JACK (*pleasantly*): Never. Not even of any kind.

GWENDOLEN: I am afraid it is quite clear, Cecily, that neither of us is engaged to be married to any one.

CECILY: It is not a very pleasant position for a young girl suddenly to find herself in. Is it?

GWENDOLEN: Let us go into the garden. They will hardly venture to come after us there.

CECILY: No, men are so cowardly, aren't they?

They retire into the garden with scornful looks.

JACK: Pretty mess you have got me into.

ALGERNON *sits down at tea table and pours out some tea. He seems quite unconcerned.*

What on earth do you mean by coming down here and pretending to be my brother? Perfectly monstrous of you!

ALGERNON (*eating muffin*): What on earth do you mean by pretending to have a brother! It was absolutely disgraceful! (*Eats another muffin.*)

JACK: I told you to go away by the three-fifty. I ordered the dog-cart for you. Why on earth didn't you take it?

ALGERNON: I hadn't had my tea.

JACK: This ghastly state of things is what you call Bunburying, I suppose?

ALGERNON: Yes, and a perfectly wonderful Bunbury it is. The most wonderful Bunbury I have ever had in my life.

JACK: Well, you've no right whatsoever to Bunbury here.

ALGERNON: That is absurd. One has a right to Bunbury anywhere one chooses. Every serious Bunburyist knows that.

JACK: Serious Bunburyist! Good heavens!

ALGERNON: Well, one must be serious about something, if one wants to have any amusement in life. I happen to be serious about Bunburying. What on earth you are serious about I haven't got the remotest idea. About everything, I should fancy. You have such an absolutely trivial nature.

JACK: Well, the only small satisfaction I have in the whole of this wretched business is that your friend Bunbury is quite exploded. You won't be able to run down to the country quite so often as you used to do, dear Algy. And a very good thing too.

ALGERNON: Your brother is a little off colour, isn't he, dear Jack? You won't be able to disappear to London quite so frequently as your wicked custom was. And not a bad thing either.

JACK: As for your conduct towards Miss Cardew, I must say that your taking in a sweet, simple, innocent girl like that is quite inexcusable. To say nothing of the fact that she is my ward.

ALGERNON: I can see no possible defence at all for your deceiving a brilliant, clever, thoroughly experienced young lady like Miss Fairfax. To say nothing of the fact that she is my cousin.

JACK: I wanted to be engaged to Gwendolen, that is all. I love her.

ALGERNON: Well, I simply wanted to be engaged to Cecily. I adore her.

JACK: There is certainly no chance of your marrying Miss Cardew.

ALGERNON: I don't think there is much likelihood, Jack, of you and Miss Fairfax being united.

JACK: Well, that is no business of yours.

ALGERNON: If it was my business, I wouldn't talk about it. It is very vulgar to talk about one's business. Only people like stock-brokers do that, and then merely at dinner parties.

JACK: How can you sit there, calmly eating muffins when we are in this horrible trouble, I can't make out. You seem to me to be perfectly heartless.

ALGERNON: Well, I can't eat muffins in an agitated manner. The butter would probably get on my cuffs. One should always eat muffins quite calmly. It is the only way to eat them.

JACK: I say it's perfectly heartless your eating muffins at all, under the circumstances.

ALGERNON: When I am in trouble, eating is the only thing that consoles me. Indeed, when I am in really great trouble, as any one who knows me intimately will tell you, I refuse everything except food and drink. At the present moment I am eating muffins because I am unhappy. Besides, I am particularly fond of muffins. *(Rising.)*

JACK *(rising)*: Well, that is no reason why you should eat them all in that greedy way. *(Takes muffins from* ALGERNON.*)*

ALGERNON *(offering tea-cake)*: I wish you would have tea-cake instead. I don't like tea-cake.

JACK: Good heavens! I suppose a man may eat his own muffins in his own house!

ALGERNON: But you have just said it was perfectly heartless to eat muffins.

JACK: I said it was perfectly heartless of you, under the circumstances. That is a very different thing.

ALGERNON: That may be. But the muffins are the same. *(He seizes the muffin-dish from* JACK.*)*

JACK: Algy, I wish to goodness you would go.

ALGERNON: You can't possibly ask me to go without having some dinner. It's absurd. I never go without my dinner. No one ever does, except vegetarians and people like that. Besides, I have just made arrangements with Dr. Chasuble to be christened at a quarter to six under the name of Ernest.

JACK: My dear fellow, the sooner you give up that nonsense the better. I made arrangements this morning with Dr. Chasuble to be christened myself at 5.30, and I naturally will take the name of Ernest. Gwendolen would wish it. We can't both be christened Ernest. It's absurd. Besides, I have a perfect right to be christened if I like. There is no evidence at all that I have ever been christened by anybody. I should think it extremely probable I never was, and so does Dr. Chasuble. It is entirely different in your case. You have been christened already.

ALGERNON: Yes, but I have not been christened for years.

JACK: Yes, but you have been christened. That is the important thing.

ALGERNON: Quite so. So I know my constitution can stand it. If you are not quite sure about your ever having been christened, I must say I think it rather dangerous your venturing on it now. It might make you very unwell. You can hardly have forgotten that some one very closely connected with you was very nearly carried off this week in Paris by a severe chill.

JACK: Yes; but you said yourself it was not hereditary, or anything of that kind.

ALGERNON: It usen't to be, I know—but I dare say it is now. Science is always making wonderful improvements in things.

JACK: May I ask, Algy, what on earth do you propose to do?

ALGERNON: Nothing. That is what I have been trying to do for the last ten minutes, and you have kept on doing everything in your power to distract my attention from my work.

JACK: Well, I shall go out into the garden, and see Gwendolen. I feel quite sure she expects me.

ALGERNON: I know from her extremely cold manner that Cecily expects me so I certainly shan't go out into the garden. When a man does exactly what a woman expects him to do she doesn't think much of him. One should always do what a woman doesn't expect, just as one should always say what she doesn't understand. The result is invariably perfect sympathy on both sides.

JACK: Oh, that is nonsense. You are always talking nonsense.

ALGERNON: It is much cleverer to talk nonsense than to listen to it, my dear fellow, and a much rarer thing too, in spite of all the public may say.

JACK: I don't listen to you. I can't listen to you.

ALGERNON: Oh, that is merely false modesty. You know perfectly well you could listen to me if you tried. You always under-rate yourself, an absurd thing to do nowadays when there are such a lot of conceited people about. Jack, you are eating the muffins again! I wish you wouldn't. There are only two left. *(Removes plate.)* I told you I was particularly fond of muffins.

JACK: But I hate tea-cake.

ALGERNON: Why on earth do you allow tea-cake to be served up to your guests, then? What ideas you have of hospitality!

JACK *(irritably)*: Oh! that is not the point. We are not discussing tea-cakes. *(Crosses.)* Algy! you are perfectly maddening. You never can stick to the point in any conversation.

ALGERNON *(slowly)*: No: it always hurts me.

JACK: Good Heavens! What affectation! I loathe affectation.

ALGERNON: Well, my dear fellow, if you don't like affectation, I really don't see what you can like. Besides, it isn't affectation. The point always does hurt me, and I hate physical pain, of any kind.

JACK *(glares at* ALGERNON; *walks up and down stage. Finally comes up to table)*: Algy! I have already told you to go. I don't want you here. Why don't you go?

ALGERNON: I haven't quite finished my tea yet. And there is still one muffin left. *(Takes the last muffin.)*

JACK *groans and sinks down in a chair and buries his face in his hands.*

Act Drop

Act Four

SCENE: *The same.*

JACK *and* ALGERNON *discovered in the same position as at the close of Act Three. Enter behind,* GWENDOLEN *and* CECILY.

GWENDOLEN: The fact that they did not follow us at once into the garden, as any one else would have done, seems to me to show that they have some sense of shame left.

CECILY: They have been eating muffins. That looks like repentance.

GWENDOLEN (*after a pause*): They don't seem to notice us at all. Couldn't you cough?

CECILY: But I haven't got a cough.

GWENDOLEN: They're looking at us. What effrontery!

CECILY: They're approaching. That's very forward of them.

GWENDOLEN: Let us preserve a dignified silence.

CECILY: Certainly. It's the only thing to do now.

JACK *and* ALGERNON *whistle some dreadful popular air from a British Opera.*[1]

GWENDOLEN: This dignified silence seems to produce an unpleasant effect.

CECILY: A most distasteful one.

GWENDOLEN: But we will not be the first to speak.

CECILY: Certainly not.

GWENDOLEN: Mr. Worthing, I have something very particular to ask you. Much depends on your reply.

CECILY: Gwendolen, your common sense is invaluable. Mr. Moncrieff, kindly answer me the following question. Why did you pretend to be my guardian's brother?

ALGERNON: In order that I might have an opportunity of meeting you.

CECILY (*to* GWENDOLEN): That certainly seems a satisfactory explanation, does it not?

GWENDOLEN: Yes, dear, if you can believe him.

CECILY: I don't. But that does not affect the wonderful beauty of his answer.

GWENDOLEN: True. In matters of grave importance, style, not sincerity, is the vital thing. Mr. Worthing, what explanation can you offer to me for pretending to have a brother? Was it in order that you might have an opportunity of coming up to town to see me as often as possible?

JACK: Can you doubt it, Miss Fairfax?

GWENDOLEN: I have the greatest doubts upon the subject. But I intend to crush them. This is not the moment for German scepticism. (*Moving to* CECILY.) Their explanations appear to be quite satisfactory, especially Mr. Worthing's. That seems to me to have the stamp of truth upon it.

CECILY: I am more than content with what Mr. Moncrieff said. His voice alone inspires one with absolute credulity.

GWENDOLEN: Then you think we should forgive them?

CECILY: Yes. I mean no.

GWENDOLEN: True! I had forgotten. There are principles at stake that one cannot surrender. Which of us should tell them? The task is not a pleasant one.

CECILY: Could we not both speak at the same time?

GWENDOLEN: An excellent idea! I always speak at the same time as other people. Will you take the time from me?

CECILY: Certainly.

GWENDOLEN *beats time with uplifted finger.*

GWENDOLEN *and* CECILY (*speaking together*): Your Christian names are still an insuperable barrier. That is all!

JACK *and* ALGERNON (*speaking together*): Our Christian names! Is that all? But we are going to be christened this afternoon.

GWENDOLEN (*to* JACK): For my sake you are prepared to do this terrible thing?

JACK: I am.

CECILY (*to* ALGERNON): To please me you are ready to face this fearful ordeal?

ALGERNON: I am!

GWENDOLEN: How absurd to talk of the equality of the sexes! Where questions of self-sacrifice are concerned, men are infinitely beyond us.

JACK: We are. (*Clasps hands with* ALGERNON.)

CECILY: They have moments of physical courage of which we women know absolutely nothing.

GWENDOLEN (*to* JACK): Darling.

ALGERNON (*to* CECILY): Darling!

They fall into each other's arms.
Enter MERRIMAN. *When he enters he coughs loudly, seeing the situation.*

MERRIMAN: Ahem! Ahem! Lady Bracknell!

JACK: Good heavens!

Enter LADY BRACKNELL. *The couples separate in alarm.*
Exit MERRIMAN.

LADY BRACKNELL: Gwendolen! What does this mean?

GWENDOLEN: Merely that I am engaged to be married to Mr. Worthing, mamma.

LADY BRACKNELL: Come here. Sit down. Sit down immediately. Hesitation of any kind is a sign of mental decay in the young, of physical weakness in the old. (*Turns to* JACK.) Apprised, sir, of my daughter's sudden flight by her trusty maid, whose confidence I purchased by means of a small coin, I followed her at once by a luggage train. Her unhappy father is, I am glad to say, under the impression that she is attending a more than usually lengthy lecture by the University Extension Scheme on the Influence of a permanent income on Thought. I do not propose to undeceive him. Indeed I have never undeceived him on any question. I would consider it wrong. But, of course, you will clearly understand that all communication between yourself and my daughter must cease immediately from this moment. On this point, as indeed on all points, I am firm.

JACK: I am engaged to be married to Gwendolen, Lady Bracknell!

LADY BRACKNELL: You are nothing of the kind, sir. And now, as regards Algernon! . . . Algernon!

ALGERNON: Yes, Aunt Augusta.

LADY BRACKNELL: May I ask if it is in this house that your invalid friend Mr. Bunbury resides?

ALGERNON (*stammering*): Oh! No! Bunbury doesn't live here. Bunbury is somewhere else at present. In fact, Bunbury is dead.

LADY BRACKNELL: Dead! When did Mr. Bunbury die? His death must have been extremely sudden.

ALGERNON *(airily)*: Oh! I killed Bunbury this afternoon. I mean poor Bunbury died this afternoon.

LADY BRACKNELL: What did he die of?

ALGERNON: Bunbury? Oh, he was quite exploded.

LADY BRACKNELL: Exploded! Was he the victim of a revolutionary outrage? I was not aware that Mr. Bunbury was interested in social legislation. If so, he is well punished for his morbidity.

ALGERNON: My dear Aunt Augusta, I mean he was found out! The doctors found out that Bunbury could not live, that is what I mean—so Bunbury died.

LADY BRACKNELL: He seems to have had great confidence in the opinion of his physicians. I am glad, however, that he made up his mind at the last to some definite course of action, and acted under proper medical advice. And now that we have finally got rid of this Mr. Bunbury, may I ask, Mr. Worthing, who is that young person whose hand my nephew Algernon is now holding in what seems to me a peculiarly unnecessary manner?

JACK: That lady is Miss Cecily Cardew, my ward.

LADY BRACKNELL *bows coldly to* CECILY.

ALGERNON: I am engaged to be married to Cecily, Aunt Augusta.

LADY BRACKNELL: I beg your pardon?

CECILY: Mr. Moncrieff and I are engaged to be married, Lady Bracknell.

LADY BRACKNELL *(with a shiver, crossing to the sofa and sitting down)*: I do not know whether there is anything peculiarly exciting in the air of this particular part of Hertfordshire, but the number of engagements that go on seems to me considerably above the proper average that statistics have laid down for our guidance. I think some preliminary inquiry on my part would not be out of place. Mr. Worthing, is Miss Cardew at all connected with any of the larger railway stations in London? I merely desire information. Until yesterday I had no idea that there were any families or persons whose origin was a Terminus.

JACK *looks perfectly furious, but restrains himself.*

JACK *(in a clear, cold voice)*: Miss Cardew is the grand-daughter of the late Mr. Thomas Cardew of 149 Belgrave Square, S.W.; Gervase Park, Dorking, Surrey; and the Sporran, Fifeshire, N.B.

LADY BRACKNELL: That sounds not unsatisfactory. Three addresses always inspire confidence, even in tradesmen. But what proof have I of their authenticity?

JACK: I have carefully preserved the Court Guides of the period. They are open to your inspection, Lady Bracknell.

LADY BRACKNELL *(grimly)*: I have known strange errors in that publication.

JACK: Miss Cardew's family solicitors are Messrs. Markby, Markby, and Markby of 149a Lincoln's Inn Fields, Western Central District, London. I have no doubt they will be happy to supply you with any further information. Their office hours are from ten till four.

LADY BRACKNELL: Markby, Markby, and Markby? A firm of the very highest position in their profession. Indeed I am told that one of the Mr. Markbys is occasionally to be seen at dinner parties. So far I am satisfied.

JACK *(very irritably)*: How extremely kind of you, Lady Bracknell! I have also in my possession, you will be pleased to hear, certificates of Miss Cardew's birth, baptism, whooping cough, registration, vaccination, confirmation, and the measles; both the German and the English variety.

LADY BRACKNELL: Ah! A life crowded with incident, I see; though perhaps somewhat too exciting for a young girl. I am not myself in favour of premature experiences. *(Rises, looks at her watch.)* Gwendolen! the time approaches for our departure. We have not a moment to lose. As a matter of form, Mr. Worthing, I had better ask you if Miss Cardew has any little fortune?

JACK: Oh! about a hundred and thirty thousand pounds in the Funds. That is all. Good-bye, Lady Bracknell. So pleased to have seen you.

LADY BRACKNELL *(sitting down again)*: A moment, Mr. Worthing. A hundred and thirty thousand pounds! And in the Funds! Miss Cardew seems to me a most attractive young lady, now that I look at her. Few girls of the present day have any really solid qualities, any of the qualities that last, and improve with time. We live, I regret to say, in an age of surfaces. *(To* CECILY): Come over here, dear. (CECILY *goes across.*) Pretty child! your dress is sadly simple, and your hair seems almost as Nature might have left it. But we can soon alter all that. A thoroughly experienced French maid produces a really marvellous result in a very brief space of time. I remember recommending one to young Lady Lancing, and after three months her own husband did not know her.

JACK: And after six months nobody knew her.

LADY BRACKNELL *(glares at* JACK *for a few moments. Then bends, with a practised smile, to* CECILY): Kindly turn round, sweet child. (CECILY *turns completely round.*) No, the side view is what I want. (CECILY *presents her profile.*) Yes, quite as I expected. There are distinct social possibilities in your profile. The two weak points in our age are its want of principle and its want of profile. The chin a little higher, dear. Style largely depends on the way the chin is worn. They are worn very high, just at present. Algernon!

ALGERNON: Yes, Aunt Augusta!

LADY BRACKNELL: There are distinct social possibilities in Miss Cardew's profile.

ALGERNON: Cecily is the sweetest, dearest, prettiest girl in the whole world. And I don't care twopence about social possibilities.

LADY BRACKNELL: Never speak disrespectfully of Society, Algernon. Only people who can't get into it do that. (*To* CECILY): Dear child, of course you know that Algernon has nothing but his debts to depend upon. But I do not approve of mercenary marriages. When I married Lord Bracknell I had no fortune of any kind. But I never dreamed for a moment of allowing that to stand in my way. Well, I suppose I must give my consent.

ALGERNON: Thank you, Aunt Augusta.

LADY BRACKNELL: Cecily, you may kiss me!

CECILY (*kisses her*): Thank you, Lady Bracknell.

LADY BRACKNELL: You may also address me as Aunt Augusta for the future.

CECILY: Thank you, Aunt Augusta.

LADY BRACKNELL: The marriage, I think, had better take place quite soon.

ALGERNON: Thank you, Aunt Augusta.

CECILY: Thank you, Aunt Augusta.

LADY BRACKNELL: To speak frankly, I am not in favour of long engagements. They give people the opportunity of finding out each other's character before marriage, which I think is never advisable.

JACK: I beg your pardon for interrupting you, Lady Bracknell, but this engagement is quite out of the question. I am Miss Cardew's guardian, and she cannot marry without my consent until she comes of age. That consent I absolutely decline to give.

LADY BRACKNELL: Upon what grounds, may I ask? Algernon is an extremely, I may almost say an ostentatiously,

eligible young man. He has nothing, but he looks everything. What more can one desire?

JACK: It pains me very much to have to speak frankly to you,
Lady Bracknell, about your nephew, but the fact is that I
do not approve at all of his moral character. I suspect him
of being untruthful.

ALGERNON *and* CECILY *look at him in indignant amazement.*

LADY BRACKNELL: Untruthful! My nephew Algernon? Impossible! He is an Oxonian.

JACK: I fear there can be no possible doubt about the matter. This afternoon during my temporary absence in
London on an important question of romance, he obtained admission to my house by means of the false pre-
tence of being my brother. Under an assumed name he
drank, I've just been informed by my butler, an entire
pint bottle of my Perrier-Jouet, Brut, '89; wine I was specially reserving for myself. Continuing his disgraceful
deception, he succeeded in the course of the afternoon
in alienating the affections of my only ward. He subse-
quently stayed to tea, and devoured every single muffin.
And what makes his conduct all the more heartless is,
that he was perfectly well aware from the first that I have
no brother, that I never had a brother, and that I don't intend to have a brother, not even of any kind. I distinctly
told him so myself yesterday afternoon.

CECILY: But, dear Uncle Jack, for the last year you have
been telling us all that you had a brother. You dwelt continually on the subject. Algy merely corroborated your
statement. It was noble of him.

JACK: Pardon me, Cecily, you are a little too young to understand these matters. To invent anything at all is an act
of sheer genius, and, in a commercial age like ours,

shows considerable physical courage. Few of our modern novelists dare to invent a single thing. It is an open secret that they don't know how to do it. Upon the other hand, to corroborate a falsehood is a distinctly cowardly action. I know it is a thing that the newspapers do one for the other, every day. But it is not the act of a gentleman. No gentleman ever corroborates anything.

ALGERNON (*furiously*): Upon my word Jack!

LADY BRACKNELL: Ahem! Mr. Worthing, after careful consideration I have decided entirely to overlook my nephew's conduct to you.

JACK: That is very generous of you, Lady Bracknell. My own decision, however, is unalterable. I decline to give my consent.

LADY BRACKNELL (*to* CECILY): Come here, sweet child. (CECILY *goes over*). How old are you, dear?

CECILY: Well, I am really only eighteen, but I always admit to twenty when I go to evening parties.

LADY BRACKNELL: You are perfectly right in making some slight alteration. Indeed, no woman should ever be quite accurate about her age. It looks so calculating. . . . (*In a meditative manner.*) Eighteen, but admitting to twenty at evening parties. Well, it will not be very long before you are of age and free from the restraints of tutelage. So I don't think your guardian's consent is, after all, a matter of any importance.

JACK: Pray excuse me, Lady Bracknell, for interrupting you again, but it is only fair to tell you that according to the terms of her grandfather's will Miss Cardew does not come legally of age till she is thirty-five.

LADY BRACKNELL: That does not seem to me to be a grave objection. Thirty-five is a very attractive age. London society is full of women of the very highest birth who have, of their own free choice, remained thirty-five for years. Lady Dumbleton is an instance in point. To my own knowledge she has been thirty-five ever since she arrived at the age of forty, which was many years ago now. I see no reason why our dear Cecily should not be even still more attractive at the age you mention than she is at present. There will be a large accumulation of property.

CECILY (*to* JACK): You are quite sure that I can't marry without your consent till I am thirty-five?

JACK: That is the wise provision of your grandfather's will, Cecily. He undoubtedly foresaw the sort of difficulty that would be likely to occur.

CECILY: Then grandpapa must have had a very extraordinary imagination. Algy . . . could you wait for me till I was thirty-five? Don't speak hastily. It is a very serious question, and much of my future happiness, as well as all of yours, depends on your answer.

ALGERNON: Of course I could, Cecily. How can you ask me such a question? I could wait for ever for you. You know I could.

CECILY: Yes, I felt it instinctively, but I couldn't wait all that time. I hate waiting even five minutes for anybody. It always makes me rather cross. I am not punctual myself, I know, but I do like punctuality in others, and waiting, even to be married, is quite out of the question.

ALGERNON: Then what is to be done, Cecily?

CECILY: I don't know, Mr. Moncrieff.

LADY BRACKNELL: My dear Mr. Worthing, as Miss Cecily states positively that she cannot wait till she is thirty-five—a remark which I am bound to say seems to me to show a somewhat impatient nature—I would beg of you to reconsider your decision.

JACK: But my dear Lady Bracknell, the matter is entirely in your own hands. The moment you consent to my marriage with Gwendolen, I will most gladly allow your nephew to form an alliance with my ward.

LADY BRACKNELL (*rising and drawing herself up*): You

must be quite aware that what you propose is out of the question.

JACK: Then a passionate celibacy is all that any of us can look forward to.

LADY BRACKNELL: That is not the destiny I propose for Gwendolen. Algernon, of course, can choose for himself. *(Pulls out her watch.)* Come, dear—(GWENDOLEN *rises*)—we have already missed five, if not six, trains. To miss any more might expose us to comment on the platform.

Enter DR. CHASUBLE.

CHASUBLE: Everything is quite ready for the christenings.

LADY BRACKNELL: The christenings, sir! Is not that somewhat premature?

CHASUBLE (*looking rather puzzled, and pointing to* JACK *and* ALGERNON): Both these gentleman have expressed a desire for immediate baptism.

LADY BRACKNELL: At their age? The idea is grotesque and irreligious! Algernon, I forbid you to be baptized. I will not hear of such excess. Lord Bracknell would be highly displeased if he learned that that was the way in which you wasted your time and money.

CHASUBLE: Am I to understand then that there are to be no christenings at all this afternoon?

JACK: I don't think that, as things are now, it would be of much practical value to either of us, Dr. Chasuble.

CHASUBLE: I am grieved to hear such sentiments from you, Mr. Worthing. They savour of the heretical views of the Anabaptists, views that I have completely refuted in four of my unpublished sermons. Baptismal regeneration is not to be lightly spoken of. Indeed, by the unanimous opinion of the fathers, baptism is a form of new birth. However, where adults are concerned, compulsory christening, except in the case of savage tribes, is, I regret to say, uncanonical, so I shall return to the church at once. Indeed, I have just been informed by the pew-opener that for the last hour and a half Miss Prism has been waiting for me in the vestry.

LADY BRACKNELL (*starting*): Miss Prism! Did I hear you mention a Miss Prism?

CHASUBLE: Yes, Lady Bracknell. I am on my way to join her.

LADY BRACKNELL: Pray allow me to detain you for a moment. This matter may prove to be one of vital importance to Lord Bracknell and myself. Is this Miss Prism a female of repellent aspect, remotely connected with education?

CHASUBLE (*somewhat indignantly*): She is the most cultivated of ladies, and the very picture of respectability.

LADY BRACKNELL: It is obviously the same person. May I ask what position she holds in your household?

CHASUBLE (*severely*): I am a celibate, madam.

JACK (*interposing*): Lady Bracknell, Miss Prism has been for the last three years Miss Cardew's esteemed governess and valued companion.

LADY BRACKNELL: In spite of what I hear of her, I must see her at once. Let her be sent for.

CHASUBLE (*looking off*): She approaches; she is nigh.

Enter MISS PRISM *hurriedly.*

MISS PRISM: I was told you expected me in the vestry, dear Canon. I have been waiting for you there for an hour and three-quarters. (*Catches sight of* LADY BRACKNELL, *who has fixed her with a stony glare.* MISS PRISM *grows pale and quails. She looks anxiously round as if desirous to escape.*)

LADY BRACKNELL (*in a severe, judicial voice*): Prism! (MISS PRISM *bows her head in shame.*) Come here, Prism! (MISS PRISM *approaches in a humble manner.*) Prism! Where is that baby? (*General consternation. The* CANON *starts back in horror.* ALGERNON *and* JACK *pretend to be anxious to shield* CECILY *and* GWENDOLEN *from hearing the details of a terrible public scandal.*) Twenty-eight years ago, Prism, you left Lord Bracknell's house, Number 104, Upper Grosvenor Street, in charge of a perambulator that contained a baby of the male sex. You never returned. A few weeks later, through the elaborate investigations of the Metropolitan police, the perambulator was discovered at midnight standing by itself in a remote corner of Bayswater. It contained the manuscript of a three-volume novel of more than usually revolting sentimentality. (MISS PRISM *starts in involuntary indignation.*) But the baby was not there. (*Every one looks at* MISS PRISM.) Prism! Where is that baby? (*A pause.*)

MISS PRISM: Lady Bracknell, I admit with shame that I do not know. I only wish I did. The plain facts of the case are these. On the morning of the day you mention, a day that is for ever branded on my memory, I prepared as usual to take the baby out in its perambulator. I had also with me a somewhat old, capacious hand-bag in which I had intended to place the manuscript of a work of fiction that I had written during my few unoccupied hours. In a moment of mental abstraction, for which I never can forgive myself, I deposited the manuscript in the basinette, and placed the baby in the hand-bag.

JACK (*who has been listening attentively*): But where did you deposit the hand-bag?

MISS PRISM: Do not ask me, Mr. Worthing.

JACK: Miss Prism, this is a matter of no small importance to me. I insist on knowing where you deposited the hand-bag that contained that infant.

MISS PRISM: I left it in the cloak-room of one of the larger railway stations in London.

JACK: What railway station?

MISS PRISM *(quite crushed)*: Victoria. The Brighton line. *(Sinks into a chair.)*

LADY BRACKNELL *(looking at Jack)*: I sincerely hope nothing improbable is going to happen. The improbable is always in bad, or at any rate, questionable taste.

JACK: I must retire to my room for a moment.

CHASUBLE: This news seems to have upset you, Mr. Worthing. I trust your indisposition is merely temporary.

JACK: I will be back in a few moments, dear Canon. Gwendolen! Wait here for me!

GWENDOLEN: If you are not too long, I will wait here for you all my life.

Exit JACK *in great excitement.*

CHASUBLE: What do you think this means, Lady Bracknell?

LADY BRACKNELL: I dare not even suspect, Dr. Chasuble. I need hardly tell you that in families of high position strange coincidences are not supposed to occur. They are hardly considered the thing.

Noises heard overhead as if some one was throwing trunks about. Every one looks up.

CECILY: Uncle Jack seems strangely agitated.

CHASUBLE: Your guardian has a very emotional nature.

LADY BRACKNELL: This noise is extremely unpleasant. It sounds as if he was having an argument with the furniture. I dislike arguments of any kind. They are always vulgar, and often convincing.

CHASUBLE *(looking up)*: It has stopped now. *(The noise is redoubled.)*

LADY BRACKNELL: I wish he would arrive at some conclusion.

GWENDOLEN: This suspense is terrible. I hope it will last.

Enter JACK *with a hand-bag of black leather in his hand.*

JACK (*rushing over to* MISS PRISM): Is this the hand-bag, Miss Prism? Examine it carefully before you speak. The happiness of more than one life depends on your answer.

MISS PRISM (*calmly*): It seems to be mine. Yes, here is the injury it received through the upsetting of a Gower Street omnibus in younger and happier days. Here is the stain on the lining caused by the explosion of a temperance beverage,² an incident that occurred at Leamington. And here, on the lock, are my initials. I had forgotten that in an extravagant mood I had had them placed there. The bag is undoubtedly mine. I am delighted to have it so unexpectedly restored to me. It has been a great inconvenience being without it all these years.

JACK (*in a pathetic voice*): Miss Prism, more is restored to you than this hand-bag. I was the baby you placed in it.

MISS PRISM (*amazed*): You?

JACK (*embracing her*): Yes . . . mother!

MISS PRISM (*recoiling in indignant astonishment*): Mr. Worthing, I am unmarried!

JACK: Unmarried! I do not deny that is a serious blow. But after all, who has the right to cast a stone against one who has suffered? Cannot repentance wipe out an act of folly? Why should there be one law for men, and another for women. Mother, I forgive you. (*Tries to embrace her again.*)

MISS PRISM (*still more indignant*): But Mr. Worthing, there is some error. Maternity has never been an incident in my life. The suggestion, if it were not made before such a large number of people, would be almost indelicate. (*Pointing to* LADY BRACKNELL.) There stands the lady who can tell you who you really are. (*Retires to back of stage.*)

JACK (*after a pause*): Lady Bracknell, I hate to seem inquisitive, but would you kindly inform me who I am?

LADY BRACKNELL: I am afraid that the news I have to give you will not altogether please you. You are the son of my poor sister, Mrs. Moncrieff, and consequently Algernon's elder brother.

JACK: Algy's elder brother! Then I have a brother after all. I knew I had a brother! I always said I had a brother! Cecily,—how could you have ever doubted that I had a brother! (*Seizes hold of* ALGERNON.) Dr. Chasuble, my unfortunate brother. Miss Prism, my unfortunate brother. Gwendolen, my unfortunate brother. Algy, you young scoundrel, you will have to treat me with more respect in the future. You have never behaved to me like a brother in all your life.

ALGERNON: Well, not till to-day, old boy, I admit. (*Shakes hands.*) I did my best, however, though I was out of practice.

GWENDOLEN (*to* JACK): Darling!

JACK: Darling!

LADY BRACKNELL: Under these strange and unforeseen circumstances you can kiss your Aunt Augusta.

JACK (*staying where he is*): I am dazed with happiness. (*Kisses* GWENDOLEN.) I hardly know who I am kissing.

ALGERNON *takes the opportunity to kiss* CECILY.

GWENDOLEN: I hope that will be the last time I shall ever hear you make such an observation.

JACK: It will, darling.

MISS PRISM (*advancing, after coughing slightly*): Mr. Worthing,—Mr. Moncrieff as I should call you now—after what has just occurred I feel it my duty to resign my position in this household. Any inconvenience I may have caused you in your infancy through placing you inadvertently in this hand-bag I sincerely apologise for.

JACK: Don't mention it, dear Miss Prism. Don't mention anything. I am sure I had a very pleasant time in your nice hand-bag in spite of the slight damage it received through the overturning of an omnibus in your happier days. As for leaving us, the suggestion is absurd.

MISS PRISM: It is my duty to leave. I have really nothing more to teach dear Cecily. In the very difficult accomplishment of getting married I fear my sweet and clever pupil has far outstripped her teacher.

CHASUBLE: A moment—Lætitia!

MISS PRISM: Dr. Chasuble!

CHASUBLE: Lætitia, I have come to the conclusion that the Primitive Church was in error on certain points. Corrupt readings seem to have crept into the text. I beg to solicit the honour of your hand.

MISS PRISM: Frederick, at the present moment words fail me to express my feelings. But I will forward you, this evening, the three last volumes of my diary. In these you will be able to peruse a full account of the sentiments that I have entertained towards you for the last eighteen months.

Enter MERRIMAN.

MERRIMAN: Lady Bracknell's flyman says he cannot wait any longer.

LADY BRACKNELL (*rising*): True! I must return to town at once. (*Pulls out watch.*) I see I have now missed no less than nine trains. There is only one more.

MERRIMAN *goes out.* LADY BRACKNELL *moves towards the door.*

Prism, from your last observation to Dr. Chasuble, I learn with regret that you have not yet given up your passion for fiction in three volumes. And, if you really are going to enter into the state of matrimony which at your age seems to me, I feel bound to say, rather like flying in the face of an all-wise Providence, I trust you will be more careful of your husband than you were of your infant charge, and not leave poor Dr. Chasuble lying about at railway stations in hand-bags or receptacles of any kind. Cloak-rooms are notoriously draughty places. (MISS PRISM *bows her head meekly.*) Dr. Chasuble, you have my sincere good wishes, and if baptism be, as you say it is, a form of new birth, I would strongly advise you to have Miss Prism baptised without delay. To be born again would be of considerable advantage to her. Whether such a procedure be in accordance with the practice of the Primitive Church I do not know. But it is hardly probable, I should fancy, that they had to grapple with such extremely advanced problems. (*Turning sweetly to* CECILY *and patting her cheek.*) Sweet child! We will expect you at Upper Grosvenor Street in a few days.

CECILY: Thank you, Aunt Augusta!

LADY BRACKNELL: Come, Gwendolen.

GWENDOLEN (*to* JACK): My own! But what own are you? What is your Christian name, now that you have become some one else?

JACK: Good heavens! . . . I had quite forgotten that point. Your decision on the subject of my name is irrevocable, I suppose?

GWENDOLEN: I never change, except in my affections.

CECILY: What a noble nature you have, Gwendolen!

JACK: Then the question had better be cleared up at once. Aunt Augusta, a moment. At the time when Miss Prism left me in the hand-bag, had I been christened already? Pray be calm, Aunt Augusta. This is a terrible crisis and much depends on your answer.

LADY BRACKNELL (*quite calmly*): Every luxury that money could buy, including christening, had been lavished on you by your fond and doting parents.

JACK: Then I was christened! That is settled. Now, what name was I given? Let me know the worst.

LADY BRACKNELL (*after a pause*): Being the eldest son you were naturally christened after your father.

JACK (*irritably*): Yes, but what was my father's Christian name? Pray don't be so calm, Aunt Augusta. This is a terrible crisis and everything hangs on the nature of your reply. What was my father's Christian name?

LADY BRACKNELL (*meditatively*): I cannot at the present moment recall what the General's Christian name was. Your poor dear mother always addressed him as "General." That I remember perfectly. Indeed, I don't think she would have dared to have called him by his Christian name. But I have no doubt he had one. He was violent in his manner, but there was nothing eccentric about him in any way. That was rather the result of the Indian climate, and marriage, and indigestion, and other things of that kind. In fact he was rather a martinet about the little details of daily life. Too much so, I used to tell my sister.

JACK: Algy! Can't you recollect what our father's Christian name was?

ALGERNON: My dear boy, we were never even on speaking terms. He died before I was a year old.

JACK: His name would appear in the Army Lists of the period, I suppose, Aunt Augusta?

LADY BRACKNELL: The General was essentially a man of peace, except in his domestic life. But I have no doubt his name would appear in any military directory.

JACK: The Army Lists for the last forty years are here. (*Rushes to the bookcase and tears the books out. Distributes them rapidly.*) Here, Dr. Chasuble—Miss Prism, two for you—Cecily, Cecily, an Army List. Make a précis of it at once. Algernon, pray search English history for our father's Christian name if you have the smallest filial affection left. Aunt Augusta, I beg you to bring your masculine mind to bear on this subject. Gwendolen—

no, it would agitate you too much. Leave these researches to less philosophic natures like ours.

GWENDOLEN *(heroically)*: Give me six copies of any period, this century or the last. I do not care which!

JACK: Noble girl! Here are a dozen. More might be an inconvenience to you. *(Brings her a pile of Army Lists—rushes through them himself, taking each one from her hands as she tries to examine it.)* No, just let me look. No, allow me, dear. Darling, I think I can find it out sooner. Just allow me, my love.

CHASUBLE: What station, Mr. Moncrieff, did you say you wished to go to?

JACK *(pausing in despair)*: Station! Who on earth is talking about a station? I merely want to find out my father's Christian name.

CHASUBLE: But you have handed me a Bradshaw. *(Looks at it.)* Of 1869, I observe. A book of considerable antiquarian interest: but not in any way bearing on the question of the names usually conferred on Generals at baptism.

CECILY: I am so sorry, Uncle Jack. But Generals don't seem to be even alluded to in the "History of our own times," although it is the best edition. The one written in collaboration with the typewriting machine.

MISS PRISM: To me, Mr. Moncrieff, you have given two copies of the Price Lists of the Civil Service Stores. I do not find Generals marked anywhere. There seems to be either no demand or no supply.

LADY BRACKNELL: This treatise, "The Green Carnation," as I see it is called, seems to be a book about the culture of exotics. It contains no reference to Generals in it. It seems a morbid and middle-class affair.

JACK *(very irritable indeed)*: Good Heavens! and what nonsense are you reading, Algy? *(Takes book from him.)* The Army List? Well, I don't suppose you knew it was the Army List. And you have got it open at the wrong page.

Besides, there is the thing staring you in the face. M. Generals . . . Malam—what ghastly names they have— Markby, Migsby, Mobbs, Moncrieff, Moncrieff! Lieutenant 1840, Captain, Lieutenant-Colonel, Colonel, General 1860. Christian names, Ernest John. (*Puts book quietly down and speaks quite calmly.*) I always told you Gwendolen, my name was Ernest, didn't I? Well, it is Ernest after all. I mean it naturally is Ernest.

LADY BRACKNELL: Yes, I remember now that the General was called Ernest. I knew I had some particular reason for disliking the name. Come, Gwendolen. (*Goes out.*)

GWENDOLEN: Ernest! My own Ernest! I felt from the first that you could have no other name!

JACK: Gwendolen, it is a terrible thing for a man to find out suddenly that all his life he has been speaking nothing but the truth. Can you forgive me?

GWENDOLEN: I can. For I feel that you are sure to change.

JACK: My own one!

CHASUBLE (*to* MISS PRISM): Lætitia! (*Embraces her.*)

MISS PRISM (*enthusiastically*): Frederick! At last!

ALGERNON: Cecily! (*Embraces her.*) At last!

JACK: Gwendolen! (*Embraces her.*) At last!

Enter LADY BRACKNELL.

LADY BRACKNELL: I have missed the last train!—My nephew, you seem to be displaying signs of triviality.

JACK: On the contrary, Aunt Augusta, I've now realised for the first time in my life the vital Importance of Being Earnest.

Curtain

LADY WINDERMERE'S FAN

The Persons of the Play

LORD WINDERMERE

LORD DARLINGTON

LORD AUGUSTUS LORTON

MR. DUMBY

MR. CECIL GRAHAM

MR. HOPPER

PARKER, Butler

LADY WINDERMERE

THE DUCHESS OF BERWICK

LADY AGATHA CARLISLE

LADY PLYMDALE

LADY STUTFIELD

LADY JEDBURGH

MRS. COWPER-COWPER

MRS. ERLYNNE

ROSALIE, Maid

ACT ONE

SCENE: *Morning-room of Lord Windermere's house in Carlton House Terrace,[1] London. The action of the play takes place within twenty-four hours, beginning on a Tuesday afternoon at five o'clock, and ending the next day at 1:30 p.m.* TIME: *The present. Doors C. and R. Bureau with books and papers R. Sofa with small tea-table L. Window opening on to terrace L. Table R.*

LADY WINDERMERE *is at table R., arranging roses in a blue bowl.*
    Enter PARKER.

PARKER: Is your ladyship at home this afternoon?[2]
LADY WINDERMERE: Yes—who has called?
PARKER: Lord Darlington, my lady.
LADY WINDERMERE (*hesitates for a moment*): Show him up—and I'm at home to any one who calls.
PARKER: Yes, my lady. (*Exit C.*)
LADY WINDERMERE: It's best for me to see him before tonight. I'm glad he's come.

Enter PARKER *C.*

PARKER: Lord Darlington.

Enter LORD DARLINGTON *C. Exit* PARKER.

LORD DARLINGTON: How do you do, Lady Windermere?

LADY WINDERMERE: How do you do, Lord Darlington? No, I can't shake hands with you. My hands are all wet with these roses. Aren't they lovely? They came up from Selby[3] this morning.

LORD DARLINGTON: They are quite perfect. *(Sees a fan lying on the table.)* And what a wonderful fan! May I look at it?

LADY WINDERMERE: Do. Pretty, isn't it? It's got my name on it, and everything. I have only just seen it myself. It's my husband's birthday present to me. You know to-day is my birthday?

LORD DARLINGTON: No? Is it really?

LADY WINDERMERE: Yes, I'm of age to-day.[4] Quite an important day in my life, isn't it? That is why I am giving this party tonight. Do sit down. *(Still arranging flowers.)*

LORD DARLINGTON *(sitting down)*: I wish I had known it was your birthday, Lady Windermere. I would have covered the whole street in front of your house with flowers for you to walk on. They are made for you. *(A short pause.)*

LADY WINDERMERE: Lord Darlington, you annoyed me last night at the Foreign Office. I am afraid you are going to annoy me again.

LORD DARLINGTON: I, Lady Windermere?

Enter PARKER *and* FOOTMAN *C., with tray and tea things.*

LADY WINDERMERE: Put it there, Parker. That will do. *(Wipes her hands with her pocket-handkerchief, goes to*

tea-table L., and sits down.) Won't you come over, Lord
Darlington?

Exit PARKER C.

LORD DARLINGTON *(takes chair and goes across L.C.)*: I am
quite miserable, Lady Windermere. You must tell me
what I did. *(Sits down at table L.)*

LADY WINDERMERE: Well, you kept paying me elaborate
compliments the whole evening.

LORD DARLINGTON *(smiling)*: Ah, nowadays we are all of us
so hard up, that the only pleasant things to pay *are* compliments. They're the only things we *can* pay.

LADY WINDERMERE *(shaking her head)*: No, I am talking
very seriously. You mustn't laugh, I am quite serious. I
don't like compliments, and I don't see why a man should
think he is pleasing a woman enormously when he says to
her a whole heap of things that he doesn't mean.

LORD DARLINGTON: Ah, but I did mean them. *(Takes tea
which she offers him.)*

LADY WINDERMERE *(gravely)*: I hope not. I should be sorry
to have to quarrel with you, Lord Darlington. I like you
very much, you know that. But I shouldn't like you at all
if I thought you were what most other men are. Believe
me, you are better than most other men, and I sometimes think you pretend to be worse.

LORD DARLINGTON: We all have our little vanities, Lady
Windermere.

LADY WINDERMERE: Why do you make that your special
one? *(Still seated at table L.)*

LORD DARLINGTON *(still seated L.C.)*: Oh, nowadays so
many conceited people go about Society pretending to
be good, that I think it shows rather a sweet and modest
disposition to pretend to be bad. Besides, there is this to
be said. If you pretend to be good, the world takes you

very seriously. If you pretend to be bad, it doesn't. Such is the astounding stupidity of optimism.

LADY WINDERMERE: Don't you *want* the world to take you seriously then, Lord Darlington?

LORD DARLINGTON: No, not the world. Who are the people the world takes seriously? All the dull people one can think of, from the Bishops down to the bores. I should like *you* to take me very seriously, Lady Windermere, *you* more than any one else in life.

LADY WINDERMERE: Why—why me?

LORD DARLINGTON *(after a slight hesitation)*: Because I think we might be great friends. Let us be great friends. You may want a friend some day.

LADY WINDERMERE: Why do you say that?

LORD DARLINGTON: Oh!—we all want friends at times.

LADY WINDERMERE: I think we're very good friends already, Lord Darlington. We can always remain so as long as you don't—

LORD DARLINGTON: Don't what?

LADY WINDERMERE: Don't spoil it by saying extravagant silly things to me. You think I am a Puritan, I suppose? Well, I have something of the Puritan in me. I was brought up like that. I am glad of it. My mother died when I was a mere child. I lived always with Lady Julia, my father's elder sister, you know. She was stern to me, but she taught me what the world is forgetting, the difference that there is between what is right and what is wrong. *She* allowed of no compromise. *I* allow of none.

LORD DARLINGTON: My dear Lady Windermere!

LADY WINDERMERE *(leaning back on the sofa)*: You look on me as being behind the age.—Well, I am! I should be sorry to be on the same level as an age like this.

LORD DARLINGTON: You think the age very bad?

LADY WINDERMERE: Yes. Nowadays people seem to look on life as a speculation. It is not a speculation. It is a sacrament. Its ideal is Love. Its purification is Sacrifice.

LORD DARLINGTON (*smiling*): Oh, anything is better than being sacrificed!

LADY WINDERMERE (*leaning forward*): Don't say that.

LORD DARLINGTON: I do say it. I felt it—I know it.

Enter PARKER *C.*

PARKER: The men want to know if they are to put the carpets on the terrace for to-night, my lady?

LADY WINDERMERE: You don't think it will rain, Lord Darlington, do you?

LORD DARLINGTON: I won't hear of its raining on your birthday.

LADY WINDERMERE: Tell them to do it at once, Parker.

Exit PARKER *C.*

LORD DARLINGTON (*still seated*): Do you think then—of course I am only putting an imaginary instance—do you think that in the case of a young married couple, say about two years married, if the husband suddenly becomes the intimate friend of a woman of—well, more than doubtful character—is always calling upon her, lunching with her, and probably paying her bills—do you think that the wife should not console herself?

LADY WINDERMERE (*frowning*): Console herself?

LORD DARLINGTON: Yes, I think she should—I think she has the right.

LADY WINDERMERE: Because the husband is vile—should the wife be vile also?

LORD DARLINGTON: Vileness is a terrible word, Lady Windermere.

LADY WINDERMERE: It is a terrible thing, Lord Darlington.

LORD DARLINGTON: Do you know I am afraid that good people do a great deal of harm in this world. Certainly the greatest harm they do is that they make badness of such extraordinary importance. It is absurd to divide people into good and bad. People are either charming or tedious. I take the side of the charming, and you, Lady Windermere, can't help belonging to them.

LADY WINDERMERE: Now, Lord Darlington. (*Rising and crossing R., front of him.*) Don't stir, I am merely going to finish my flowers. (*Goes to table R.C.*)

LORD DARLINGTON (*rising and moving chair*): And I must say I think you are very hard on modern life, Lady Windermere. Of course there is much against it, I admit. Most women, for instance, nowadays, are rather mercenary.

LADY WINDERMERE: Don't talk about such people.

LORD DARLINGTON: Well then, setting mercenary people aside, who, of course, are dreadful, do you think seriously that women who have committed what the world calls a fault should never be forgiven?

LADY WINDERMERE (*standing at table*): I think they should never be forgiven.

LORD DARLINGTON: And men? Do you think that there should be the same laws for men as there are for women?

LADY WINDERMERE: Certainly!

LORD DARLINGTON: I think life too complex a thing to be settled by these hard and fast rules.

LADY WINDERMERE: If we had "these hard and fast rules," we should find life much more simple.

LORD DARLINGTON: You allow of no exceptions?

LADY WINDERMERE: None!

LORD DARLINGTON: Ah, what a fascinating Puritan you are, Lady Windermere!

LADY WINDERMERE: The adjective was unnecessary, Lord Darlington.

LORD DARLINGTON: I couldn't help it. I can resist everything except temptation.

LADY WINDERMERE: You have the modern affectation of
weakness.

LORD DARLINGTON (*looking at her*): It's only an affectation,
Lady Windermere.

Enter PARKER *C.*

PARKER: The Duchess of Berwick and Lady Agatha Carlisle.

Enter the DUCHESS OF BERWICK *and* LADY AGATHA
CARLISLE *C.*
  Exit PARKER *C.*

DUCHESS OF BERWICK (*coming down C. and shaking
hands*): Dear Margaret, I am so pleased to see you. You
remember Agatha, don't you? (*Crossing L.C.*) How do
you do, Lord Darlington? I won't let you know my
daughter, you are far too wicked.

LORD DARLINGTON: Don't say that, Duchess. As a wicked
man I am a complete failure. Why, there are lots of people who say I have never really done anything wrong in
the whole course of my life. Of course they only say it
behind my back.

DUCHESS OF BERWICK: Isn't he dreadful? Agatha, this is
Lord Darlington. Mind you don't believe a word he says.
(LORD DARLINGTON *crosses R.C.*) No, no tea, thank
you, dear. (*Crosses and sits on sofa.*) We have just had tea
at Lady Markby's. Such bad tea, too. It was quite un-
drinkable. I wasn't at all surprised. Her own son-in-law
supplies it. Agatha is looking forward so much to your
ball to-night, dear Margaret.

LADY WINDERMERE (*seated L.C.*): Oh, you mustn't think it
is going to be a ball, Duchess. It is only a dance in honour
of my birthday. A small and early.

LORD DARLINGTON (*standing L.C.*): Very small, very early,
and very select, Duchess.

DUCHESS OF BERWICK (*on sofa L.*): Of course it's going to

be select. But we know *that,* dear Margaret, about *your* house. It is really one of the few houses in London where I can take Agatha, and where I feel perfectly secure about dear Berwick. I don't know what society is coming to. The most dreadful people seem to go everywhere. They certainly come to my parties—the men get furious if one doesn't ask them. Really, some one should make a stand against it.

LADY WINDERMERE: I will, Duchess. I will have no one in my house about whom there is any scandal.

LORD DARLINGTON *(R.C.)*: Oh, don't say that, Lady Windermere. I should never be admitted! *(Sitting.)*

DUCHESS OF BERWICK: Oh, men don't matter. With women it is different. We're good. Some of us are, at least. But we are positively getting elbowed into the corner. Our husbands would really forget our existence if we didn't nag at them from time to time, just to remind them that we have a perfect legal right to do so.

LORD DARLINGTON: It's a curious thing, Duchess, about the game of marriage—a game, by the way, that is going out of fashion—the wives hold all the honours, and invariably lose the odd trick.

DUCHESS OF BERWICK: The odd trick? Is that the husband, Lord Darlington?

LORD DARLINGTON: It would be rather a good name for the modern husband.

DUCHESS OF BERWICK: Dear Lord Darlington, how thoroughly depraved you are!

LADY WINDERMERE: Lord Darlington is trivial.

LORD DARLINGTON: Ah, don't say that, Lady Windermere.

LADY WINDERMERE: Why do you *talk* so trivially about life, then?

LORD DARLINGTON: Because I think that life is far too important a thing ever to talk seriously about it. *(Moves up C.)*

DUCHESS OF BERWICK: What does he mean? Do, as a concession to my poor wits, Lord Darlington, just explain to me what you really mean.

LORD DARLINGTON (*coming down back of table*): I think I had better not, Duchess. Nowadays to be intelligible is to be found out. Good-bye! (*Shakes hands with* DUCHESS.) And now—(*goes up stage*)—Lady Windermere, good-bye. I may come to-night, mayn't I? Do let me come.

LADY WINDERMERE (*standing up stage with* LORD DARLINGTON): Yes, certainly. But you are not to say foolish, insincere things to people.

LORD DARLINGTON (*smiling*): Ah! you are beginning to reform me. It is a dangerous thing to reform any one, Lady Windermere. (*Bows, and exit C.*)

DUCHESS OF BERWICK (*who has risen, goes C.*): What a charming, wicked creature! I like him so much. I'm quite delighted he's gone! How sweet you're looking! Where *do* you get your gowns? And now I must tell you how sorry I am for you, dear Margaret. (*Crosses to sofa and sits with* LADY WINDERMERE.) Agatha, darling!

LADY AGATHA: Yes, mamma. (*Rises.*)

DUCHESS OF BERWICK: Will you go and look over the photograph album that I see there?

LADY AGATHA: Yes, mamma. (*Goes to table up L.*)

DUCHESS OF BERWICK: Dear girl! She is so fond of photographs of Switzerland. Such a pure taste, I think. But I really am so sorry for you, Margaret.

LADY WINDERMERE (*smiling*): Why, Duchess?

DUCHESS OF BERWICK: Oh, on account of that horrid woman. She dresses so well, too, which makes it much worse, sets such a dreadful example. Augustus—you know my disreputable brother—such a trial to us all— well, Augustus is completely infatuated about her. It is quite scandalous, for she is absolutely inadmissible into society. Many a woman has a past, but I am told that she has at least a dozen, and that they all fit.

LADY WINDERMERE: Whom are you talking about, Duchess?

DUCHESS OF BERWICK: About Mrs. Erlynne.

LADY WINDERMERE: Mrs. Erlynne? I never heard of her, Duchess. And what has she to do with me?

DUCHESS OF BERWICK: My poor child! Agatha, darling!

LADY AGATHA: Yes, mamma.

DUCHESS OF BERWICK: Will you go out on the terrace and look at the sunset?

LADY AGATHA: Yes, mamma. (*Exit through window L.*)

DUCHESS OF BERWICK: Sweet girl! So devoted to sunsets! Shows such refinement of feeling, does it not? After all, there is nothing like Nature, is there?

LADY WINDERMERE: But what is it, Duchess? Why do you talk to me about this person?

DUCHESS OF BERWICK: Don't you really know? I assure you we're all so distressed about it. Only last night at dear Lady Jansen's every one was saying how extraordinary it was that, of all men in London, Windermere should behave in such a way.

LADY WINDERMERE: My husband—what has *he* got to do with any woman of that kind?

DUCHESS OF BERWICK: Ah, what indeed, dear? That is the point. He goes to see her continually, and stops for hours at a time, and while he is there she is not at home to any one. Not that many ladies call on her, dear, but she has a great many disreputable men friends—my own brother particularly, as I told you—and that is what makes it so dreadful about Windermere. We looked upon *him* as being such a model husband, but I am afraid there is no doubt about it. My dear nieces—you know the Saville girls, don't you?—such nice domestic creatures—plain, dreadfully plain,—but so good—well, they're always at

the window doing fancy work, and making ugly things
for the poor, which I think so useful of them in these
dreadful socialistic days, and this terrible woman has
taken a house in Curzon Street,[5] right opposite them—
such a respectable street, too! I don't know what we're
coming to! And they tell me that Windermere goes there
four and five times a week—they *see* him. They can't
help it—and although they never talk scandal, they—
well, of course—they remark on it to every one. And the
worst of it all is that I have been told that this woman has
got a great deal of money out of somebody, for it seems
that she came to London six months ago without anything at all to speak of, and now she has this charming
house in Mayfair,[6] drives her ponies in the Park every afternoon and all—well, all—since she has known poor
dear Windermere.

LADY WINDERMERE: Oh, I can't believe it!

DUCHESS OF BERWICK: But it's quite true, my dear. The
whole of London knows it. That is why I felt it was better
to come and talk to you, and advise you to take Windermere away at once to Homburg or to Aix, where he'll
have something to amuse him, and where you can watch
him all day long. I assure you, my dear, that on several
occasions after I was first married, I had to pretend to be
very ill, and was obliged to drink the most unpleasant
mineral waters, merely to get Berwick out of town. He
was so extremely susceptible. Though I am bound to say
he never gave away any large sums of money to anybody.
He is far too high-principled for that!

LADY WINDERMERE *(interrupting)*: Duchess, Duchess, it's
impossible! *(Rising and crossing stage to C.)* We are only
married two years. Our child is but six months old. *(Sits
in chair R. of L. table.)*

DUCHESS OF BERWICK: Ah, the dear pretty baby! How is
the little darling? Is it a boy or a girl? I hope a girl—ah,

no, I remember it's a boy! I'm so sorry. Boys are so wicked. My boy is excessively immoral. You wouldn't believe at what hours he comes home. And he's only left Oxford a few months—I really don't know what they teach them there.

LADY WINDERMERE: Are *all* men bad?

DUCHESS OF BERWICK: Oh, all of them, my dear, all of them, without any exception. And they never grow any better. Men become old, but they never become good.

LADY WINDERMERE: Windermere and I married for love.

DUCHESS OF BERWICK: Yes, we begin like that. It was only Berwick's brutal and incessant threats of suicide that made me accept him at all, and before the year was out, he was running after all kinds of petticoats, every colour, every shape, every material. In fact, before the honeymoon was over, I caught him winking at my maid, a most pretty, respectable girl. I dismissed her at once without a character.—No, I remember I passed her on to my sister; poor dear Sir George is so short-sighted, I thought it wouldn't matter. But it did, though—it was most unfortunate. *(Rises.)* And now, my dear child, I must go, as we are dining out. And mind you don't take this little aberration of Windermere's too much to heart. Just take him abroad, and he'll come back to you all right.

LADY WINDERMERE: Come back to me? *(C.)*

DUCHESS OF BERWICK *(L.C.)*: Yes, dear, these wicked women get our husbands away from us, but they always come back, slightly damaged, of course. And don't make scenes, men hate them!

LADY WINDERMERE: It is very kind of you, Duchess, to come and tell all this. But I can't believe that my husband is untrue to me.

DUCHESS OF BERWICK: Pretty child! I was like that once. Now I know that all men are monsters. (LADY WINDERMERE *rings bell.*) The only thing to do is to feed the wretches well. A good cook does wonders, and that I know you have. My dear Margaret, you are not going to cry?

LADY WINDERMERE: You needn't be afraid, Duchess, I never cry.

DUCHESS OF BERWICK: That's quite right, dear. Crying is the refuge of plain women but the ruin of pretty ones. Agatha, darling!

LADY AGATHA (*entering L.*): Yes, mamma. (*Stands back of table L.C.*)

DUCHESS OF BERWICK: Come and bid good-bye to Lady Windermere, and thank her for your charming visit. (*Coming down again.*): And by the way, I must thank you for sending a card to Mr. Hopper—he's that rich young Australian people are taking such notice of just at present. His father made a great fortune by selling some kind of food in circular tins—most palatable, I believe—I fancy it is the thing the servants always refuse to eat. But the son is quite interesting. I think he's attracted by dear Agatha's clever talk. Of course, we should be very sorry to lose her, but I think that a mother who doesn't part with a daughter every season has no real affection. We're coming to-night, dear. (PARKER *opens C. doors.*) And remember my advice, take the poor fellow out of town at once, it is the only thing to do. Good-bye, once more; come, Agatha.

Exeunt DUCHESS *and* LADY AGATHA *C.*

LADY WINDERMERE: How horrible! I understand now what Lord Darlington meant by the imaginary instance of the couple not two years married. Oh! it can't be true—she spoke of enormous sums of money paid to this woman. I know where Arthur keeps his bank book—in one of the drawers of that desk. I might find out by that. I *will* find out. (*Opens drawer.*) No, it is some hideous mistake.

(Rises and goes C.) Some silly scandal! He loves *me!* He loves *me!* But why should I not look? I am his wife, I have a right to look! *(Returns to bureau, takes out book and examines it page by page, smiles and gives a sigh of relief.)* I knew it! there is not a word of truth in this stupid story. *(Puts book back in drawer. As she does so, starts and takes out another book.)* A second book—private—locked! *(Tries to open it, but fails. Sees paper knife on bureau, and with it cuts cover from book. Begins to start at the first page.)* "Mrs. Erlynne—£600—Mrs. Erlynne—£700—Mrs. Erlynne—£400."[7] Oh! it is true! It is true! How horrible! *(Throws book on floor.)*

Enter LORD WINDERMERE *C.*

LORD WINDERMERE: Well, dear, has the fan been sent home yet? *(Going R.C. Sees book.)* Margaret, you have cut my bank book. You have no right to do such a thing!

LADY WINDERMERE: You think it wrong that you are found out, don't you?

LORD WINDERMERE: I think it wrong that a wife should spy on her husband.

LADY WINDERMERE: I did not spy on you. I never knew of this woman's existence till half an hour ago. Some one who pitied me was kind enough to tell me what every one in London knows already—your daily visits to Curzon Street, your mad infatuation, the monstrous sums of money you squander on this infamous woman! *(Crossing L.)*

LORD WINDERMERE: Margaret! don't talk like that of Mrs. Erlynne, you don't know how unjust it is!

LADY WINDERMERE *(turning to him)*: You are very jealous of Mrs. Erlynne's honour. I wish you had been as jealous of mine.

LORD WINDERMERE: Your honour is untouched, Margaret.

You don't think for a moment that—(*Puts book back into desk.*)

LADY WINDERMERE: I think that you spend your money strangely. That is all. Oh, don't imagine I mind about the money. As far as I am concerned, you may squander everything we have. But what I *do* mind is that you have loved me, you who have taught me to love you, should pass from the love that is given to the love that is bought. Oh, it's horrible! (*Sits on sofa.*) And it is I who feel degraded! *you* don't feel anything. I feel stained, utterly stained. You can't realise how hideous the last six months seems to me now—every kiss you have given me is tainted in my memory.

LORD WINDERMERE (*crossing to her*): Don't say that, Margaret. I never loved any one in the whole world but you.

LADY WINDERMERE (*rises*): Who is this woman, then? Why do you take a house for her?

LORD WINDERMERE: I did not take a house for her.

LADY WINDERMERE: You gave her the money to do it, which is the same thing.

LORD WINDERMERE: Margaret, as far as I have known Mrs. Erlynne—

LADY WINDERMERE: Is there a Mr. Erlynne—or is he a myth?

LORD WINDERMERE: Her husband died many years ago. She is alone in the world.

LADY WINDERMERE: No relations? (*A pause.*)

LORD WINDERMERE: None.

LADY WINDERMERE: Rather curious, isn't it? (*L.*)

LORD WINDERMERE (*L.C.*): Margaret, I was saying to you—and I beg you to listen to me—that as far as I have known Mrs. Erlynne, she has conducted herself well. If years ago—

LADY WINDERMERE: Oh! (*Crossing R.C.*) I don't want details about her life!

LORD WINDERMERE *(C.)*: I am not going to give you any details about her life. I tell you simply this—Mrs. Erlynne was once honoured, loved, respected. She was well born, she had position—she lost everything—threw it away, if you like. That makes it all the more bitter. Misfortunes one can endure—they come from outside, they are accidents. But to suffer for one's own faults—ah!—there is the sting of life. It was twenty years ago, too. She was little more than a girl then. She had been a wife for even less time than you have.

LADY WINDERMERE: I am not interested in her—and—you should not mention this woman and me in the same breath. It is an error of taste. *(Sitting R. at desk.)*

LORD WINDERMERE: Margaret, you could save this woman. She wants to get back into society, and she wants you to help her. *(Crossing to her.)*

LADY WINDERMERE: Me!

LORD WINDERMERE: Yes, you.

LADY WINDERMERE: How impertinent of her! *(A pause.)*

LORD WINDERMERE: Margaret, I came to ask you a great favour, and I still ask it of you, though you have discovered what I had intended you should never have known, that I have given Mrs. Erlynne a large sum of money. I want you to send her an invitation for our party to-night. *(Standing L. of her.)*

LADY WINDERMERE: You are mad! *(Rises.)*

LORD WINDERMERE: I entreat you. People may chatter about her, do chatter about her, of course, but they don't know anything definite against her. She has been to several houses—not to houses where you would go, I admit, but still to houses where women who are in what is called Society nowadays do go. That does not content her. She wants you to receive her once.[8]

LADY WINDERMERE: As a triumph for her, I suppose?

LORD WINDERMERE: No; but because she knows that you

are a good woman—and that if she comes here once she will have a chance of a happier, a surer life than she has had. She will make no further effort to know you. Won't you help a woman who is trying to get back?

LADY WINDERMERE: No! If a woman really repents, she never wishes to return to the society that has made or seen her ruin.

LORD WINDERMERE: I beg of you.

LADY WINDERMERE (*crossing to door R.*): I am going to dress for dinner, and don't mention the subject again this evening. Arthur—(*going to him C.*)—you fancy because I have no father or mother that I am alone in the world, and that you can treat me as you choose. You are wrong, I have friends, many friends.

LORD WINDERMERE (*L.C.*): Margaret, you are talking foolishly, recklessly. I won't argue with you, but I insist upon your asking Mrs. Erlynne to-night.

LADY WINDERMERE (*R.C.*): I shall do nothing of the kind. (*Crossing L.C.*)

LORD WINDERMERE: You refuse? (*C.*)

LADY WINDERMERE: Absolutely!

LORD WINDERMERE: Ah, Margaret, do this for my sake; it is her last chance.

LADY WINDERMERE: What has that to do with me?

LORD WINDERMERE: How hard good women are!

LADY WINDERMERE: How weak bad men are!

LORD WINDERMERE: Margaret, none of us men may be good enough for the women we marry—that is quite true—but you don't imagine I would ever—oh, the suggestion is monstrous!

LADY WINDERMERE: Why should *you* be different from other men? I am told that there is hardly a husband in London who does not waste his life over *some* shameful passion.

LORD WINDERMERE: I am not one of them.

LADY WINDERMERE: I am not sure of that!

LORD WINDERMERE: You are sure in your heart. But don't make chasm after chasm between us. God knows the last few minutes have thrust us wide enough apart. Sit down and write the card.

LADY WINDERMERE: Nothing in the whole world would induce me.

LORD WINDERMERE (*crossing to bureau*): Then I will! (*Rings electric bell, sits and writes card.*)

LADY WINDERMERE: You are going to invite this woman? (*Crossing to him.*)

LORD WINDERMERE: Yes.

    Pause. Enter PARKER.

    Parker!

PARKER: Yes, my lord. (*Comes down L.C.*)

LORD WINDERMERE: Have this note sent to Mrs. Erlynne at No. 84A Curzon Street. (*Crossing to L.C. and giving note to* PARKER.) There is no answer!

    Exit PARKER *C*.

LADY WINDERMERE: Arthur, if that woman comes here, I shall insult her.

LORD WINDERMERE: Margaret, don't say that.

LADY WINDERMERE: I mean it.

LORD WINDERMERE: Child, if you did such a thing, there's not a woman in London who wouldn't pity you.

LADY WINDERMERE: There is not a *good* woman in London who would not applaud me. We have been too lax. We must make an example. I propose to begin to-night. (*Picking up fan.*) Yes, you gave me this fan to-day; it was your birthday present. If that woman crosses my threshold, I shall strike her across the face with it.

LORD WINDERMERE: Margaret, you couldn't do such a thing.

LADY WINDERMERE: You don't know me! (*Moves R.*)

Enter PARKER.

Parker!

PARKER: Yes, my lady.

LADY WINDERMERE: I shall dine in my own room. I don't want dinner, in fact. See that everything is ready by half-past ten. And, Parker, be sure you pronounce the names of the guests very distinctly to-night. Sometimes you speak so fast that I miss them. I am particularly anxious to hear the names quite clearly, so as to make no mistake. You understand, Parker?

PARKER: Yes, my lady.

LADY WINDERMERE: That will do!

Exit PARKER *C*.

(*Speaking to* LORD WINDERMERE): Arthur, if that woman comes here—I warn you—

LORD WINDERMERE: Margaret, you'll ruin us!

LADY WINDERMERE: Us! From this moment my life is separate from yours. But if you wish to avoid a public scandal, write at once to this woman, and tell her that I forbid her to come here!

LORD WINDERMERE: I will not—I cannot—she must come!

LADY WINDERMERE: Then I shall do exactly as I have said. (*Goes R.*) You leave me no choice. (*Exit R.*)

LORD WINDERMERE (*calling after her*): Margaret! Margaret! (*A pause.*) My God! What shall I do? I dare not tell her who this woman really is. The shame would kill her. (*Sinks down into a chair and buries his face in his hands.*)

Act Drop

Act Two

SCENE: *Drawing-room in Lord Windermere's house. Door R.U. opening into ballroom, where band is playing. Door L. through which guests are entering. Door L.U. opens on to illuminated terrace. Palms, flowers, and brilliant lights. Room crowded with guests. Lady Windermere is receiving them.*

DUCHESS OF BERWICK *(up C.)*: So strange Lord Windermere isn't here. Mr. Hopper is very late, too. You have kept those five dances for him, Agatha? *(Comes down.)*

LADY AGATHA: Yes, mamma.

DUCHESS OF BERWICK *(sitting on sofa)*: Just let me see your card. I'm so glad Lady Windermere has revived cards.—They're a mother's only safeguard. You dear simple little thing! *(Scratches out two names.)* No nice girl should ever waltz with such particularly younger sons! It looks so fast! The last two dances you might pass on the terrace with Mr. Hopper.

Enter MR. DUMBY *and* LADY PLYMDALE *from the ball-room.*

LADY AGATHA: Yes, mamma.

DUCHESS OF BERWICK (*fanning herself*): The air is so pleasant there.

PARKER: Mrs. Cowper-Cowper. Lady Stutfield. Sir James Royston. Mr. Guy Berkeley.

These people enter as announced.

DUMBY: Good evening, Lady Stutfield. I suppose this will be the last ball of the season?

LADY STUTFIELD: I suppose so, Mr. Dumby. It's been a delightful season, hasn't it?

DUMBY: Quite delightful! Good evening, Duchess. I suppose this will be the last ball of the season?

DUCHESS OF BERWICK: I suppose so, Mr. Dumby. It has been a very dull season, hasn't it?

DUMBY: Dreadfully dull! Dreadfully dull!

MRS. COWPER-COWPER: Good evening, Mr. Dumby. I suppose this will be the last ball of the season?

DUMBY: Oh, I think not. There'll probably be two more. (*Wanders back to* LADY PLYMDALE.)

PARKER: Mr. Rufford. Lady Jedburgh and Miss Graham. Mr. Hopper.

These people enter as announced.

HOPPER: How do you do, Lady Windermere? How do you do, Duchess? (*Bows to* LADY AGATHA.)

DUCHESS OF BERWICK: Dear Mr. Hopper, how nice of you to come so early. We all know how you are run after in London.

HOPPER: Capital place, London! They are not nearly so exclusive in London as they are in Sydney.[1]

DUCHESS OF BERWICK: Ah! we know your value, Mr. Hopper. We wish there were more like you. It would make life so much easier. Do you know, Mr. Hopper, dear Agatha and I are so much interested in Australia. It must be so pretty with all the dear little kangaroos flying about. Agatha has found it on the map. What a curious shape it is! Just like a large packing case. However, it is a very young country, isn't it?

HOPPER: Wasn't it made at the same time as the others, Duchess?

DUCHESS OF BERWICK: How clever you are, Mr. Hopper. You have a cleverness quite of your own. Now I mustn't keep you.

HOPPER: But I should like to dance with Lady Agatha, Duchess.

DUCHESS OF BERWICK: Well, I *hope* she has a dance left. Have you a dance left, Agatha?

LADY AGATHA: Yes, mamma.

DUCHESS OF BERWICK: The next one?

LADY AGATHA: Yes, mamma.

HOPPER: May I have the pleasure? (LADY AGATHA *bows.*)

DUCHESS OF BERWICK: Mind you take great care of my little chatter-box, Mr. Hopper.

LADY AGATHA *and* MR. HOPPER *pass into ballroom.*
Enter LORD WINDERMERE *L.*

LORD WINDERMERE: Margaret, I want to speak to you.

LADY WINDERMERE: In a moment. *(The music stops.)*

PARKER: Lord Augustus Lorton.

Enter LORD AUGUSTUS.

LORD AUGUSTUS: Good evening, Lady Windermere.

DUCHESS OF BERWICK: Sir James, will you take me into the ballroom? Augustus has been dining with us to-night. I really have had quite enough of dear Augustus for the moment.

SIR JAMES ROYSTON *gives the* DUCHESS *his arm and escorts her into the ballroom.*

PARKER: Mr. and Mrs. Arthur Bowden. Lord and Lady Paisley. Lord Darlington.

These people enter as announced.

LORD AUGUSTUS (*coming up to* LORD WINDERMERE): Want to speak to you particularly, dear boy. I'm worn to a shadow. Know I don't look it. None of us men do look what we really are. Demmed good thing, too. What I want to know is this. Who is she? Where does she come from? Why hasn't she got any demmed relations! Demmed nuisance, relations! But they make one so demmed respectable.

LORD WINDERMERE: You are talking of Mrs. Erlynne, I suppose? I only met her six months ago. Till then, I never knew of her existence.

LORD AUGUSTUS: You have seen a good deal of her since then.

LORD WINDERMERE (*coldly*): Yes, I have seen a good deal of her since then. I have just seen her.

LORD AUGUSTUS: Egad! the women are very down on her. I have been dining with Arabella this evening! By Jove! you should have heard what she said about Mrs. Erlynne. She didn't leave a rag on her. . . . (*Aside.*) Berwick and I told her that didn't matter much, as the lady in question must have an extremely fine figure. You should have seen Arabella's expression. . . . But, look here, dear boy. I don't know what to do about Mrs. Erlynne. Egad! I might be married to her; she treats me with such demmed indifference. She's deuced clever, too! She explains everything. Egad! she explains you. She has got any amount of explanations for you—and all of them different.

LORD WINDERMERE: No explanations are necessary about
my friendship with Mrs. Erlynne.

LORD AUGUSTUS: Hem! Well, look here, dear old fellow.
Do you think she will ever get into this demmed thing
called Society? Would you introduce her to your wife?
No use beating about the confounded bush. Would you
do that?

LORD WINDERMERE: Mrs. Erlynne is coming here
to-night.

LORD AUGUSTUS: Your wife has sent her a card?

LORD WINDERMERE: Mrs. Erlynne has received a card.

LORD AUGUSTUS: Then she's all right, dear boy. But why
didn't you tell me that before? It would have saved me a
heap of worry and demmed misunderstandings!

LADY AGATHA *and* MR. HOPPER *cross and exit on terrace
L.U.E.*

PARKER: Mr. Cecil Graham!

Enter MR. CECIL GRAHAM.

CECIL GRAHAM (*bows to* LADY WINDERMERE, *passes over
and shakes hands with* LORD WINDERMERE): Good
evening, Arthur. Why don't you ask me how I am? I like
people to ask me how I am. It shows a wide-spread interest in my health. Now, to-night I am not at all well. Been
dining with my people. Wonder why it is one's people are
always so tedious? My father would talk morality after
dinner. I told him he was old enough to know better. But
my experience is that as soon as people are old enough to
know better, they don't know anything at all. Hullo,
Tuppy! Hear you're going to be married again; thought
you were tired of that game.

LORD AUGUSTUS: You're excessively trivial, my dear boy,
excessively trivial!

CECIL GRAHAM: By the way, Tuppy, which is it? Have you

been twice married and once divorced, or twice divorced and once married? I say you've been twice divorced and once married. It seems so much more
probable.

LORD AUGUSTUS: I have a very bad memory. I really don't
remember which. (*Moves away R.*)

LADY PLYMDALE: Lord Windermere, I've something most
particular to ask you.

LORD WINDERMERE: I am afraid—if you will excuse me—I
must join my wife.

LADY PLYMDALE: Oh, you mustn't dream of such a thing.
It's most dangerous nowadays for a husband to pay any
attention to his wife in public. It always makes people
think that he beats her when they're alone. The world
has grown so suspicious of anything that looks like a
happy married life. But I'll tell you what it is at supper.
(*Moves towards door of ballroom.*)

LORD WINDERMERE (*C.*): Margaret! I must speak to you.

LADY WINDERMERE: Will you hold my fan for me, Lord
Darlington? Thanks. (*Comes down to him.*)

LORD WINDERMERE (*crossing to her*): Margaret, what you
said before dinner was, of course, impossible?

LADY WINDERMERE: That woman is not coming here
to-night.

LORD WINDERMERE (*R.C.*): Mrs. Erlynne is coming here,
and if you in any way annoy or wound her, you will bring
shame and sorrow on us both. Remember that! Ah, Margaret, only trust me! A wife should trust her husband!

LADY WINDERMERE (*C.*): London is full of women who
trust their husbands. One can always recognise them.
They look so thoroughly unhappy. I am not going to be
one of them. (*Moves up.*) Lord Darlington, will you give
me back my fan, please? Thanks. . . . A useful thing a
fan, isn't it? . . . I want a friend to-night, Lord Darlington; I didn't know I would want one so soon.

LORD DARLINGTON: Lady Windermere! I knew the time would come some day; but why to-night?

LORD WINDERMERE: I *will* tell her. I must. It would be terrible if there were any scene. Margaret . . .

PARKER: Mrs. Erlynne!

LORD WINDERMERE starts. MRS. ERLYNNE enters, very beautifully dressed and very dignified. LADY WINDERMERE clutches at her fan, then lets it drop on the floor. She bows coldly to MRS. ERLYNNE, who bows to her sweetly in turn, and sails into the room.

LORD DARLINGTON: You have dropped your fan, Lady Windermere. *(Picks it up and hands it to her.)*

MRS. ERLYNNE *(C.)*: How do you do, again, Lord Windermere? How charming your sweet wife looks! Quite a picture!

LORD WINDERMERE *(in a low voice)*: It was terribly rash of you to come!

MRS. ERLYNNE *(smiling)*: The wisest thing I ever did in my life. And, by the way, you must pay me a good deal of attention this evening. I am afraid of the women. You must introduce me to some of them. The men I can always manage. How do you do, Lord Augustus? You have quite neglected me lately. I have not seen you since yesterday. I am afraid you're faithless. Every one told me so.

LORD AUGUSTUS *(R.)*: Now really, Mrs. Erlynne, allow me to explain.

MRS. ERLYNNE *(R.C.)*: No, dear Lord Augustus, you can't explain anything. It is your chief charm.

LORD AUGUSTUS: Ah! if you find charms in me, Mrs. Erlynne—

They converse together. LORD WINDERMERE moves uneasily about the room watching MRS. ERLYNNE.

LORD DARLINGTON (*to* LADY WINDERMERE): How pale you are!

LADY WINDERMERE: Cowards are always pale!

LORD DARLINGTON: You look faint. Come out on the terrace.

LADY WINDERMERE: Yes. (*To* PARKER): Parker, send my cloak out.

MRS. ERLYNNE (*crossing to her*): Lady Windermere, how beautifully your terrace is illuminated. Reminds me of Prince Doria's at Rome.

LADY WINDERMERE *bows coldly, and goes off with* LORD DARLINGTON.

Oh, how do you do, Mr. Graham? Isn't that your aunt, Lady Jedburgh? I should so much like to know her.

CECIL GRAHAM (*after a moment's hesitation and embarrassment*): Oh, certainly, if you wish it. Aunt Caroline, allow me to introduce Mrs. Erlynne.

MRS. ERLYNNE: So pleased to meet you, Lady Jedburgh. (*Sits beside her on the sofa.*) Your nephew and I are great friends. I am so much interested in his political career. I think he's sure to be a wonderful success. He thinks like a Tory, and talks like a Radical, and that's so important nowadays. He's such a brilliant talker, too. But we all know from whom he inherits that. Lord Allandale was saying to me only yesterday, in the Park, that Mr. Graham talks almost as well as his aunt.

LADY JEDBURGH (*R*): Most kind of you to say these charming things to me! (MRS. ERLYNNE *smiles, and continues conversation.*)

DUMBY (*to* CECIL GRAHAM): Did you introduce Mrs. Erlynne to Lady Jedburgh?

CECIL GRAHAM: Had to, my dear fellow. Couldn't help it! That woman can make one do anything she wants. How, I don't know.

DUMBY: Hope to goodness she won't speak to me! (*Saunters towards* LADY PLYMDALE.)

MRS. ERLYNNE (*C. To* LADY JEDBURGH): On Thursday? With great pleasure. (*Rises, and speaks to* LORD WINDERMERE, *laughing.*) What a bore it is to have to be civil to these old dowagers! But they always insist on it!

LADY PLYMDALE (*to* MR. DUMBY): Who is that well-dressed woman talking to Windermere?

DUMBY: Haven't got the slightest idea! Looks like an *édition de luxe* of a wicked French novel,[2] meant specially for the English market.

MRS. ERLYNNE: So that is poor Dumby with Lady Plymdale? I hear she is frightfully jealous of him. He doesn't seem anxious to speak to me to-night. I suppose he is afraid of her. Those straw-coloured women have dreadful tempers. Do you know, I think I'll dance with you first, Windermere. (LORD WINDERMERE *bites his lip and frowns.*) It will make Lord Augustus so jealous! Lord Augustus! (LORD AUGUSTUS *comes down.*) Lord Windermere insists on my dancing with him first; as it's his own house, I can't well refuse. You know I would much sooner dance with you.

LORD AUGUSTUS (*with a low bow*): I wish I could think so, Mrs. Erlynne.

MRS. ERLYNNE: You know it far too well. I can fancy a person dancing through life with you and finding it charming.

LORD AUGUSTUS (*placing his hand on his white waistcoat*): Oh, thank you, thank you. You are the most adorable of all ladies!

MRS. ERLYNNE: What a nice speech! So simple and so sincere! Just the sort of speech I like. Well, you shall hold my bouquet. (*Goes towards ballroom on* LORD WINDERMERE's *arm.*) Ah, Mr. Dumby, how are you? I am so sorry I have been out the last three times you have called. Come and lunch on Friday.

DUMBY (*with perfect nonchalance*): Delighted!

LADY PLYMDALE *glares with indignation at* MR. DUMBY. LORD AUGUSTUS *follows* MRS. ERLYNNE *and* LORD WINDERMERE *into the ballroom holding bouquet.*

LADY PLYMDALE (*to* MR. DUMBY): What an absolute brute you are! I never can believe a word you say! Why did you tell me you didn't know her? What do you mean by calling on her three times running? You are not to go to lunch there; of course you understand that?

DUMBY: My dear Laura, I wouldn't dream of going!

LADY PLYMDALE: You haven't told me her name yet! Who is she?

DUMBY (*coughs slightly and smooths his hair*): She's a Mrs. Erlynne.

LADY PLYMDALE: That woman!

DUMBY: Yes; that is what every one calls her.

LADY PLYMDALE: How very interesting! How intensely interesting! I really must have a good stare at her. (*Goes to door of ballroom and looks in.*) I have heard the most shocking things about her. They say she is ruining poor Windermere. And Lady Windermere, who goes in for being so proper, invites her! How extremely amusing! It takes a thoroughly good woman to do a thoroughly stupid thing. You are to lunch there on Friday!

DUMBY: Why?

LADY PLYMDALE: Because I want you to take my husband with you. He has been so attentive lately, that he has become a perfect nuisance. Now, this woman's just the thing for him. He'll dance attendance upon her as long as she lets him, and won't bother me. I assure you, women of that kind are most useful. They form the basis of other people's marriages.

DUMBY: What a mystery you are!

LADY PLYMDALE *(looking at him)*: I wish *you* were!

DUMBY: I am—to myself. I am the only person in the world I should like to know thoroughly; but I don't see any chance of it just at present.

They pass into the ballroom, and LADY WINDERMERE *and* LORD DARLINGTON *enter from the terrace.*

LADY WINDERMERE: Yes. Yes. Her coming here is monstrous, unbearable. I know now what you meant to-day at tea time. Why didn't you tell me right out? You should have!

LORD DARLINGTON: I couldn't! A man can't tell these things about another man! But if I had known he was going to make you ask her here to-night, I think I would have told you. That insult, at any rate, you would have been spared.

LADY WINDERMERE: I did not ask her. He insisted on her coming—against my entreaties—against my commands. Oh! the house is tainted for me! I feel that every woman here sneers at me as she dances by with my husband. What have I done to deserve this? I gave him all my life. He took it—used it—spoiled it! I am degraded in my own eyes, and I lack courage—I am a coward! *(Sits down on sofa.)*

LORD DARLINGTON: If I know you at all, I know that you can't live with a man who treats you like this! What sort of life would you have with him? You would feel that he was lying to you every moment of the day. You would feel that the look in his eyes was false, his voice false, his touch false, his passion false. He would come to you when he was weary of others; you would have to comfort him. He would come to you when he was devoted to others; you would have to charm him. You would have to be to him the mask of his real life, the cloak to hide his secret.

LADY WINDERMERE: You are right—you are terribly right. But where am I to turn? You said you would be my friend, Lord Darlington.—Tell me, what am I to do? Be my friend now.

LORD DARLINGTON: Between men and women there is no friendship possible. There is passion, enmity, worship, love, but no friendship. I love you—

LADY WINDERMERE: No, no! *(Rises.)*

LORD DARLINGTON: Yes, I love you! You are more to me than anything in the whole world. What does your husband give you? Nothing. Whatever is in him he gives to this wretched woman, whom he has thrust into your society, into your home, to shame you before every one. I offer you my life—

LADY WINDERMERE: Lord Darlington!

LORD DARLINGTON: My life—my whole life. Take it, and do with it what you will. . . . I love you—love you as I have never loved any living thing. From the moment I met you I loved you, loved you blindly, adoringly, madly! You did not know it then—you know it now! Leave this house to-night. I won't tell you that the world matters nothing, or the world's voice, or the voice of society. They matter a great deal. They matter far too much. But there are moments when one has to choose between living one's own life, fully, entirely, completely—or dragging out some false, shallow, degrading existence that the world in its hypocrisy demands. You have that moment now. Choose! Oh, my love, choose.

LADY WINDERMERE *(moving slowly away from him, and looking at him with startled eyes)*: I have not the courage.

LORD DARLINGTON *(following her)*: Yes; you have the

courage. There may be six months of pain, of disgrace even, but when you no longer bear his name, when you bear mine, all will be well. Margaret, my love, my wife that shall be some day—yes, my wife! You know it! What are you now? This woman has the place that belongs by right to you. Oh! go—go out of this house, with head erect, with a smile upon your lips, with courage in your eyes. All London will know why you did it; and who will blame you? No one. If they do, what matter? Wrong? What is wrong? It's wrong for a man to abandon his wife for a shameless woman. It is wrong for a wife to remain with a man who so dishonours her. You said once you would make no compromise with things. Make none now. Be brave! Be yourself!

LADY WINDERMERE: I am afraid of being myself. Let me think. Let me wait! My husband may return to me. (*Sits down on sofa.*)

LORD DARLINGTON: And you would take him back! You are not what I thought you were. You are just the same as every other woman. You would stand anything rather than face the censure of a world whose praise you would despise. In a week you will be driving with this woman in the Park. She will be your constant guest—your dearest friend. You would endure anything rather than break with one blow this monstrous tie. You are right. You have no courage; none!

LADY WINDERMERE: Ah, give me time to think. I cannot answer you now. (*Passes her hand nervously over her brow.*)

LORD DARLINGTON: It must be now or not at all.

LADY WINDERMERE (*rising from the sofa*): Then, not at all! (*A pause.*)

LORD DARLINGTON: You break my heart!

LADY WINDERMERE: Mine is already broken. (*A pause.*)

LORD DARLINGTON: To-morrow I leave England. This is

the last time I shall ever look on you. You will never see me again. For one moment our lives met—our souls touched. They must never meet or touch again. Good-bye, Margaret. (*Exit.*)

LADY WINDERMERE: How alone I am in life. How terribly alone!

The music stops. Enter the DUCHESS OF BERWICK *and* LORD PAISLEY *laughing and talking. Other guests come in from ballroom.*

DUCHESS OF BERWICK: Dear Margaret, I've just been having such a delightful chat with Mrs. Erlynne. I am so sorry for what I said to you this afternoon about her. Of course, she must be all right if *you* invite her. A most attractive woman, and has such sensible views on life. Told me she entirely disapproved of people marrying more than once, so I feel quite safe about poor Augustus. Can't imagine why people speak against her. It's those horrid nieces of mine—the Saville girls—they're always talking scandal. Still, I should go to Homburg, dear, I really should. She is just a little too attractive. But where is Agatha? Oh, there she is. (LADY AGATHA *and* MR. HOPPER *enter from terrace L.U.E.*) Mr. Hopper, I am very, very angry with you. You have taken Agatha out on the terrace, and she is so delicate.

HOPPER (*L.C.*): Awfully sorry, Duchess. We went out for a moment and then got chatting together.

DUCHESS OF BERWICK (*C.*): Ah, about dear Australia, I suppose?

HOPPER: Yes!

DUCHESS OF BERWICK: Agatha, darling! (*Beckons her over.*)

LADY AGATHA: Yes, mamma!

DUCHESS OF BERWICK (*aside*): Did Mr. Hopper definitely—

LADY AGATHA: Yes, mamma!

DUCHESS OF BERWICK: And what answer did you give him, dear child?

LADY AGATHA: Yes, mamma.

DUCHESS OF BERWICK (*affectionately*): My dear one! You always say the right thing. Mr. Hopper! James! Agatha has told me everything. How cleverly you have both kept your secret.

HOPPER: You don't mind my taking Agatha off to Australia, then, Duchess?

DUCHESS OF BERWICK (*indignantly*): To Australia? Oh, don't mention that dreadful vulgar place.

HOPPER: But she said she'd like to come with me.

DUCHESS OF BERWICK (*severely*): Did you say that, Agatha?

LADY AGATHA: Yes, mamma.

DUCHESS OF BERWICK: Agatha, you say the most silly things possible. I think on the whole that Grosvenor Square[3] would be a more healthy place to reside in. There are lots of vulgar people live in Grosvenor Square, but at any rate there are no horrid kangaroos crawling about. But we'll talk about that to-morrow. James, you can take Agatha down. You'll come to lunch, of course, James. At half-past one, instead of two. The Duke will wish to say a few words to you, I am sure.

HOPPER: I should like to have a chat with the Duke, Duchess. He has not said a single word to me yet.

DUCHESS OF BERWICK: I think you'll find he will have a great deal to say to you to-morrow. (*Exit* LADY AGATHA *with* MR. HOPPER.) And now good-night, Margaret. I'm afraid it's the old, old story, dear. Love—well, not love at first sight, but love at the end of the season, which is so much more satisfactory.

LADY WINDERMERE: Good-night, Duchess.

Exit the DUCHESS OF BERWICK *on* LORD PAISLEY'S *arm.*

LADY PLYMDALE: My dear Margaret, what a handsome woman your husband has been dancing with! I should be quite jealous if I were you! Is she a great friend of yours?

LADY WINDERMERE: No!

LADY PLYMDALE: Really? Good-night, dear. *(Looks at* MR. DUMBY *and exit.)*

DUMBY: Awful manners young Hopper has!

CECIL GRAHAM: Ah! Hopper is one of Nature's gentlemen, the worst type of gentleman I know.

DUMBY: Sensible woman, Lady Windermere. Lots of wives would have objected to Mrs. Erlynne coming. But Lady Windermere has that uncommon thing called common sense.

CECIL GRAHAM: And Windermere knows that nothing looks so like innocence as an indiscretion.

DUMBY: Yes; dear Windermere is becoming almost modern. Never thought he would. *(Bows to* LADY WINDERMERE *and exit.)*

LADY JEDBURGH: Good-night, Lady Windermere. What a fascinating woman Mrs. Erlynne is! She is coming to lunch on Thursday, won't you come too? I expect the Bishop and dear Lady Merton.

LADY WINDERMERE: I am afraid I am engaged, Lady Jedburgh.

LADY JEDBURGH: So sorry. Come, dear.

Exeunt LADY JEDBURGH *and* MISS GRAHAM.

Enter MRS. ERLYNNE *and* LORD WINDERMERE.

MRS. ERLYNNE: Charming ball it has been! Quite reminds me of old days. *(Sits on sofa.)* And I see that there are just as many fools in society as there used to be. So pleased to find that nothing has altered! Except Margaret. She's grown quite pretty. The last time I saw her—twenty years ago, she was a fright in flannel. Positive fright, I assure you. The dear Duchess! and that sweet Lady Agatha! Just the type of girl I like! Well, really, Windermere, if I am to be the Duchess's sister-in-law—

LORD WINDERMERE (*sitting L. of her*): But are you—?

Exit MR. CECIL GRAHAM *with rest of guests.* LADY WINDERMERE *watches, with a look of scorn and pain,* MRS. ERLYNNE *and her husband. They are unconscious of her presence.*

MRS. ERLYNNE: Oh, yes! He's to call to-morrow at twelve o'clock. He wanted to propose to-night. In fact he did. He kept on proposing. Poor Augustus; you know how he repeats himself. Such a bad habit! But I told him I wouldn't give him an answer till to-morrow. Of course I am going to take him. And I dare say I'll make him an admirable wife, as wives go. And there is a great deal of good in Lord Augustus. Fortunately it is all on the surface. Just where good qualities should be. Of course you must help me in this matter.

LORD WINDERMERE: I am not called on to encourage Lord Augustus, I suppose?

MRS. ERLYNNE: Oh, no! I do the encouraging. But you will make me a handsome settlement,[4] Windermere, won't you?

LORD WINDERMERE (*frowning*): Is that what you want to talk to me about to-night?

MRS. ERLYNNE: Yes.

LORD WINDERMERE (*with a gesture of impatience*): I will not talk of it here.

MRS. ERLYNNE (*laughing*): Then we will talk of it on the terrace. Even business should have a picturesque background. Should it not, Windermere? With a proper background women can do anything.

LORD WINDERMERE: Won't to-morrow do as well?

MRS. ERLYNNE: No; you see, to-morrow I am going to accept him. And I think it would be a good thing if I was
able to tell him that I had—well, what shall I say?—
£2000 a year left to me by a third cousin—or a second
husband—or some distant relative of that kind. It would
be an additional attraction, wouldn't it? You have a delightful opportunity now of paying me a compliment,
Windermere. But you are not very clever at paying compliments. I am afraid Margaret doesn't encourage you in
that excellent habit. It's a great mistake on her part.
When men give up saying what is charming, they give up
thinking what is charming. But seriously, what do you say
to £2000? £2500, I think. In modern life margin is everything. Windermere, don't you think the world an intensely amusing place? I do!

Exit on terrace with LORD WINDERMERE. *Music strikes
up in ballroom.*

LADY WINDERMERE: To stay in this house any longer is impossible. To-night a man who loves me offered me his
whole life. I refused it. It was foolish of me. I will offer
him mine now. I will give him mine. I will go to him!
(*Puts on cloak and goes to the door, then turns back. Sits
down at table and writes a letter, puts it into an envelope,
and leaves it on table.*) Arthur has never understood me.
When he reads this, he will. He may do as he chooses
now with his life. I have done with mine as I think best,
as I think right. It is he who has broken the bond of marriage—not I. I only break its bondage. (*Exit.*)

PARKER *enters L. and crosses towards the ballroom R.
Enter* MRS. ERLYNNE.

MRS. ERLYNNE: Is Lady Windermere in the ballroom?

PARKER: Her ladyship has just gone out.

MRS. ERLYNNE: Gone out? She's not on the terrace?

PARKER: No, madam. Her ladyship has just gone out of the house.

MRS. ERLYNNE (*starts, and looks at the servant with a puzzled expression in her face*): Out of the house?

PARKER: Yes, madam—her ladyship told me she had left a letter for his lordship on the table.

MRS. ERLYNNE: A letter for Lord Windermere?

PARKER: Yes, madam.

MRS. ERLYNNE: Thank you.

Exit PARKER. *The music in the ballroom stops.*

Gone out of her house! A letter addressed to her husband! (*Goes over to bureau and looks at letter. Takes it up and lays it down again with a shudder of fear.*) No, no! It would be impossible! Life doesn't repeat its tragedies like that! Oh, why does this horrible fancy come across me? Why do I remember now the one moment of my life I most wish to forget? Does life repeat its tragedies? (*Tears letter open and reads it, then sinks down into a chair with a gesture of anguish.*) Oh, how terrible! The same words that twenty years ago I wrote to her father! and how bitterly I have been punished for it! No; my punishment, my real punishment is tonight, is now! (*Still seated R.*)

Enter LORD WINDERMERE *L.U.E.*

LORD WINDERMERE: Have you said good-night to my wife? (*Comes C.*)

MRS. ERLYNNE (*crushing letter in her hand*): Yes.

LORD WINDERMERE: Where is she?

MRS. ERLYNNE: She is very tired. She has gone to bed. She said she had a headache.

LORD WINDERMERE: I must go to her. You'll excuse me?

MRS. ERLYNNE (*rising hurriedly*): Oh, no! It's nothing serious. She's only very tired, that is all. Besides, there are people still in the supper-room. She wants you to make her apologies to them. She said she didn't wish to be disturbed. *(Drops letter.)* She asked me to tell you!

LORD WINDERMERE *(picks up letter)*: You have dropped something.

MRS. ERLYNNE: Oh yes, thank you, that is mine. *(Puts out her hand to take it.)*

LORD WINDERMERE *(still looking at letter)*: But it's my wife's handwriting, isn't it?

MRS. ERLYNNE *(takes the letter quickly)*: Yes, it's—an address. Will you ask them to call my carriage, please?

LORD WINDERMERE: Certainly. *(Goes L. and exit.)*

MRS. ERLYNNE: Thanks! What can I do? What can I do? I feel a passion awakening within me that I never felt before. What can it mean? The daughter must not be like the mother—that would be terrible. How can I save her? How can I save my child? A moment may ruin a life. Who knows that better than I? Windermere must be got out of the house; that is absolutely necessary. *(Goes L.)* But how shall I do it? It must be done somehow. Ah!

Enter LORD AUGUSTUS *R.U.E. carrying bouquet.*

LORD AUGUSTUS: Dear lady, I am in such suspense! May I not have an answer to my request?

MRS. ERLYNNE: Lord Augustus, listen to me. You are to take Lord Windermere down to your club at once, and keep him there as long as possible. You understand?

LORD AUGUSTUS: But you said you wished me to keep early hours!

MRS. ERLYNNE *(nervously)*: Do what I tell you. Do what I tell you.

LORD AUGUSTUS: And my reward?

MRS. ERLYNNE: Your reward? Your reward? Oh! ask me that to-morrow. But don't let Windermere out of your sight to-night. If you do I will never forgive you. I will never speak to you again. I'll have nothing to do with you. Remember you are to keep Windermere at your club, and don't let him come back to-night. (*Exit L.*)

LORD AUGUSTUS: Well, really, I might be her husband already. Positively I might. (*Follows her in a bewildered manner.*)

Act Drop

ACT THREE

SCENE: *Lord Darlington's rooms. A large sofa is in front of fireplace R. At the back of the stage a curtain is drawn across the window. Doors L. and R. Table R. with writing materials. Table C. with syphons, glasses, and Tantalus frame. Table L. with cigar and cigarette box. Lamps lit.*

LADY WINDERMERE (*standing by the fireplace*): Why doesn't he come? This waiting is horrible. He should be here. Why is he not here, to wake by passionate words some fire within me? I am cold—cold as a loveless thing. Arthur must have read my letter by this time. If he cared for me, he would have come after me, would have taken me back by force. But he doesn't care. He's entrammelled by this woman—fascinated by her—dominated by her. If a woman wants to hold a man, she has merely to appeal to what is worst in him. We make gods of men and they leave us. Others make brutes of them and they fawn and are faithful. How hideous life is! . . . Oh! it was mad of me to come here, horribly mad. And yet, which is the worst, I wonder, to be at the mercy of a man who loves one, or the wife of a man who in one's own house dishonours one? What woman knows? What woman in the whole world? But will he love me always, this man to whom I am giving my life? What do I bring him? Lips that have lost the note of joy, eyes that are blinded by tears, chill hands and icy heart. I bring him nothing. I must go back—no; I can't go back, my letter has put me in their power—Arthur would not take me back! That fatal letter! No! Lord Darlington leaves England to-morrow. I will go with him—I have no choice. (*Sits down for a few moments. Then starts up and puts on her cloak.*) No, no! I will go back, let Arthur do with me what he pleases. I can't wait here. It has been madness my coming. I must go at once. As for Lord Darlington.— Oh! here he is! What shall I do? What can I say to him? Will he let me go away at all? I have heard that men are brutal, horrible . . . Oh! (*Hides her face in her hands.*)

Enters MRS. ERLYNNE *L.*

MRS. ERLYNNE: Lady Windermere! (LADY WINDERMERE *starts and looks up. Then recoils in contempt.*) Thank Heaven I am in time. You must go back to your husband's house immediately.

LADY WINDERMERE: Must?

MRS. ERLYNNE (*authoritatively*): Yes, you must! There is not a second to be lost. Lord Darlington may return at any moment.

LADY WINDERMERE: Don't come near me!

MRS. ERYLYNNE: Oh! You are on the brink of ruin, you are on the brink of a hideous precipice. You must leave this place at once; my carriage is waiting at the corner of the street. You must come with me and drive straight home.

LADY WINDERMERE *throws off her cloak and flings it on the sofa.*

What are you doing?

LADY WINDERMERE: Mrs. Erlynne—if you had not come here, I would have gone back. But now that I see you, I feel that nothing in the whole world would induce me to live under the same roof as Lord Windermere. You fill me with horror. There is something about you that stirs the wildest—rage within me. And I know why you are here. My husband sent you to lure me back that I might serve as a blind to whatever relations exist between you and him.

MRS. ERLYNNE: Oh! You don't think that—you can't.

LADY WINDERMERE: Go back to my husband, Mrs. Erlynne. He belongs to you and not to me. I suppose he is afraid of a scandal. Men are such cowards. They outrage every law of the world, and are afraid of the world's tongue. But he had better prepare himself. He shall have a scandal. He shall have the worst scandal there has been in London for years. He shall see his name in every vile paper, mine on every hideous placard.

MRS. ERLYNNE: No—no—

LADY WINDERMERE: Yes! he shall. Had he come himself, I admit I would have gone back to the life of degradation you and he had prepared for me—I was going back—but to stay himself at home, and to send you as his messenger—oh! it was infamous—infamous.

MRS. ERLYNNE (*C.*): Lady Windermere, you wrong me horribly—you wrong your husband horribly. He doesn't know you are here—he thinks you are safe in your own house. He thinks you are asleep in your own room. He never read the mad letter you wrote to him!

LADY WINDERMERE (*R.*): Never read it!

MRS. ERLYNNE: No—he knows nothing about it.

LADY WINDERMERE: How simple you think me! (*Going to her.*) You are lying to me!

MRS. ERLYNNE (*restraining herself*): I am not. I am telling you the truth.

LADY WINDERMERE: If my husband didn't read my letter, how is it that you are here? Who told you I had left the house you were shameless enough to enter? Who told you where I had gone to? My husband told you, and sent you to decoy me back. (*Crosses L.*)

MRS. ERLYNNE (*R.C.*): Your husband has never seen the letter. I—saw it, I opened it. I—read it.

LADY WINDERMERE (*turning to her*): You opened a letter of mine to my husband? You wouldn't dare!

MRS. ERLYNNE: Dare! Oh! to save you from the abyss into which you are falling, there is nothing in the world I would not dare, nothing in the whole world. Here is the letter. Your husband has never read it. He never shall read it. (*Going to fireplace.*) It should never have been written. (*Tears it and throws it into the fire.*)

LADY WINDERMERE (*with infinite contempt in her voice and look*): How do I know that that was my letter after all? You seem to think that commonest device can take me in!

MRS. ERLYNNE: Oh! why do you disbelieve everything I tell you? What object do you think I have in coming here, except to save you from utter ruin, to save you from the consequence of a hideous mistake? That letter that is burnt now *was* your letter. I swear it to you!

LADY WINDERMERE (*slowly*): You took good care to burn it before I had examined it. I cannot trust you. You, whose whole life is a lie, how could you speak the truth about anything? (*Sits down.*)

MRS. ERLYNNE (*hurriedly*): Think as you like about me— say what you choose against me, but go back, go back to the husband you love.

LADY WINDERMERE (*sullenly*): I do *not* love him!

MRS. ERLYNNE: You do, and you know that he loves you.

LADY WINDERMERE: He does not understand what love is. He understands it as little as you do—but I see what you want. It would be a great advantage for you to get me back. Dear Heaven! what a life I would have then! Living at the mercy of a woman who has neither mercy nor pity in her, a woman whom it is an infamy to meet, a degradation to know, a vile woman, a woman who comes between husband and wife!

MRS. ERLYNNE (*with a gesture of despair*): Lady Windermere, Lady Windermere, don't say such terrible things. You don't know how terrible they are, how terrible and how unjust. Listen, you must listen! Only go back to your husband, and I promise you never to communicate with him again on any pretext—never to see him—never to have anything to do with his life or yours. The money that he gave me, he gave me not through love, but through hatred, not in worship, but in contempt. The hold I have over him—

LADY WINDERMERE (*rising*): Ah! you admit you have a hold!

MRS. ERLYNNE: Yes, and I will tell you what it is. It is his love for you, Lady Windermere.

LADY WINDERMERE: You expect me to believe that?

MRS. ERYLYNNE: You must believe it! it is true. It is his love for you that has made him submit to—oh! call it what you like, tyranny, threats, anything you choose. But it is his love for you. His desire to spare you—shame, yes, shame and disgrace.

LADY WINDERMERE: What do you mean? You are insolent! What have I to do with you?

MRS. ERLYNNE (*humbly*): Nothing. I know it—but I tell you that your husband loves you—that you may never meet with such love again in your whole life—that such love you will never meet—and that if you throw it away, the day may come when you will starve for love and it will not be given to you, beg for love and it will be denied you.—Oh! Arthur loves you!

LADY WINDERMERE: Arthur? And you tell me there is nothing between you?

MRS. ERLYNNE: Lady Windermere, before Heaven your husband is guiltless of all offence towards you! And I—I tell you that had it ever occurred to me that such a monstrous suspicion would have entered your mind, I would have died rather than have crossed your life or his—oh! died, gladly died! (*Moves away to sofa R.*)

LADY WINDERMERE: You talk as if you had a heart. Women like you have no hearts. Heart is not in you. You are bought and sold. (*Sits L. C.*)

MRS. ERLYNNE (*starts, with a gesture of pain. Then restrains herself, and comes over to where* LADY WINDERMERE *is sitting. As she speaks, she stretches out her hands towards her, but does not dare to touch her*): Believe what you choose about me. I am not worth a moment's sorrow. But don't spoil your beautiful young life on my account! You don't know what may be in store for you, unless you leave this house at once. You don't know what it is to fall into the pit, to be despised, mocked, abandoned, sneered at—to be an outcast! to find the door shut against one, to have to creep in by hideous byways, afraid every moment lest the mask should be stripped from one's face, and all the while to hear the laughter, the horrible laughter of the world, a thing more tragic than all the tears the world has ever shed. You don't know what it is. One pays for one's sin, and then one pays again, and all one's life one pays. You must never know that.—As for me, if suffering be an expiation, then at this moment I have expiated all my faults, whatever they have been; for to-night you have made a heart in one who had it not, made it and broken it.—But let that pass. I may have wrecked my own life, but I will not let you wreck yours. You—why, you are a mere girl, you would be lost. You haven't got the kind of

brains that enables a woman to get back. You have neither the wit nor the courage. You couldn't stand dishonour! No! Go back, Lady Windermere, to the husband
who loves you, whom you love. You have a child, Lady
Windermere. Go back to that child who even now, in
pain or in joy, may be calling to you. (LADY WINDER-
MERE *rises*.) God gave you that child. He will require
from you that you make his life fine, that you watch over
him. What answer will you make to God if his life is
ruined through you? Back to your house, Lady Windermere—your husband loves you! He has never swerved
for a moment from the love he bears you. But even if he
had a thousand loves, you must stay with your child. If he
was harsh to you, you must stay with your child. If he ill-
treated you, you must stay with your child. If he abandoned you, your place is with your child.

LADY WINDERMERE *bursts into tears and buries her
face in her hands.*

(Rushing to her): Lady Windermere!

LADY WINDERMERE *(holding out her hands to her, help-
lessly, as a child might do)*: Take me home. Take me
home.

MRS. ERLYNNE *(is about to embrace her. Then restrains herself. There is a look of wonderful joy in her face)*: Come!
Where is your cloak? *(Getting it from sofa.)* Here. Put it
on. Come at once!

They go to the door.

LADY WINDERMERE: Stop! Don't you hear voices?

MRS. ERLYNNE: No, no! There is no one!

LADY WINDERMERE: Yes, there is! Listen! Oh! that is my
husband's voice! He is coming in! Save me! Oh, it's some
plot! You have sent for him.

Voices outside.

MRS. ERLYNNE: Silence! I'm here to save you, if I can. But I fear it is too late! There! *(Points to the curtain across the window.)* The first chance you have slip out, if you ever get a chance!

LADY WINDERMERE: But you?

MRS. ERLYNNE: Oh! never mind me. I'll face them.

LADY WINDERMERE *hides herself behind the curtain.*

LORD AUGUSTUS *(outside)*: Nonsense, dear Windermere, you must not leave me!

MRS. ERLYNNE: Lord Augustus! Then it is I who am lost! *(Hesitates for a moment, then looks round and sees door R., and exit through it.)*

Enter LORD DARLINGTON, MR. DUMBY, LORD WINDERMERE, LORD AUGUSTUS LORTON, *and* MR. CECIL GRAHAM.

DUMBY: What a nuisance their turning us out of the club at this hour! It's only two o'clock. *(Sinks into a chair.)* The lively part of the evening is only just beginning. *(Yawns and closes his eyes.)*

LORD WINDERMERE: It is very good of you, Lord Darlington, allowing Augustus to force our company on you, but I'm afraid I can't stay long.

LORD DARLINGTON: Really! I am so sorry! You'll take a cigar, won't you?

LORD WINDERMERE: Thanks! *(Sits down.)*

LORD AUGUSTUS *(to* LORD WINDERMERE*)*: My dear boy, you must not dream of going. I have a great deal to talk to you about, of demmed importance, too. *(Sits down with him at L. table.)*

CECIL GRAHAM: Oh! We all know what that is! Tuppy can't talk about anything but Mrs. Erlynne.

LORD WINDERMERE: Well, that is no business of yours, is it, Cecil?

CECIL GRAHAM: None! That is why it interests me. My own

business always bores me to death. I prefer other people's.

LORD DARLINGTON: Have something to drink, you fellows. Cecil, you'll have a whisky and soda?

CECIL GRAHAM: Thanks. (*Goes to table with* LORD DAR-LINGTON) Mrs. Erlynne looked very handsome to-night, didn't she?

LORD DARLINGTON: I am not one of her admirers.

CECIL GRAHAM: I usen't to be, but I am now. Why! she actually made me introduce her to poor dear Aunt Caroline. I believe she is going to lunch there.

LORD DARLINGTON (*in surprise*): No?

CECIL GRAHAM: She is, really.

LORD DARLINGTON: Excuse me, you fellows. I'm going away to-morrow. And I have to write a few letters. (*Goes to writing-table and sits down.*)

DUMBY: Clever woman, Mrs. Erlynne.

CECIL GRAHAM: Hallo, Dumby! I thought you were asleep.

DUMBY: I am, I usually am!

LORD AUGUSTUS: A very clever woman. Knows perfectly well what a demmed fool I am—knows it as well as I do myself.

    CECIL GRAHAM *comes towards him laughing.*

    Ah, you may laugh, my boy, but it is a great thing to come across a woman who thoroughly understands one.

DUMBY: It is an awfully dangerous thing. They always end by marrying one.

CECIL GRAHAM: But I thought, Tuppy, you were never going to see her again! Yes! you told me so yesterday evening at the club. You said you'd heard—

Whispering to him.

LORD AUGUSTUS: Oh, she's explained that.

CECIL GRAHAM: And the Wiesbaden[1] affair?

LORD AUGUSTUS: She's explained that too.

DUMBY: And her income, Tuppy? Has she explained that?

LORD AUGUSTUS (*in a very serious voice*): She's going to explain that to-morrow.

CECIL GRAHAM *goes back to C. table*.

DUMBY: Awfully commercial, women nowadays. Our grandmothers threw their caps over the mills, of course, but, by Jove, their grand-daughters only throw their caps over mills that can raise the wind for them.[2]

LORD AUGUSTUS: You want to make her out a wicked woman. She is not!

CECIL GRAHAM: Oh! Wicked women bother one. Good women bore one. That is the only difference between them.

LORD AUGUSTUS (*puffing a cigar*): Mrs. Erlynne has a future before her.

DUMBY: Mrs. Erlynne has a past before her.

LORD AUGUSTUS: I prefer women with a past. They're always so demmed amusing to talk to.

CECIL GRAHAM: Well, you'll have lots of topics of conversation with *her*, Tuppy. (*Rising and going to him.*)

LORD AUGUSTUS: You're getting annoying, dear boy; you're getting demmed annoying.

CECIL GRAHAM (*puts his hands on his shoulders*): Now, Tuppy, you've lost your figure and you've lost your character. Don't lose your temper; you have only got one.

LORD AUGUSTUS: My dear boy, if I wasn't the most good-natured man in London—

CECIL GRAHAM: We'd treat you with more respect, wouldn't we, Tuppy? (*Strolls away.*)

DUMBY: The youth of the present day are quite monstrous. They have absolutely no respect for dyed hair.[3]

LORD AUGUSTUS *looks round angrily*.

CECIL GRAHAM: Mrs. Erlynne has a very great respect for dear Tuppy.

DUMBY: Then Mrs. Erlynne sets an admirable example to the rest of her sex. It is perfectly brutal the way most women nowadays behave to men who are not their husbands.

LORD WINDERMERE: Dumby, you are ridiculous, and Cecil, you let your tongue run away with you. You must leave Mrs. Erlynne alone. You don't really know anything about her, and you're always talking scandal against her.

CECIL GRAHAM (*coming towards him L.C.*): My dear Arthur, I never talk scandal. *I* only talk gossip.

LORD WINDERMERE: What is the difference between scandal and gossip?

CECIL GRAHAM: Oh! gossip is charming! History is merely gossip. But scandal is gossip made tedious by morality. Now, I never moralise. A man who moralises is usually a hypocrite, and a woman who moralises is invariably plain. There is nothing in the whole world so unbecoming to a woman as a Nonconformist conscience. And most women know it, I'm glad to say.

LORD AUGUSTUS: Just my sentiments, dear boy, just my sentiments.

CECIL GRAHAM: Sorry to hear it, Tuppy; whenever people agree with me, I always feel I must be wrong.

LORD AUGUSTUS: My dear boy, when I was your age—

CECIL GRAHAM: But you never were, Tuppy, and you never will be. (*Goes up to C.*) I say, Darlington, let us have some cards. You'll play, Arthur, won't you?

LORD WINDERMERE: No, thanks, Cecil.

DUMBY (*with a sigh*): Good heavens! how marriage ruins a man! It's as demoralising as cigarettes, and far more expensive.

CECIL GRAHAM: You'll play, of course, Tuppy?

LORD AUGUSTUS (*pouring himself out a brandy and soda at table*): Can't, dear boy. Promised Mrs. Erlynne never to play or drink again.

CECIL GRAHAM: Now, my dear Tuppy, don't be led astray into the paths of virtue. Reformed, you would be perfectly tedious. That is the worst of women. They always want one to be good. And if we are good, when they meet us, they don't love us at all. They like to find us quite irretrievably bad, and to leave us quite unattractively good.

LORD DARLINGTON (*rising from R. table, where he has been writing letters*): They always do find us bad!

DUMBY: I don't think we are bad. I think we are all good, except Tuppy.

LORD DARLINGTON: No, we are all in the gutter, but some of us are looking at the stars. (*Sits down at C. table.*)

DUMBY: We are all in the gutter, but some of us are looking at the stars? Upon my word, you are very romantic to-night, Darlington.

CECIL GRAHAM: Too romantic! You must be in love. Who is the girl?

LORD DARLINGTON: The woman I love is not free, or thinks she isn't. (*Glances instinctively at* LORD WINDERMERE *while he speaks.*)

CECIL GRAHAM: A married woman, then! Well, there's nothing in the world like the devotion of a married woman. It's a thing no married man knows anything about.

LORD DARLINGTON: Oh! she doesn't love me. She is a good woman. She is the only woman I have ever met in my life.

CECIL GRAHAM: The only good woman you have ever met in your life.

LORD DARLINGTON: Yes!

CECIL GRAHAM (*lighting a cigarette*): Well, you are a lucky fellow! Why, I have met hundreds of good women. I never seem to meet any but good women. The world is perfectly packed with good women. To know them is a middle-class education.

LORD DARLINGTON: This woman has purity and innocence. She has everything we men have lost.

CECIL GRAHAM: My dear fellow, what on earth should we men do going about with purity and innocence? A carefully thought-out buttonhole is much more effective.

DUMBY: She doesn't really love you then?

LORD DARLINGTON: No, she does not!

DUMBY: I congratulate you, my dear fellow. In this world there are only two tragedies. One is not getting what one wants, and the other is getting it. The last is much the worst; the last is a real tragedy! But I am interested to hear she does not love you. How long could you love a woman who didn't love you, Cecil?

CECIL GRAHAM: A woman who didn't love me? Oh, all my life!

DUMBY: So could I. But it's so difficult to meet one.

LORD DARLINGTON: How can you be so conceited, Dumby?

DUMBY: I didn't say it as a matter of conceit. I said it as a matter of regret. I have been wildly, madly adored. I am sorry I have. It has been an immense nuisance. I should like to be allowed a little time to myself now and then.

LORD AUGUSTUS (*looking round*): Time to educate yourself, I suppose.

DUMBY: No, time to forget all I have learned. That is much more important, dear Tuppy.

LORD AUGUSTUS *moves uneasily in his chair.*

LORD DARLINGTON: What cynics you fellows are!

CECIL GRAHAM: What is a cynic? (*Sitting on the back of the sofa.*)

LORD DARLINGTON: A man who knows the price of everything and the value of nothing.

CECIL GRAHAM: And a sentimentalist, my dear Darlington,
is a man who sees an absurd value in everything, and
doesn't know the market price of any single thing.

LORD DARLINGTON: You always amuse me, Cecil. You talk
as if you were a man of experience.

CECIL GRAHAM: I am. (*Moves up to front of fireplace.*)

LORD DARLINGTON: You are far too young!

CECIL GRAHAM: That is a great error. Experience is a question of instinct about life. I have got it. Tuppy hasn't. Experience is the name Tuppy gives to his mistakes. That
is all.

LORD AUGUSTUS *looks round indignantly.*

DUMBY: Experience is the name every one gives to their
mistakes.

CECIL GRAHAM (*standing with his back to the fireplace*):
One shouldn't commit any. (*Sees* LADY WINDERMERE'S
fan on sofa.)

DUMBY: Life would be very dull without them.

CECIL GRAHAM: Of course you are quite faithful to this
woman you are in love with, Darlington, to this good
woman?

LORD DARLINGTON: Cecil, if one really loves a woman, all
other women in the world become absolutely meaning-
less to one. Love changes one—I am changed.

CECIL GRAHAM: Dear me! How very interesting! Tuppy, I
want to talk to you.

LORD AUGUSTUS *takes no notice.*

DUMBY: It's no use talking to Tuppy. You might just as well
talk to a brick wall.

CECIL GRAHAM: But I like talking to a brick wall—it's the

only thing in the world that never contradicts me!
Tuppy!

LORD AUGUSTUS: Well, what is it? What is it? (*Rising and
going over to* CECIL GRAHAM.)

CECIL GRAHAM: Come over here. I want you particularly.
(*Aside.*) Darlington has been moralising and talking
about the purity of love, and that sort of thing, and he has
got some woman in his rooms all the time.

LORD AUGUSTUS: No, really! really!

CECIL GRAHAM (*in a low voice*): Yes, here is her fan. (*Points
to the fan.*)

LORD AUGUSTUS (*chuckling*): By Jove! By Jove!

LORD WINDERMERE (*up by door*): I am really off now, Lord
Darlington. I am sorry you are leaving England so soon.
Pray call on us when you come back! My wife and I will
be charmed to see you!

LORD DARLINGTON (*up stage with* LORD WINDERMERE): I
am afraid I shall be away for many years. Good-night!

CECIL GRAHAM: Arthur!

LORD WINDERMERE: What?

CECIL GRAHAM: I want to speak to you for a moment. No,
do come!

LORD WINDERMERE (*putting on his coat*): I can't—I'm off.

CECIL GRAHAM: It is something very particular. It will interest you enormously.

LORD WINDERMERE (*smiling*): It is some of your nonsense,
Cecil.

CECIL: It isn't! It isn't really.

LORD AUGUSTUS (*going to him*): My dear fellow, you
mustn't go yet. I have a lot to talk to you about. And Cecil
has something to show you.

LORD WINDERMERE (*walking over*): Well, what is it?

CECIL GRAHAM: Darlington has got a woman here in his
rooms. Here is her fan. Amusing, isn't it? (*A pause.*)

LORD WINDERMERE: Good God! (*Seizes the fan*—DUMBY *rises.*)

CECIL GRAHAM: What is the matter?

LORD WINDERMERE: Lord Darlington!

LORD DARLINGTON (*turning round*): Yes!

LORD WINDERMERE: What is my wife's fan doing here in your rooms? Hands off, Cecil. Don't touch me.

LORD DARLINGTON: Your wife's fan?

LORD WINDERMERE: Yes, here it is!

LORD DARLINGTON (*walking towards him*): I don't know!

LORD WINDERMERE: You must know. I demand an explanation. Don't hold me, you fool. (*To* CECIL GRAHAM.)

LORD DARLINGTON (*aside*): She is here after all!

LORD WINDERMERE: Speak, sir! Why is my wife's fan here? Answer me! By God! I'll search your rooms, and if my wife's here, I'll——(*Moves.*)

LORD DARLINGTON: You shall not search my rooms. You have no right to do so. I forbid you!

LORD WINDERMERE: You scoundrel! I'll not leave your room till I have searched every corner of it! What moves behind that curtain? (*Rushes towards the curtain C.*)

MRS ERLYNNE (*enters behind R.*): Lord Windermere!

LORD WINDERMERE: Mrs. Erlynne!

Every one starts and turns round. LADY WINDERMERE *slips out from behind the curtain and glides from the room L.*

MRS. ERLYNNE: I am afraid I took your wife's fan in mistake for my own, when I was leaving your house to-night. I am so sorry. (*Takes fan from him.* LORD WINDERMERE *looks at her in contempt.* LORD DARLINGTON *in mingled astonishment and anger.* LORD AUGUSTUS *turns away. The other men smile at each other.*)

Act Drop

ACT FOUR

SCENE: *Same as in Act One.*

LADY WINDERMERE (*lying on sofa*): How can I tell him? I can't tell him. It would kill me. I wonder what happened after I escaped from that horrible room. Perhaps she told them the true reason of her being there, and the real meaning of that—fatal fan of mine. Oh, if he knows—how can I look him in the face again? He would never forgive me. (*Touches bell.*) How securely one thinks one lives—out of reach of temptation, sin, folly. And then suddenly—Oh! Life is terrible. It rules us, we do not rule it.

Enter ROSALIE *R.*

ROSALIE: Did your ladyship ring for me?
LADY WINDERMERE: Yes. Have you found out at what time Lord Windermere came in last night?
ROSALIE: His lordship did not come in till five o'clock.
LADY WINDERMERE: Five o'clock? He knocked at my door this morning, didn't he?

ROSALIE: Yes, my lady—at half-past nine. I told him your ladyship was not awake yet.

LADY WINDERMERE: Did he say anything?

ROSALIE: Something about your ladyship's fan. I didn't quite catch what his lordship said. Has the fan been lost, my lady? I can't find it, and Parker says it was not left in any of the rooms. He has looked in all of them and on the terrace as well.

LADY WINDERMERE: It doesn't matter. Tell Parker not to trouble. That will do.

Exit ROSALIE.

LADY WINDERMERE *(rising)*: She is sure to tell him. I can fancy a person doing a wonderful act of self-sacrifice, doing it spontaneously, recklessly, nobly—and afterwards finding out that it costs too much. Why should she hesitate between her ruin and mine? . . . How strange! I would have publicly disgraced her in my own house. She accepts public disgrace in the house of another to save me. . . . There is a bitter irony in things, a bitter irony in the way we talk of good and bad women. . . . Oh, what a lesson! and what a pity that in life we only get our lessons when they are of no use to us! For even if she doesn't tell, I must. Oh! the shame of it, the shame of it. To tell it is to live through it all again. Actions are the first tragedy in life, words are the second. Words are perhaps the worst. Words are merciless. . . . Oh! *(Starts as* LORD WINDERMERE *enters.)*

LORD WINDERMERE *(kisses her)*: Margaret—how pale you look!

LADY WINDERMERE: I slept very badly.

LORD WINDERMERE *(sitting on sofa with her)*: I am so sorry. I came in dreadfully late, and didn't like to wake you. You are crying, dear.

LADY WINDERMERE: Yes, I am crying, for I have something to tell you, Arthur.

LORD WINDERMERE: My dear child, you are not well. You've been doing too much. Let us go away to the country. You'll be all right at Selby. The season is almost over. There is no use staying on. Poor darling! We'll go away to-day, if you like. *(Rises.)* We can easily catch the 3.40. I'll send a wire to Fannen. *(Crosses and sits down at table to write a telegram.)*

LADY WINDERMERE: Yes; let us go away to-day. No; I can't go to-day, Arthur. There is some one I must see before I leave town—some one who has been kind to me.

LORD WINDERMERE *(rising and leaning over sofa)*: Kind to you?

LADY WINDERMERE: Far more than that. *(Rises and goes to him.)* I will tell you, Arthur, but only love me, love me as you used to love me.

LORD WINDERMERE: Used to? You are not thinking of that wretched woman who came here last night? *(Coming round and sitting R. of her.)* You don't still imagine—no, you couldn't.

LADY WINDERMERE: I don't. I know now I was wrong and foolish.

LORD WINDERMERE: It was very good of you to receive her last night—but you are never to see her again.

LADY WINDERMERE: Why do you say that? *(A pause.)*

LORD WINDERMERE *(holding her hand)*: Margaret, I thought Mrs. Erlynne was a woman more sinned against than sinning, as the phrase goes. I thought she wanted to be good, to get back into a place that she had lost by a moment's folly, to lead again a decent life. I believed what she told me—I was mistaken in her. She is bad—as bad as a woman can be.

LADY WINDERMERE: Arthur, Arthur, don't talk so bitterly about any woman. I don't think now that people can be divided into the good and the bad as though they were two separate races or creations. What are called good women may have terrible things in them, mad moods of recklessness, assertion, jealousy, sin. Bad women, as they are termed, may have in them sorrow, repentance, pity, sacrifice. And I don't think Mrs. Erlynne a bad woman— I know she's not.

LORD WINDERMERE: My dear child, the woman's impossible. No matter what harm she tries to do us, you must never see her again. She is inadmissible anywhere.

LADY WINDERMERE: But I want to see her. I want her to come here.

LORD WINDERMERE: Never!

LADY WINDERMERE: She came here once as *your* guest. She must come now as *mine*. That is but fair.

LORD WINDERMERE: She should never have come here.

LADY WINDERMERE (*rising*): It is too late, Arthur, to say that now. (*Moves away.*)

LORD WINDERMERE (*rising*): Margaret, if you knew where Mrs. Erlynne went last night, after she left this house, you would not sit in the same room with her. It was absolutely shameless, the whole thing.

LADY WINDERMERE: Arthur, I can't bear it any longer. I must tell you. Last night—

Enter PARKER *with a tray on which lie* LADY WINDERMERE's *fan and a card.*

PARKER: Mrs. Erlynne has called to return your ladyship's fan which she took away by mistake last night. Mrs. Erlynne has written a message on the card.

LADY WINDERMERE: Oh, ask Mrs. Erlynne to be kind enough to come up. (*Reads card.*) Say I shall be very glad to see her.

Exit PARKER.

She wants to see me, Arthur.

LORD WINDERMERE (*takes card and looks at it*): Margaret,

I *beg* you not to. Let me see her first, at any rate. She's a dangerous woman. She is the most dangerous woman I know. You don't realise what you're doing.

LADY WINDERMERE: It is right that I should see her.

LORD WINDERMERE: My child, you may be on the brink of a great sorrow. Don't go to meet it. It is absolutely necessary that I should see her before you do.

LADY WINDERMERE: Why should it be necessary?

Enter PARKER.

PARKER: Mrs. Erlynne.

Enter MRS. ERYLNNE. *Exit* PARKER.

MRS. ERLYNNE: How do you do, Lady Windermere? (*To* LORD WINDERMERE): How do you do? Do you know, Lady Windermere, I am so sorry about your fan. I can't imagine how I made such a silly mistake. Most stupid of me. And as I was driving in your direction, I thought I would take the opportunity of returning your property in person with many apologies for my carelessness, and of bidding you good-bye.

LADY WINDERMERE: Good-bye? (*Moves towards sofa with* MRS. ERLYNNE *and sits down beside her.*) Are you going away, then, Mrs. Erlynne?

MRS. ERLYNNE: Yes; I am going to live abroad again. The English climate doesn't suit me. My—heart is affected here, and that I don't like. I prefer living in the south. London is too full of fogs and—and serious people, Lord Windermere. Whether the fogs produce the serious people or whether the serious people produce the fogs, I don't know, but the whole thing rather gets on my nerves, and so I'm leaving this afternoon by the Club Train.[1]

LADY WINDERMERE: This afternoon? But I wanted so much to come and see you.

MRS. ERLYNNE: How kind of you! But I am afraid I have to go.

LADY WINDERMERE: Shall I never see you again, Mrs. Erlynne?

MRS. ERLYNNE: I am afraid not. Our lives lie too far apart. But there is a little thing I would like you to do for me. I want a photograph of you, Lady Windermere— would you give me one? You don't know how gratified I should be.

LADY WINDERMERE: Oh, with pleasure. There is one on that table. I'll show it to you. (*Goes across to the table.*)

LORD WINDERMERE (*coming up to* MRS. ERLYNNE *and speaking in a low voice*): It is monstrous your intruding yourself here after your conduct last night.

MRS. ERLYNNE (*with an amused smile*): My dear Windermere, manners before morals!

LADY WINDERMERE (*returning*): I'm afraid it is very flattering—I am not so pretty as that. (*Showing photograph.*)

MRS. ERLYNNE: You are much prettier. But haven't you got one of yourself with your little boy?

LADY WINDERMERE: I have. Would you prefer one of those?

MRS. ERLYNNE: Yes.

LADY WINDERMERE: I'll go and get it for you, if you'll excuse me for a moment. I have one upstairs.

MRS. ERLYNNE: So sorry, Lady Windermere, to give you so much trouble.

LADY WINDERMERE (*moves to door R.*): No trouble at all, Mrs. Erlynne.

MRS. ERLYNNE: Thanks so much.

Exit LADY WINDERMERE *R.*

You seem rather out of temper this morning, Windermere. Why should you be? Margaret and I get on charmingly together.

LORD WINDERMERE: I can't bear to see you with her. Besides, you have not told me the truth, Mrs. Erlynne.

MRS. ERLYNNE: I have not told *her* the truth, you mean.

LORD WINDERMERE *(standing C.)*: I sometimes wish you had. I should have been spared then the misery, the anxiety, the annoyance of the last six months. But rather than my wife should know—that the mother whom she was taught to consider as dead, the mother whom she has mourned as dead, is living—a divorced woman, going about under an assumed name, a bad woman preying upon life, as I know you now to be—rather than that, I was ready to supply you with money to pay bill after bill, extravagance after extravagance, to risk what occurred yesterday, the first quarrel I have ever had with my wife. You don't understand what that means to me. How could you? But I tell you that the only bitter words that ever came from those sweet lips of hers were on your account, and I hate to see you next her. You sully the innocence that is in her. *(Moves L.C.)* And then I used to think that with all your faults you were frank and honest. You are not.

MRS. ERLYNNE: Why do you say that?

LORD WINDERMERE: You made me get you an invitation to my wife's ball.

MRS. ERLYNNE: For my daughter's ball—yes.

LORD WINDERMERE: You came, and within an hour of your leaving the house you are found in a man's rooms—you are disgraced before every one. *(Goes up stage C.)*

MRS. ERLYNNE: Yes.

LORD WINDERMERE *(turning round on her)*: Therefore I have a right to look upon you as what you are—a worthless, vicious woman. I have the right to tell you never to enter this house, never to attempt to come near my wife—

MRS. ERLYNNE *(coldly)*: My daughter, you mean.

LORD WINDERMERE: You have no right to claim her as your daughter. You left her, abandoned her when she was but a child in the cradle, abandoned her for your lover, who abandoned you in turn.

MRS. ERLYNNE (*rising*): Do you count that to his credit, Lord Windermere—or to mine?

LORD WINDERMERE: To his, now that I know you.

MRS. ERLYNNE: Take care—you had better be careful.

LORD WINDERMERE: Oh, I am not going to mince words for you. I know you thoroughly.

MRS. ERLYNNE (*looking steadily at him*): I question that.

LORD WINDERMERE: I *do* know you. For twenty years of your life you lived without your child, without a thought of your child. One day you read in the papers that she had married a rich man. You saw your hideous chance. You knew that to spare her the ignominy of learning that a woman like you was her mother, I would endure anything. You began your blackmailing.

MRS. ERLYNNE (*shrugging her shoulders*): Don't use ugly words, Windermere. They are vulgar. I saw my chance, it is true, and took it.

LORD WINDERMERE: Yes, you took it—and spoiled it all last night by being found out.

MRS. ERLYNNE (*with a strange smile*): You are quite right, I spoiled it all last night.

LORD WINDERMERE: And as for your blunder in taking my wife's fan from here and then leaving it about in Darlington's rooms, it is unpardonable. I can't bear the sight of it now. I shall never let my wife use it again. The thing is soiled for me. You should have kept it and not brought it back.

MRS. ERLYNNE: I think I *shall* keep it. (*Goes up.*) It's extremely pretty. (*Takes up fan.*) I shall ask Margaret to give it to me.

LORD WINDERMERE: I hope my wife will give it to you.

MRS. ERLYNNE: Oh, I'm sure she will have no objection.

LORD WINDERMERE: I wish that at the same time she would give you a miniature she kisses every night before she prays.—It's the miniature of a young innocent-looking girl with beautiful *dark* hair.

MRS. ERLYNNE: Ah, yes, I remember. How long ago that seems! *(Goes to sofa and sits down.)* It was done before I was married. Dark hair and an innocent expression were the fashion then, Windermere! *(A pause.)*

LORD WINDERMERE: What do you mean by coming here this morning? What is your object? *(Crossing L.C. and sitting.)*

MRS. ERLYNNE *(with a note of irony in her voice)*: To bid good-bye to my dear daughter, of course.

LORD WINDERMERE *bites his under lip in anger.* MRS. ERLYNNE *looks at him, and her voice and manner become serious. In her accents as she talks there is a note of deep tragedy. For a moment she reveals herself.*

Oh, don't imagine I am going to have a pathetic scene with her, weep on her neck and tell her who I am, and all that kind of thing. I have no ambition to play the part of a mother. Only once in my life have I known a mother's feelings. That was last night. They were terrible—they made me suffer—they made me suffer too much. For twenty years, as you say, I have lived childless—I want to live childless still. *(Hiding her feelings with a trivial laugh.)* Besides, my dear Windermere, how on earth could I pose as a mother with a grown-up daughter? Margaret is twenty-one, and I have never admitted that I am more than twenty-nine, or thirty at the most. Twenty-nine when there are pink shades,[2] thirty when there are not. So you see what difficulties it would involve. No, as far as I am concerned, let your wife cherish the memory of this dead, stainless mother. Why should I interfere with her illusions? I find it hard enough to keep my own. I lost one illusion last night. I thought I had no heart. I find I have, and a heart doesn't suit me, Windermere. Somehow it doesn't go with modern dress. It makes one look old. *(Takes up hand-mirror from table and looks into it.)* And it spoils one's career at critical moments.

LORD WINDERMERE: You fill me with horror—with absolute horror.

MRS. ERLYNNE *(rising)*: I suppose, Windermere, you would like me to retire into a convent, or become a hospital nurse, or something of that kind, as people do in silly modern novels. That is stupid of you, Arthur; in real life we don't do such things—not as long as we have any good looks left, at any rate. No—what consoles one nowadays is not repentance, but pleasure. Repentance is quite out of date. And besides, if a woman really repents, she has to go to a bad dressmaker, otherwise no one believes in her. And nothing in the world would induce me to do that. No; I am going to pass entirely out of your two lives. My coming into them has been a mistake—I discovered that last night.

LORD WINDERMERE: A fatal mistake.

MRS. ERLYNNE *(smiling)*: Almost fatal.

LORD WINDERMERE: I am sorry now I did not tell my wife the whole thing at once.

MRS. ERLYNNE: I regret my bad actions. You regret your good ones—that is the difference between us.

LORD WINDERMERE: I don't trust you. I *will* tell my wife. It's better for her to know, and from me. It will cause her infinite pain—it will humiliate her terribly, but it's right that she should know.

MRS. ERLYNNE: You propose to tell her?

LORD WINDERMERE: I am going to tell her.

MRS. ERLYNNE (*going up to him*): If you do, I will make my name so infamous that it will mar every moment of her life. It will ruin her, and make her wretched. If you dare to tell her, there is no depth of degradation I will not sink to, no pit of shame I will not enter. You shall not tell her—I forbid you.

LORD WINDERMERE: Why?

MRS. ERLYNNE (*after a pause*): If I said to you that I cared for her, perhaps loved her even—you would sneer at me, wouldn't you?

LORD WINDERMERE: I should feel it was not true. A mother's love means devotion, unselfishness, sacrifice. What could you know of such things?

MRS. ERLYNNE: You are right. What could I know of such things? Don't let us talk any more about it—as for telling my daughter who I am, that I do not allow. It is my secret, it is not yours. If I make up my mind to tell her, and I think I will, I shall tell her before I leave the house—if not, I shall never tell her.

LORD WINDERMERE (*angrily*): Then let me beg of you to leave our house at once. I will make your excuses to Margaret.

Enter LADY WINDERMERE *R. She goes over to* MRS. ERLYNNE *with the photograph in her hand.* LORD WINDERMERE *moves to back of sofa, and anxiously watches* MRS. ERLYNNE *as the scene progresses.*

LADY WINDERMERE: I am so sorry, Mrs. Erlynne, to have kept you waiting. I couldn't find the photograph anywhere. At last I discovered it in my husband's dressing-room—he had stolen it.

MRS. ERLYNNE (*takes the photograph from her and looks at it*): I am not surprised—it is charming. (*Goes over to sofa with* LADY WINDERMERE, *and sits down beside her.*

Looks again at the photograph.) And so that is your little boy! What is he called?

LADY WINDERMERE: Gerard, after my dear father.

MRS. ERLYNNE (*laying the photograph down*): Really?

LADY WINDERMERE: Yes. If it had been a girl, I would have called it after my mother. My mother had the same name as myself, Margaret.

MRS. ERLYNNE: My name is Margaret too.

LADY WINDERMERE: Indeed!

MRS. ERLYNNE: Yes. (*Pause.*) You are devoted to your mother's memory, Lady Windermere, your husband tells me.

LADY WINDERMERE: We all have ideals in life. At least we all should have. Mine is my mother.

MRS. ERLYNNE: Ideals are dangerous things. Realities are better. They wound, but they're better.

LADY WINDERMERE (*shaking her head*): If I lost my ideals, I should lose everything.

MRS. ERLYNNE: Everything?

LADY WINDERMERE: Yes. (*Pause.*)

MRS. ERLYNNE: Did your father often speak to you of your mother?

LADY WINDERMERE: No, it gave him too much pain. He told me how my mother had died a few months after I was born. His eyes filled with tears as he spoke. Then he begged me never to mention her name to him again. It made him suffer even to hear it. My father—my father really died of a broken heart. His was the most ruined life I know.

MRS. ERLYNNE (*rising*): I am afraid I must go now, Lady Windermere.

LADY WINDERMERE (*rising*): Oh no, don't.

MRS. ERLYNNE: I think I had better. My carriage must have come back by this time. I sent it to Lady Jedburgh's with a note.

LADY WINDERMERE: Arthur, would you mind seeing if Mrs. Erlynne's carriage has come back?

MRS. ERLYNNE: Pray don't trouble, Lord Windermere.

LADY WINDERMERE: Yes, Arthur, do go, please.

LORD WINDERMERE *hesitates for a moment and looks at* MRS. ERLYNNE. *She remains quite impassive. He leaves the room.*

(*To* MRS. ERLYNNE): Oh! What am I to say to you? You saved me last night. (*Goes towards her.*)

MRS. ERLYNNE: Hush—don't speak of it.

LADY WINDERMERE: I must speak of it. I can't let you think that I am going to accept this sacrifice. I am not. It is too great. I am going to tell my husband everything. It is my duty.

MRS. ERLYNNE: It is not your duty—at least you have duties to others besides him. You say you owe me something?

LADY WINDERMERE: I owe you everything.

MRS. ERLYNNE: Then pay your debt by silence. That is the only way in which it can be paid. Don't spoil the one good thing I have done in my life by telling it to any one. Promise me that what passed last night will remain a secret between us. You must not bring misery into your husband's life. Why spoil his love? You must not spoil it. Love is easily killed. Oh! how easily love is killed. Pledge me your word, Lady Windermere, that you will *never* tell him. I insist upon it.

LADY WINDERMERE (*with bowed head*): It is your will, not mine.

MRS. ERLYNNE: Yes, it is my will. And never forget your child—I like to think of you as a mother. I like you to think of yourself as one.

LADY WINDERMERE (*looking up*): I always will now. Only once in my life I have forgotten my own mother—that was last night. Oh, if I had remembered her I should not have been so foolish, so wicked.

MRS. ERLYNNE *(with a slight shudder)*: Hush, last night is quite over.

Enter LORD WINDERMERE.

LORD WINDERMERE: Your carriage has not come back yet, Mrs. Erlynne.

MRS. ERLYNNE: It makes no matter. I'll take a hansom. There is nothing in the world so respectable as a good Shrewsbury and Talbot.[3] And now, dear Lady Windermere, I am afraid it is really good-bye. *(Moves up C.)* Oh, I remember. You'll think me absurd, but do you know I've taken a great fancy to this fan that I was silly enough to run away with last night from your ball. Now, I wonder would you give it to me? Lord Windermere says you may. I know it is his present.

LADY WINDERMERE: Oh, certainly, if it will give you any pleasure. But it has my name on it. It has "Margaret" on it.

MRS. ERLYNNE: But we have the same Christian name.

LADY WINDERMERE: Oh, I forgot. Of course, do have it. What a wonderful chance our names being the same!

MRS. ERLYNNE: Quite wonderful. Thanks—it will always remind me of you. *(Shakes hands with her.)*

Enter PARKER.

PARKER: Lord Augustus Lorton. Mrs. Erlynne's carriage has come.

Enter LORD AUGUSTUS.

LORD AUGUSTUS: Good-morning, dear boy. Good-morning, Lady Windermere. *(Sees* MRS. ERLYNNE.*)* Mrs. Erlynne!

MRS. ERLYNNE: How do you do, Lord Augustus? Are you quite well this morning?

LORD AUGUSTUS (*coldly*): Quite well, thank you, Mrs. Erlynne.

MRS. ERLYNNE: You don't look at all well, Lord Augustus. You stop up too late—it is so bad for you. You really should take more care of yourself. Good-bye, Lord Windermere. (*Goes towards door with a bow to* LORD AUGUSTUS. *Suddenly smiles and looks back at him.*) Lord Augustus! Won't you see me to my carriage? You might carry the fan.

LORD WINDERMERE: Allow me!

MRS. ERLYNNE: No; I want Lord Augustus. I have a special message for the dear Duchess. Won't you carry the fan, Lord Augustus?

LORD AUGUSTUS: If you really desire it, Mrs. Erlynne.

MRS. ERLYNNE (*laughing*): Of course I do. You'll carry it so gracefully. You would carry off anything gracefully, dear Lord Augustus. (*When she reaches the door she looks back for a moment at* LADY WINDERMERE. *Their eyes meet. Then she turns, and exit C. followed by* LORD AUGUSTUS.)

LADY WINDERMERE: You will never speak against Mrs. Erlynne again, Arthur, will you?

LORD WINDERMERE (*gravely*): She is better than one thought her.

LADY WINDERMERE: She is better than I am.

LORD WINDERMERE (*smiling as he strokes her hair*): Child, you and she belong to different worlds. Into your world evil has never entered.

LADY WINDERMERE: Don't say that, Arthur. There is the same world for all of us, and good and evil, sin and innocence, go through it hand in hand. To shut one's eyes to half of life that one may live securely is as though one blinded oneself that one might walk with more safety in a land of pit and precipice.

LORD WINDERMERE (*moves down with her*): Darling, why do you say that?

LADY WINDERMERE (*sits on sofa*): Because I, who had shut my eyes to life, came to the brink. And one who had separated us—

LORD WINDERMERE: We were never separated.

LADY WINDERMERE: We never must be again. O Arthur, don't love me less, and I will trust you more. I will trust you absolutely. Let us go to Selby. In the Rose Garden at Selby the roses are white and red.

Enter LORD AUGUSTUS *C.*

LORD AUGUSTUS: Arthur, she has explained everything!

    LADY WINDERMERE *looks horribly frightened at this.* LORD WINDERMERE *starts.* LORD AUGUSTUS *takes* WINDERMERE *by the arm and brings him to front of stage. He talks rapidly and in a low voice.* LADY WINDERMERE *stands watching them in terror.*

    My dear fellow, she has explained every demmed thing. We all wronged her immensely. It was entirely for my sake she went to Darlington's rooms. Called first at the Club—fact is, wanted to put me out of suspense—and being told I had gone on—followed—naturally frightened when she heard a lot of us coming in—retired to another room—I assure you, most gratifying to me, the whole thing. We all behaved brutally to her. She is just the woman for me. Suits me down to the ground. All the conditions she makes are that we live entirely out of England. A very good thing too. Demmed clubs, demmed climate, demmed cooks, demmed everything. Sick of it all!

LADY WINDERMERE (*frightened*): Has Mrs. Erlynne—?

LORD AUGUSTUS (*advancing towards her with a low bow*):

Yes, Lady Windermere—Mrs. Erlynne has done me the honour of accepting my hand.

LORD WINDERMERE: Well, you are certainly marrying a very clever woman!

LADY WINDERMERE *(taking her husband's hand)*: Ah, you're marrying a very good woman!

Curtain

An Ideal Husband

The Persons of the Play

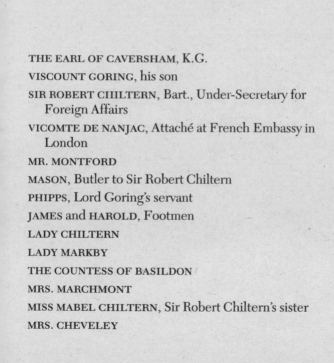

THE EARL OF CAVERSHAM, K.G.

VISCOUNT GORING, his son

SIR ROBERT CHILTERN, Bart., Under-Secretary for Foreign Affairs

VICOMTE DE NANJAC, Attaché at French Embassy in London

MR. MONTFORD

MASON, Butler to Sir Robert Chiltern

PHIPPS, Lord Goring's servant

JAMES and HAROLD, Footmen

LADY CHILTERN

LADY MARKBY

THE COUNTESS OF BASILDON

MRS. MARCHMONT

MISS MABEL CHILTERN, Sir Robert Chiltern's sister

MRS. CHEVELEY

ACT ONE

$$\text{───────────────⚜───────────────}$$

SCENE: *The octagon room at Sir Robert Chiltern's house in Grosvenor Square, London. The action of the play is completed within twenty-four hours.* TIME: *The present.*

The room is brilliantly lighted and full of guests.

    At the top of the staircase stands LADY CHILTERN, *a woman of grave Greek beauty, about twenty-seven years of age. She receives the guests as they come up. Over the well of the staircase hangs a great chandelier with wax lights, which illumine a large eighteenth-century French tapestry—representing the Triumph of Love, from a design by Boucher—that is stretched on the staircase wall. On the right is the entrance to the music-room. The sound of a string quartette is faintly heard. The entrance on the left leads to other reception-rooms.* MRS. MARCHMONT *and* LADY BASILDON, *two very pretty women, are seated together on a Louis Seize sofa. They are types of exquisite fragility. Their affectation of manner has a delicate charm. Watteau would have loved to paint them.*[1]

MRS. MARCHMONT: Going on to the Hartlocks' to-night, Margaret?

LADY BASILDON: I suppose so. Are you?

MRS. MARCHMONT: Yes. Horribly tedious parties they give, don't they?

LADY BASILDON: Horribly tedious! Never know why I go. Never know why I go anywhere.

MRS. MARCHMONT: I come here to be educated.

LADY BASILDON: Ah! I hate being educated!

MRS. MARCHMONT: So do I. It puts one almost on a level with the commercial classes, doesn't it? But dear Gertrude Chiltern is always telling me that I should have some serious purpose in life. So I come here to try to find one.

LADY BASILDON (*looking round through her lorgnette*): I don't see anybody here to-night whom one could possibly call a serious purpose. The man who took me in to dinner talked to me about his wife the whole time.

MRS. MARCHMONT: How very trivial of him!

LADY BASILDON: Terribly trivial! What did your man talk about?

MRS. MARCHMONT: About myself.

LADY BASILDON (*languidly*): And were you interested?

MRS. MARCHMONT (*shaking her head*): Not in the smallest degree.

LADY BASILDON: What martyrs we are, dear Margaret!

MRS. MARCHMONT (*rising*): And how well it becomes us, Olivia!

They rise and go towards the music-room. The VICOMTE DE NANJAC, *a young attaché known for his neckties and his Anglomania, approaches with a low bow, and enters into conversation.*

MASON (*announcing guests from the top of the staircase*): Mr. and Lady Jane Barford. Lord Caversham.

Enter LORD CAVERSHAM, *an old gentleman of seventy, wearing the riband and star of the Garter. A fine Whig type. Rather like a portrait by Lawrence.*[2]

LORD CAVERSHAM: Good-evening, Lady Chiltern! Has my good-for-nothing young son been here?

LADY CHILTERN (*smiling*): I don't think Lord Goring has arrived yet.

MABEL CHILTERN (*coming up to* LORD CAVERSHAM): Why do you call Lord Goring good-for-nothing?

MABEL CHILTERN *is a perfect example of the English type of prettiness, the apple-blossom type. She has all the fragrance and freedom of a flower. There is ripple after ripple of sunlight in her hair, and the little mouth, with its parted lips, is expectant, like the mouth of a child. She has the fascinating tyranny of youth, and the astonishing courage of innocence. To sane people she is not reminiscent of any work of art. But she is really like a Tanagra statuette,*[3] *and would be rather annoyed if she were told so.*

LORD CAVERSHAM: Because he leads such an idle life.

MABEL CHILTERN: How can you say such a thing? Why, he rides in the Row at ten o'clock in the morning, goes to the Opera three times a week, changes his clothes at least five times a day, and dines out every night of the season. You don't call that leading an idle life, do you?

LORD CAVERSHAM (*looking at her with a kindly twinkle in his eyes*): You are a very charming young lady!

MABEL CHILTERN: How sweet of you to say that, Lord Caversham! Do come to us more often. You know we are always at home on Wednesdays,[4] and you look so well with your star!

LORD CAVERSHAM: Never go anywhere now. Sick of London Society. Shouldn't mind being introduced to my own tailor; he always votes on the right side. But object strongly to being sent down to dinner with my wife's milliner.[5] Never could stand Lady Caversham's bonnets.

MABEL CHILTERN: Oh, I love London Society! I think it has immensely improved. It is entirely composed now of beautiful idiots and brilliant lunatics. Just what Society should be.

LORD CAVERSHAM: Hum! Which is Goring? Beautiful idiot, or the other thing?

MABEL CHILTERN (*gravely*): I have been obliged for the present to put Lord Goring into a class quite by himself. But he is developing charmingly!

LORD CAVERSHAM: Into what?

MABEL CHILTERN (*with a little curtsey*): I hope to let you know very soon, Lord Caversham!

MASON (*announcing guests*): Lady Markby. Mrs. Cheveley.

Enter LADY MARKBY *and* MRS. CHEVELEY. LADY MARKBY *is a pleasant, kindly, popular woman, with gray hair à la marquise and good lace.* MRS. CHEVELEY, *who accompanies her, is tall and rather slight. Lips very thin and highly-coloured, a line of scarlet on a pallid face. Venetian red hair, aquiline nose, and long throat. Rouge accentuates the natural paleness of her complexion. Gray-green eyes that move restlessly. She is in heliotrope, with diamonds. She looks rather like an orchid, and makes great demands on one's curiosity. In all her movements she is extremely graceful. A work of art, on the whole, but showing the influence of too many schools.*[6]

LADY MARKBY: Good-evening, dear Gertrude! So kind of you to let me bring my friend, Mrs. Cheveley. Two such charming women should know each other!

LADY CHILTERN (*advances towards* MRS. CHEVELEY *with a sweet smile. Then suddenly stops, and bows rather dis-*

tantly): I think Mrs. Cheveley and I have met before. I did not know she had married a second time.

LADY MARKBY (*genially*): Ah, nowadays people marry as often as they can, don't they? It is most fashionable. (*To* DUCHESS OF MARYBOROUGH): Dear Duchess, and how is the Duke? Brain still weak, I suppose? Well, that is only to be expected, is it not? His good father was just the same. There is nothing like race, is there?

MRS. CHEVELEY (*playing with her fan*): But have we really met before, Lady Chiltern? I can't remember where. I have been out of England for so long.

LADY CHILTERN: We were at school together, Mrs. Cheveley.

MRS. CHEVELEY (*superciliously*): Indeed? I have forgotten all about my schooldays. I have a vague impression that they were detestable.

LADY CHILTERN (*coldly*): I am not surprised!

MRS. CHEVELEY (*in her sweetest manner*): Do you know, I am quite looking forward to meeting your clever husband, Lady Chiltern. Since he has been at the Foreign Office, he has been so much talked of in Vienna. They actually succeed in spelling his name right in the newspapers. That in itself is fame, on the continent.

LADY CHILTERN: I hardly think there will be much in common between you and my husband, Mrs. Cheveley! (*Moves away.*)

VICOMTE DE NANJAC: Ah, chère Madame, quelle surprise! I have not seen you since Berlin!

MRS. CHEVELEY: Not since Berlin, Vicomte. Five years ago!

VICOMTE DE NANJAC: And you are younger and more beautiful than ever. How do you manage it?

MRS. CHEVELEY: By making it a rule only to talk to perfectly charming people like yourself.

VICOMTE DE NANJAC: Ah! you flatter me. You butter me, as they say here.

MRS. CHEVELEY: Do they say that here? How dreadful of them!

VICOMTE DE NANJAC: Yes, they have a wonderful language. It should be more widely known.

> SIR ROBERT CHILTERN *enters. A man of forty, but looking somewhat younger. Clean-shaven, with finely-cut features, dark-haired and dark-eyed. A personality of mark. Not popular—few personalities are. But intensely admired by the few, and deeply respected by the many. The note of his manner is that of perfect distinction, with a slight touch of pride. One feels that he is conscious of the success he has made in life. A nervous temperament, with a tired look. The firmly-chiselled mouth and chin contrast strikingly with the romantic expression in the deep-set eyes. The variance is suggestive of an almost complete separation of passion and intellect, as though thought and emotion were each isolated in its own sphere through some violence of will-power. There is nervousness in the nostrils, and in the pale, thin, pointed hands. It would be inaccurate to call him picturesque. Picturesqueness cannot survive the House of Commons. But Vandyck*[7] *would have liked to have painted his head.*

SIR ROBERT CHILTERN: Good-evening, Lady Markby. I hope you have brought Sir John with you?

LADY MARKBY: Oh! I have brought a much more charming person than Sir John. Sir John's temper since he has taken seriously to politics has become quite unbearable. Really, now that the House of Commons is trying to become useful, it does a great deal of harm.

SIR ROBERT CHILTERN: I hope not, Lady Markby. At any rate we do our best to waste the public time, don't we? But who is this charming person you have been kind enough to bring to us?

LADY MARKBY: Her name is Mrs. Cheveley! One of the Dorsetshire Cheveleys, I suppose. But I really don't know. Families are so mixed nowadays. Indeed, as a rule, everybody turns out to be somebody else.

SIR ROBERT CHILTERN: Mrs. Cheveley? I seem to know the name.

LADY MARKBY: She has just arrived from Vienna.[8]

SIR ROBERT CHILTERN: Ah! yes. I think I know whom you mean.

LADY MARKBY: Oh! she goes everywhere there, and has such pleasant scandals about all her friends. I really must go to Vienna next winter. I hope there is a good chef at the Embassy.

SIR ROBERT CHILTERN: If there is not, the Ambassador will certainly have to be recalled. Pray point out Mrs. Cheveley to me. I should like to see her.

LADY MARKBY: Let me introduce you. (*To* MRS. CHEVELEY): My dear, Sir Robert Chiltern is dying to know you!

SIR ROBERT CHILTERN (*bowing*): Every one is dying to know the brilliant Mrs. Cheveley. Our attachés at Vienna write to us about nothing else.

MRS. CHEVELEY: Thank you, Sir Robert. An acquaintance that begins with a compliment is sure to develop into a real friendship. It starts in the right manner. And I find that I know Lady Chiltern already.

SIR ROBERT CHILTERN: Really?

MRS. CHEVELEY: Yes. She has just reminded me that we were at school together. I remember it perfectly now. She always got the good conduct prize. I have a distinct recollection of Lady Chiltern always getting the good conduct prize!

SIR ROBERT CHILTERN (*smiling*): And what prizes did you get, Mrs. Cheveley?

MRS. CHEVELEY: My prizes came a little later on in life. I don't think any of them were for good conduct. I forget!

SIR ROBERT CHILTERN: I am sure they were for something charming!

MRS. CHEVELEY: I don't know that women are always rewarded for being charming. I think they are usually punished for it! Certainly, more women grow old nowadays through the faithfulness of their admirers than through anything else! At least that is the only way I can account for the terribly haggard look of most of your pretty women in London!

SIR ROBERT CHILTERN: What an appalling philosophy that sounds! To attempt to classify you, Mrs. Cheveley, would be an impertinence. But may I ask, at heart, are you an optimist or a pessimist? Those seem to be the only two fashionable religions left to us nowadays.

MRS. CHEVELEY: Oh, I'm neither. Optimism begins in a broad grin, and Pessimism ends with blue spectacles.[9] Besides, they are both of them merely poses.

SIR ROBERT CHILTERN: You prefer to be natural?

MRS. CHEVELEY: Sometimes. But it is such a very difficult pose to keep up.

SIR ROBERT CHILTERN: What would those modern psychological novelists,[10] of whom we hear so much, say to such a theory as that?

MRS. CHEVELEY: Ah! the strength of women comes from the fact that psychology cannot explain us. Men can be analysed, women . . . merely adored.

SIR ROBERT CHILTERN: You think science cannot grapple with the problem of women?

MRS. CHEVELEY: Science can never grapple with the irrational. That is why it has no future before it, in this world.

SIR ROBERT CHILTERN: And women represent the irrational.

MRS. CHEVELEY: Well-dressed women do.

SIR ROBERT CHILTERN (*with a polite bow*): I fear I could hardly agree with you there. But do sit down. And now tell me, what makes you leave your brilliant Vienna for our gloomy London—or perhaps the question is indiscreet?

MRS. CHEVELEY: Questions are never indiscreet. Answers sometimes are.

SIR ROBERT CHILTERN: Well, at any rate, may I know if it is politics or pleasure?

MRS. CHEVELEY: Politics are my only pleasure. You see, nowadays it is not fashionable to flirt till one is forty, or to be romantic till one is forty-five, so we poor women who are under thirty, or say we are, have nothing open to us but politics or philanthropy. And philanthropy seems to me to have become simply the refuge of people who wish to annoy their fellow-creatures. I prefer politics. I think they are more . . . becoming!

SIR ROBERT CHILTERN: A political life is a noble career!

MRS. CHEVELEY: Sometimes. And sometimes it is a clever game, Sir Robert. And sometimes it is a great nuisance.

SIR ROBERT CHILTERN: Which do you find it?

MRS. CHEVELEY: A combination of all three. (Drops her fan.)

SIR ROBERT CHILTERN (picks up fan): Allow me!

MRS. CHEVELEY: Thanks.

SIR ROBERT CHILTERN: But you have not told me yet what makes you honour London so suddenly. Our season is almost over.

MRS. CHEVELEY: Oh! I don't care about the London season! It is too matrimonial. People are either hunting for husbands, or hiding from them. I wanted to meet you. It is quite true. You know what a woman's curiosity is. Almost as great as a man's! I wanted immensely to meet you, and . . . to ask you to do something for me.

SIR ROBERT CHILTERN: I hope it is not a little thing, Mrs. Cheveley. I find that little things are so very difficult to do.

MRS. CHEVELEY *(after a moment's reflection)*: No, I don't think it is quite a little thing.

SIR ROBERT CHILTERN: I am so glad. Do tell me what it is.

MRS. CHEVELEY: Later on. *(Rises.)* And now may I walk through your beautiful house? I hear your pictures are charming. Poor Baron Arnheim—you remember the Baron?—used to tell me you had some wonderful Corots.[11]

SIR ROBERT CHILTERN *(with an almost imperceptible start)*: Did you know Baron Arnheim well?

MRS. CHEVELEY *(smiling)*: Intimately. Did you?

SIR ROBERT CHILTERN: At one time.

MRS. CHEVELEY: Wonderful man, wasn't he?

SIR ROBERT CHILTERN *(after a pause)*: He was very remarkable, in many ways.

MRS. CHEVELEY: I often think it such a pity he never wrote his memoirs. They would have been most interesting.

SIR ROBERT CHILTERN: Yes: he knew men and cities well, like the old Greek.[12]

MRS. CHEVELEY: Without the dreadful disadvantage of having a Penelope waiting at home for him.

MASON: Lord Goring.

Enter LORD GORING. *Thirty-four, but always says he is younger. A well-bred, expressionless face. He is clever, but would not like to be thought so. A flawless dandy[13] he would be annoyed if he were considered romantic. He plays with life, and is on perfectly good terms with the world. He is fond of being misunderstood. It gives him a post of vantage.*

SIR ROBERT CHILTERN: Good-evening, my dear Arthur! Mrs. Cheveley, allow me to introduce to you Lord Goring, the idlest man in London.

MRS. CHEVELEY: I have met Lord Goring before.

LORD GORING (*bowing*): I did not think you would remember me, Mrs. Cheveley.

MRS. CHEVELEY: My memory is under admirable control. And are you still a bachelor?

LORD GORING: I . . . believe so.

MRS. CHEVELEY: How very romantic.

LORD GORING: Oh! I am not at all romantic. I am not old enough. I leave romance to my seniors.

SIR ROBERT CHILTERN: Lord Goring is the result of Boodle's Club, Mrs. Cheveley.

MRS. CHEVELEY: He reflects every credit on the institution.

LORD GORING: May I ask are you staying in London long?

MRS. CHEVELEY: That depends partly on the weather, partly on the cooking, and partly on Sir Robert.

SIR ROBERT CHILTERN: You are not going to plunge us into a European war, I hope?

MRS. CHEVELEY: There is no danger, at present!

She nods to LORD GORING, *with a look of amusement in her eyes, and goes out with* SIR ROBERT CHILTERN. LORD GORING *saunters over to* MABEL CHILTERN.

MABEL CHILTERN: You are very late!

LORD GORING: Have you missed me?

MABEL CHILTERN: Awfully!

LORD GORING: Then I am sorry I did not stay away longer. I like being missed.

MABEL CHILTERN: How very selfish of you!

LORD GORING: I am very selfish.

MABEL CHILTERN: You are always telling me of your bad qualities, Lord Goring.

LORD GORING: I have only told you half of them as yet, Miss Mabel!

MABEL CHILTERN: Are the others very bad?

LORD GORING: Quite dreadful! When I think of them at night I go to sleep at once.

MABEL CHILTERN: Well, I delight in your bad qualities. I wouldn't have you part with one of them.

LORD GORING: How very nice of you! But then you are always nice. By the way, I want to ask you a question, Miss Mabel. Who brought Mrs. Cheveley here? That woman in heliotrope, who has just gone out of the room with your brother?

MABEL CHILTERN: Oh, I think Lady Markby brought her. Why do you ask?

LORD GORING: I haven't seen her for years, that is all.

MABEL CHILTERN: What an absurd reason!

LORD GORING: All reasons are absurd.

MABEL CHILTERN: What sort of a woman is she?

LORD GORING: Oh! a genius in the daytime and a beauty at night!

MABEL CHILTERN: I dislike her already.

LORD GORING: That shows your admirable good taste.

VICOMTE DE NANJAC (*approaching*): Ah, the English young lady is the dragon of good taste, is she not? Quite the dragon of good taste.

LORD GORING: So the newspapers are always telling us.

VICOMTE DE NANJAC: I read all your English newspapers. I find them so amusing.

LORD GORING: Then, my dear Nanjac, you must certainly read between the lines.

VICOMTE DE NANJAC: I should like to, but my professor objects. (*To* MABEL CHILTERN): May I have the pleasure of escorting you to the music-room, Mademoiselle?

MABEL CHILTERN (*looking very disappointed*): Delighted, Vicomte, quite delighted! (*Turning to* LORD GORING): Aren't you coming to the music-room?

LORD GORING: Not if there is any music going on, Miss Mabel.

MABEL CHILTERN (*severely*): The music is in German. You would not understand it.

Goes out with the VICOMTE DE NANJAC. LORD CAVERSHAM *comes up to his son.*

LORD CAVERSHAM: Well, sir! what are you doing here? Wasting your life as usual! You should be in bed, sir. You keep too late hours! I heard of you the other night at Lady Rufford's dancing till four o'clock in the morning!

LORD GORING: Only a quarter to four, father.

LORD CAVERSHAM: Can't make out how you stand London Society. The thing has gone to the dogs, a lot of damned nobodies talking about nothing.

LORD GORING: I love talking about nothing, father. It is the only thing I know anything about.

LORD CAVERSHAM: You seem to me to be living entirely for pleasure.

LORD GORING: What else is there to live for, father? Nothing ages like happiness.

LORD CAVERSHAM: You are heartless, sir, very heartless.

LORD GORING: I hope not, father. Good-evening, Lady Basildon!

LADY BASILDON (*arching two pretty eyebrows*): Are you here? I had no idea you ever came to political parties.

LORD GORING: I adore political parties. They are the only place left to us where people don't talk politics.

LADY BASILDON: I delight in talking politics. I talk them all day long. But I can't bear listening to them. I don't know how the unfortunate men in the House stand these long debates.

LORD GORING: By never listening.

LADY BASILDON: Really?

LORD GORING (*in his most serious manner*): Of course. You see, it is a very dangerous thing to listen. If one listens one may be convinced; and a man who allows himself to be convinced by an argument is a thoroughly unreasonable person.

LADY BASILDON: Ah! that accounts for so much in men that I have never understood, and so much in women that their husbands never appreciate in them!

MRS. MARCHMONT (*with a sigh*): Our husbands never appreciate anything in us. We have to go to others for that!

LADY BASILDON (*emphatically*): Yes, always to others, have we not?

LORD GORING (*smiling*): And those are the views of the two ladies who are known to have the most admirable husbands in London.

MRS. MARCHMONT: That is exactly what we can't stand. My Reginald is quite hopelessly faultless. He is really unendurably so, at times! There is not the smallest element of excitement in knowing him.

LORD GORING: How terrible! Really, the thing should be more widely known!

LADY BASILDON: Basildon is quite as bad; he is as domestic as if he was a bachelor.

MRS. MARCHMONT (*pressing* LADY BASILDON's *hand*): My poor Olivia! We have married perfect husbands, and we are well punished for it.

LORD GORING: I should have thought it was the husbands who were punished.

MRS. MARCHMONT (*drawing herself up*): Oh, dear no! They are as happy as possible! And as for trusting us, it is tragic how much they trust us.

LADY BASILDON: Perfectly tragic!

LORD GORING: Or comic, Lady Basildon?

LADY BASILDON: Certainly not comic, Lord Goring. How unkind of you to suggest such a thing!

MRS. MARCHMONT: I am afraid Lord Goring is in the camp of the enemy, as usual. I saw him talking to that Mrs. Cheveley when he came in.

LORD GORING: Handsome woman, Mrs. Cheveley!

LADY BASILDON (*stiffly*): Please don't praise other women in our presence. You might wait for us to do that!

LORD GORING: I did wait.

MRS. MARCHMONT: Well, we are not going to praise her. I hear she went to the Opera on Monday night, and told Tommy Rufford at supper that, as far as she could see, London Society was entirely made up of dowdies and dandies.

LORD GORING: She is quite right, too. The men are all dowdies and the women are all dandies, aren't they?

MRS. MARCHMONT (*after a pause*): Oh! do you really think that is what Mrs. Cheveley meant?

LORD GORING: Of course. And a very sensible remark for Mrs. Cheveley to make, too.

Enter MABEL CHILTERN. *She joins the group.*

MABEL CHILTERN: Why are you talking about Mrs. Cheveley? Everybody is talking about Mrs. Cheveley! Lord Goring says—what did you say, Lord Goring, about Mrs. Cheveley? Oh! I remember, that she was a genius in the daytime and a beauty at night.

LADY BASILDON: What a horrid combination! So very unnatural!

MRS. MARCHMONT (*in her most dreamy manner*): I like looking at geniuses, and listening to beautiful people!

LORD GORING: Ah! that is morbid of you, Mrs. Marchmont!

MRS. MARCHMONT (*brightening to a look of real pleasure*): I am so glad to hear you say that. Marchmont and I have been married for seven years, and he has never once told me that I was morbid. Men are so painfully unobservant.

LADY BASILDON (*turning to her*): I have always said, dear Margaret, that you were the most morbid person in London.

MRS. MARCHMONT: Ah! but you are always sympathetic, Olivia!

MABEL CHILTERN: Is it morbid to have a desire for food? I have a great desire for food. Lord Goring, will you give me some supper?

LORD GORING: With pleasure, Miss Mabel. *(Moves away with her.)*

MABEL CHILTERN: How horrid you have been! You have never talked to me the whole evening!

LORD GORING: How could I? You went away with the child-diplomatist.

MABEL CHILTERN: You might have followed us. Pursuit would have been only polite. I don't think I like you at all this evening!

LORD GORING: I like you immensely.

MABEL CHILTERN: Well, I wish you'd show it in a more marked way!

They go downstairs.

MRS. MARCHMONT: Olivia, I have a curious feeling of absolute faintness. I think I should like some supper very much. I know I should like some supper.

LADY BASILDON: I am positively dying for supper, Margaret!

MRS. MARCHMONT: Men are so horribly selfish, they never think of these things.

LADY BASILDON: Men are grossly material, grossly material!

The VICOMTE DE NANJAC *enters from the music-room with some other guests. After having carefully examined all the people present, he approaches* LADY BASILDON.

VICOMTE DE NANJAC: May I have the honour of taking you down to supper, Countess?

LADY BASILDON *(coldly)*: I never take supper, thank you,

Vicomte. (*The* VICOMTE *is about to retire.* LADY BASIL-
DON, *seeing this, rises at once and takes his arm.*) But I
will come down with you with pleasure.

VICOMTE DE NANJAC: I am so fond of eating! I am very English in all my tastes.

LADY BASILDON: You look quite English, Vicomte, quite
English.

They pass out. MR. MONTFORD, *a perfectly groomed
young dandy, approaches* MRS. MARCHMONT.

MR. MONTFORD: Like some supper, Mrs. Marchmont?

MRS. MARCHMONT (*languidly*): Thank you, Mr. Montford,
I never touch supper. (*Rises hastily and takes his arm.*)
But I will sit beside you, and watch you.

MR. MONTFORD: I don't know that I like being watched
when I am eating!

MRS. MARCHMONT: Then I will watch some one else.

MR. MONTFORD: I don't know that I should like that either.

MRS. MARCHMONT (*severely*): Pray, Mr. Montford, do not
make these painful scenes of jealousy in public!

They go downstairs with the other guests, passing SIR
ROBERT CHILTERN *and* MRS. CHEVELEY, *who now
enter.*

SIR ROBERT CHILTERN: And are you going to any of our
country houses before you leave England, Mrs. Cheveley?

MRS. CHEVELEY: Oh, no! I can't stand your English house-
parties. In England people actually try to be brilliant at
breakfast. That is dreadful of them! Only dull people are
brilliant at breakfast. And then the family skeleton is always reading family prayers. My stay in England really
depends on you, Sir Robert. (*Sits down on the sofa.*)

SIR ROBERT CHILTERN (*taking a seat beside her*): Seriously?

MRS. CHEVELEY: Quite seriously. I want to talk to you about a great political and financial scheme, about this Argentine Canal Company, in fact.

SIR ROBERT CHILTERN: What a tedious, practical subject for you to talk about, Mrs. Cheveley!

MRS. CHEVELEY: Oh, I like tedious, practical subjects. What I don't like are tedious, practical people. There is a wide difference. Besides, you are interested, I know, in International Canal schemes. You were Lord Radley's secretary, weren't you, when the Government bought the Suez Canal shares?

SIR ROBERT CHILTERN: Yes. But the Suez Canal was a very great and splendid undertaking. It gave us our direct route to India. It had imperial value. It was necessary that we should have control. This Argentine scheme is a commonplace Stock Exchange swindle.[14]

MRS. CHEVELEY: A speculation, Sir Robert! A brilliant, daring speculation.

SIR ROBERT CHILTERN: Believe me, Mrs. Cheveley, it is a swindle. Let us call things by their proper names. It makes matters simpler. We have all the information about it at the Foreign Office. In fact, I sent out a special Commission to inquire into the matter privately, and they report that the works are hardly begun, and as for the money already subscribed, no one seems to know what has become of it. The whole thing is a second Panama,[15] and with not a quarter of the chance of success that miserable affair ever had. I hope you have not invested in it. I am sure you are far too clever to have done that.

MRS. CHEVELEY: I have invested very largely in it.

SIR ROBERT CHILTERN: Who could have advised you to do such a foolish thing?

MRS. CHEVELEY: Your old friend—and mine.

SIR ROBERT CHILTERN: Who?

MRS. CHEVELEY: Baron Arnheim.

SIR ROBERT CHILTERN (*frowning*): Ah! yes. I remember hearing, at the time of his death, that he had been mixed up in the whole affair.

MRS. CHEVELEY: It was his last romance. His last but one, to do him justice.

SIR ROBERT CHILTERN (*rising*): But you have not seen my Corots yet. They are in the music-room. Corots seem to go with music, don't they? May I show them to you?

MRS. CHEVELEY (*shaking her head*): I am not in a mood to-night for silver twilights, or rose-pink dawns. I want to talk business. (*Motions to him with her fan to sit down again beside her.*)

SIR ROBERT CHILTERN: I fear I have no advice to give you, Mrs. Cheveley, except to interest yourself in something less dangerous. The success of the Canal depends, of course, on the attitude of England, and I am going to lay the report of the Commissioners before the House[16] to-morrow night.

MRS. CHEVELEY: That you must not do. In your own interests, Sir Robert, to say nothing of mine, you must not do that.

SIR ROBERT CHILTERN (*looking at her in wonder*): In my own interests? My dear Mrs. Cheveley, what do you mean? (*Sits down beside her.*)

MRS. CHEVELEY: Sir Robert, I will be quite frank with you. I want you to withdraw the report that you had intended to lay before the House, on the ground that you have reasons to believe that the Commissioners have been prejudiced or misinformed, or something. Then I want you to say a few words to the effect that the Government is going to reconsider the question, and that you have reason to believe that the Canal, if completed, will be of great international value. You know the sort of things ministers say in cases of this kind. A few ordinary platitudes will do. In modern life nothing produces such an effect as a good platitude. It makes the whole world kin. Will you do that for me?

SIR ROBERT CHILTERN: Mrs. Cheveley, you cannot be serious in making me such a proposition!

MRS. CHEVELEY: I am quite serious.

SIR ROBERT CHILTERN (*coldly*): Pray allow me to believe that you are not.

MRS. CHEVELEY (*speaking with great deliberation and emphasis*): Ah! but I am. And if you do what I ask you, I . . . will pay you very handsomely!

SIR ROBERT CHILTERN: Pay me!

MRS. CHEVELEY: Yes.

SIR ROBERT CHILTERN: I am afraid I don't quite understand what you mean.

MRS. CHEVELEY (*leaning back on the sofa and looking at him*): How very disappointing! And I have come all the way from Vienna in order that you should thoroughly understand me.

SIR ROBERT CHILTERN: I fear I don't.

MRS. CHEVELEY (*in her most nonchalant manner*): My dear Sir Robert, you are a man of the world, and you have your price, I suppose. Everybody has nowadays. The drawback is that most people are so dreadfully expensive. I know I am. I hope you will be more reasonable in your terms.

SIR ROBERT CHILTERN (*rises indignantly*): If you will allow me, I will call your carriage for you. You have lived so long abroad, Mrs. Cheveley, that you seem to be unable to realise that you are talking to an English gentleman.

MRS. CHEVELEY (*detains him by touching his arm with her fan, and keeping it there while she is talking*): I realise that I am talking to a man who laid the foundation of his fortune by selling to a Stock Exchange speculator a Cabinet secret.

SIR ROBERT CHILTERN *(biting his lip)*: What do you mean?

MRS. CHEVELEY *(rising and facing him)*: I mean that I know the real origin of your wealth and your career, and I have got your letter, too.

SIR ROBERT CHILTERN: What letter?

MRS. CHEVELEY *(contemptuously)*: The letter you wrote to Baron Arnheim, when you were Lord Radley's secretary, telling the Baron to buy Suez Canal shares—a letter written three days before the Government announced its own purchase.

SIR ROBERT CHILTERN *(hoarsely)*: It is not true.

MRS. CHEVELEY: You thought that letter had been destroyed. How foolish of you! It is in my possession.

SIR ROBERT CHILTERN: The affair to which you allude was no more than a speculation. The House of Commons had not yet passed the bill; it might have been rejected.

MRS. CHEVELEY: It was a swindle, Sir Robert. Let us call things by their proper names. It makes everything simpler. And now I am going to sell you that letter, and the price I ask for it is your public support of the Argentine scheme. You made your own fortune out of one canal. You must help me and my friends to make our fortunes out of another!

SIR ROBERT CHILTERN: It is infamous, what you propose— infamous!

MRS. CHEVELEY: Oh, no! This is the game of life as we all have to play it, Sir Robert, sooner or later!

SIR ROBERT CHILTERN: I cannot do what you ask me.

MRS. CHEVELEY: You mean you cannot help doing it. You know you are standing on the edge of a precipice. And it is not for you to make terms. It is for you to accept them. Supposing you refuse——

SIR ROBERT CHILTERN: What then?

MRS. CHEVELEY: My dear Sir Robert, what then? You are ruined, that is all! Remember to what a point your Puritanism in England has brought you. In old days nobody pretended to be a bit better than his neighbours. In fact, to be a bit better than one's neighbour was considered excessively vulgar and middle-class. Nowadays, with our modern mania for morality, every one has to pose as a paragon of purity, incorruptibility, and all the other seven deadly virtues—and what is the result? You all go over like ninepins—one after the other. Not a year passes in England without somebody disappearing. Scandals used to lend charm, or at least interest, to a man—now they crush him. And yours is a very nasty scandal. You couldn't survive it. If it were known that as a young man, secretary to a great and important minister, you sold a Cabinet secret for a large sum of money, and that was the origin of your wealth and career, you would be hounded out of public life, you would disappear completely. And after all, Sir Robert, why should you sacrifice your entire future rather than deal diplomatically with your enemy? For the moment I am your enemy. I admit it! And I am much stronger than you are. The big battalions are on my side. You have a splendid position, but it is your splendid position that makes you so vulnerable. You can't defend it! And I am in attack. Of course I have not talked morality to you. You must admit in fairness that I have spared you that. Years ago you did a clever, unscrupulous thing; it turned out a great success. You owe to it your fortune and position. And now you have got to pay for it. Sooner or later we have all to pay for what we do. You have to pay now. Before I leave you to-night, you have got to promise me to suppress your report, and to speak in the House in favour of this scheme.

SIR ROBERT CHILTERN: What you ask is impossible.

MRS. CHEVELEY: You must make it possible. You are going to make it possible. Sir Robert, you know what your English newspapers are like. Suppose that when I leave this

house I drive down to some newspaper office, and give
them this scandal and the proofs of it. Think of their
loathsome joy, of the delight they would have in dragging
you down, of the mud and mire they would plunge you
in. Think of the hypocrite with his greasy smile penning
his leading article, and arranging the foulness of the public placard.

SIR ROBERT CHILTERN: Stop! You want me to withdraw the
report and to make a short speech stating that I believe
there are possibilities in the scheme?

MRS. CHEVELEY *(sitting down on the sofa)*: Those are my
terms.

SIR ROBERT CHILTERN *(in a low voice)*: I will give you any
sum of money you want.

MRS. CHEVELEY: Even you are not rich enough, Sir Robert,
to buy back your past. No man is.

SIR ROBERT CHILTERN: I will not do what you ask me. I will
not.

MRS. CHEVELEY: You have to. If you don't. . . . *(Rises from
the sofa.)*

SIR ROBERT CHILTERN *(bewildered and unnerved)*: Wait a
moment! What did you propose? You said that you
would give me back my letter, didn't you?

MRS. CHEVELEY: Yes. That is agreed. I will be in the Ladies'
Gallery[17] to-morrow night at half-past eleven. If by that
time—and you will have had heaps of opportunity—you
have made an announcement to the House in the terms
I wish, I shall hand you back your letter with the prettiest
thanks, and the best, or at any rate the most suitable,
compliment I can think of. I intend to play quite fairly
with you. One should always play fairly . . . when one has
the winning cards. The Baron taught me that . . .
amongst other things.

SIR ROBERT CHILTERN: You must let me have time to consider your proposal.

MRS. CHEVELEY: No; you must settle now!

SIR ROBERT CHILTERN: Give me a week—three days!

MRS. CHEVELEY: Impossible! I have got to telegraph to Vienna to-night.

SIR ROBERT CHILTERN: My God! what brought you into my life?

MRS. CHEVELEY: Circumstances. (*Moves towards the door.*)

SIR ROBERT CHILTERN: Don't go. I consent. The report shall be withdrawn. I will arrange for a question to be put to me on the subject.

MRS. CHEVELEY: Thank you. I knew we should come to an amicable agreement. I understood your nature from the first. I analysed you, though you did not adore me. And now you can get my carriage for me, Sir Robert. I see the people coming up from supper, and Englishmen always get romantic after a meal, and that bores me dreadfully. (*Exit* SIR ROBERT CHILTERN.)

Enter Guests, LADY CHILTERN, LADY MARKBY, LORD CAVERSHAM, LADY BASILDON, MRS. MARCHMONT, VICOMTE DE NANJAC, MR. MONTFORD.

LADY MARKBY: Well, dear Mrs. Cheveley, I hope you have enjoyed yourself. Sir Robert is very entertaining, is he not?

MRS. CHEVELEY: Most entertaining! I have enjoyed my talk with him immensely.

LADY MARKBY: He has had a very interesting and brilliant career. And he has married a most admirable wife. Lady Chiltern is a woman of the very highest principles, I am glad to say. I am a little too old now, myself, to trouble about setting a good example, but I always admire people who do. And Lady Chiltern has a very ennobling effect on life, though her dinner-parties are rather dull sometimes. But one can't have everything, can one? And now I must go, dear. Shall I call for you to-morrow?

MRS. CHEVELEY: Thanks.

LADY MARKBY: We might drive in the Park at five. Everything looks so fresh in the Park now!

MRS. CHEVELEY: Except the people!

LADY MARKBY: Perhaps the people are a little jaded. I have often observed that the Season as it goes on produces a kind of softening of the brain. However, I think anything is better than high intellectual pressure. That is the most unbecoming thing there is. It makes the noses of the young girls so particularly large. And there is nothing so difficult to marry as a large nose; men don't like them. Good-night, dear! (*To* LADY CHILTERN): Good-night, Gertrude! (*Goes out on* LORD CAVERSHAM's *arm.*)

MRS. CHEVELEY: What a charming house you have, Lady Chiltern! I have spent a delightful evening. It has been so interesting getting to know your husband.

LADY CHILTERN: Why did you wish to meet my husband, Mrs. Cheveley?

MRS. CHEVELEY: Oh, I will tell you. I wanted to interest him in this Argentine Canal scheme, of which I dare say you have heard. And I found him most susceptible—susceptible to reason, I mean. A rare thing in a man. I converted him in ten minutes. He is going to make a speech in the House to-morrow night in favour of the idea. We must go to the Ladies' Gallery and hear him! It will be a great occasion!

LADY CHILTERN: There must be some mistake. That scheme could never have my husband's support.

MRS. CHEVELEY: Oh, I assure you it's all settled. I don't regret my tedious journey from Vienna now. It has been a great success. But, of course, for the next twenty-four hours the whole thing is a dead secret.

LADY CHILTERN (*gently*): A secret? Between whom?

MRS. CHEVELEY (*with a flash of amusement in her eyes*): Between your husband and myself.

SIR ROBERT CHILTERN (*entering*): Your carriage is here, Mrs. Cheveley!

MRS. CHEVELEY: Thanks! Good-evening Lady Chiltern! Good-night, Lord Goring! I am at Claridge's. Don't you think you might leave a card?[18]

LORD GORING: If you wish it, Mrs. Cheveley!

MRS. CHEVELEY: Oh, don't be so solemn about it, or I shall be obliged to leave a card on you. In England I suppose that would hardly be considered *en règle*.[19] Abroad, we are more civilised. Will you see me down, Sir Robert? Now that we have both the same interests at heart we shall be great friends, I hope!

Sails out on SIR ROBERT CHILTERN's *arm.* LADY CHILTERN *goes to the top of the staircase and looks down at them as they descend. Her expression is troubled. After a little time she is joined by some of the guests, and passes with them into another reception-room.*

MABEL CHILTERN: What a horrid woman!

LORD GORING: You should go to bed, Miss Mabel.

MABEL CHILTERN: Lord Goring!

LORD GORING: My father told me to go to bed an hour ago. I don't see why I shouldn't give you the same advice. I always pass on good advice. It is the only thing to do with it. It is never of any use to oneself.

MABEL CHILTERN: Lord Goring, you are always ordering me out of the room. I think it most courageous of you. Especially as I am not going to bed for hours. (*Goes over to the sofa.*) You can come and sit down if you like, and talk about anything in the world, except the Royal Academy, Mrs. Cheveley, or novels in Scotch dialect.[20] They are not improving subjects. (*Catches sight of something that is lying on the sofa half-hidden by the cushion.)* What is this? Some one has dropped a diamond brooch! Quite beautiful, isn't it? *(Shows it to him.)* I wish it was mine, but Gertrude won't let me wear anything but pearls, and I am thoroughly sick of pearls. They make one look so plain, so good and so intellectual. I wonder whom the brooch belongs to.

LORD GORING: I wonder who dropped it.

MABEL CHILTERN: It is a beautiful brooch.

LORD GORING: It is a handsome bracelet.

MABEL CHILTERN: It isn't a bracelet. It's a brooch.

LORD GORING: It can be used as a bracelet. *(Takes it from her, and, pulling out a green letter-case, puts the ornament carefully in it, and replaces the whole thing in his breast-pocket with the most perfect sang froid.)*

MABEL CHILTERN: What are you doing?

LORD GORING: Miss Mabel, I am going to make a rather strange request to you.

MABEL CHILTERN *(eagerly)*: Oh, pray do! I have been waiting for it all the evening.

LORD GORING *(is a little taken aback, but recovers himself)*: Don't mention to anybody that I have taken charge of this brooch. Should any one write and claim it, let me know at once.

MABEL CHILTERN: That is a strange request.

LORD GORING: Well, you see I gave this brooch to somebody once, years ago.

MABEL CHILTERN: You did?

LORD GORING: Yes.

LADY CHILTERN *enters alone. The other guests have gone.*

MABEL CHILTERN: Then I shall certainly bid you good-night. Good-night, Gertrude! *(Exit.)*

LADY CHILTERN: Good-night, dear! (*To* LORD GORING): You saw whom Lady Markby brought here to-night?

LORD GORING: Yes. It was an unpleasant surprise. What did she come here for?

LADY CHILTERN: Apparently to try and lure Robert to uphold some fraudulent scheme in which she is interested. The Argentine Canal, in fact.

LORD GORING: She has mistaken her man, hasn't she?

LADY CHILTERN: She is incapable of understanding an upright nature like my husband's!

LORD GORING: Yes. I should fancy she came to grief if she tried to get Robert into her toils. It is extraordinary what astounding mistakes clever women make.

LADY CHILTERN: I don't call women of that kind clever. I call them stupid!

LORD GORING: Same thing often. Good-night, Lady Chiltern!

LADY CHILTERN: Good-night!

Enter SIR ROBERT CHILTERN.

SIR ROBERT CHILTERN: My dear Arthur, you are not going? Do stop a little!

LORD GORING: Afraid I can't, thanks. I have promised to look in at the Hartlocks'. I believe they have got a mauve Hungarian band that plays mauve Hungarian music. See you soon. Good-bye! (*Exit.*)

SIR ROBERT CHILTERN: How beautiful you look to-night, Gertrude!

LADY CHILTERN: Robert, it is not true, is it? You are not going to lend your support to this Argentine speculation? You couldn't!

SIR ROBERT CHILTERN (*starting*): Who told you I intended to do so?

LADY CHILTERN: That woman who has just gone out, Mrs. Cheveley, as she calls herself now. She seemed to taunt me with it. Robert, I know this woman. You don't. We were at school together. She was untruthful, dishonest, an evil influence on every one whose trust or friendship she could win. I hated, I despised her. She stole things, she was a thief. She was sent away for being a thief. Why do you let her influence you?

SIR ROBERT CHILTERN: Gertrude, what you tell me may be true, but it happened many years ago. It is best forgotten! Mrs. Cheveley may have changed since then. No one should be entirely judged by their past.

LADY CHILTERN (*sadly*): One's past is what one is. It is the only way by which people should be judged.

SIR ROBERT CHILTERN: That is hard saying, Gertrude!

LADY CHILTERN: It is a true saying, Robert. And what did she mean by boasting that she had got you to lend your support, your name, to a thing I have heard you describe as the most dishonest and fraudulent scheme there has ever been in political life?

SIR ROBERT CHILTERN (*biting his lip*): I was mistaken in the view I took. We all may make mistakes.

LADY CHILTERN: But you told me yesterday that you had received the report from the Commission, and that it entirely condemned the whole thing.

SIR ROBERT CHILTERN (*walking up and down*): I have reasons now to believe that the Commission was prejudiced, or, at any rate, misinformed. Besides, Gertrude, public and private life are different things. They have different laws, and move on different lines.

LADY CHILTERN: They should both represent man at his highest. I see no difference between them.

SIR ROBERT CHILTERN (*stopping*): In the present case, on a matter of practical politics, I have changed my mind. That is all.

LADY CHILTERN: All!

SIR ROBERT CHILTERN (*sternly*): Yes!

LADY CHILTERN: Robert! Oh! it is horrible that I should have to ask you such a question—Robert, are you telling me the whole truth?

SIR ROBERT CHILTERN: Why do you ask me such a question?

LADY CHILTERN *(after a pause)*: Why do you not answer it?

SIR ROBERT CHILTERN *(sitting down)*: Gertrude, truth is a very complex thing, and politics is a very complex business. There are wheels within wheels. One may be under certain obligations to people that one must pay. Sooner or later in political life one has to compromise. Every one does.

LADY CHILTERN: Compromise? Robert, why do you talk so differently to-night from the way I have always heard you talk? Why are you changed?

SIR ROBERT CHILTERN: I am not changed. But circumstances alter things.

LADY CHILTERN: Circumstances should never alter principles.

SIR ROBERT CHILTERN: But if I told you—

LADY CHILTERN: What?

SIR ROBERT CHILTERN: That it was necessary, vitally necessary?

LADY CHILTERN: It can never be necessary to do what is not honourable. Or if it be necessary, then what is it that I have loved! But it is not, Robert; tell me it is not. Why should it be? What gain would you get? Money? We have no need of that! And money that comes from a tainted source is a degradation. Power? But power is nothing in itself. It is power to do good that is fine—that, and that only. What is it, then? Robert, tell me why you are going to do this dishonourable thing!

SIR ROBERT CHILTERN: Gertrude, you have no right to use that word. I told you it was a question of rational compromise. It is no more than that.

LADY CHILTERN: Robert, that is all very well for other men, for men who treat life simply as a sordid speculation; but not for you, Robert, not for you. You are different. All your life you have stood apart from others. You have never let the world soil you. To the world, as to myself, you have been an ideal always. Oh! be that ideal still. That great inheritance throw not away—that tower of ivory do not destroy. Robert, men can love what is beneath them—things unworthy, stained, dishonoured. We women worship when we love; and when we lose our worship, we lose everything. Oh! don't kill my love for you, don't kill that!

SIR ROBERT CHILTERN: Gertrude!

LADY CHILTERN: I know that there are men with horrible secrets in their lives—men who have done some shameful thing, and who in some critical moment have to pay for it, by doing some other act of shame—oh! don't tell me you are such as they are! Robert, is there in your life any secret dishonour or disgrace? Tell me, tell me at once, that—

SIR ROBERT CHILTERN: That what?

LADY CHILTERN (*speaking very slowly*): That our lives may drift apart.

SIR ROBERT CHILTERN: Drift apart?

LADY CHILTERN: That they may entirely separate. It would be better for us both.

SIR ROBERT CHILTERN: Gertrude, there is nothing in my past life that you might not know.

LADY CHILTERN: I was sure of it, Robert, I was sure of it. But why did you say those dreadful things, things so unlike your real self? Don't let us ever talk about the subject again. You will write, won't you, to Mrs. Cheveley, and tell her that you cannot support this scandalous scheme of hers? If you have given her any promise you must take it back, that is all!

SIR ROBERT CHILTERN: Must I write and tell her that?

LADY CHILTERN: Surely, Robert! What else is there to do?

SIR ROBERT CHILTERN: I might see her personally. It would be better.

LADY CHILTERN: You must never see her again, Robert. She is not a woman you should ever speak to. She is not worthy to talk to a man like you. No; you must write to her at once, now, this moment, and let your letter show her that your decision is quite irrevocable!

SIR ROBERT CHILTERN: Write this moment!

LADY CHILTERN: Yes.

SIR ROBERT CHILTERN: But it is so late. It is close on twelve.

LADY CHILTERN: That makes no matter. She must know at once that she has been mistaken in you—and that you are not a man to do anything base or underhand or dishonourable. Write here, Robert. Write that you decline to support this scheme of hers, as you hold it to be a dishonest scheme. Yes—write the word dishonest. She knows what that word means. (SIR ROBERT CHILTERN *sits down and writes a letter. His wife takes it up and reads it.*) Yes; that will do. (*Rings bell.*) And now the envelope. (*He writes the envelope slowly. Enter* MASON.) Have this letter sent at once to Claridge's Hotel. There is no answer. (*Exit* MASON. LADY CHILTERN *kneels down beside her husband and puts her arms around him.*) Robert, love gives one an instinct to things. I feel to-night that I have saved you from something that might have been a danger to you, from something that might have made men honour you less than they do. I don't think you realise sufficiently, Robert, that you have brought into the political life of our time a nobler atmosphere, a finer attitude towards life, a freer air of purer aims and higher ideals—I know it, and for that I love you, Robert.

SIR ROBERT CHILTERN: Oh, love me always, Gertrude, love me always!

LADY CHILTERN: I will love you always, because you will always be worthy of love. We needs must love the highest when we see it! (*Kisses him and rises and goes out.*)

SIR ROBERT CHILTERN *walks up and down for a moment; then sits down and buries his face in his hands. The Servant enters and begins putting out the lights.* SIR ROBERT CHILTERN *looks up.*

SIR ROBERT CHILTERN: Put out the lights, Mason, put out the lights!

The Servant puts out the lights. The room becomes almost dark. The only light there is comes from the great chandelier that hangs over the staircase and illumines the tapestry of the Triumph of Love.

Act Drop

Act Two

SCENE: *Morning-room at Sir Robert Chiltern's house.*

LORD GORING, *dressed in the height of fashion, is loung-ing in an arm-chair.* SIR ROBERT CHILTERN *is standing in front of the fireplace. He is evidently in a state of great mental excitement and distress. As the scene progresses he paces nervously up and down the room.*

LORD GORING: My dear Robert, it's a very awkward busi-ness, very awkward indeed. You should have told your wife the whole thing. Secrets from other people's wives are a necessary luxury in modern life. So, at least, I am al-ways told at the club by people who are bald enough to know better. But no man should have a secret from his own wife. She invariably finds it out. Women have a won-derful instinct about things. They can discover every-thing except the obvious.

SIR ROBERT CHILTERN: Arthur, I couldn't tell my wife. When could I have told her? Not last night. It would have made a life-long separation between us, and I would have lost the love of the one woman in the world I worship, of the only woman who had ever stirred love within me. Last night it would have been quite impossible. She would have turned from me in horror . . . in horror and in contempt.

LORD GORING: Is Lady Chiltern as perfect as all that?

SIR ROBERT CHILTERN: Yes; my wife is as perfect as all that.

LORD GORING (*taking off his left-hand glove*): What a pity! I beg your pardon, my dear fellow, I didn't quite mean that. But if what you tell me is true, I should like to have a serious talk about life with Lady Chiltern.

SIR ROBERT CHILTERN: It would be quite useless.

LORD GORING: May I try?

SIR ROBERT CHILTERN: Yes; but nothing could make her alter her views.

LORD GORING: Well, at the worst it would simply be a psychological experiment.

SIR ROBERT CHILTERN: All such experiments are terribly dangerous.

LORD GORING: Everything is dangerous, my dear fellow. If it wasn't so, life wouldn't be worth living. . . . Well, I am bound to say that I think you should have told her years ago.

SIR ROBERT CHILTERN: When? When we were engaged? Do you think she would have married me if she had known that the origin of my fortune is such as it is, the basis of my career such as it is, and that I had done a thing that I suppose most men would call shameful and dishonourable?

LORD GORING (*slowly*): Yes; most men would call it ugly names. There is no doubt of that.

SIR ROBERT CHILTERN (*bitterly*): Men who every day do something of the same kind themselves. Men who, each one of them, have worse secrets in their own lives.

LORD GORING: That is the reason they are so pleased to find

out other people's secrets. It distracts public attention from their own.

SIR ROBERT CHILTERN: And, after all, whom did I wrong by what I did? No one.

LORD GORING (*looking at him steadily*): Except yourself, Robert.

SIR ROBERT CHILTERN (*after a pause*): Of course I had private information about a certain transaction contemplated by the Government of the day, and I acted on it. Private information is practically the source of every large modern fortune.

LORD GORING (*tapping his boot with his cane*): And public scandal invariably the result.

SIR ROBERT CHILTERN (*pacing up and down the room*): Arthur, do you think that what I did nearly eighteen years ago should be brought up against me now? Do you think it fair that a man's whole career should be ruined for a fault done in one's boyhood almost? I was twenty-two at the time, and I had the double misfortune of being well-born and poor, two unforgivable things nowadays. Is it fair that the folly, the sin of one's youth, if men choose to call it a sin, should wreck a life like mine, should place me in the pillory, should shatter all that I have worked for, all that I have built up? Is it fair, Arthur?

LORD GORING: Life is never fair, Robert. And perhaps it is a good thing for most of us that it is not.

SIR ROBERT CHILTERN: Every man of ambition has to fight his century with its own weapons. What this century worships is wealth. The God of this century is wealth. To succeed one must have wealth. At all costs one must have wealth.

LORD GORING: You underrate yourself, Robert. Believe me, without your wealth you could have succeeded just as well.

SIR ROBERT CHILTERN: When I was old, perhaps. When I had lost my passion for power, or could not use it. When I was tired, worn out, disappointed. I wanted my success when I was young. Youth is the time for success. I couldn't wait.

LORD GORING: Well, you certainly have had your success while you are still young. No one in our day has had such a brilliant success. Under-Secretary for Foreign Affairs at the age of forty—that's good enough for any one, I should think.

SIR ROBERT CHILTERN: And if it is all taken away from me now? If I lose everything over a horrible scandal? If I am hounded from public life?

LORD GORING: Robert, how could you have sold yourself for money?

SIR ROBERT CHILTERN (excitedly): I did not sell myself for money. I bought success at a great price. That is all.

LORD GORING (gravely): Yes; you certainly paid a great price for it. But what first made you think of doing such a thing?

SIR ROBERT CHILTERN: Baron Arnheim.

LORD GORING: Damned scoundrel!

SIR ROBERT CHILTERN: No; he was a man of a most subtle and refined intellect. A man of culture, charm, and distinction. One of the most intellectual men I ever met.

LORD GORING: Ah! I prefer a gentlemanly fool any day. There is more to be said for stupidity than people imagine. Personally, I have a great admiration for stupidity. It is a sort of fellow-feeling, I suppose. But how did he do it? Tell me the whole thing.

SIR ROBERT CHILTERN (throws himself into an arm-chair by the writing-table): One night after dinner at Lord Radley's the Baron began talking about success in modern life as something that one could reduce to an absolutely definite science. With that wonderfully fascinating quiet voice of his he expounded to us the most terrible of all philosophies, the philosophy of power, preached to us the most marvellous of all gospels, the gospel of gold. I think he saw the effect he had produced on me, for some days afterwards he wrote and asked me to come and see him. He was living then in Park Lane, in the house Lord Woolcomb has now. I remember so well how, with a strange smile on his pale, curved lips, he led me through his wonderful picture gallery, showed me his tapestries, his enamels, his jewels, his carved ivories, made me wonder at the strange loveliness of the luxury in which he lived; and then told me that luxury was nothing but a background, a painted scene in a play, and that power, power over other men, power over the world, was the one thing worth having, the one supreme pleasure worth knowing, the one joy one never tired of, and that in our century only the rich possessed it.

LORD GORING (*with great deliberation*): A thoroughly shallow creed.

SIR ROBERT CHILTERN (*rising*): I didn't think so then. I don't think so now. Wealth has given me enormous power. It gave me at the very outset of my life freedom, and freedom is everything. You have never been poor, and never known what ambition is. You cannot understand what a wonderful chance the Baron gave me. Such a chance as few men get.

LORD GORING: Fortunately for them, if one is to judge by results. But tell me definitely, how did the Baron finally persuade you to—well, to do what you did?

SIR ROBERT CHILTERN: When I was going away he said to me that if I ever could give him any private information of real value he would make me a very rich man. I was dazed at the prospect he held out to me, and my ambition and my desire for power were at that time boundless. Six weeks later certain private documents passed through my hands.

LORD GORING (*keeping his eyes steadily fixed on the carpet*): State documents?

SIR ROBERT CHILTERN: Yes.

LORD GORING *sighs, then passes his hand across his forehead and looks up.*

LORD GORING: I had no idea that you, of all men in the world, could have been so weak, Robert, as to yield to such a temptation as Baron Arnheim held out to you.

SIR ROBERT CHILTERN: Weak? Oh, I am sick of hearing that phrase. Sick of using it about others. Weak! Do you really think, Arthur, that it is weakness that yields to temptation? I tell you that there are terrible temptations that it requires strength, strength and courage, to yield to. To stake all one's life on a single moment, to risk everything on one throw, whether the stake be power or pleasure, I care not—there is no weakness in that. There is a horrible, a terrible courage. I had that courage. I sat down the same afternoon and wrote Baron Arnheim the letter this woman now holds. He made three-quarters of a million over the transaction.

LORD GORING: And you?

SIR ROBERT CHILTERN: I received from the Baron £110,000.

LORD GORING: You were worth more, Robert.

SIR ROBERT CHILTERN: No; that money gave me exactly what I wanted, power over others. I went into the House immediately. The Baron advised me in finance from time to time. Before five years I had almost trebled my fortune. Since then everything that I have touched has turned out a success. In all things connected with money I have had a luck so extraordinary that sometimes it has

made me almost afraid. I remember having read somewhere, in some strange book, that when the gods wish to
punish us they answer our prayers.

LORD GORING: But tell me, Robert, did you never suffer
any regret for what you had done?

SIR ROBERT CHILTERN: No. I felt that I had fought the century with its own weapons, and won.

LORD GORING (*sadly*): You thought you had won.

SIR ROBERT CHILTERN: I thought so. (*After a long pause*):
Arthur, do you despise me for what I have told you?

LORD GORING (*with deep feeling in his voice*): I am very
sorry for you, Robert, very sorry indeed.

SIR ROBERT CHILTERN: I don't say that I suffered any remorse. I didn't. Not remorse in the ordinary, rather silly
sense of the word. But I have paid conscience money
many times. I had a wild hope that I might disarm destiny. The sum Baron Arnheim gave me I have distributed
twice over in public charities since then.

LORD GORING (*looking up*): In public charities? Dear me!
what a lot of harm you must have done, Robert!

SIR ROBERT CHILTERN: Oh, don't say that, Arthur; don't
talk like that!

LORD GORING: Never mind what I say, Robert! I am always
saying what I shouldn't say. In fact, I usually say what I
really think. A great mistake nowadays. It makes one so
liable to be understood. As regards this dreadful business, I will help you in whatever way I can. Of course you
know that.

SIR ROBERT CHILTERN: Thank you, Arthur, thank you. But
what is to be done? What can be done?

LORD GORING (*leaning back with his hands in his pockets*):
Well, the English can't stand a man who is always saying
he is in the right, but they are very fond of a man who admits that he has been in the wrong. It is one of the best
things in them. However, in your case, Robert, a confes-

sion would not do. The money, if you will allow me to say so, is . . . awkward. Besides, if you did make a clean breast of the whole affair, you would never be able to talk morality again. And in England a man who can't talk morality twice a week to a large, popular, immoral audience is quite over as a serious politician. There would be nothing left for him as a profession except Botany or the Church. A confession would be of no use. It would ruin you.

SIR ROBERT CHILTERN: It would ruin me. Arthur, the only thing for me to do now is to fight the thing out.

LORD GORING *(rising from his chair)*: I was waiting for you to say that, Robert. It is the only thing to do now. And you must begin by telling your wife the whole story.

SIR ROBERT CHILTERN: That I will not do.

LORD GORING: Robert, believe me, you are wrong.

SIR ROBERT CHILTERN: I couldn't do it. It would kill her love for me. And now about this woman, this Mrs. Cheveley. How can I defend myself against her? You knew her before, Arthur, apparently.

LORD GORING: Yes.

SIR ROBERT CHILTERN: Did you know her well?

LORD GORING *(arranging his necktie)*: So little that I got engaged to be married to her once, when I was staying at the Tenbys'. The affair lasted for three days . . . nearly.

SIR ROBERT CHILTERN: Why was it broken off?

LORD GORING *(airily)*: Oh, I forget. At least, it makes no matter. By the way, have you tried her with money? She used to be confoundedly fond of money.

SIR ROBERT CHILTERN: I offered her any sum she wanted. She refused.

LORD GORING: Then the marvellous gospel of gold breaks down sometimes. The rich can't do everything, after all.

SIR ROBERT CHILTERN: Not everything. I suppose you are right. Arthur, I feel that public disgrace is in store for me.

I feel certain of it. I never knew what terror was before. I know it now. It is as if a hand of ice were laid upon one's heart. It is as if one's heart were beating itself to death in some empty hollow.

LORD GORING (*striking the table*): Robert, you must fight her. You must fight her.

SIR ROBERT CHILTERN: But how?

LORD GORING: I can't tell you how at present. I have not the smallest idea. But every one has some weak point. There is some flaw in each one of us. (*Strolls over to the fire-place and looks at himself in the glass.*) My father tells me that even I have faults. Perhaps I have. I don't know.

SIR ROBERT CHILTERN: In defending myself against Mrs. Cheveley I have a right to use any weapon I can find, have I not?

LORD GORING (*still looking in the glass*): In your place I don't think I should have the smallest scruple in doing so. She is thoroughly well able to take care of herself.

SIR ROBERT CHILTERN (*sits down at the table and takes a pen in his hand*): Well, I shall send a cipher telegram to the Embassy at Vienna, to inquire if there is anything known against her. There may be some secret scandal she might be afraid of.

LORD GORING (*settling his buttonhole*): Oh, I should fancy Mrs. Cheveley is one of those very modern women of our time who find a new scandal as becoming as a new bonnet, and air them both in the Park every afternoon at five-thirty. I am sure she adores scandals, and that the sorrow of her life at present is that she can't manage to have enough of them.

SIR ROBERT CHILTERN (*writing*): Why do you say that?

LORD GORING (*turning round*): Well, she wore far too much rouge last night, and not quite enough clothes. That is always a sign of despair in a woman.

SIR ROBERT CHILTERN (*striking a bell*): But it is worth while my wiring to Vienna, is it not?

LORD GORING: It is always worth while asking a question, though it is not always worth while answering one.

Enter MASON.

SIR ROBERT CHILTERN: Is Mr. Trafford in his room?

MASON: Yes, Sir Robert.

SIR ROBERT CHILTERN (*puts what he has written into an envelope, which he then carefully closes*): Tell him to have this sent off in cipher at once. There must not be a moment's delay.

MASON: Yes, Sir Robert.

SIR ROBERT CHILTERN: Oh! just give that back to me again.

Writes something on the envelope. MASON *then goes out with the letter.*

SIR ROBERT CHILTERN: She must have had some curious hold over Baron Arnheim. I wonder what it was.

LORD GORING (*smiling*): I wonder.

SIR ROBERT CHILTERN: I will fight her to the death, as long as my wife knows nothing.

LORD GORING (*strongly*): Oh, fight in any case—in any case.

SIR ROBERT CHILTERN (*with a gesture of despair*): If my wife found out, there would be little left to fight for. Well, as soon as I hear from Vienna, I shall let you know the result. It is a chance, just a chance, but I believe in it. And as I fought the age with its own weapons, I will fight her with her weapons. It is only fair, and she looks like a woman with a past, doesn't she?

LORD GORING: Most pretty women do. But there is a fashion in pasts just as there is a fashion in frocks. Perhaps Mrs. Cheveley's past is merely a slightly *décolleté*[1] one, and they are excessively popular nowadays. Besides, my dear Robert, I should not build too high hopes on frightening Mrs. Cheveley. I should not fancy Mrs. Cheveley is a woman who would be easily frightened. She has survived all her creditors, and she shows wonderful presence of mind.

SIR ROBERT CHILTERN: Oh! I live on hopes now. I clutch at every chance. I feel like a man on a ship that is sinking. The water is round my feet, and the very air is bitter with storm. Hush! I hear my wife's voice.

Enter LADY CHILTERN *in walking dress.*

LADY CHILTERN: Good-afternoon, Lord Goring.

LORD GORING: Good-afternoon, Lady Chiltern! Have you been in the Park?

LADY CHILTERN: No; I have just come from the Woman's Liberal Association,[2] where, by the way, Robert, your name was received with loud applause, and now I have come in to have my tea. (*To* LORD GORING): You will wait and have some tea, won't you?

LORD GORING: I'll wait for a short time, thanks.

LADY CHILTERN: I will be back in a moment. I am only going to take my hat off.

LORD GORING (*in his most earnest manner*): Oh! please don't. It is so pretty. One of the prettiest hats I ever saw. I hope the Woman's Liberal Association received it with loud applause.

LADY CHILTERN (*with a smile*): We have much more important work to do than look at each other's bonnets, Lord Goring.

LORD GORING: Really? What sort of work?

LADY CHILTERN: Oh! dull, useful, delightful things, Factory Acts, Female Inspectors, the Eight Hours' Bill, the Parliamentary Franchise. . . . Everything, in fact, that you would find thoroughly uninteresting.

LORD GORING: And never bonnets?

LADY CHILTERN (*with mock indignation*): Never bonnets, never!

LADY CHILTERN goes out through the door leading to her boudoir.

SIR ROBERT CHILTERN (*takes* LORD GORING's *hand*): You have been a good friend to me, Arthur, a thoroughly good friend.

LORD GORING: I don't know that I have been able to do much for you, Robert, as yet. In fact, I have not been able to do anything for you, as far as I can see. I am thoroughly disappointed with myself.

SIR ROBERT CHILTERN: You have enabled me to tell you the truth. That is something. The truth has always stifled me.

LORD GORING: Ah! the truth is a thing I get rid of as soon as possible! Bad habit, by the way. Makes one very unpopular at the club . . . with the older members. They call it being conceited. Perhaps it is.

SIR ROBERT CHILTERN: I would to God that I had been able to tell the truth . . . to live the truth. Ah! that is the great thing in life, to live the truth. (*Sighs, and goes towards the door.*) I'll see you soon again, Arthur, shan't I?

LORD GORING: Certainly. Whenever you like. I'm going to look in at the Bachelors' Ball to-night, unless I find something better to do. But I'll come round to-morrow morning. If you should want me to-night by any chance, send round a note to Curzon Street.

SIR ROBERT CHILTERN: Thank you.

As he reaches the door, LADY CHILTERN *enters from her boudoir.*

LADY CHILTERN: You are not going, Robert?

SIR ROBERT CHILTERN: I have some letters to write, dear.

LADY CHILTERN (*going to him*): You work too hard, Robert. You seem never to think of yourself; and you are looking so tired.

SIR ROBERT CHILTERN: It is nothing, dear, nothing. (*He kisses her and goes out.*)

LADY CHILTERN (*to* LORD GORING): Do sit down. I am so glad you have called. I want to talk to you about . . . well, not about bonnets, or the Woman's Liberal Association. You take far too much interest in the first subject, and not nearly enough in the second.

LORD GORING: You want to talk to me about Mrs. Cheveley?

LADY CHILTERN: Yes. You have guessed it. After you left last night I found out that what she had said was really true. Of course I made Robert write her a letter at once, withdrawing his promise.

LORD GORING: So he gave me to understand.

LADY CHILTERN: To have kept it would have been the first stain on a career that has been stainless always. Robert must be above reproach. He is not like other men. He cannot afford to do what other men do. (*She looks at* LORD GORING, *who remains silent.*) Don't you agree with me? You are Robert's greatest friend. You are our greatest friend, Lord Goring. No one, except myself, knows Robert better than you do. He has no secrets from me, and I don't think he has any from you.

LORD GORING: He certainly has no secrets from me. At least I don't think so.

LADY CHILTERN: Then am I not right in my estimate of him? I know I am right. But speak to me frankly.

LORD GORING (*looking straight at her*): Quite frankly?

LADY CHILTERN: Surely. You have nothing to conceal, have you?

LORD GORING: Nothing. But, my dear Lady Chiltern, I

think, if you will allow me to say so, that in practical life—

LADY CHILTERN (*smiling*): Of which you know so little, Lord Goring—

LORD GORING: Of which I know nothing by experience, though I know something by observation. I think that in practical life there is something about success, actual success, that is a little unscrupulous, something about ambition that is unscrupulous always. Once a man has set his heart and soul on getting to a certain point, if he has to climb the crag, he climbs the crag; if he has to walk in the mire—

LADY CHILTERN: Well?

LORD GORING: He walks in the mire. Of course I am only talking generally about life.

LADY CHILTERN (*gravely*): I hope so. Why do you look at me so strangely, Lord Goring?

LORD GORING: Lady Chiltern, I have sometimes thought that . . . perhaps you are a little hard in some of your views on life. I think that . . . often you don't make sufficient allowances. In every nature there are elements of weakness, or worse than weakness. Supposing, for instance, that—that any public man, my father, or Lord Merton, or Robert, say, had, years ago, written some foolish letter to some one. . . .

LADY CHILTERN: What do you mean by a foolish letter?

LORD GORING: A letter gravely compromising one's position. I am only putting an imaginary case.

LADY CHILTERN: Robert is as incapable of doing a foolish thing as he is of doing a wrong thing.

LORD GORING (*after a long pause*): Nobody is incapable of doing a foolish thing. Nobody is incapable of doing a wrong thing.

LADY CHILTERN: Are you a Pessimist? What will the other dandies say? They will all have to go into mourning.

LORD GORING (*rising*): No, Lady Chiltern, I am not a Pessimist. Indeed I am not sure that I quite know what pessimism really means. All I do know is that life cannot be understood without much charity, cannot be lived without much charity. It is love, and not German philosophy, that is the true explanation of this world, whatever may be the explanation of the next. And if you are ever in trouble, Lady Chiltern, trust me absolutely, and I will help you in every way I can. If you ever want me, come to me for my assistance, and you shall have it. Come at once to me.

LADY CHILTERN (*looking at him in surprise*): Lord Goring, you are talking quite seriously. I don't think I ever heard you talk seriously before.

LORD GORING (*laughing*): You must excuse me, Lady Chiltern. It won't occur again, if I can help it.

LADY CHILTERN: But I like you to be serious.

Enter MABEL CHILTERN, *in the most ravishing frock.*

MABEL CHILTERN: Dear Gertrude, don't say such a dreadful thing to Lord Goring. Seriousness would be very unbecoming to him. Good-afternoon, Lord Goring! Pray be as trivial as you can.

LORD GORING: I should like to, Miss Mabel, but I am afraid I am . . . a little out of practice this morning; and besides, I have to be going now.

MABEL CHILTERN: Just when I have come in! What dreadful manners you have! I am sure you were very badly brought up.

LORD GORING: I was.

MABEL CHILTERN: I wish I had brought you up!

LORD GORING: I am so sorry you didn't.

MABEL CHILTERN: It is too late now, I suppose?

LORD GORING (*smiling*): I am not so sure.

MABEL CHILTERN: Will you ride to-morrow morning?

LORD GORING: Yes, at ten.

MABEL CHILTERN: Don't forget.

LORD GORING: Of course I shan't. By the way, Lady Chiltern, there is no list of your guests in *The Morning Post* of to-day. It has apparently been crowded out by the County Council, or the Lambeth Conference,[3] or something equally boring. Could you let me have a list? I have a particular reason for asking you.

LADY CHILTERN: I am sure Mr. Trafford will be able to give you one.

LORD GORING: Thanks, so much.

MABEL CHILTERN: Tommy is the most useful person in London.

LORD GORING (*turning to her*): And who is the most ornamental?

MABEL CHILTERN (*triumphantly*): I am.

LORD GORING: How clever of you to guess it! (*Takes up his hat and cane.*) Good-bye, Lady Chiltern! You will remember what I said to you, won't you?

LADY CHILTERN: Yes; but I don't know why you said it to me.

LORD GORING: I hardly know myself. Good-bye, Miss Mabel!

MABEL CHILTERN (*with a little moue of disappointment*): I wish you were not going. I have had four wonderful adventures this morning; four and a half, in fact. You might stop and listen to some of them.

LORD GORING: How very selfish of you to have four and a half! There won't be any left for me.

MABEL CHILTERN: I don't want you to have any. They would not be good for you.

LORD GORING: That is the first unkind thing you have ever said to me. How charmingly you said it! Ten to-morrow.

MABEL CHILTERN: Sharp.

LORD GORING: Quite sharp. But don't bring Mr. Trafford.

MABEL CHILTERN *(with a little toss of her head)*: Of course I shan't bring Tommy Trafford. Tommy Trafford is in great disgrace.

LORD GORING: I am delighted to hear it. *(Bows and goes out.)*

MABEL CHILTERN: Gertrude, I wish you would speak to Tommy Trafford.

LADY CHILTERN: What has poor Mr. Trafford done this time? Robert says he is the best secretary he has ever had.

MABEL CHILTERN: Well, Tommy has proposed to me again. Tommy really does nothing but propose to me. He proposed to me last night in the music-room, when I was quite unprotected, as there was an elaborate trio going on. I didn't dare to make the smallest repartee, I need hardly tell you. If I had, it would have stopped the music at once. Musical people are so absurdly unreasonable. They always want one to be perfectly dumb at the very moment when one is longing to be absolutely deaf. Then he proposed to me in broad daylight this morning, in front of that dreadful statue of Achilles. Really, the things that go on in front of that work of art are quite appalling. The police should interfere. At luncheon I saw by the glare in his eye that he was going to propose again, and I just managed to check him in time by assuring him that I was a bimetallist.[4] Fortunately I don't know what bimetallism means. And I don't believe anybody else does either. But the observation crushed Tommy for ten minutes. He looked quite shocked. And then Tommy is so annoying in the way he proposes. If he proposed at the top of his voice, I should not mind so much. That might produce some effect on the public. But he does it in a horrid confidential way. When Tommy wants to be romantic he talks to one just like a doctor. I am very fond of Tommy, but his methods of proposing are quite out of date. I wish, Gertrude, you would speak to him, and tell him that once a week is quite often enough to propose to any one, and that it should always be done in a manner that attracts some attention.

LADY CHILTERN: Dear Mabel, don't talk like that. Besides, Robert thinks very highly of Mr. Trafford. He believes he has a brilliant future before him.

MABEL CHILTERN: Oh! I wouldn't marry a man with a future before him for anything under the sun.

LADY CHILTERN: Mabel!

MABEL CHILTERN: I know, dear. You married a man with a future, didn't you! But then Robert was a genius, and you have a noble, self-sacrificing character. You can stand geniuses. I have no character at all, and Robert is the only genius I could ever bear. As a rule, I think they are quite impossible. Geniuses talk so much, don't they? Such a bad habit! And they are always thinking about themselves, when I want them to be thinking about me. I must go round now and rehearse at Lady Basildon's. You remember, we are having tableaux, don't you? The Triumph of something, I don't know what! I hope it will be triumph of me. Only triumph I am really interested in at present. (*Kisses* LADY CHILTERN *and goes out; then comes running back*). Oh, Gertrude, do you know who is coming to see you? That dreadful Mrs. Cheveley, in a most lovely gown. Did you ask her?

LADY CHILTERN (*rising*): Mrs. Cheveley! Coming to see me? Impossible!

MABEL CHILTERN: I assure you she is coming upstairs, as large as life and not nearly so natural.

LADY CHILTERN: You need not wait, Mabel. Remember, Lady Basildon is expecting you.

MABEL CHILTERN: Oh! I must shake hands with Lady Markby. She is delightful. I love being scolded by her.

Enter MASON.

MASON: Lady Markby. Mrs. Cheveley.

Enter LADY MARKBY *and* MRS. CHEVELEY.

LADY CHILTERN (*advancing to meet them*): Dear Lady
Markby, how nice of you to come and see me! (*Shakes
hands with her, and bows somewhat distantly to* MRS.
CHEVELEY.) Won't you sit down, Mrs. Cheveley?

MRS. CHEVELEY: Thanks. Isn't that Miss Chiltern? I should
like so much to know her.

LADY CHILTERN: Mabel, Mrs. Cheveley wishes to know
you. (MABEL CHILTERN *gives a little nod.*)

MRS. CHEVELEY (*sitting down*): I thought your frock so
charming, last night, Miss Chiltern. So simple and . . .
suitable.

MABEL CHILTERN: Really? I must tell my dressmaker. It
will be such a surprise to her. Good-bye, Lady Markby!

LADY MARKBY: Going already?

MABEL CHILTERN: I am so sorry but I am obliged to. I am
just off to rehearsal. I have got to stand on my head in
some tableaux.

LADY MARKBY: On your head, child? Oh! I hope not. I believe it is most unhealthy. (*Takes a seat on the sofa next to*
LADY CHILTERN.)

MABEL CHILTERN: But it is for an excellent charity; in aid
of the Undeserving, the only people I am really interested in. I am the secretary, and Tommy Trafford is
treasurer.

MRS. CHEVELEY: And what is Lord Goring?

MABEL CHILTERN: Oh! Lord Goring is president.

MRS. CHEVELEY: The post should suit him admirably, unless he has deteriorated since I knew him first.

LADY MARKBY (*reflecting*): You are remarkably modern,
Mabel. A little too modern, perhaps. Nothing is so dan-

gerous as being too modern. One is apt to grow old-fashioned quite suddenly. I have known many instances of it.

MABEL CHILTERN: What a dreadful prospect!

LADY MARKBY: Ah! my dear, you need not be nervous. You will always be as pretty as possible. That is the best fashion there is, and the only fashion that England succeeds in setting.

MABEL CHILTERN *(with a curtsey)*: Thank you so much, Lady Markby, for England . . . and myself. *(Goes out.)*

LADY MARKBY *(turning to* LADY CHILTERN*)*: Dear Gertrude, we just called to know if Mrs. Cheveley's diamond brooch has been found.

LADY CHILTERN: Here?

MRS. CHEVELEY: Yes. I missed it when I got back to Claridge's, and I thought I might possibly have dropped it here.

LADY CHILTERN: I have heard nothing about it. But I will send for the butler and ask. *(Touches the bell.)*

MRS. CHEVELEY: Oh, pray don't trouble, Lady Chiltern. I dare say I lost it at the Opera, before we came on here.

LADY MARKBY: Ah yes, I suppose it must have been at the Opera. The fact is, we all scramble and jostle so much nowadays that I wonder we have anything at all left on us at the end of an evening. I know myself that, when I am coming back from the Drawing room, I always feel as if I hadn't a shred on me, except a small shred of decent reputation, just enough to prevent the lower classes making painful observations through the windows of the carriage. The fact is that our Society is terribly over-populated. Really, some one should arrange a proper scheme of assisted emigration. It would do a great deal of good.

MRS. CHEVELEY: I quite agree with you, Lady Markby. It is nearly six years since I have been in London for the Sea-

son, and I must say Society has become dreadfully
mixed. One sees the oddest people everywhere.

LADY MARKBY: That is quite true, dear. But one needn't
know them. I'm sure I don't know half the people who
come to my house. Indeed, from all I hear, I shouldn't
like to.

Enter MASON.

LADY CHILTERN: What sort of brooch was it that you lost,
Mrs. Cheveley?

MRS. CHEVELEY: A diamond snake-brooch with a ruby, a
rather large ruby.

LADY MARKBY: I thought you said there was a sapphire on
the head, dear?

MRS. CHEVELEY (*smiling*): No. Lady Markby—a ruby.

LADY MARKBY (*nodding her head*): And very becoming, I
am quite sure.

LADY CHILTERN: Has a ruby and diamond brooch been
found in any of the rooms this morning, Mason?

MASON: No, my lady.

MRS. CHEVELEY: It really is of no consequence, Lady
Chiltern. I am so sorry to have put you to any inconvenience.

LADY CHILTERN (*coldly*): Oh, it has been no inconvenience. That will do, Mason. You can bring tea. (*Exit*
MASON.)

LADY MARKBY: Well, I must say it is most annoying to lose
anything. I remember once at Bath, years ago, losing in
the Pump Room⁵ an exceedingly handsome cameo
bracelet that Sir John had given me. I don't think he has
ever given me anything since, I am sorry to say. He has
sadly degenerated. Really, this horrid House of Commons quite ruins our husbands for us. I think the Lower
House by far the greatest blow to a happy married life

that there has been since that terrible thing called the Higher Education of Women was invented.

LADY CHILTERN: Ah! it is heresy to say that in this house, Lady Markby. Robert is a great champion of the Higher Education of Women, and so, I am afraid, am I.

MRS. CHEVELEY: The higher education of men is what I should like to see. Men need it so sadly.

LADY MARKBY: They do, dear. But I am afraid such a scheme would be quite unpractical. I don't think man has much capacity for development. He has got as far as he can, and that is not far, is it? With regard to women, well, dear Gertrude, you belong to the younger generation, and I am sure it is all right if you approve of it. In my time, of course, we were taught not to understand anything. That was the old system, and wonderfully interesting it was. I assure you that the amount of things I and my poor dear sister were taught not to understand was quite extraordinary. But modern women understand everything, I am told.

MRS. CHEVELEY: Except their husbands. That is the one thing the modern woman never understands.

LADY MARKBY: And a very good thing too, dear, I dare say. It might break up many a happy home if they did. Not yours, I need hardly say, Gertrude. You have married a pattern husband. I wish I could say as much for myself. But since Sir John has taken to attending the debates regularly, which he never used to do in the good old days, his language has become quite impossible. He always seems to think that he is addressing the House, and consequently whenever he discusses the state of the agricultural labourer, or the Welsh Church,[6] or something quite improper of that kind, I am obliged to send all the servants out of the room. It is not pleasant to see one's own butler, who has been with one for twenty-three years, actually blushing at the sideboard, and the footmen making contortions in corners like persons in circuses. I assure you my life will be quite ruined unless they send John at once to the Upper House. He won't take any interest in politics then, will he? The House of Lords is so sensible. An assembly of gentlemen. But in his present state, Sir John is really a great trial. Why, this morning before breakfast was half over, he stood up on the hearth-rug, put his hands in his pockets, and appealed to the country at the top of his voice. I left the table as soon as I had my second cup of tea, I need hardly say. But his violent language could be heard all over the house! I trust, Gertrude, that Sir Robert is not like that?

LADY CHILTERN: But I am very much interested in politics, Lady Markby. I love to hear Robert talk about them.

LADY MARKBY: Well, I hope he is not as devoted to Blue Books as Sir John is. I don't think they can be quite improving reading for any one.

MRS. CHEVELEY (*languidly*): I have never read a Blue Book. I prefer books . . . in yellow covers.[7]

LADY MARKBY (*genially unconscious*): Yellow is a gayer colour, is it not? I used to wear yellow a good deal in my early days, and would do so now if Sir John was not so painfully personal in his observations, and a man on the question of dress is always ridiculous, is he not?

MRS. CHEVELEY: Oh, no! I think men are the only authorities on dress.

LADY MARKBY: Really? One wouldn't say so from the sort of hats they wear? Would one?

The butler enters, followed by the footman. Tea is set on a small table close to LADY CHILTERN.

LADY CHILTERN: May I give you some tea, Mrs. Cheveley?

MRS. CHEVELEY: Thanks. (*The butler hands* MRS. CHEVELEY *a cup of tea on a salver.*)

LADY CHILTERN: Some tea, Lady Markby?

LADY MARKBY: No thanks, dear. (*The servants go out.*) The fact is, I have promised to go round for ten minutes to see poor Lady Brancaster, who is in very great trouble. Her daughter, quite a well-brought-up girl, too, has actually become engaged to be married to a curate in Shropshire. It is very sad, very sad indeed. I can't understand this modern mania for curates. In my time we girls saw them, of course, running about the place like rabbits. But we never took any notice of them, I need hardly say. But I am told that nowadays country society is quite honeycombed with them. I think it most irreligious. And then the eldest son has quarrelled with his father, and it is said that when they meet at the club Lord Brancaster always hides himself behind the money article in *The Times*. However, I believe that is quite a common occurrence nowadays and that they have to take in extra copies of *The Times* at all the clubs in St. James's Street; there are so many sons who won't have anything to do with their fathers, and so many fathers who won't speak to their sons. I think myself, it is very much to be regretted.

MRS. CHEVELEY: So do I. Fathers have so much to learn from their sons nowadays.

LADY MARKBY: Really, dear? What?

MRS. CHEVELEY: The art of living. The only really Fine Art we have produced in modern times.

LADY MARKBY (*shaking her head*): Ah! I am afraid Lord Brancaster knew a good deal about that. More than his poor wife ever did. (*Turning to* LADY CHILTERN): You know Lady Brancaster, don't you, dear?

LADY CHILTERN: Just slightly. She was staying at Langton last autumn, when we were there.

LADY MARKBY: Well, like all stout women, she looks the very picture of happiness, as no doubt you noticed. But there are many tragedies in her family, besides this affair of the curate. Her own sister, Mrs. Jekyll, had a most un-

happy life; through no fault of her own, I am sorry to say.
She ultimately was so broken-hearted that she went into
a convent, or on to the operatic stage, I forget which. No;
I think it was decorative art-needlework she took up. I
know she had lost all sense of pleasure in life. *(Rising)*:
And now, Gertrude, if you will allow me, I shall leave
Mrs. Cheveley in your charge and call back for her in a
quarter of an hour. Or perhaps, dear Mrs. Cheveley, you
wouldn't mind waiting in the carriage while I am with
Lady Brancaster. As I intend it to be a visit of condolence, I shan't stay long.

MRS. CHEVELEY *(rising)*: I don't mind waiting in the carriage at all, provided there is somebody to look at one.

LADY MARKBY: Well, I hear the curate is always prowling
about the house.

MRS. CHEVELEY: I am afraid I am not fond of girl friends.

LADY CHILTERN *(rising)*: Oh, I hope Mrs. Cheveley will
stay here a little. I should like to have a few minutes' conversation with her.

MRS. CHEVELEY: How very kind of you, Lady Chiltern! Believe me, nothing would give me greater pleasure.

LADY MARKBY: Ah! no doubt you both have many pleasant
reminiscences of your schooldays to talk over together.
Good-bye, dear Gertrude! Shall I see you at Lady
Bonar's to-night? She has discovered a wonderful new
genius. He does . . . nothing at all, I believe. That is a
great comfort, is it not?

LADY CHILTERN: Robert and I are dining at home by ourselves to-night, and I don't think I shall go anywhere afterwards. Robert, of course, will have to be in the House.
But there is nothing interesting on.

LADY MARKBY: Dining at home by yourselves? Is that quite
prudent? Ah, I forgot, your husband is an exception.
Mine is the general rule, and nothing ages a woman so
rapidly as having married the general rule.

Exit LADY MARKBY.

MRS. CHEVELEY: Wonderful woman, Lady Markby, isn't she? Talks more and says less than anybody I ever met. She is made to be a public speaker. Much more so than her husband, though he is a typical Englishman, always dull and usually violent.

LADY CHILTERN (*makes no answer, but remains standing. There is a pause. Then the eyes of the two women meet. LADY CHILTERN looks stern and pale. MRS. CHEVELEY seems rather amused*): Mrs. Cheveley, I think it is right to tell you quite frankly that, had I known who you really were, I should not have invited you to my house last night.

MRS. CHEVELEY (*with an impertinent smile*): Really?

LADY CHILTERN: I could not have done so.

MRS. CHEVELEY: I see that after all these years you have not changed a bit, Gertrude.

LADY CHILTERN: I never change.

MRS. CHEVELEY (*elevating her eyebrows*): Then life has taught you nothing?

LADY CHILTERN: It has taught me that a person who has once been guilty of a dishonest and dishonourable action may be guilty of it a second time, and should be shunned.

MRS. CHEVELEY: Would you apply that rule to every one?

LADY CHILTERN: Yes, to every one, without exception.

MRS. CHEVELEY: Then I am sorry for you, Gertrude, very sorry for you.

LADY CHILTERN: You see now, I am sure, that for many reasons any further acquaintance between us during your stay in London is quite impossible?

MRS. CHEVELEY (*leaning back in her chair*): Do you know, Gertrude, I don't mind your talking morality a bit. Morality is simply the attitude we adopt towards people whom we personally dislike. You dislike me. I am quite aware of that. And I have always detested you. And yet I have come here to do you a service.

LADY CHILTERN *(contemptuously)*: Like the service you wished to render my husband last night, I suppose. Thank heaven, I saved him from that.

MRS. CHEVELEY *(starting to her feet)*: It was you who made him write that insolent letter to me? It was you who made him break his promise?

LADY CHILTERN: Yes.

MRS. CHEVELEY: Then you must make him keep it. I give you till to-morrow morning—no more. If by that time your husband does not solemnly bind himself to help me in this great scheme in which I am interested—

LADY CHILTERN: This fraudulent speculation—

MRS. CHEVELEY: Call it what you choose. I hold your husband in the hollow of my hand, and if you are wise you will make him do what I tell him.

LADY CHILTERN *(rising and going towards her)*: You are impertinent. What has my husband to do with you? With a woman like you?

MRS. CHEVELEY *(with a bitter laugh)*: In this world like meets with like. It is because your husband is himself fraudulent and dishonest that we pair so well together. Between you and him there are chasms. He and I are closer than friends. We are enemies linked together. The same sin binds us.

LADY CHILTERN: How dare you class my husband with yourself? How dare you threaten him or me? Leave my house. You are unfit to enter it.

SIR ROBERT CHILTERN *enters from behind. He hears his wife's last words, and sees to whom they are addressed. He grows deadly pale.*

MRS. CHEVELEY: Your house! A house bought with the price of dishonour. A house, everything in which has been paid for by fraud. (*Turns round and sees* SIR ROBERT CHILTERN.) Ask him what the origin of his fortune is! Get him to tell you how he sold to a stockbroker a Cabinet secret. Learn from him to what you owe your position.

LADY CHILTERN: It is not true! Robert! It is not true!

MRS. CHEVELEY (*pointing at him with outstretched finger*): Look at him! Can he deny it! Does he dare to?

SIR ROBERT CHILTERN: Go! Go at once. You have done your worst now.

MRS. CHEVELEY: My worst? I have not yet finished with you, with either of you. I give you both till to-morrow at noon. If by then you don't do what I bid you to do, the whole world shall know the origin of Robert Chiltern.

SIR ROBERT CHILTERN *strikes the bell. Enter* MASON.

SIR ROBERT CHILTERN: Show Mrs. Cheveley out.

MRS. CHEVELEY *starts; then bows with somewhat exaggerated politeness to* LADY CHILTERN, *who makes no sign of response. As she passes by* SIR ROBERT CHILTERN, *who is standing close to the door, she pauses for a moment and looks him straight in the face. She then goes out, followed by the servant, who closes the door after him. The husband and wife are left alone.* LADY CHILTERN *stands like some one in a dreadful dream. Then she turns round and looks at her husband. She looks at him with strange eyes, as though she was seeing him for the first time.*

LADY CHILTERN: You sold a Cabinet secret for money! You began your life with fraud! You built up your career on dishonour! Oh, tell me it is not true! Lie to me! Lie to me! Tell me it is not true.

SIR ROBERT CHILTERN: What this woman said is quite true. But, Gertrude, listen to me. You don't realise how I was tempted. Let me tell you the whole thing. (*Goes towards her.*)

LADY CHILTERN: Don't come near me. Don't touch me. I feel as if you had soiled me for ever. Oh! what a mask you have been wearing all these years! A horrible painted mask! You sold yourself for money. Oh! a common thief were better. You put yourself up to sale to the highest bidder! You were bought in the market. You lied to the whole world. And yet you will not lie to me.

SIR ROBERT CHILTERN (*rushing towards her*): Gertrude! Gertrude!

LADY CHILTERN (*thrusting him back with outstretched hands*): No, don't speak! Say nothing! Your voice wakes terrible memories—memories of things that made me love you—memories of words that made me love you—memories that now are horrible to me. And how I worshipped you! You were to me something apart from common life, a thing pure, noble, honest, without stain. The world seemed to me finer because you were in it, and goodness more real because you lived. And now—oh, when I think that I made of a man like you my ideal! the ideal of my life!

SIR ROBERT CHILTERN: There was your mistake. There was your error. The error all women commit. Why can't you women love us, faults and all? Why do you place us on monstrous pedestals? We have all feet of clay, women as well as men; but when we men love women, we love them knowing their weaknesses, their follies, their imperfections, love them all the more, it may be, for that reason. It is not the perfect, but the imperfect, who have need of love. It is when we are wounded by our own hands, or by the hands of others, that love should come to cure us—else what use is love at all? All sins, except a sin against itself, Love should forgive. All lives, save loveless lives, true Love should pardon. A man's love is like that. It is wider, larger, more human than a woman's. Women think that they are making ideals of men. What they are making of us are false idols merely. You made your false idol of me, and I had not the courage to come down, show you my wounds, tell you my weaknesses. I was afraid that I might lose your love, as I have lost it now. And so, last night you ruined my life for me —yes, ruined it! What this woman asked of me was nothing compared to what she offered to me. She offered security, peace, stability. The sin of my youth, that I had thought was buried, rose up in front of me, hideous, horrible, with its hands at my throat. I could have killed it for ever, sent it back into its tomb, destroyed its record, burned the one witness against me. You prevented me. No one but you, you know it. And now what is there before me but public disgrace, ruin, terrible shame, the mockery of the world, a lonely dishonoured life, a lonely dishonoured death, it may be, some day? Let women make no more ideals of men! let them not put them on altars and bow before them or they may ruin other lives as completely as you—you whom I have so wildly loved—have ruined mine!

He passes from the room. LADY CHILTERN *rushes towards him, but the door is closed when she reaches it. Pale with anguish, bewildered, helpless, she sways like a plant in the water. Her hands, outstretched, seem to tremble in the air like blossoms in the wind. Then she flings herself down beside a sofa and buries her face. Her sobs are like the sobs of a child.*

Act Drop

ACT THREE

♣

SCENE: *The Library in Lord Goring's house in Curzon Street, London. An Adam room. On the right is the door leading into the hall. On the left, the door of the smoking-room. A pair of folding doors at the back open into the drawing-room. The fire is lit. Phipps, the butler, is arranging some newspapers on the writing-table. The distinction of Phipps is his impassivity. He has been termed by enthusiasts the Ideal Butler. The Sphinx is not so incommunicable. He is a mask with a manner. Of his intellectual or emotional life, history knows nothing. He represents the dominance of form.*

Enter LORD GORING *in evening dress with a buttonhole. He is wearing a silk hat and Inverness cape. White-gloved, he carries a Louis Seize cane.*[1] *His are all the delicate fopperies of Fashion. One sees that he stands in immediate relation to modern life, makes it indeed, and so masters it. He is the first well-dressed philosopher in the history of thought.*

LORD GORING: Got my second buttonhole for me, Phipps?

PHIPPS: Yes, my lord. (*Takes his hat, cane, and cape, and presents new buttonhole on salver.*)

LORD GORING: Rather distinguished thing, Phipps. I am the only person of the smallest importance in London at present who wears a buttonhole.

PHIPPS: Yes, my lord. I have observed that.

LORD GORING (*taking out old buttonhole*): You see, Phipps, Fashion is what one wears oneself. What is unfashionable is what other people wear.

PHIPPS: Yes, my lord.

LORD GORING: Just as vulgarity is simply the conduct of other people.

PHIPPS: Yes, my lord.

LORD GORING (*putting in new buttonhole*): And falsehoods the truths of other people.

PHIPPS: Yes, my lord.

LORD GORING: Other people are quite dreadful. The only possible society is oneself.

PHIPPS: Yes, my lord.

LORD GORING: To love oneself is the beginning of a lifelong romance, Phipps.

PHIPPS: Yes, my lord.

LORD GORING (*looking at himself in the glass*): Don't think I quite like this buttonhole, Phipps. Makes me look a little too old. Makes me almost in the prime of life, eh, Phipps?

PHIPPS: I don't observe any alteration in your lordship's appearance.

LORD GORING: You don't, Phipps?

PHIPPS: No, my lord.

LORD GORING: I am not quite sure. For the future a more trivial buttonhole, Phipps, on Thursday evenings.

PHIPPS: I will speak to the florist, my lord. She has had a loss in her family lately, which perhaps accounts for the lack of triviality your lordship complains of in the button-hole.

LORD GORING: Extraordinary thing about the lower classes in England—they are always losing their relations.

PHIPPS: Yes, my lord! They are extremely fortunate in that respect.

LORD GORING (*turns round and looks at him.* PHIPPS *remains impassive*): Hum! Any letters, Phipps?

PHIPPS: Three, my lord. (*Hands letters on a salver.*)

LORD GORING (*takes letters*): Want my cab round in twenty minutes.

PHIPPS: Yes, my lord. (*Goes towards door.*)

LORD GORING (*holds up letter in pink envelope*): Ahem, Phipps, when did this letter arrive?

PHIPPS: It was brought by hand just after your lordship went to the club.

LORD GORING: That will do. (*Exit* PHIPPS.) Lady Chiltern's handwriting on Lady Chiltern's pink notepaper. That is rather curious. I thought Robert was to write. Wonder what Lady Chiltern has got to say to me? (*Sits at bureau and opens letter, and reads it.*) 'I want you. I trust you. I am coming to you. Gertrude.' (*Puts down the letter with a puzzled look. Then takes it up, and reads it again slowly.*) 'I want you. I trust you. I am coming to you.' She has found out everything! Poor woman! Poor woman! (*Pulls out watch and looks at it.*) But what an hour to call! Ten o'clock! I shall have to give up going to the Berkshires. However, it is always nice to be expected, and not to arrive. I am not expected at the Bachelors', so I shall certainly go there. Well, I will make her stand by her husband. That is the only thing for any woman to do. It is the growth of the moral sense of women that makes marriage such a hopeless, one-sided institution. Ten o'clock. She should be here soon. I must tell Phipps I am not in to any one else. (*Goes towards bell.*)

Enter PHIPPS.

PHIPPS: Lord Caversham.

LORD GORING: Oh, why will parents always appear at the wrong time? Some extraordinary mistake in nature, I suppose. (*Enter* LORD CAVERSHAM.) Delighted to see you, my dear father. (*Goes to meet him.*)

LORD CAVERSHAM: Take my cloak off.

LORD GORING: Is it worth while, father?

LORD CAVERSHAM: Of course it is worth while, sir. Which is the most comfortable chair?

LORD GORING: This one, father. It is the chair I use myself, when I have visitors.

LORD CAVERSHAM: Thank ye. No draught, I hope, in this room?

LORD GORING: No, father.

LORD CAVERSHAM (*sitting down*): Glad to hear it. Can't stand draughts. No draughts at home.

LORD GORING: Good many breezes, father.

LORD CAVERSHAM: Eh? Eh? Don't understand what you mean. Want to have a serious conversation with you, sir.

LORD GORING: My dear father! At this hour?

LORD CAVERSHAM: Well, sir, it is only ten o'clock. What is your objection to the hour? I think the hour is an admirable hour!

LORD GORING: Well, the fact is, father, this is not my day for talking seriously. I am very sorry, but it is not my day.

LORD CAVERSHAM: What do you mean, sir?

LORD GORING: During the Season, father, I only talk seriously on the first Tuesday in every month, from four to seven.

LORD CAVERSHAM: Well, make it Tuesday, sir, make it Tuesday.

LORD GORING: But it is after seven, father, and my doctor

says I must not have any serious conversation after seven. It makes me talk in my sleep.

LORD CAVERSHAM: Talk in your sleep, sir? What does that matter? You are not married.

LORD GORING: No, father, I am not married.

LORD CAVERSHAM: Hum! That is what I have come to talk to you about, sir. You have got to get married, and at once. Why, when I was your age, sir, I had been an inconsolable widower for three months, and was already paying my addresses to your admirable mother. Damme, sir, it is your duty to get married. You can't be always living for pleasure. Every man of position is married nowadays. Bachelors are not fashionable any more. They are a damaged lot. Too much is known about them. You must get a wife, sir. Look where your friend Robert Chiltern has got to by probity, hard work, and a sensible marriage with a good woman. Why don't you imitate him, sir? Why don't you take him for your model?

LORD GORING: I think I shall, father.

LORD CAVERSHAM: I wish you would, sir. Then I should be happy. At present I make your mother's life miserable on your account. You are heartless, sir, quite heartless.

LORD GORING: I hope not, father.

LORD CAVERSHAM: And it is high time for you to get married. You are thirty-four years of age, sir.

LORD GORING: Yes, father, but I only admit to thirty-two—thirty-one and a half when I have a really good buttonhole. This buttonhole is not . . . trivial enough.

LORD CAVERSHAM: I tell you, you are thirty-four, sir. And there is a draught in your room, besides, which makes your conduct worse. Why did you tell me there was no draught, sir? I feel a draught, sir, I feel it distinctly.

LORD GORING: So do I, father. It is a dreadful draught. I will come and see you to-morrow, father. We can talk over anything you like. Let me help you on with your cloak, father.

LORD CAVERSHAM: No, sir; I have called this evening for a definite purpose, and I am going to see it through at all costs to my health or yours. Put down my cloak, sir.

LORD GORING: Certainly, father. But let us go into another room. (*Rings bell.*) There is a dreadful draught here. (*Enter* PHIPPS.) Phipps, is there a good fire in the smoking-room?

PHIPPS: Yes, my lord.

LORD GORING: Come in there, father. Your sneezes are quite heartrending.

LORD CAVERSHAM: Well, sir, I suppose I have a right to sneeze when I choose?

LORD GORING (*apologetically*): Quite so, father. I was merely expressing sympathy.

LORD CAVERSHAM: Oh, damn sympathy. There is a great deal too much of that sort of thing going on nowadays.

LORD GORING: I quite agree with you, father. If there was less sympathy in the world there would be less trouble in the world.

LORD CAVERSHAM (*going towards the smoking-room*): That is a paradox, sir. I hate paradoxes.

LORD GORING: So do I, father. Everybody one meets is a paradox nowadays. It is a great bore. It makes society so obvious.

LORD CAVERSHAM (*turning round, and looking at his son beneath his bushy eyebrows*): Do you always really understand what you say, sir?

LORD GORING (*after some hesitation*): Yes, father, if I listen attentively.

LORD CAVERSHAM (*indignantly*): If you listen attentively! . . . Conceited young puppy!

Goes off grumbling into the smoking-room. PHIPPS *enters.*

LORD GORING: Phipps, there is a lady coming to see me this evening on particular business. Show her into the drawing-room when she arrives. You understand?

PHIPPS: Yes, my lord.

LORD GORING: It is a matter of the gravest importance, Phipps.

PHIPPS: I understand, my lord.

LORD GORING: No one else is to be admitted, under any circumstances.

PHIPPS: I understand, my lord. (*Bell rings.*)

LORD GORING: Ah! that is probably the lady. I shall see her myself.

Just as he is going towards the door LORD CAVERSHAM *enters from the smoking-room.*

LORD CAVERSHAM: Well, sir? am I to wait attendance on you?

LORD GORING (*considerably perplexed*): In a moment, father. Do excuse me. (LORD CAVERSHAM *goes back.*) Well, remember my instructions, Phipps—into that room.

PHIPPS: Yes, my lord.

LORD GORING goes into the smoking-room. HAROLD, *the footman, shows* MRS. CHEVELEY *in. Lamia-like,*[2] *she is in green and silver. She has a cloak of black satin, lined with dead rose-leaf silk.*

HAROLD: What name, madam?

MRS. CHEVELEY (*to* PHIPPS, *who advances towards her*): Is Lord Goring not here? I was told he was at home?

PHIPPS: His lordship is engaged at present with Lord Caversham, madam.

Turns a cold, glassy eye on HAROLD, *who at once retires.*

MRS. CHEVELEY *(to herself)*: How very filial!

PHIPPS: His lordship told me to ask you, madam, to be kind enough to wait in the drawing-room for him. His lordship will come to you there.

MRS. CHEVELEY *(with a look of surprise)*: Lord Goring expects me?

PHIPPS: Yes, madam.

MRS. CHEVELEY: Are you quite sure?

PHIPPS: His lordship told me that if a lady called I was to ask her to wait in the drawing-room. *(Goes to the door of the drawing-room and opens it.)* His lordship's directions on the subject were very precise.

MRS. CHEVELEY *(to herself)*: How thoughtful of him! To expect the unexpected shows a thoroughly modern intellect. *(Goes towards the drawing-room and looks in.)* Ugh! How dreary a bachelor's drawing-room always looks. I shall have to alter this. (PHIPPS *brings the lamp from the writing-table.)* No, I don't care for that lamp. It is far too glaring. Light some candles.

PHIPPS *(replaces lamp)*: Certainly, madam.

MRS. CHEVELEY: I hope the candles have very becoming shades.

PHIPPS: We have had no complaints about them, madam, as yet.

Passes into the drawing-room and begins to light the candles.

MRS. CHEVELEY *(to herself)*: I wonder what woman he is waiting for to-night. It will be delightful to catch him. Men always look so silly when they are caught. And they are always being caught. *(Looks about room and approaches the writing-table.)* What a very interesting room! What a very interesting picture! Wonder what his correspondence is like. *(Takes up letters.)* Oh, what a very uninteresting correspondence! Bills and cards, debts and dowagers! Who on earth writes to him on pink paper? How silly to write on pink paper! It looks like the beginning of a middle-class romance. Romance should never begin with sentiment. It should begin with science and end with a settlement. *(Puts letter down, then takes it up again.)* I know that handwriting. That is Gertrude Chiltern's. I remember it perfectly. The ten commandments in every stroke of the pen, and the moral law all over the page. Wonder what Gertrude is writing to him about? Something horrid about me, I suppose. How I detest that woman! *(Reads it.)* 'I trust you. I want you. I am coming to you. Gertrude.' 'I trust you. I want you. I am coming to you.'

A look of triumph comes over her face. She is just about to steal the letter, when PHIPPS *comes in.*

PHIPPS: The candles in the drawing-room are lit, madam, as you directed.

MRS. CHEVELEY: Thank you. *(Rises hastily and slips the letter under a large silver-cased blotting-book that is lying on the table.)*

PHIPPS: I trust the shades will be to your liking, madam. They are the most becoming we have. They are the same as his lordship uses himself when he is dressing for dinner.

MRS. CHEVELEY *(with a smile)*: Then I am sure they will be perfectly right.

PHIPPS *(gravely)*: Thank you, madam.

MRS. CHEVELEY *goes into the drawing-room.* PHIPPS *closes the door and retires. The door is then slowly opened, and* MRS. CHEVELEY *comes out and creeps stealthily towards the writing-table. Suddenly voices are heard from the smoking-room.* MRS. CHEVELEY *grows pale, and stops. The voices grow louder, and she goes back into the drawing-room, biting her lip.*

Enter LORD GORING *and* LORD CAVERSHAM.

LORD GORING *(expostulating)*: My dear father, if I am to get married, surely you will allow me to choose the time, place, and person? Particularly the person.

LORD CAVERSHAM *(testily)*: That is a matter for me, sir. You would probably make a very poor choice. It is I who should be consulted, not you. There is property at stake. It is not a matter for affection. Affection comes later on in married life.

LORD GORING: Yes. In married life affection comes when people thoroughly dislike each other, father, doesn't it? *(Puts on* LORD CAVERSHAM's *cloak for him.)*

LORD CAVERSHAM: Certainly, sir. I mean certainly not, sir. You are talking very foolishly to-night. What I say is that marriage is a matter for common sense.

LORD GORING: But women who have common sense are so curiously plain, father, aren't they? Of course I only speak from hearsay.

LORD CAVERSHAM: No woman, plain or pretty, has any common sense at all, sir. Common sense is the privilege of our sex.

LORD GORING: Quite so. And we men are so self-sacrificing that we never use it, do we, father?

LORD CAVERSHAM: I use it, sir. I use nothing else.

LORD GORING: So my mother tells me.

LORD CAVERSHAM: It is the secret of your mother's happiness. You are very heartless, sir, very heartless.

LORD GORING: I hope not, father.

Goes out for a moment. Then returns, looking rather put out, with SIR ROBERT CHILTERN.

SIR ROBERT CHILTERN: My dear Arthur, what a piece of good luck meeting you on the doorstep! Your servant had just told me you were not at home. How extraordinary!

LORD GORING: The fact is, I am horribly busy to-night, Robert, and I gave orders I was not at home to any one. Even my father had a comparatively cold reception. He complained of a draught the whole time.

SIR ROBERT CHILTERN: Ah! you must be at home to me, Arthur. You are my best friend. Perhaps by to-morrow you will be my only friend. My wife has discovered everything.

LORD GORING: Ah! I guessed as much!

SIR ROBERT CHILTERN (*looking at him*): Really! How!

LORD GORING (*after some hesitation*): Oh, merely by something in the expression of your face as you came in. Who told her?

SIR ROBERT CHILTERN: Mrs. Cheveley herself. And the woman I love knows that I began my career with an act of low dishonesty, that I built up my life upon sands of shame—that I sold, like a common huckster, the secret that had been intrusted to me as a man of honour. I thank heaven poor Lord Radley died without knowing that I betrayed him. I would to God I had died before I had been so horribly tempted, or had fallen so low. (*Burying his face in his hands.*)

LORD GORING (*after a pause*): You have heard nothing from Vienna yet, in answer to your wire?

SIR ROBERT CHILTERN (*looking up*): Yes; I got a telegram from the first secretary at eight o'clock to-night.

LORD GORING: Well?

SIR ROBERT CHILTERN: Nothing is absolutely known against her. On the contrary, she occupies a rather high position in society. It is a sort of open secret that Baron

Arnheim left her the greater portion of his immense fortune. Beyond that I can learn nothing.

LORD GORING: She doesn't turn out to be a spy, then?

SIR ROBERT CHILTERN: Oh! spies are of no use nowadays. Their profession is over. The newspapers do their work instead.

LORD GORING: And thunderingly well they do it.

SIR ROBERT CHILTERN: Arthur, I am parched with thirst. May I ring for something? Some hock and seltzer?[3]

LORD GORING: Certainly. Let me. (*Rings the bell.*)

SIR ROBERT CHILTERN: Thanks! I don't know what to do, Arthur, I don't know what to do, and you are my only friend. But what a friend you are—the one friend I can trust. I can trust you absolutely, can't I?

Enter PHIPPS.

LORD GORING: My dear Robert, of course. (*To* PHIPPS): Bring some hock and seltzer.

PHIPPS: Yes, my lord.

LORD GORING: And Phipps!

PHIPPS: Yes, my lord.

LORD GORING: Will you excuse me for a moment, Robert? I want to give some directions to my servant.

SIR ROBERT CHILTERN: Certainly.

LORD GORING: When that lady calls, tell her that I am not expected home this evening. Tell her that I have been suddenly called out of town. You understand?

PHIPPS: The lady is in that room, my lord. You told me to show her into that room, my lord.

LORD GORING: You did perfectly right. (*Exit* PHIPPS.) What a mess I am in. No; I think I shall get through it. I'll give her a lecture through the door. Awkward thing to manage, though.

SIR ROBERT CHILTERN: Arthur, tell me what I should do.

My life seems to have crumbled about me. I am a ship without a rudder in a night without a star.

LORD GORING: Robert, you love your wife, don't you?

SIR ROBERT CHILTERN: I love her more than anything in the world. I used to think ambition the great thing. It is not. Love is the great thing in the world. There is nothing but love, and I love her. But I am defamed in her eyes. I am ignoble in her eyes. There is a wide gulf between us now. She had found me out, Arthur, she has found me out.

LORD GORING: Has she never in her life done some folly— some indiscretion—that she should not forgive your sin?

SIR ROBERT CHILTERN: My wife! Never! She does not know what weakness or temptation is. I am of clay like other men. She stands apart as good women do—pitiless in her perfection—cold and stern and without mercy. But I love her, Arthur. We are childless, and I have no one else to love, no one else to love me. Perhaps if God had sent us children she might have been kinder to me. But God has given us a lonely house. And she has cut my heart in two. Don't let us talk of it. I was brutal to her this evening. But I suppose when sinners talk to saints they are brutal always. I said to her things that were hideously true, on my side, from my standpoint, from the standpoint of men. But don't let us talk of that.

LORD GORING: Your wife will forgive you. Perhaps at this moment she is forgiving you. She loves you, Robert. Why should she not forgive?

SIR ROBERT CHILTERN: God grant it! God grant it! (*Buries his face in his hands.*) But there is something more I have to tell you, Arthur.

Enter PHIPPS *with drinks.*

PHIPPS (*hands hock and seltzer to* SIR ROBERT CHILTERN): Hock and seltzer, sir.

SIR ROBERT CHILTERN: Thank you.

LORD GORING: Is your carriage here, Robert?

SIR ROBERT CHILTERN: No; I walked from the club.

LORD GORING: Sir Robert will take my cab, Phipps.

PHIPPS: Yes, my lord.

Exit.

LORD GORING: Robert, you don't mind my sending you away?

SIR ROBERT CHILTERN: Arthur, you must let me stay for five minutes. I have made up my mind what I am going to do to-night in the House. The debate on the Argentine Canal is to begin at eleven. *(A chair falls in the drawing-room.)* What is that!

LORD GORING: Nothing.

SIR ROBERT CHILTERN: I heard a chair fall in the next room. Some one has been listening.

LORD GORING: No, no; there is no one there.

SIR ROBERT CHILTERN: There is some one. There are lights in the room, and the door is ajar. Some one has been listening to every secret of my life. Arthur, what does this mean?

LORD GORING: Robert, you are excited, unnerved. I tell you there is no one in that room. Sit down, Robert.

SIR ROBERT CHILTERN: Do you give me your word that there is no one there?

LORD GORING: Yes.

SIR ROBERT CHILTERN: Your word of honour? *(Sits down.)*

LORD GORING: Yes.

SIR ROBERT CHILTERN *(rises)*: Arthur, let me see for myself.

LORD GORING: No, no.

SIR ROBERT CHILTERN: If there is no one there why should I not look in that room? Arthur, you must let me go into that room and satisfy myself. Let me know that no eavesdropper has heard my life's secret. Arthur, you don't realise what I am going through.

LORD GORING: Robert, this must stop. I have told you that there is no one in that room—that is enough.

SIR ROBERT CHILTERN (*rushes to the door of the room*): It is not enough. I insist on going into this room. You have told me there is no one there, so what reason can you have for refusing me?

LORD GORING: For God's sake, don't! There is some one there. Some one whom you must not see.

SIR ROBERT CHILTERN: Ah, I thought so!

LORD GORING: I forbid you to enter that room.

SIR ROBERT CHILTERN: Stand back. My life is at stake. And I don't care who is there. I will know who it is to whom I have told my secret and my shame. (*Enters room.*)

LORD GORING: Great heavens! his own wife!

SIR ROBERT CHILTERN *comes back, with a look of scorn and anger on his face.*

SIR ROBERT CHILTERN: What explanation have you to give for the presence of that woman here?

LORD GORING: Robert, I swear to you on my honour that that lady is stainless and guiltless of all offence towards you.

SIR ROBERT CHILTERN: She is vile, an infamous thing!

LORD GORING: Don't say that, Robert! It was for your sake she came here. It was to try and save you she came here. She loves you and no one else.

SIR ROBERT CHILTERN: You are mad. What have I to do with her intrigues with you? Let her remain your mistress! You are well suited to each other. She, corrupt and shameful—you, false as a friend, treacherous as an enemy even—

LORD GORING: It is not true, Robert. Before heaven, it is not true. In her presence and in yours I will explain all.

SIR ROBERT CHILTERN: Let me pass, sir. You have lied enough upon your word of honour.

SIR ROBERT CHILTERN *goes out.* LORD GORING *rushes to the door of the drawing-room, when* MRS. CHEVELEY *comes out, looking radiant and much amused.*

MRS. CHEVELEY *(with a mock curtsey)*: Good-evening, Lord Goring!

LORD GORING: Mrs. Cheveley! Great heavens . . . May I ask what were you doing in my drawing-room?

MRS. CHEVELEY: Merely listening. I have a perfect passion for listening through keyholes. One always hears such wonderful things through them.

LORD GORING: Doesn't that sound rather like tempting Providence?

MRS. CHEVELEY: Oh! surely Providence can resist temptation by this time. *(Makes a sign to him to take her cloak off, which he does.)*

LORD GORING: I am glad you have called. I am going to give you some good advice.

MRS. CHEVELEY: Oh! pray don't. One should never give a woman anything that she can't wear in the evening.

LORD GORING: I see you are quite as wilful as you used to be.

MRS. CHEVELEY: Far more! I have greatly improved. I have had more experience.

LORD GORING: Too much experience is a dangerous thing. Pray have a cigarette. Half the pretty women in London smoke cigarettes. Personally I prefer the other half.

MRS. CHEVELEY: Thanks. I never smoke. My dressmaker wouldn't like it, and a woman's first duty in life is to her dressmaker, isn't it? What the second duty is, no one has as yet discovered.

LORD GORING: You have come here to sell me Robert Chiltern's letter, haven't you?

MRS. CHEVELEY: To offer it to you on conditions! How did you guess that?

LORD GORING: Because you haven't mentioned the subject. Have you got it with you?

MRS. CHEVELEY (*sitting down*): Oh, no! A well-made dress has no pockets.

LORD GORING: What is your price for it?

MRS. CHEVELEY: How absurdly English you are! The English think that a cheque-book can solve every problem in life. Why, my dear Arthur, I have very much more money than you have, and quite as much as Robert Chiltern has got hold of. Money is not what I want.

LORD GORING: What do you want then, Mrs. Cheveley?

MRS. CHEVELEY: Why don't you call me Laura?

LORD GORING: I don't like the name.

MRS. CHEVELEY: You used to adore it.

LORD GORING: Yes; that's why. (MRS. CHEVELEY *motions to him to sit down beside her. He smiles, and does so.*)

MRS. CHEVELEY: Arthur, you loved me once.

LORD GORING: Yes.

MRS. CHEVELEY: And you asked me to be your wife.

LORD GORING: That was the natural result of my loving you.

MRS. CHEVELEY: And you threw me over because you saw, or said you saw, poor old Lord Mortlake trying to have a violent flirtation with me in the conservatory at Tenby.

LORD GORING: I am under the impression that my lawyer settled that matter with you on certain terms . . . dictated by yourself.

MRS. CHEVELEY: At that time I was poor; you were rich.

LORD GORING: Quite so. That is why you pretended to love me.

MRS. CHEVELEY (*shrugging her shoulders*): Poor old Lord Mortlake, who had only two topics of conversation, his gout and his wife! I never could quite make out which of the two he was talking about. He used the most horrible language about them both. Well, you were silly, Arthur. Why, Lord Mortlake was never anything more to me than an amusement. One of those utterly tedious amusements one only finds at an English country house on an English country Sunday. I don't think any one at all morally responsible for what he or she does at an English country house.

LORD GORING: Yes. I know lots of people think that.

MRS. CHEVELEY: I loved you, Arthur.

LORD GORING: My dear Mrs. Cheveley, you have always been far too clever to know anything about love.

MRS. CHEVELEY: I did love you. And you loved me. You know you loved me; and love is a very wonderful thing. I suppose that when a man has once loved a woman, he will do anything for her, except continue to love her? *(Puts her hand on his.)*

LORD GORING *(taking his hand away quietly)*: Yes; except that.

MRS. CHEVELEY *(after a pause)*: I am tired of living abroad. I want to come back to London. I want to have a charming house here. I want to have a salon. If one could only teach the English how to talk, and the Irish how to listen, society here would be quite civilised. Besides, I have arrived at the romantic stage. When I saw you last night at the Chilterns', I knew you were the only person I had ever cared for, if I ever have cared for anybody, Arthur. And so, on the morning of the day you marry me, I will give you Robert Chiltern's letter. That is my offer. I will give it to you now, if you promise to marry me.

LORD GORING: Now?

MRS. CHEVELEY *(smiling)*: To-morrow.

LORD GORING: Are you really serious?

MRS. CHEVELEY: Yes, quite serious.

LORD GORING: I should make you a very bad husband.

MRS. CHEVELEY: I don't mind bad husbands. I have had two. They amused me immensely.

LORD GORING: You mean that you amused yourself immensely, don't you?

MRS. CHEVELEY: What do you know about my married life?

LORD GORING: Nothing; but I can read it like a book.

MRS. CHEVELEY: What book?

LORD GORING (*rising*): The Book of Numbers.

MRS. CHEVELEY: Do you think it is quite charming of you to be so rude to a woman in your own house?

LORD GORING: In the case of very fascinating women, sex is a challenge, not a defence.

MRS. CHEVELEY: I suppose that is meant for a compliment. My dear Arthur, women are never disarmed by compliments. Men always are. That is the difference between the two sexes.

LORD GORING: Women are never disarmed by anything, as far as I know them.

MRS. CHEVELEY (*after a pause*): Then you are going to allow your greatest friend, Robert Chiltern, to be ruined, rather than marry some one who really has considerable attractions left. I thought you would have risen to some great height of self-sacrifice, Arthur. I think you should. And the rest of your life you could spend in contemplating your own perfections.

LORD GORING: Oh! I do that as it is. And self-sacrifice is a thing that should be put down by law. It is so demoralising to the people for whom one sacrifices oneself. They always go to the bad.

MRS. CHEVELEY: As if anything could demoralise Robert Chiltern! You seem to forget that I know his real character.

LORD GORING: What you know about him is not his real character. It was an act of folly done in his youth, dishonourable, I admit, shameful, I admit, unworthy of him, I admit, and therefore . . . not his true character.

MRS. CHEVELEY: How you men stand up for each other!

LORD GORING: How you women war against each other!

MRS. CHEVELEY (*bitterly*): I only war against one woman, against Gertrude Chiltern. I hate her. I hate her now more than ever.

LORD GORING: Because you have brought a real tragedy into her life, I suppose.

MRS. CHEVELEY (*with a sneer*): Oh, there is only one real tragedy in a woman's life. The fact that her past is always her lover, and her future invariably her husband.

LORD GORING: Lady Chiltern knows nothing of the kind of life to which you are alluding.

MRS. CHEVELEY: A woman whose size in gloves is seven and three-quarters never knows much about anything. You know Gertrude has always worn seven and three-quarters? That is one of the reasons why there was never any moral sympathy between us. . . . Well, Arthur, I suppose this romantic interview may be regarded as at an end. You admit it was romantic, don't you? For the privilege of being your wife I was ready to surrender a great prize, the climax of my diplomatic career. You decline. Very well. If Sir Robert doesn't uphold my Argentine scheme, I expose him. *Voila tout.*[4]

LORD GORING: You mustn't do that. It would be vile, horrible, infamous.

MRS. CHEVELEY (*shrugging her shoulders*): Oh, don't use big words. They mean so little. It is a commercial transaction. That is all. There is no good mixing up sentimentality in it. I offered to sell Robert Chiltern a certain thing. If he won't pay me my price, he will have to pay the world a greater price. There is no more to be said. I must go. Good-bye. Won't you shake hands?

LORD GORING: With you? No. Your transaction with Robert

Chiltern may pass as a loathsome commercial transaction of a loathsome commercial age; but you seem to have forgotten that you came here to-night to talk of love, you whose lips desecrated the word love, you to whom the thing is a book closely sealed, went this afternoon to the house of one of the most noble and gentle women in the world to degrade her husband in her eyes, to try and kill her love for him, to put poison in her heart, and bitterness in her life, to break her idol, and, it may be, spoil her soul. That I cannot forgive you. That was horrible. For that there can be no forgiveness.

MRS. CHEVELEY: Arthur, you are unjust to me. Believe me, you are quite unjust to me. I didn't go to taunt Gertrude at all. I had no idea of doing anything of the kind when I entered. I called with Lady Markby simply to ask whether an ornament, a jewel, that I lost somewhere last night, had been found at the Chilterns'. If you don't believe me, you can ask Lady Markby. She will tell you it is true. The scene that occurred happened after Lady Markby had left, and was really forced on me by Gertrude's rudeness and sneers. I called, oh!—a little out of malice if you like—but really to ask if a diamond brooch of mine had been found. That was the origin of the whole thing.

LORD GORING: A diamond snake-brooch with a ruby?

MRS. CHEVELEY: Yes. How do you know?

LORD GORING: Because it is found. In point of fact, I found it myself, and stupidly forgot to tell the butler anything about it as I was leaving. (*Goes over to the writing-table and pulls out the drawers.*) It is in this drawer. No, that one. This is the brooch, isn't it? (*Holds up the brooch.*)

MRS. CHEVELEY: Yes. I am so glad to get it back. It was . . . a present.

LORD GORING: Won't you wear it?

MRS. CHEVELEY: Certainly, if you pin it in. (LORD GORING

suddenly clasps it on her arm.) Why do you put it on as a bracelet? I never knew it could be worn as a bracelet.

LORD GORING: Really?

MRS. CHEVELEY (*holding out her handsome arm*): No; but it looks very well on me as a bracelet, doesn't it?

LORD GORING: Yes; much better than when I saw it last.

MRS. CHEVELEY: When did you see it last?

LORD GORING (*calmly*): Oh, ten years ago, on Lady Berkshire, from whom you stole it.

MRS. CHEVELEY (*starting*): What do you mean?

LORD GORING: I mean that you stole that ornament from my cousin, Mary Berkshire, to whom I gave it when she was married. Suspicion fell on a wretched servant, who was sent away in disgrace. I recognised it last night. I determined to say nothing about it till I had found the thief. I have found the thief now, and I have heard her own confession.

MRS. CHEVELEY (*tossing her head*): It is not true.

LORD GORING: You know it is true. Why, thief is written across your face at this moment.

MRS. CHEVELEY: I will deny the whole affair from beginning to end. I will say that I have never seen this wretched thing, that it was never in my possession.

MRS. CHEVELEY *tries to get the bracelet off her arm, but fails.* LORD GORING *looks on amused. Her thin fingers tear at the jewel to no purpose. A curse breaks from her.*

LORD GORING: The drawback of stealing a thing, Mrs. Cheveley, is that one never knows how wonderful the thing that one steals is. You can't get that bracelet off, unless you know where the spring is. And I see you don't know where the spring is. It is rather difficult to find.

MRS. CHEVELEY: You brute! You coward! (*She tries again to unclasp the bracelet, but fails.*)

LORD GORING: Oh! don't use big words. They mean so little.

MRS. CHEVELEY (*again tears at the bracelet in a paroxysm of rage, with inarticulate sounds. Then stops, and looks at* LORD GORING): What are you going to do?

LORD GORING: I am going to ring for my servant. He is an admirable servant. Always comes in the moment one rings for him. When he comes I will tell him to fetch the police.

MRS. CHEVELEY (*trembling*): The police? What for?

LORD GORING: To-morrow the Berkshires will prosecute you. That is what the police are for.

MRS. CHEVELEY (*is now in an agony of physical terror. Her face is distorted. Her mouth awry. A mask has fallen from her. She is, for the moment, dreadful to look at*): Don't do that. I will do anything you want. Anything in the world you want.

LORD GORING: Give me Robert Chiltern's letter.

MRS. CHEVELEY: Stop! Stop! Let me have time to think.

LORD GORING: Give me Robert Chiltern's letter.

MRS. CHEVELEY: I have not got it with me. I will give it to you to-morrow.

LORD GORING: You know you are lying. Give it to me at once. (MRS. CHEVELEY *pulls the letter out, and hands it to him. She is horribly pale.*) This is it?

MRS. CHEVELEY (*in a hoarse voice*): Yes.

LORD GORING (*takes the letter, examines it, sighs, and burns it over the lamp*): For so well-dressed a woman, Mrs. Cheveley, you have moments of admirable common sense. I congratulate you.

MRS. CHEVELEY (*catches sight of* LADY CHILTERN's *letter, the cover of which is just showing from under the blotting-book*): Please get me a glass of water.

LORD GORING: Certainly. (*Goes to the corner of the room and pours out a glass of water. While his back is turned*

MRS. CHEVELEY *steals* LADY CHILTERN's *letter. When* LORD GORING *returns with the glass she refuses it with a gesture.)*

MRS. CHEVELEY: Thank you. Will you help me on with my cloak?

LORD GORING: With pleasure. *(Puts her cloak on.)*

MRS. CHEVELEY: Thanks. I am never going to try to harm Robert Chiltern again.

LORD GORING: Fortunately you have not the chance, Mrs. Cheveley.

MRS. CHEVELEY: Well, if even I had the chance, I wouldn't. On the contrary, I am going to render him a great service.

LORD GORING: I am charmed to hear it. It is a reformation.

MRS. CHEVELEY: Yes. I can't bear so upright a gentleman, so honourable an English gentleman, being so shamefully deceived and so—

LORD GORING: Well?

MRS. CHEVELEY: I find that somehow Gertrude Chiltern's dying speech and confession has strayed into my pocket.

LORD GORING: What do you mean?

MRS. CHEVELEY *(with a bitter note of triumph in her voice)*: I mean that I am going to send Robert Chiltern the love-letter his wife wrote to you to-night.

LORD GORING: Love-letter?

MRS. CHEVELEY *(laughing)*: 'I want you. I trust you. I am coming to you. Gertrude.'

LORD GORING *rushes to the bureau and takes up the envelope, finds it empty, and turns round.*

LORD GORING: You wretched woman, must you always be thieving? Give me back that letter. I'll take it from you by force. You shall not leave my room till I have got it.

He rushes towards her, but MRS. CHEVELEY *at once puts her hand on the electric bell that is on the table. The bell sounds with shrill reverberations, and* PHIPPS *enters.*

MRS. CHEVELEY (*after a pause*): Lord Goring merely rang that you should show me out. Good-night, Lord Goring!

Goes out followed by PHIPPS. *Her face is illumined with evil triumph. There is joy in her eyes. Youth seems to have come back to her. Her last glance is like a swift arrow.* LORD GORING *bites his lip, and lights a cigarette.*

Act Drop

Act Four

SCENE: *Same as Act Two.*

LORD GORING *is standing by the fireplace with his hands in his pockets. He is looking rather bored.*

LORD GORING (*pulls out his watch, inspects it, and rings the bell*): It is a great nuisance. I can't find any one in this house to talk to. And I am full of interesting information. I feel like the latest edition of something or other.

Enter servant.

JAMES: Sir Robert is still at the Foreign Office, my lord.
LORD GORING: Lady Chiltern not down yet?
JAMES: Her ladyship has not yet left her room. Miss Chiltern has just come in from riding.
LORD GORING (*to himself*): Ah! that is something.
JAMES: Lord Caversham has been waiting some time in the library for Sir Robert. I told him your lordship was here.
LORD GORING: Thank you. Would you kindly tell him I've gone?

JAMES *(bowing)*: I shall do so, my lord.

Exit servant.

LORD GORING: Really, I don't want to meet my father three days running. It is a great deal too much excitement for any son. I hope to goodness he won't come up. Fathers should be neither seen nor heard. That is the only proper basis for family life. Mothers are different. Mothers are darlings. *(Throws himself down into a chair, picks up a paper and begins to read it.)*

Enter LORD CAVERSHAM.

LORD CAVERSHAM: Well, sir, what are you doing here? Wasting your time as usual, I suppose?

LORD GORING *(throws down paper and rises)*: My dear father, when one pays a visit it is for the purpose of wasting other people's time, not one's own.

LORD CAVERSHAM: Have you been thinking over what I spoke to you about last night?

LORD GORING: I have been thinking about nothing else.

LORD CAVERSHAM: Engaged to be married yet?

LORD GORING *(genially)*: Not yet; but I hope to be before lunch-tune.

LORD CAVERSHAM *(caustically)*: You can have till dinner-time if it would be of any convenience to you.

LORD GORING: Thanks awfully, but I think I'd sooner be engaged before lunch.

LORD CAVERSHAM: Humph! Never know when you are serious or not.

LORD GORING: Neither do I, father.

A pause.

LORD CAVERSHAM: I suppose you have read *The Times* this morning?

LORD GORING *(airily)*: *The Times?* Certainly not. I only

read *The Morning Post.* All that one should know about modern life is where the Duchesses are; anything else is quite demoralising.

LORD CAVERSHAM: Do you mean to say you have not read *The Times* leading article on Robert Chiltern's career?

LORD GORING: Good heavens! No. What does it say?

LORD CAVERSHAM: What should it say, sir? Everything complimentary, of course. Chiltern's speech last night on this Argentine Canal scheme was one of the finest pieces of oratory ever delivered in the House since Canning.[1]

LORD GORING: Ah! Never heard of Canning. Never wanted to. And did . . . did Chiltern uphold the scheme?

LORD CAVERSHAM: Uphold it, sir? How little you know him! Why, he denounced it roundly, and the whole system of modern political finance. This speech is the turning-point in his career, as *The Times* points out. You should read this article, sir. (*Opens* The Times.) 'Sir Robert Chiltern . . . most rising of our young statesmen . . . Brilliant orator. . . . Unblemished career. . . . Well-known integrity of character. . . . Represents what is best in English public life. . . . Noble contrast to the lax morality so common among foreign politicians.' They will never say that of you, sir.

LORD GORING: I sincerely hope not, father. However, I am delighted at what you tell me about Robert, thoroughly delighted. It shows he has got pluck.

LORD CAVERSHAM: He has got more than pluck, sir, he has got genius.

LORD GORING: Ah! I prefer pluck. It is not so common, nowadays, as genius is.

LORD CAVERSHAM: I wish you would go into Parliament.

LORD GORING: My dear father, only people who look dull ever get into the House of Commons, and only people who are dull ever succeed there.

LORD CAVERSHAM: Why don't you try to do something useful in life?

LORD GORING: I am far too young.

LORD CAVERSHAM (*testily*): I hate this affectation of youth, sir. It is a great deal too prevalent nowadays.

LORD GORING: Youth isn't an affectation. Youth is an art.

LORD CAVERSHAM: Why don't you propose to that pretty Miss Chiltern?

LORD GORING: I am of a very nervous disposition, especially in the morning.

LORD CAVERSHAM: I don't suppose there is the smallest chance of her accepting you.

LORD GORING: I don't know how the betting stands to-day.

LORD CAVERSHAM: If she did accept you she would be the prettiest fool in England.

LORD GORING: That is just what I should like to marry. A thoroughly sensible wife would reduce me to a condition of absolute idiocy in less than six months.

LORD CAVERSHAM: You don't deserve her, sir.

LORD GORING: My dear father, if we men married the women we deserved, we should have a very bad time of it.

Enter MABEL CHILTERN.

MABEL CHILTERN: Oh! . . . How do you do, Lord Caversham? I hope Lady Caversham is quite well?

LORD CAVERSHAM: Lady Caversham is as usual, as usual.

LORD GORING: Good-morning, Miss Mabel!

MABEL CHILTERN (*taking no notice at all of* LORD GORING, *and addressing herself exclusively to* LORD CAVERSHAM): And Lady Caversham's bonnets . . . are they at all better?

LORD CAVERSHAM: They have had a serious relapse, I am sorry to say.

LORD GORING: Good-morning, Miss Mabel.

MABEL CHILTERN (*to* LORD CAVERSHAM): I hope an operation will not be necessary.

LORD CAVERSHAM (*smiling at her pertness*): If it is, we shall have to give Lady Caversham a narcotic. Otherwise she would never consent to have a feather touched.

LORD GORING (*with increased emphasis*): Good-morning, Miss Mabel!

MABEL CHILTERN (*turning round with feigned surprise*): Oh, are you here? Of course you understand that after your breaking your appointment I am never going to speak to you again.

LORD GORING: Oh, please don't say such a thing. You are the one person in London I really like to have to listen to me.

MABEL CHILTERN: Lord Goring, I never believe a single word that either you or I say to each other.

LORD CAVERSHAM: You are quite right, my dear, quite right as far as he is concerned, I mean.

MABEL CHILTERN: Do you think you could possibly make your son behave a little better occasionally? Just as a change.

LORD CAVERSHAM: I regret to say, Miss Chiltern, that I have no influence at all over my son. I wish I had. If I had, I know what I would make him do.

MABEL CHILTERN: I am afraid that he has one of those terribly weak natures that are not susceptible to influence.

LORD CAVERSHAM: He is very heartless, very heartless.

LORD GORING: It seems to me that I am a little in the way here.

MABEL CHILTERN: It is very good for you to be in the way, and to know what people say of you behind your back.

LORD GORING: I don't at all like knowing what people say of me behind my back. It makes me far too conceited.

LORD CAVERSHAM: After that, my dear, I really must bid you good-morning.

MABEL CHILTERN: Oh! I hope you are not going to leave me all alone with Lord Goring? Especially at such an early hour in the day.

LORD CAVERSHAM: I am afraid I can't take him with me to Downing Street. It is not the Prime Minister's day for seeing the unemployed.

Shakes hands with MABEL CHILTERN, *takes up his hat and stick, and goes out, with a parting glare of indignation at* LORD GORING.

MABEL CHILTERN (*takes up roses and begins to arrange them in a bowl on the table*): People who don't keep their appointments in the Park are horrid.

LORD GORING: Detestable.

MABEL CHILTERN: I am glad you admit it. But I wish you wouldn't look so pleased about it.

LORD GORING: I can't help it. I always look pleased when I am with you.

MABEL CHILTERN (*sadly*): Then I suppose it is my duty to remain with you?

LORD GORING: Of course it is.

MABEL CHILTERN: Well, my duty is a thing I never do, on principle. It always depresses me. So I am afraid I must leave you.

LORD GORING: Please don't, Miss Mabel. I have something very particular to say to you.

MABEL CHILTERN (*rapturously*): Oh! is it a proposal?

LORD GORING (*somewhat taken aback*): Well, yes, it is—I am bound to say it is.

MABEL CHILTERN (*with a sigh of pleasure*): I am so glad. That makes the second to-day.

LORD GORING (*indignantly*): The second to-day? What conceited ass has been impertinent enough to dare to propose to you before I had proposed to you?

MABEL CHILTERN: Tommy Trafford, of course. It is one of

Tommy's days for proposing. He always proposes on
Tuesdays and Thursdays, during the Season.

LORD GORING: You didn't accept him, I hope?

MABEL CHILTERN: I make it a rule never to accept Tommy.
That is why he goes on proposing. Of course, as you
didn't turn up this morning, I very nearly said yes. It
would have been an excellent lesson both for him and for
you if I had. It would have taught you both better manners.

LORD GORING: Oh! bother Tommy Trafford. Tommy is a
silly little ass. I love you.

MABEL CHILTERN: I know. And I think you might have
mentioned it before. I am sure I have given you heaps of
opportunities.

LORD GORING: Mabel, do be serious. Please be serious.

MABEL CHILTERN: Ah! that is the sort of thing a man always
says to a girl before he has been married to her. He never
says it afterwards.

LORD GORING (*taking hold of her hand*): Mabel, I have told
you that I love you. Can't you love me a little in return?

MABEL CHILTERN: You silly Arthur! If you knew anything
about . . . anything, which you don't, you would know
that I adore you. Every one in London knows it except
you. It is a public scandal the way I adore you. I have
been going about for the last six months telling the whole
of society that I adore you. I wonder you consent to have
anything to say to me. I have no character left at all. At
least, I feel so happy that I am quite sure I have no character left at all.

LORD GORING (*catches her in his arms and kisses her. Then
there is a pause of bliss*): Dear! Do you know I was awfully afraid of being refused!

MABEL CHILTERN (*looking up at him*): But you never have
been refused yet by anybody, have you, Arthur? I can't
imagine any one refusing you.

LORD GORING (*after kissing her again*): Of course I'm not nearly good enough for you, Mabel.

MABEL CHILTERN (*nestling close to him*): I am so glad, darling. I was afraid you were.

LORD GORING (*after some hesitation*): And I'm . . . I'm a little over thirty.

MABEL CHILTERN: Dear, you look weeks younger than that.

LORD GORING (*enthusiastically*): How sweet of you to say so! . . . And it is only fair to tell you frankly that I am fearfully extravagant.

MABEL CHILTERN: But so am I, Arthur. So we're sure to agree. And now I must go and see Gertrude.

LORD GORING: Must you really? (*Kisses her.*)

MABEL CHILTERN: Yes.

LORD GORING: Then do tell her I want to talk to her particularly. I have been waiting here all the morning to see either her or Robert.

MABEL CHILTERN: Do you mean to say you didn't come here expressly to propose to me?

LORD GORING (*triumphantly*): No; that was a flash of genius.

MABEL CHILTERN: Your first.

LORD GORING (*with determination*): My last.

MABEL CHILTERN: I am delighted to hear it. Now don't stir. I'll be back in five minutes. And don't fall into any temptations while I am away.

LORD GORING: Dear Mabel, while you are away, there are none. It makes me horribly dependent on you.

Enter LADY CHILTERN.

LADY CHILTERN: Good-morning, dear! How pretty you are looking!

MABEL CHILTERN: How pale you are looking, Gertrude! It is most becoming!

LADY CHILTERN: Good-morning, Lord Goring!

LORD GORING (*bowing*): Good-morning, Lady Chiltern!

MABEL CHILTERN (*aside to* LORD GORING): I shall be in the conservatory, under the second palm tree on the left.

LORD GORING: Second on the left?

MABEL CHILTERN (*with a look of mock surprise*): Yes; the usual palm tree.

Blows a kiss to him, unobserved by LADY CHILTERN, *and goes out.*

LORD GORING: Lady Chiltern, I have a certain amount of very good news to tell you. Mrs. Cheveley gave me up Robert's letter last night, and I burned it. Robert is safe.

LADY CHILTERN (*sinking on the sofa*): Safe! Oh! I am so glad of that. What a good friend you are to him—to us!

LORD GORING: There is only one person now that could be said to be in any danger.

LADY CHILTERN: Who is that?

LORD GORING (*sitting down beside her*): Yourself.

LADY CHILTERN: I! In danger? What do you mean?

LORD GORING: Danger is too great a word. It is a word I should not have used. But I admit I have something to tell you that may distress you, that terribly distresses me. Yesterday evening you wrote me a very beautiful, womanly letter, asking me for my help. You wrote to me as one of your oldest friends, one of your husband's oldest friends. Mrs. Cheveley stole that letter from my rooms.

LADY CHILTERN: Well, what use is it to her? Why should she not have it?

LORD GORING (*rising*): Lady Chiltern, I will be quite frank with you. Mrs. Cheveley puts a certain construction on that letter and proposes to send it to your husband.

LADY CHILTERN: But what construction could she put on it? . . . Oh! not that! not that! If I in—in trouble, and wanting your help, trusting you, propose to come to you . . . that you may advise me . . . assist me. . . . Oh!

are there women so horrible as that . . . ? And she proposes to send it to my husband? Tell me what happened. Tell me all that happened.

LORD GORING: Mrs. Cheveley was concealed in a room adjoining my library, without my knowledge. I thought that the person who was waiting in that room to see me was yourself. Robert came in unexpectedly. A chair or something fell in the room. He forced his way in, and he discovered her. We had a terrible scene. I still thought it was you. He left me in anger. At the end of everything Mrs. Cheveley got possession of your letter—she stole it, when or how, I don't know.

LADY CHILTERN: At what hour did this happen?

LORD GORING: At half-past ten. And now I propose that we tell Robert the whole thing at once.

LADY CHILTERN (*looking at him with amazement that is almost terror*): You want me to tell Robert that the woman you expected was not Mrs. Cheveley, but myself? That it was I whom you thought was concealed in a room in your house, at half-past ten o'clock at night? You want me to tell him that?

LORD GORING: I think it is better that he should know the exact truth.

LADY CHILTERN (*rising*): Oh, I couldn't, I couldn't!

LORD GORING: May I do it?

LADY CHILTERN: No.

LORD GORING (*gravely*): You are wrong, Lady Chiltern.

LADY CHILTERN: No. The letter must be intercepted. That is all. But how can I do it? Letters arrive for him every moment of the day. His secretaries open them and hand them to him. I dare not ask the servants to bring me his letters. It would be impossible. Oh! why don't you tell me what to do?

LORD GORING: Pray be calm, Lady Chiltern, and answer

the questions I am going to put to you. You said his secretaries open his letters.

LADY CHILTERN: Yes.

LORD GORING: Who is with him to-day? Mr. Trafford,
isn't it?

LADY CHILTERN: No, Mr. Montford, I think.

LORD GORING: You can trust him?

LADY CHILTERN (*with a gesture of despair*): Oh! how do I
know?

LORD GORING: He would do what you asked him,
wouldn't he?

LADY CHILTERN: I think so.

LORD GORING: Your letter was on pink paper. He could
recognise it without reading it, couldn't he? By the
colour?

LADY CHILTERN: I suppose so.

LORD GORING: Is he in the house now?

LADY CHILTERN: Yes.

LORD GORING: Then I will go and see him myself, and tell
him that a certain letter, written on pink paper, is to be
forwarded to Robert to-day, and that at all costs it must
not reach him. (*Goes to the door, and opens it.*) Oh!
Robert is coming upstairs with the letter in his hand. It
has reached him already.

LADY CHILTERN (*with a cry of pain*): Oh! you have saved
his life; what have you done with mine?

Enter SIR ROBERT CHILTERN. *He has the letter in his
hand, and is reading it. He comes towards his wife, not
noticing* LORD GORING'*s presence.*

SIR ROBERT CHILTERN: 'I want you. I trust you. I am coming to you. Gertrude.' Oh, my love! Is this true? Do you
indeed trust me, and want me? If so, it was for me to
come to you, not for you to write of coming to me. This

letter of yours, Gertrude, makes me feel that nothing that the world may do can hurt me now. You want me, Gertrude.

LORD GORING, *unseen by* SIR ROBERT CHILTERN, *makes an imploring sign to* LADY CHILTERN *to accept the situation and* SIR ROBERT's *error.*

LADY CHILTERN: Yes.

SIR ROBERT CHILTERN: You trust me, Gertrude?

LADY CHILTERN: Yes.

SIR ROBERT CHILTERN: Ah! why did you not add you loved me?

LADY CHILTERN (*taking his hand*): Because I loved you.

LORD GORING *passes into the conservatory.*

SIR ROBERT CHILTERN (*kisses her*): Gertrude, you don't know what I feel. When Montford passed me your letter across the table—he had opened it by mistake, I suppose, without looking at the hand-writing on the envelope and I read it—oh! I did not care what disgrace or punishment was in store for me, I only thought you loved me still.

LADY CHILTERN: There is no disgrace in store for you, nor any public shame. Mrs. Cheveley has handed over to Lord Goring the document that was in her possession, and he has destroyed it.

SIR ROBERT CHILTERN: Are you sure of this, Gertrude?

LADY CHILTERN: Yes; Lord Goring has just told me.

SIR ROBERT CHILTERN: Then I am safe! Oh! what a wonderful thing to be safe! For two days I have been in terror. I am safe now. How did Arthur destroy my letter? Tell me.

LADY CHILTERN: He burned it.

SIR ROBERT CHILTERN: I wish I had seen that one sin of my youth burning to ashes. How many men there are in modern life who would like to see their past burning to white ashes before them! Is Arthur still here?

LADY CHILTERN: Yes; he is in the conservatory.

SIR ROBERT CHILTERN: I am so glad now I made that speech last night in the House, so glad. I made it thinking that public disgrace might be the result. But it has not been so.

LADY CHILTERN: Public honour has been the result.

SIR ROBERT CHILTERN: I think so. I fear so, almost. For although I am safe from detection, although every proof against me is destroyed, I suppose, Gertrude . . . I suppose I should retire from public life? *(He looks anxiously at his wife.)*

LADY CHILTERN *(eagerly)*: Oh yes, Robert, you should do that. It is your duty to do that.

SIR ROBERT CHILTERN: It is much to surrender.

LADY CHILTERN: No; it will be much to gain.

SIR ROBERT CHILTERN *walks up and down the room with a troubled expression. Then comes over to his wife, and puts his hand on her shoulder.*

SIR ROBERT CHILTERN: And you would be happy living somewhere alone with me, abroad perhaps, or in the country away from London, away from public life? You would have no regrets?

LADY CHILTERN: Oh! none, Robert.

SIR ROBERT CHILTERN *(sadly)*: And your ambition for me? You used to be ambitious for me.

LADY CHILTERN: Oh, my ambition! I have none now, but that we two may love each other. It was your ambition that led you astray. Let us not talk about ambition.

LORD GORING *returns from the conservatory, looking very pleased with himself, and with an entirely new buttonhole that some one has made for him.*

SIR ROBERT CHILTERN (*going towards him*): Arthur, I have to thank you for what you have done for me. I don't know how I can repay you. (*Shakes hands with him.*)

LORD GORING: My dear fellow, I'll tell you at once. At the present moment, under the usual palm tree . . . I mean in the conservatory . . .

Enter MASON.

MASON: Lord Caversham.

LORD GORING: That admirable father of mine really makes a habit of turning up at the wrong moment. It is very heartless of him, very heartless indeed.

Enter LORD CAVERSHAM. MASON *goes out.*

LORD CAVERSHAM: Good-morning, Lady Chiltern! Warmest congratulations to you, Chiltern, on your brilliant speech last night. I have just left the Prime Minister, and you are to have the vacant seat in the Cabinet.

SIR ROBERT CHILTERN (*with a look of joy and triumph*): A seat in the Cabinet?

LORD CAVERSHAM: Yes; here is the Prime Minister's letter. (*Hands letter.*)

SIR ROBERT CHILTERN (*takes letter and reads it*): A seat in the Cabinet!

LORD CAVERSHAM: Certainly, and you well deserve it too. You have got what we want so much in political life nowadays—high character, high moral tone, high principles. (*To* LORD GORING): Everything that you have not got, sir, and never will have.

LORD GORING: I don't like principles, father. I prefer prejudices.

SIR ROBERT CHILTERN *is on the brink of accepting the Prime Minister's offer, when he sees his wife looking at him with her clear, candid eyes. He then realises that it is impossible.*

SIR ROBERT CHILTERN: I cannot accept this offer, Lord Caversham. I have made up my mind to decline it.

LORD CAVERSHAM: Decline it, sir?

SIR ROBERT CHILTERN: My intention is to retire at once from public life.

LORD CAVERSHAM (*angrily*): Decline a seat in the Cabinet, and retire from public life? Never heard such damned nonsense in the whole course of my existence. I beg your pardon, Lady Chiltern. Chiltern, I beg your pardon. (*To* LORD GORING): Don't grin like that, sir.

LORD GORING: No, father.

LORD CAVERSHAM: Lady Chiltern, you are a sensible woman, the most sensible woman in London, the most sensible woman I know. Will you kindly prevent your husband from making such a . . . from talking such. . . . Will you kindly do that, Lady Chiltern?

LADY CHILTERN: I think my husband is right in his determination, Lord Caversham. I approve of it.

LORD CAVERSHAM: You approve of it? Good heavens!

LADY CHILTERN (*taking her husband's hand*): I admire him for it. I admire him immensely for it. I have never admired him so much before. He is finer than even I thought him. (*To* SIR ROBERT CHILTERN): You will go and write your letter to the Prime Minister now, won't you? Don't hesitate about it, Robert.

SIR ROBERT CHILTERN (*with a touch of bitterness*): I suppose I had better write it at once. Such offers are not repeated. I will ask you to excuse me for a moment, Lord Caversham.

LADY CHILTERN: I may come with you, Robert, may I not?

SIR ROBERT CHILTERN: Yes, Gertrude.

LADY CHILTERN *goes with him.*

LORD CAVERSHAM: What is the matter with this family? Something wrong here, eh? (*Tapping his forehead.*)

Idiocy? Hereditary, I suppose. Both of them, too. Wife as well as husband. Very sad. Very sad indeed! And they are not an old family. Can't understand it.

LORD GORING: It is not idiocy, father, I assure you.

LORD CAVERSHAM: What is it then, sir?

LORD GORING (*after some hesitation*): Well, it is what is called nowadays a high moral tone, father. That is all.

LORD CAVERSHAM: Hate these new-fangled names. Same thing as we used to call idiocy fifty years ago. Shan't stay in this house any longer.

LORD GORING (*taking his arm*): Oh! just go in there for a moment, father. Third palm tree to the left, the usual palm tree.

LORD CAVERSHAM: What, sir?

LORD GORING: I beg your pardon, father, I forgot. The conservatory, father, the conservatory—there is some one there I want you to talk to.

LORD CAVERSHAM: What about, sir?

LORD GORING: About me, father.

LORD CAVERSHAM (*grimly*): Not a subject on which much eloquence is possible.

LORD GORING: No, father; but the lady is like me. She doesn't care much for eloquence in others. She thinks it a little loud.

LORD CAVERSHAM *goes into the conservatory.* LADY CHILTERN *enters.*

LORD GORING: Lady Chiltern, why are you playing Mrs. Cheveley's cards?

LADY CHILTERN (*startled*): I don't understand you.

LORD GORING: Mrs. Cheveley made an attempt to ruin your husband. Either to drive him from public life, or to make him adopt a dishonourable position. From the latter tragedy you saved him. The former you are now

thrusting on him. Why should you do him the wrong
Mrs. Cheveley tried to do and failed?

LADY CHILTERN: Lord Goring?

LORD GORING (*pulling himself together for a great effort,
and showing the philosopher that underlies the dandy*):
Lady Chiltern, allow me. You wrote me a letter last night
in which you said you trusted me and wanted my help.
Now is the moment when you really want my help, now
is the time when you have got to trust me, to trust in my
counsel and judgment. You love Robert. Do you want to
kill his love for you? What sort of existence will he have if
you rob him of the fruits of his ambition, if you take him
from the splendour of a great political career, if you close
the doors of public life against him, if you condemn him
to sterile failure, he who was made for triumph and success? Women are not meant to judge us, but to forgive us
when we need forgiveness. Pardon, not punishment, is
their mission. Why should you scourge him with rods for
a sin done in his youth, before he knew you, before he
knew himself? A man's life is of more value than a
woman's. It has larger issues, wider scope, greater ambitions. A woman's life revolves in curves of emotions. It is
upon lines of intellect that a man's life progresses. Don't
make any terrible mistake, Lady Chiltern. A woman who
can keep a man's love, and love him in return, has done
all the world wants of women, or should want of them.

LADY CHILTERN (*troubled and hesitating*): But it is my husband himself who wishes to retire from public life. He
feels it is his duty. It was he who first said so.

LORD GORING: Rather than lose your love, Robert would do
anything, wreck his whole career, as he is on the brink of
doing now. He is making for you a terrible sacrifice. Take
my advice, Lady Chiltern, and do not accept a sacrifice
so great. If you do, you will live to repent it bitterly. We

men and women are not made to accept such sacrifices from each other. We are not worthy of them. Besides, Robert has been punished enough.

LADY CHILTERN: We have both been punished. I set him up too high.

LORD GORING *(with deep feeling in his voice)*: Do not for that reason set him down now too low. If he has fallen from his altar, do not thrust him into the mire. Failure to Robert would be the very mire of shame. Power is his passion. He would lose everything, even his power to feel love. Your husband's life is at this moment in your hands, your husband's love is in your hands. Don't mar both for him.

Enter SIR ROBERT CHILTERN.

SIR ROBERT CHILTERN: Gertrude, here is the draft of my letter. Shall I read it to you?

LADY CHILTERN: Let me see it.

SIR ROBERT *hands her the letter. She reads it, and then, with a gesture of passion, tears it up.*

SIR ROBERT CHILTERN: What are you doing?

LADY CHILTERN: A man's life is of more value than a woman's. It has larger issues, wider scope, greater ambitions. Our lives revolve in curves of emotions. It is upon lines of intellect that a man's life progresses. I have just learnt this, and much else with it, from Lord Goring. And I will not spoil your life for you, nor see you spoil it as a sacrifice to me, a useless sacrifice!

SIR ROBERT CHILTERN: Gertrude! Gertrude!

LADY CHILTERN: You can forget. Men easily forget. And I forgive. That is how women help the world. I see that now.

SIR ROBERT CHILTERN *(deeply overcome by emotion, em*

braces her): My wife! my wife! (*To* LORD GORING):
Arthur, it seems that I am always to be in your debt.

LORD GORING: Oh dear no, Robert. Your debt is to Lady
Chiltern, not to me!

SIR ROBERT CHILTERN: I owe you much. And now tell me
what you were going to ask me just now as Lord Caversham came in.

LORD GORING: Robert, you are your sister's guardian, and I
want your consent to my marriage with her. That is all.

LADY CHILTERN: Oh, I am so glad! I am so glad! (*Shakes
hands with* LORD GORING.)

LORD GORING: Thank you, Lady Chiltern.

SIR ROBERT CHILTERN (*with a troubled look*): My sister to
be your wife?

LORD GORING: Yes.

SIR ROBERT CHILTERN (*speaking with great firmness*):
Arthur, I am very sorry, but the thing is quite out of the
question. I have to think of Mabel's future happiness.
And I don't think her happiness would be safe in your
hands. And I cannot have her sacrificed!

LORD GORING: Sacrificed!

SIR ROBERT CHILTERN: Yes, utterly sacrificed. Loveless
marriages are horrible. But there is one thing worse than
an absolutely loveless marriage. A marriage in which
there is love, but on one side only; faith, but on one side
only; devotion, but on one side only and in which of the
two hearts one is sure to be broken.

LORD GORING: But I love Mabel. No other woman has any
place in my life.

LADY CHILTERN: Robert, if they love each other, why
should they not be married?

SIR ROBERT CHILTERN: Arthur cannot bring Mabel the
love that she deserves.

LORD GORING: What reason have you for saying that?

SIR ROBERT CHILTERN (*after a pause*): Do you really require me to tell you?

LORD GORING: Certainly I do.

SIR ROBERT CHILTERN: As you choose. When I called on you yesterday evening I found Mrs. Cheveley concealed in your rooms. It was between ten and eleven o'clock at night. I do not wish to say anything more. Your relations with Mrs. Cheveley have, as I said to you last night, nothing whatsoever to do with me. I know you were engaged to be married to her once. The fascination she exercised over you then seems to have returned. You spoke to me last night of her as of a woman pure and stainless, a woman whom you respected and honoured. That may be so. But I cannot give my sister's life into your hands. It would be wrong of me. It would be unjust, infamously unjust to her.

LORD GORING: I have nothing more to say.

LADY CHILTERN: Robert, it was not Mrs. Cheveley whom Lord Goring expected last night.

SIR ROBERT CHILTERN: Not Mrs. Cheveley! Who was it then?

LORD GORING: Lady Chiltern.

LADY CHILTERN: It was your own wife. Robert, yesterday afternoon Lord Goring told me that if ever I was in trouble I could come to him for help, as he was our oldest and best friend. Later on, after that terrible scene in this room, I wrote to him telling him that I trusted him, that I had need of him, that I was coming to him for help and advice. (SIR ROBERT CHILTERN *takes the letter out of his pocket.*) Yes, that letter. I didn't go to Lord Goring's, after all. I felt that it is from ourselves alone that help can come. Pride made me think that. Mrs. Cheveley went. She stole my letter and sent it anonymously to you this morning, that you should think. . . . Oh! Robert, I cannot tell you what she wished you to think. . . .

SIR ROBERT CHILTERN: What! Had I fallen so low in your eyes that you thought that even for a moment I could have doubted your goodness? Gertrude, Gertrude, you are to me the white image of all good things, and sin can never touch you. Arthur, you can go to Mabel, and you have my best wishes! Oh! stop a moment. There is no name at the beginning of this letter. The brilliant Mrs. Cheveley does not seem to have noticed that. There should be a name.

LADY CHILTERN: Let me write yours. It is you I trust and need. You and none else.

LORD GORING: Well, really, Lady Chiltern, I think I should have back my own letter.

LADY CHILTERN (*smiling*): No; you shall have Mabel. (*Takes the letter and writes her husband's name on it.*)

LORD GORING: Well, I hope she hasn't changed her mind. It's nearly twenty minutes since I saw her last.

Enter MABEL CHILTERN *and* LORD CAVERSHAM.

MABEL CHILTERN: Lord Goring, I think your father's conversation much more improving than yours. I am only going to talk to Lord Caversham in the future, and always under the usual palm tree.

LORD GORING: Darling! (*Kisses her.*)

LORD CAVERSHAM (*considerably taken aback*): What does this mean, sir? You don't mean to say that this charming, clever young lady has been so foolish as to accept you?

LORD GORING: Certainly, father! And Chiltern's been wise enough to accept the seat in the Cabinet.

LORD CAVERSHAM: I am very glad to hear that, Chiltern . . . I congratulate you, sir. If the country doesn't go to the dogs or the Radicals, we shall have you Prime Minister, some day.

Enter MASON.

MASON: Luncheon is on the table, my Lady! (MASON *goes out.*)

MABEL CHILTERN: You'll stop to luncheon, Lord Caversham, won't you?

LORD CAVERSHAM: With pleasure, and I'll drive you down to Downing Street afterwards, Chiltern. You have a great future before you, a great future. Wish I could say the same for you, sir. (*To* LORD GORING): But your career will have to be entirely domestic.

LORD GORING: Yes, father, I prefer it domestic.

LORD CAVERSHAM: And if you don't make this young lady an ideal husband, I'll cut you off with a shilling.

MABEL CHILTERN: An ideal husband! Oh, I don't think I should like that. It sounds like something in the next world.

LORD CAVERSHAM: What do you want him to be then, dear?

MABEL CHILTERN: He can be what he chooses. All I want is to be . . . to be . . . oh! a real wife to him.

LORD CAVERSHAM: Upon my word, there is a good deal of common sense in that, Lady Chiltern.

They all go out except SIR ROBERT CHILTERN. *He sinks into a chair, wrapt in thought. After a little time* LADY CHILTERN *returns to look for him.*

LADY CHILTERN (*leaning over the back of the chair*): Aren't you coming in, Robert?

SIR ROBERT CHILTERN (*taking her hand*): Gertrude, is it love you feel for me, or is it pity merely?

LADY CHILTERN (*kisses him*): It is love, Robert. Love, and only love. For both of us a new life is beginning.

Curtain

Salomé

A TRAGEDY IN ONE ACT.
TRANSLATED FROM THE FRENCH OF
OSCAR WILDE BY LORD ALFRED DOUGLAS

THE PERSONS OF THE PLAY

HEROD ANTIPAS, Tetrarch of Judæa
JOKANAAN,[1] The Prophet
THE YOUNG SYRIAN, Captain of the Guard
TIGELLINUS, A Young Roman
A CAPPADOCIAN
A NUBIAN[2]
FIRST SOLDIER
SECOND SOLDIER
THE PAGE OF HERODIAS
JEWS, NAZARENES, ETC.
A SLAVE
NAAMAN, The Executioner
HERODIAS, Wife of the Tetrarch
SALOMÉ, Daughter of Herodias
THE SLAVES OF SALOMÉ

SCENE: *A great terrace in the Palace of* HEROD, *set above the banqueting-hall. Some soldiers are leaning over the balcony. To the right there is a gigantic staircase, to the left, at the back, an old cistern surrounded by a wall of green bronze. Moonlight.*

THE YOUNG SYRIAN: How beautiful is the Princess Salomé to-night!

THE PAGE OF HERODIAS: Look at the moon! How strange the moon seems! She is like a woman rising from a tomb. She is like a dead woman. You would fancy she was looking for dead things.

THE YOUNG SYRIAN: She has a strange look. She is like a little princess who wears a yellow veil, and whose feet are of silver. She is like a princess who has little white doves for feet. You would fancy she was dancing.

THE PAGE OF HERODIAS: She is like a woman who is dead. She moves very slowly.

Noise in the banqueting-hall.

FIRST SOLDIER: What an uproar! Who are those wild beasts howling!

SECOND SOLDIER: The Jews. They are always like that. They are disputing about their religion.

FIRST SOLDIER: Why do they dispute about their religion?

SECOND SOLDIER: I cannot tell. They are always doing it. The Pharisees, for instance, say that there are angels, and the Sadducees[1] declare that angels do not exist.

FIRST SOLDIER: I think it is ridiculous to dispute about such things.

THE YOUNG SYRIAN: How beautiful is the Princess Salomé to-night!

THE PAGE OF HERODIAS: You are always looking at her. You look at her too much. It is dangerous to look at people in such fashion. Something terrible may happen.

THE YOUNG SYRIAN: She is very beautiful to-night.

FIRST SOLDIER: The Tetrarch has a sombre look.

SECOND SOLDIER: Yes, he has a sombre look.

FIRST SOLDIER: He is looking at something.

SECOND SOLDIER: He is looking at some one.

FIRST SOLDIER: At whom is he looking?

SECOND SOLDIER: I cannot tell.

THE YOUNG SYRIAN: How pale the Princess is! Never have I seen her so pale. She is like the shadow of a white rose in a mirror of silver.

THE PAGE OF HERODIAS: You must not look at her. You look too much at her.

FIRST SOLDIER: Herodias has filled the cup of the Tetrarch.

THE CAPPADOCIAN: Is that the Queen Herodias, she who wears a black mitre sewn with pearls, and whose hair is powdered with blue dust?

FIRST SOLDIER: Yes, that is Herodias, the Tetrarch's wife.

SECOND SOLDIER: The Tetrarch is very fond of wine. He has wine of three sorts. One which is brought from the Island of Samothrace, and is purple like the cloak of Cæsar.[2]

THE CAPPADOCIAN: I have never seen Cæsar.

SECOND SOLDIER: Another that comes from a town called Cyprus,[3] and is yellow like gold.

THE CAPPADOCIAN: I love gold.

SECOND SOLDIER: And the third is a wine of Sicily. That wine is red like blood.

THE NUBIAN: The gods of my country are very fond of blood. Twice in the year we sacrifice to them young men and maidens; fifty young men and a hundred maidens. But it seems we never give them quite enough, for they are very harsh to us.

THE CAPPADOCIAN: In my country there are no gods left. The Romans have driven them out. There are some who say that they have hidden themselves in the mountains, but I do not believe it. Three nights I have been on the mountains seeking them everywhere. I did not find them. And at last I called them by their names, and they did not come. I think they are dead.

FIRST SOLDIER: The Jews worship a God that you cannot see.

THE CAPPADOCIAN: I cannot understand that.

FIRST SOLDIER: In fact, they only believe in things that you cannot see.

THE CAPPADOCIAN: That seems to me altogether ridiculous.

THE VOICE OF JOKANAAN: After me shall come another mightier than I. I am not worthy so much as to unloose the latchet of his shoes. When he cometh, the solitary places shall be glad. They shall blossom like the lily. The eyes of the blind shall see the day, and the ears of the deaf shall be opened. The new-born child shall put his hand upon the dragon's lair, he shall lead the lions by their manes.[4]

SECOND SOLDIER: Make him be silent. He is always saying ridiculous things.

FIRST SOLDIER: No, no. He is a holy man. He is very gentle, too. Every day, when I give him to eat he thanks me.

THE CAPPADOCIAN: Who is he?

FIRST SOLDIER: A prophet.

THE CAPPADOCIAN: What is his name?

FIRST SOLDIER: Jokanaan.

THE CAPPADOCIAN: Whence comes he?

FIRST SOLDIER: From the desert, where he fed on locusts and wild honey.[5] He was clothed in camel's hair, and round his loins he had a leathern belt. He was very terrible to look upon. A great multitude used to follow him. He even had disciples.

THE CAPPADOCIAN: What is he talking of?

FIRST SOLDIER: We can never tell. Sometimes he says terrible things; but it is impossible to understand what he says.

THE CAPPADOCIAN: May one see him?

FIRST SOLDIER: No. The Tetrarch has forbidden it.

THE YOUNG SYRIAN: The Princess has hidden her face behind her fan! Her little white hands are fluttering like doves that fly to their dove-cots. They are like white butterflies. They are just like white butterflies.

THE PAGE OF HERODIAS: What is that to you? Why do you look at her? You must not look at her. . . . Something terrible may happen.

THE CAPPADOCIAN (*pointing to the cistern*): What a strange prison!

SECOND SOLDIER: It is an old cistern.

THE CAPPADOCIAN: An old cistern! It must be very unhealthy.

SECOND SOLDIER: Oh, no! For instance, the Tetrarch's brother, his elder brother, the first husband of Herodias the Queen, was imprisoned there for twelve years. It did not kill him. At the end of the twelve years he had to be strangled.

THE CAPPADOCIAN: Strangled? Who dared to do that?

SECOND SOLDIER (*pointing to the Executioner, a huge Negro*): That man yonder, Naaman.

THE CAPPADOCIAN: He was not afraid?

SECOND SOLDIER: Oh, no! The Tetrarch sent him the ring.

THE CAPPADOCIAN: What ring?

SECOND SOLDIER: The death-ring. So he was not afraid.

THE CAPPADOCIAN: Yet it is a terrible thing to strangle a king.

FIRST SOLDIER: Why? Kings have but one neck, like other folk.

THE CAPPADOCIAN: I think it terrible.

THE YOUNG SYRIAN: The Princess rises! She is leaving the table! She looks very troubled. Ah, she is coming this way. Yes, she is coming towards us. How pale she is! Never have I seen her so pale.

THE PAGE OF HERODIAS: Do not look at her. I pray you not to look at her.

THE YOUNG SYRIAN: She is like a dove that has strayed. . . . She is like a narcissus trembling in the wind. . . . She is like a silver flower.

Enter SALOMÉ.

SALOMÉ: I will not stay. I cannot stay. Why does the Tetrarch look at me all the while with his mole's eyes under his shaking eyelids? It is strange that the husband of my mother looks at me like that. I know not what it means. In truth, yes I know it.

THE YOUNG SYRIAN: You have just left the feast, Princess?

SALOMÉ: How sweet the air is here! I can breathe here!

Within there are Jews from Jerusalem who are tearing each other in pieces over their foolish ceremonies, and barbarians who drink and drink, and spill their wine on the pavement, and Greeks from Smyrna with painted eyes and painted cheeks, and frizzed hair curled in twisted coils, and silent, subtle Egyptians, with long nails of jade and russett cloaks, and Romans brutal and coarse, with their uncouth jargon. Ah! how I loathe the Romans! They are rough and common, and they give themselves the airs of noble lords.

THE YOUNG SYRIAN: Will you be seated, Princess?

THE PAGE OF HERODIAS: Why do you speak to her? Why do you look at her? Oh! something terrible will happen.

SALOMÉ: How good to see the moon. She is like a little piece of money, you would think she was a little silver flower. The moon is cold and chaste. I am sure she is a virgin, she has a virgin's beauty. Yes, she is a virgin. She has never defiled herself. She has never abandoned herself to men, like the other goddesses.

THE VOICE OF JOKANAAN: The Lord hath come. The son of man hath come. The centaurs have hidden themselves in the rivers, and the sirens[6] have left the rivers, and are lying beneath the leaves of the forest.

SALOMÉ: Who was that who cried out?

SECOND SOLDIER: The prophet, Princess.

SALOMÉ: Ah, the prophet! He of whom the Tetrarch is afraid?

SECOND SOLDIER: We know nothing of that, Princess. It was the prophet Jokanaan who cried out.

THE YOUNG SYRIAN: Is it your pleasure that I bid them bring your litter, Princess? The night is fair in the garden.

SALOMÉ: He says terrible things about my mother, does he not!

SECOND SOLDIER: We never understand what he says,
Princess.

SALOMÉ: Yes; he says terrible things about her.

Enter a SLAVE.

THE SLAVE: Princess, the Tetrarch prays you to return to
the feast.

SALOMÉ: I will not go back.

THE YOUNG SYRIAN: Pardon me, Princess, but if you do not
return some misfortune may happen.

SALOMÉ: Is he an old man, this prophet?

THE YOUNG SYRIAN: Princess, it were better to return. Suffer me to lead you in.

SALOMÉ: This prophet . . . is he an old man?

FIRST SOLDIER: No, Princess, he is quite a young man.

SECOND SOLDIER: You cannot be sure. There are those who
say he is Elias.[7]

SALOMÉ: Who is Elias?

SECOND SOLDIER: A very ancient prophet of this country,
Princess.

THE SLAVE: What answer may I give the Tetrarch from the
Princess?

THE VOICE OF JOKANAAN: Rejoice not thou, land of Pales-
tine, because the rod of him who smote thee is broken.
For from the seed of the serpent shall come forth a
basilisk,[8] and that which is born of it shall devour the
birds.

SALOMÉ: What a strange voice! I would speak with him.

FIRST SOLDIER: I fear it is impossible, Princess. The
Tetrarch does not wish any one to speak with him. He
has even forbidden the high priest to speak with him.

SALOMÉ: I desire to speak with him.

FIRST SOLDIER: It is impossible, Princess.

SALOMÉ: I will speak with him.

THE YOUNG SYRIAN: Would it not be better to return to the banquet?

SALOMÉ: Bring forth this prophet.

Exit the SLAVE.

FIRST SOLDIER: We dare not, Princess.

SALOMÉ (*approaching the cistern and looking down into it*): How black it is down there! It must be terrible to be in so black a pit! It is like a tomb . . . (*To the* SOLDIERS): Did you not hear me? Bring out the prophet. I wish to see him.

SECOND SOLDIER: Princess, I beg you do not require this of us.

SALOMÉ: You keep me waiting!

FIRST SOLDIER: Princess, our lives belong to you, but we cannot do what you have asked of us. And indeed, it is not of us that you should ask this thing.

SALOMÉ (*looking at the* YOUNG SYRIAN): Ah!

THE PAGE OF HERODIAS: Oh! what is going to happen? I am sure that some misfortune will happen.

SALOMÉ (*going up to the* YOUNG SYRIAN): You will do this thing for me, will you not, Narraboth? You will do this thing for me. I have always been kind to you. You will do it for me. I would but look at this strange prophet. Men have talked so much of him. Often have I heard the Tetrarch talk of him. I think the Tetrarch is afraid of him. Are you, even you, also afraid of him, Narraboth?

THE YOUNG SYRIAN: I fear him not, Princess; there is no man I fear. But the Tetrarch has formally forbidden that any man should raise the cover of this well.

SALOMÉ: You will do this thing for me, Narraboth, and to-morrow when I pass in my litter beneath the gateway of the idol-sellers I will let fall for you a little flower, a little green flower.[9]

THE YOUNG SYRIAN: Princess, I cannot, I cannot.

SALOMÉ (*smiling*): You will do this thing for me, Narraboth. You know that you will do this thing for me. And to-morrow when I pass in my litter by the bridge of the idol-buyers, I will look at you through the muslin veils, I will look at you, Narraboth, it may be I will smile at you. Look at me, Narraboth, look at me. Ah! you know that you will do what I ask of you. You know it well. . . . I know that you will do this thing.

THE YOUNG SYRIAN (*signing to the third soldier*): Let the prophet come forth. . . . The Princess Salomé desires to see him.

SALOMÉ: Ah!

THE PAGE OF HERODIAS: Oh! How strange the moon looks. You would think it was the hand of a dead woman who is seeking to cover herself with a shroud.

THE YOUNG SYRIAN: She has a strange look! She is like a little princess, whose eyes are eyes of amber. Through the clouds of muslin she is smiling like a little princess.

The prophet comes out of the cistern. SALOMÉ *looks at him and steps slowly back.*

JOKANAAN: Where is he whose cup of abominations is now full? Where is he, who in a robe of silver shall one day die in the face of all the people? Bid him come forth, that he may hear the voice of him who had cried in the waste places and in the houses of kings.

SALOMÉ: Of whom is he speaking?

THE YOUNG SYRIAN: You never can tell, Princess.

JOKANAAN: Where is she who, having seen the images of men painted on the walls, the images of the Chaldeans limned in colours, gave herself up unto the lust of her eyes, and sent ambassadors into Chaldea?[10]

SALOMÉ: It is of my mother that he speaks.

THE YOUNG SYRIAN: Oh, no, Princess.

SALOMÉ: Yes, it is of my mother that he speaks.

JOKANAAN: Where is she who gave herself unto the Captains of Assyria, who have baldricks on their loins, and tiaras of divers colours on their heads? Where is she who hath given herself to the young men of Egypt, who are clothed in fine linen and purple, whose shields are of gold, whose helmets are of silver, whose bodies are mighty? Bid her rise up from the bed of her abominations, from the bed of her incestuousness,[11] that she may hear the words of him who prepareth the way of the Lord, that she may repent her of her iniquities. Though she will never repent, but will stick fast in her abominations; bid her come, for the fan of the Lord is in His hand.

SALOMÉ: But he is terrible, he is terrible!

THE YOUNG SYRIAN: Do not stay here, Princess, I beseech you.

SALOMÉ: It is his eyes above all that are terrible. They are like black holes burned by torches in a Tyrian tapestry. They are like black caverns where dragons dwell. They are like the black caverns of Egypt in which the dragons make their lairs. They are like black lakes troubled by fantastic moons. . . . Do you think he will speak again?

THE YOUNG SYRIAN: Do not stay here, Princess. I pray you do not stay here.

SALOMÉ: How wasted he is! He is like a thin ivory statue. He is like an image of silver. I am sure he is chaste as the moon is. He is like a moonbeam, like a shaft of silver. His flesh must be cool like ivory. I would look closer at him.

THE YOUNG SYRIAN: No, no, Princess.

SALOMÉ: I must look at him closer.

THE YOUNG SYRIAN: Princess! Princess!

JOKANAAN: Who is this woman who is looking at me? I will not have her look at me. Wherefore doth she look at me with her golden eyes, under her gilded eyelids? I know

not who she is. I do not wish to know who she is. Bid her
begone. It is not to her that I would speak.

SALOMÉ: I am Salomé, daughter of Herodias, Princess of
Judæa.

JOKANAAN: Back! Daughter of Babylon! Come not near the
chosen of the Lord. Thy mother hath filled the earth
with the wine of her iniquities, and the cry of her sins
hath come up to the ears of God.

SALOMÉ: Speak again, Jokanaan. Thy voice is wine to me.

THE YOUNG SYRIAN: Princess! Princess! Princess!

SALOMÉ: Speak again! Speak again, Jokanaan, and tell me
what I must do.

JOKANAAN: Daughter of Sodom,[12] come not near me! But
cover thy face with a veil, and scatter ashes upon thine
head, and get thee to the desert and seek out the Son of
Man.

SALOMÉ: Who is he, the Son of Man? Is he as beautiful as
thou art, Jokanaan?

JOKANAAN: Get thee behind me! I hear in the palace the
beating of the wings of the angel of death.

THE YOUNG SYRIAN: Princess, I beseech thee to go within.

JOKANAAN: Angel of the Lord God, what dost thou here
with thy sword? Whom seekest thou in this foul palace?
The day of him who shall die in a robe of silver has not
yet come.

SALOMÉ: Jokanaan!

JOKANAAN: Who speaketh?

SALOMÉ: Jokanaan, I am amorous of thy body! Thy body is
white like the lilies of a field that the mower hath never
mowed. Thy body is white like the snows that lie on the
mountains, like the snows that lie on the mountains of
Judæa, and come down into the valleys. The roses in the
garden of the Queen of Arabia are not so white as thy
body. Neither the roses in the garden of the Queen of

Arabia, nor the feet of the dawn when they light on the leaves, nor the breast of the moon when she lies on the breast of the sea. . . . There is nothing in the world so white as thy body. Let me touch thy body.

JOKANAAN: Back! Daughter of Babylon! By woman came evil into the world. Speak not to me. I will not listen to thee. I listen but to the voice of the Lord God.

SALOMÉ: Thy body is hideous. It is like the body of a leper. It is like a plastered wall where vipers have crawled; like a plastered wall where the scorpions have made their nest. It is like a whitened sepulchre full of loathsome things. It is horrible, thy body is horrible. It is of thy hair that I am enamoured, Jokanaan. Thy hair is like clusters of grapes, like the clusters of black grapes that hang from the vine-trees of Edom in the land of the Edomites. Thy hair is like the cedars of Lebanon,[13] like the great cedars of Lebanon that give their shade to the lions and to the robbers who would hide themselves by day. The long black nights, when the moon hides her face, when the stars are afraid, are not so black. The silence that dwells in the forest is not so black. There is nothing in the world so black as thy hair. . . . Let me touch thy hair.

JOKANAAN: Back, daughter of Sodom! Touch me not. Profane not the temple of the Lord God.

SALOMÉ: Thy hair is horrible. It is covered with mire and dust. It is like a crown of thorns[14] which they have placed on thy forehead. It is like a knot of black serpents writhing round thy neck. I love not thy hair. . . . It is thy mouth that I desire, Jokanaan. Thy mouth is like a band of scarlet on a tower of ivory. It is like a pomegranate cut with a knife of ivory. The pomegranate-flowers that blossom in the garden of Tyre, and are redder than roses, are not so red. The red blasts of trumpets, that herald the approach of kings, and make afraid the enemy, are not so red. Thy mouth is redder than the feet of those who tread the wine in the wine-press. Thy mouth is redder than the feet of the doves who haunt the temples and are fed by the priests. It is redder than the feet of him who cometh from a forest where he hath slain a lion, and seen gilded tigers. Thy mouth is like a branch of coral that fishers have found in the twilight of the sea, the coral that they keep for the kings . . . ! It is like the vermilion that the Moabites find in the mines of Moab, the vermilion that the kings take from them. It is like the bow of the King of the Persians, that is painted with vermilion, and is tipped with coral. There is nothing in the world so red as thy mouth. . . . Let me kiss thy mouth.

JOKANAAN: Never, daughter of Babylon! Daughter of Sodom! Never.

SALOMÉ: I will kiss thy mouth, Jokanaan. I will kiss thy mouth.

THE YOUNG SYRIAN: Princess, Princess, thou who art like a garden of myrrh, thou who art the dove of all doves, look not at this man, look not at him! Do not speak such words to him. I cannot suffer them. . . . Princess, Princess, do not speak these things.

SALOMÉ: I will kiss thy mouth, Jokanaan.

THE YOUNG SYRIAN: Ah!

He kills himself and falls between SALOMÉ *and* JOKANAAN.

THE PAGE OF HERODIAS: The young Syrian has slain himself! The young captain has slain himself! He has slain himself who was my friend! I gave him a little box of perfumes and ear-rings wrought in silver, and now he has killed himself! Ah, did he not foretell that some misfortune would happen? I, too, foretold it, and it has happened. Well, I knew that the moon was seeking a dead thing, but I knew not that it was he whom she sought. Ah! why did I not hide him from the moon? If I had hidden him in a cavern she would not have seen him.

FIRST SOLDIER: Princess, the young captain has just killed himself.

SALOMÉ: Let me kiss thy mouth, Jokanaan.

JOKANAAN: Art thou not afraid, daughter of Herodias? Did I not tell thee that I had heard in the palace the beatings of the wings of the angel of death, and hath he not come, the angel of death?

SALOMÉ: Let me kiss thy mouth.

JOKANAAN: Daughter of adultery, there is but one who can save thee, it is He of whom I spake. Go seek Him. He is in a boat on the sea of Galilee, and He talketh with His disciples. Kneel down on the shore of the sea, and call unto Him by His name. When He cometh to thee (and to all who call on Him He cometh) bow thyself at His feet and ask of Him the remission of thy sins.

SALOMÉ: Let me kiss thy mouth.

JOKANAAN: Cursed be thou! Daughter of an incestuous mother, be thou accursed!

SALOMÉ: I will kiss thy mouth, Jokanaan.

JOKANAAN: I do not wish to look at thee. I will not look at thee, thou art accursed, Salomé, thou art accursed.

He goes down into the cistern.

SALOMÉ: I will kiss thy mouth, Jokanaan. I will kiss thy mouth.

FIRST SOLDIER: We must bear away the body to another place. The Tetrarch does not care to see dead bodies, save the bodies of those whom he himself has slain.

THE PAGE OF HERODIAS: He was my brother, and nearer to me than a brother. I gave him a little box of perfumes, and a ring of agate that he wore always on his hand. In the evening we used to walk by the river, among the almond trees, and he would tell me of the things of his country. He spake ever very low. The sound of his voice was like the sound of the flute, of a flute player. Also he much loved to gaze at himself in the river. I used to reproach him for that.

SECOND SOLDIER: You are right; we must hide the body. The Tetrarch must not see it.

FIRST SOLDIER: The Tetrarch will not come to this place. He never comes on the terrace. He is too much afraid of the prophet.

Enter HEROD, HERODIAS, *and all the* COURT.

HEROD: Where is Salomé? Where is the Princess? Why did she not return to the banquet as I commanded her? Ah! There she is!

HERODIAS: You must not look at her! You are always looking at her!

HEROD: The moon has a strange look to-night. Has she not a strange look? She is like a mad woman, a mad woman who is seeking everywhere for lovers. She is naked, too. She is quite naked. The clouds are seeking to clothe her nakedness, but she will not let them. She shows herself naked in the sky. She reels through the clouds like a drunken woman. . . . I am sure she is looking for lovers. Does she not reel like a drunken woman? She is like a mad woman, is she not?

HERODIAS: No; the moon is like the moon, that is all. Let us go within. . . . You have nothing to do here.

HEROD: I will stay here! Manesseh, lay carpets there. Light torches, bring forth the ivory tables, and the tables of jasper. The air here is delicious. I will drink more wine with my guests. We must show all honours to the ambassadors of Cæsar.

HERODIAS: It is not because of them that you remain.

HEROD: Yes; the air is delicious. Come, Herodias, our

guests await us. Ah! I have slipped! I have slipped in blood! It is an ill omen. It is a very evil omen. Wherefore is there blood here . . . ? And this body, what does this body here? Think you that I am like the King of Egypt, who gives no feast to his guests but that he shows them a corpse? Whose is it? I will not look on it.

FIRST SOLDIER: It is our captain, sire. He is the young Syrian whom you made captain only three days ago.

HEROD: I gave no order that he should be slain.

SECOND SOLDIER: He killed himself, sire.

HEROD: For what reason? I had made him captain.

SECOND SOLDIER: We do not know, sire. But he killed himself.

HEROD: That seems strange to me. I thought it was only the Roman philosophers who killed themselves. Is it not true, Tigellinus, that the philosophers at Rome kill themselves?

TIGELLINUS: There are some who kill themselves, sire. They are the Stoics.[15] The Stoics are coarse people. They are ridiculous people. I myself regard them as being perfectly ridiculous.

HEROD: I also. It is ridiculous to kill oneself.

TIGELLINUS: Everybody at Rome laughs at them. The Emperor has written a satire against them. It is recited everywhere.

HEROD: Ah! he has written a satire against them? Cæsar is wonderful. He can do everything. . . . It is strange that the young Syrian has killed himself. I am sorry he has killed himself. I am very sorry, for he was fair to look upon. He was even very fair. He had very languorous eyes. I remember that I saw that he looked languorously at Salomé. Truly, I thought he looked too much at her.

HERODIAS: There are others who look at her too much.

HEROD: His father was a king. I drove him from his kingdom. And you made a slave of his mother, who was a queen, Herodias. So he was here as my guest, as it were, and for that reason I made him my captain. I am sorry he is dead. Ho! Why have you left the body here? I will not look at it—away with it. *(They take away the body.)* It is cold here. There is a wind blowing. Is there not a wind blowing?

HERODIAS: No, there is no wind.

HEROD: I tell you there is a wind that blows. . . . And I hear in the air something that is like the beating of wings, like the beating of vast wings. Do you not hear it?

HERODIAS: I hear nothing.

HEROD: I hear it no longer. But I heard it. It was the blowing of the wind, no doubt. It has passed away. But no, I hear it again. Do you not hear it? It is just like the beating of wings.

HERODIAS: I tell you there is nothing. You are ill. Let us go within.

HEROD: I am not ill. It is your daughter who is sick. She has the mien of a sick person. Never have I seen her so pale.

HERODIAS: I have told you not to look at her.

HEROD: Pour me forth wine. *(Wine is brought.)* Salomé, come drink a little wine with me. I have here a wine that is exquisite. Cæsar himself sent it me. Dip into it thy little red lips, that I may drain the cup.

SALOMÉ: I am not thirsty, Tetrarch.

HEROD: You hear how she answers me, this daughter of yours?

HERODIAS: She does right. Why are you always gazing at her?

HEROD: Bring me ripe fruits. *(Fruits are brought.)* Salomé, come and eat fruit with me. I love to see in a fruit the mark of thy little teeth. Bite but a little of this fruit and then I will eat what is left.

SALOMÉ: I am not hungry, Tetrarch.

HEROD (*to* HERODIAS): You see how you have brought up this daughter of yours.

HERODIAS: My daughter and I come of a royal race. As for thee, thy father was a camel driver! He was also a robber!

HEROD: Thou liest!

HERODIAS: Thou knowest well that it is true.

HEROD: Salomé, come and sit next to me. I will give thee the throne of thy mother.

SALOMÉ: I am not tired, Tetrarch.

HERODIAS: You see what she thinks of you.

HEROD: Bring me—what is it that I desire? I forget. Ah! ah! I remember.

THE VOICE OF JOKANAAN: Lo! the time is come! That which I foretold has come to pass, saith the Lord God. Lo! the day of which I spoke.

HERODIAS: Bid him be silent. I will not listen to his voice. This man is for ever vomiting insults against me.

HEROD: He has said nothing against you. Besides, he is a very great prophet.

HERODIAS: I do not believe in prophets. Can a man tell what will come to pass? No man knows it. Moreover, he is for ever insulting me. But I think you are afraid of him. . . . I know well that you are afraid of him.

HEROD: I am not afraid of him. I am afraid of no man.

HERODIAS: I tell you, you are afraid of him. If you are not afraid of him why do you not deliver him to the Jews, who for these six months past have been clamouring for him?

A JEW: Truly, my lord, it were better to deliver him into our hands.

HEROD: Enough on this subject. I have already given you my answer. I will not deliver him into your hands. He is a holy man. He is a man who has seen God.

A JEW: That cannot be. There is no man who hath seen God

since the prophet Elias. He is the last man who saw God. In these days God doth not show Himself. He hideth Himself. Therefore great evils have come upon the land.

ANOTHER JEW: Verily, no man knoweth if Elias the prophet did indeed see God. Peradventure it was but the shadow of God that he saw.

A THIRD JEW: God is at no time hidden. He showeth Himself at all times and in everything. God is in what is evil, even as He is in what is good.

A FOURTH JEW: That must not be said. It is a very dangerous doctrine. It is a doctrine that cometh from the schools at Alexandria, where men teach the philosophy of the Greeks. And the Greeks are Gentiles. They are not even circumcised.

A FIFTH JEW: No one can tell how God worketh. His ways are very mysterious. It may be that the things which we call evil are good, and that the things which we call good are evil. There is no knowledge of anything. We must needs submit to everything, for God is very strong. He breaketh in pieces the strong together with the weak, for He regardeth not any man.

FIRST JEW: Thou speaketh truly. God is terrible. He breaketh the strong and the weak as a man brays corn in a mortar. But this man hath never seen God. No man hath seen God since the prophet Elias.

HERODIAS: Make them be silent. They weary me.

HEROD: But I have heard it said that Jokanaan himself is your prophet Elias.

THE JEW: That cannot be. It is more than three hundred years since the days of the prophet Elias.

HEROD: There be some who say that this man is the prophet Elias.

A NAZARENE: I am sure that he is the prophet Elias.

THE JEW: Nay, but he is not the prophet Elias.

THE VOICE OF JOKANAAN: So the day is come, the day of

the Lord, and I hear upon the mountains the feet of Him who shall be the Saviour of the world.

HEROD: What does that mean? The Saviour of the world.

TIGELLINUS: It is a title that Cæsar takes.

HEROD: But Cæsar is not coming into Judæa. Only yesterday I received letters from Rome. They contained nothing concerning this matter. And you, Tigellinus, who were at Rome during the winter, you heard nothing concerning this matter, did you?

TIGELLINUS: Sire, I heard nothing concerning the matter. I was explaining the title. It is one of Cæsar's titles.

HEROD: But Cæsar cannot come. He is too gouty. They say that his feet are like the feet of an elephant. Also there are reasons of State. He who leaves Rome loses Rome. He will not come. Howbeit Cæsar is lord, he will come if he wishes. Nevertheless, I do not think he will come.

FIRST NAZARENE: It was not concerning Cæsar that the prophet spake these words, sire.

HEROD: Not of Cæsar?

FIRST NAZARENE: No, sire.

HEROD: Concerning whom, then, did he speak?

FIRST NAZARENE: Concerning Messias[16] who has come.

A JEW: Messias hath not come.

FIRST NAZARENE: He hath come, and everywhere He worketh miracles.

HERODIAS: Ho! ho! miracles! I do not believe in miracles. I have seen too many. *(To the Page):* My fan!

FIRST NAZARENE: This man worketh true miracles. Thus, at a marriage which took place in a little town of Galilee, a town of some importance, He changed water into wine. Certain persons who were present related it to me. Also He healed two lepers[17] that were seated before the Gate of Capernaum simply by touching them.

SECOND NAZARENE: Nay, it was blind men that he healed at Capernaum.

FIRST NAZARENE: Nay, they were lepers. But He hath healed blind people also, and He was seen on a mountain talking with angels.

A SADDUCEE: Angels do not exist.

A PHARISEE: Angels exist, but I do not believe that this Man has talked with them.

FIRST NAZARENE: He was seen by a great multitude of people talking with angels.

A SADDUCEE: Not with angels.

HERODIAS: How these men weary me! They are ridiculous! *(To the Page):* Well, my fan! *(The Page gives her the fan.)* You have a dreamer's look; you must not dream. It is only sick people who dream. *(She strikes the Page with her fan.)*

SECOND NAZARENE: There is also the miracle of the daughter of Jairus.

FIRST NAZARENE: Yes, that is sure. No man can gainsay it.

HERODIAS: These men are mad. They have looked too long on the moon. Command them to be silent.

HEROD: What is this miracle of the daughter of Jairus?

FIRST NAZARENE: The daughter of Jairus was dead. He raised her from the dead.

HEROD: He raises the dead?

FIRST NAZARENE: Yea, sire, He raiseth the dead.

HEROD: I do not wish Him to do that. I forbid Him to do that. I allow no man to raise the dead. This Man must be found and told that I forbid Him to raise the dead. Where is this Man at present?

SECOND NAZARENE: He is in every place, my lord, but it is hard to find Him.

FIRST NAZARENE: It is said that He is now in Samaria.[18]

A JEW: It is easy to see that this is not Messias, if He is in Samaria. It is not to the Samaritans that Messias shall come. The Samaritans are accursed. They bring no offerings to the Temple.

SECOND NAZARENE: He left Samaria a few days since. I think that at the present moment He is in the neighbourhood of Jerusalem.

FIRST NAZARENE: No, he is not there. I have just come from Jerusalem. For two months they have had no tidings of Him.

HEROD: No matter! But let them find Him, and tell Him from me, I will not allow him to raise the dead! To change water into wine, to heal the lepers and the blind. . . . He may do these things if He will. I say nothing against these things. In truth I hold it a good deed to heal a leper. But I allow no man to raise the dead. It would be terrible if the dead came back.

THE VOICE OF JOKANAAN: Ah, the wanton! The harlot! Ah! the daughter of Babylon with her golden eyes and her gilded eyelids! Thus saith the Lord God, Let there come against her a multitude of men. Let the people take stones and stone her. . . .

HERODIAS: Command him to be silent.

THE VOICE OF JOKANAAN: Let the war captains pierce her with their swords, let them crush her beneath their shields.

HERODIAS: Nay, but it is infamous.

THE VOICE OF JOKANAAN: It is thus that I will wipe out all wickedness from the earth, and that all women shall learn not to imitate her abominations.

HERODIAS: You hear what he says against me? You allow him to revile your wife?

HEROD: He did not speak your name.

HERODIAS: What does that matter? You know well that it is I whom he seeks to revile. And I am your wife, am I not?

HEROD: Of a truth, dear and noble Herodias, you are my wife, and before that you were the wife of my brother.

HERODIAS: It was you who tore me from his arms.

HEROD: Of a truth I was stronger. . . . But let us not talk of that matter. I do not desire to talk of it. It is the cause of the terrible words that the prophet has spoken. Peradventure on account of it a misfortune will come. Let us not speak of this matter. Noble Herodias, we are not mindful of our guests. Fill thou my cup, my well-beloved. Fill with wine the great goblets of silver, and the great goblets of glass. I will drink to Cæsar. There are Romans here; we must drink to Cæsar.

ALL: Cæsar! Cæsar!

HEROD: Do you not see your daughter, how pale she is?

HERODIAS: What is it to you if she be pale or not?

HEROD: Never have I seen her so pale.

HERODIAS: You must not look at her.

THE VOICE OF JOKANAAN: In that day the sun shall become black like the sackcloth of hair, and the moon shall become like blood, and the stars of the heavens shall fall upon the earth like ripe figs that fall from the fig-tree, and the kings of the earth shall be afraid.

HERODIAS: Ah! Ah! I should like to see that day of which he speaks, when the moon shall become like blood, and when the stars shall fall upon the earth like ripe figs. This prophet talks like a drunken man . . . but I cannot suffer the sound of his voice. I hate his voice. Command him to be silent.

HEROD: I will not. I cannot understand what it is that he saith, but it may be an omen.

HERODIAS: I do not believe in omens. He speaks like a drunken man.

HEROD: It may be he is drunk with the wine of God.

HERODIAS: What wine is that, the wine of God? From what vineyards is it gathered? In what winepress may one find it?

HEROD (*from this point he looks all the while at Salomé*): Tigellinus, when you were at Rome of late, did the Emperor speak with you on the subject of . . . ?

TIGELLINUS: On what subject, sire?

HEROD: On what subject? Ah! I asked you a question, did I not? I have forgotten what I would have asked you.

HERODIAS: You are looking again at my daughter. You must not look at her. I have already said so.

HEROD: You say nothing else.

HERODIAS: I say it again.

HEROD: And that restoration of the Temple about which they have talked so much, will anything be done? They say the veil of the Sanctuary has disappeared, do they not?[19]

HERODIAS: It was thyself didst steal it. Thou speakest at random. I will not stay here. Let us go within.

HEROD: Dance for me, Salomé.

HERODIAS: I will not have her dance.

SALOMÉ: I have no desire to dance, Tetrarch.

HEROD: Salomé, daughter of Herodias, dance for me.

HERODIAS: Let her alone.

HEROD: I command thee to dance, Salomé.

SALOMÉ: I will not dance, Tetrarch.

HERODIAS (*laughing*): You see how she obeys you.

HEROD: What is it to me whether she dance or not? It is naught to me. To-night I am happy, I am exceeding happy. Never have I been so happy.

FIRST SOLDIER: The Tetrarch has a sombre look. Has he not a sombre look?

SECOND SOLDIER: Yes, he has a sombre look.

HEROD: Wherefore should I not be happy? Cæsar, who is lord of the world, who is lord of all things, loves me well. He has just sent me most precious gifts. Also he has promised me to summon to Rome the King of Cappadocia, who is my enemy. It may be that at Rome he will crucify him, for he is able to do all things that he wishes. Verily, Cæsar is lord. Thus you see I have a right to be happy. Indeed, I am happy. I have never been so happy.

There is nothing in the world that can mar my happiness.

THE VOICE OF JOKANAAN: He shall be seated on this throne. He shall be clothed in scarlet and purple. In his hand he shall bear a golden cup full of his blasphemies. And the angel of the Lord shall smite him. He shall be eaten of worms.

HERODIAS: You hear what he says about you. He says that you will be eaten of worms.

HEROD: It is not of me that he speaks. He speaks never against me. It is of the King of Cappadocia that he speaks; the King of Cappadocia, who is mine enemy. It is he who shall be eaten of worms. It is not I. Never has he spoken word against me, this prophet, save that I sinned in taking to wife the wife of my brother. It may be he is right. For, of a truth, you are sterile.

HERODIAS: I am sterile, I? You say that, you that are ever looking at my daughter, you that would have her dance for your pleasure? It is absurd to say that. I have borne a child. You have gotten no child, no, not even from one of your slaves. It is you who are sterile, not I.

HEROD: Peace, woman! I say that you are sterile. You have borne me no child, and the prophet says that our marriage is not a true marriage. He says that it is an incestuous marriage, a marriage that will bring evils. . . . I fear he is right; I am sure that he is right. But it is not the moment to speak of such things. I would be happy at this moment. Of a truth, I am happy. There is nothing I lack.

HERODIAS: I am glad you are of so fair a humour to-night. It is not your custom. But it is late. Let us go within. Do not forget that we hunt at sunrise. All honours must be shown to Cæsar's ambassadors, must they not?

SECOND SOLDIER: What a sombre look the Tetrarch wears.

FIRST SOLDIER: Yes, he wears a sombre look.

HEROD: Salomé, Salomé, dance for me. I pray thee dance

for me. I am sad to-night. Yes, I am passing sad to-night. When I came hither I slipped in blood, which is an evil omen; and I heard, I am sure I heard in the air a beating of wings, a beating of giant wings. I cannot tell what they mean. . . . I am sad to-night. Therefore dance for me. Dance for me, Salomé, I beseech you. If you dance for me you may ask of me what you will, and I will give it you, even unto the half of my kingdom.

SALOMÉ (*rising*): Will you indeed give me whatsoever I shall ask, Tetrarch?

HERODIAS: Do not dance, my daughter.

HEROD: Everything, even the half of my kingdom.

SALOMÉ: You swear it, Tetrarch?

HEROD: I swear it, Salomé.

HERODIAS: Do not dance, my daughter.

SALOMÉ: By what will you swear, Tetrarch?

HEROD: By my life, by my crown, by my gods. Whatsoever you desire I will give it you, even to the half of my kingdom, if you will but dance for me. O, Salomé, Salomé, dance for me!

SALOMÉ: You have sworn, Tetrarch.

HEROD: I have sworn, Salomé.

SALOMÉ: All this I ask, even the half of your kingdom.

HERODIAS: My daughter, do not dance.

HEROD: Even to the half of my kingdom. Thou wilt be passing fair as a queen, Salomé, if it please thee to ask for the half of my kingdom. Will she not be fair as a queen? Ah! it is cold here! There is an icy wind, and I hear . . . wherefore do I hear in the air this beating of wings? Ah! one might fancy a bird, a huge black bird that hovers over the terrace. Why can I not see it, this bird? The beat of its wings is terrible. The breath of the wind of its wings is terrible. It is a chill wind. Nay, but it is not cold, it is hot. I am choking. Pour water on my hands. Give me snow to eat. Loosen my mantle. Quick, quick! Loosen my mantle. Nay, but leave it. It is my garland that hurts me, my garland of roses. The flowers are like fire. They have burned my forehead. (*He tears the wreath from his head and throws it on the table.*) Ah! I can breathe now. How red those petals are! They are like stains of blood on the cloth. That does not matter. You must not find symbols in everything you see. It makes life impossible. It were better to say that stains of blood are as lovely as rose petals. It were better far to say that. . . . But we will not speak of this. Now I am happy, I am passing happy. Have I not the right to be happy? Your daughter is going to dance for me. Will you not dance for me, Salomé? You have promised to dance for me.

HERODIAS: I will not have her dance.

SALOMÉ: I will dance for you, Tetrarch.

HEROD: You hear what your daughter says. She is going to dance for me. You do well to dance for me, Salomé. And when you have danced for me, forget not to ask of me whatsoever you wish. Whatsoever you wish I will give it you, even to the half of my kingdom. I have sworn it, have I not?

SALOMÉ: You have sworn it, Tetrarch.

HEROD: And I have never broken my word. I am not of those who break their oaths. I know not how to lie. I am the slave of my word, and my word is the word of a king. The King of Cappadocia always lies, but he is no true king. He is a coward. Also he owes me money that he will not repay. He has even insulted my ambassadors. He has spoken words that were wounding. But Cæsar will crucify him when he comes to Rome. I am sure that Cæsar will crucify him. And if not, yet will he die, being eaten of worms. The prophet has prophesied it. Well! wherefore dost thou tarry, Salomé?

SALOMÉ: I am waiting until my slaves bring perfumes to me and the seven veils, and take off my sandals. (*Slaves bring perfumes and the seven veils, and take off the sandals of* SALOMÉ.)

HEROD: Ah, you are going to dance with naked feet. 'Tis well! 'Tis well! Your little feet will be like white doves. They will be like little white flowers that dance upon the trees. . . . No, no, she is going to dance on blood. There is blood spilt on the ground. She must not dance on blood. It were an evil omen.

HERODIAS: What is it to you if she dance on blood? Thou hast waded deep enough therein. . . .

HEROD: What is it to me? Ah! Look at the moon! She has become red. She has become red as blood. Ah! the prophet prophesied truly. He prophesied that the moon would become red as blood. Did he not prophesy it? All of you heard him. And now the moon has become red as blood. Do ye not see it?

HERODIAS: Oh, yes, I see it well, and the stars are falling like ripe figs, are they not? And the sun is becoming black like sackcloth of hair, and the kings of the earth are afraid. That at least one can see. The prophet, for once in his life, was right; the kings of the earth are afraid. . . . Let us go within. You are sick. They will say at Rome that you are mad. Let us go within, I tell you.

THE VOICE OF JOKANAAN: Who is this who cometh from Edom, who is this who cometh from Bozra, whose raiment is dyed with purple, who shineth in the beauty of his garments, who walketh mighty in his greatness? Wherefore is thy raiment stained with scarlet?

HERODIAS: Let us go within. The voice of that man maddens me. I will not have my daughter dance while he is continually crying out. I will not have her dance while you look at her in this fashion. In a word I will not have her dance.

HEROD: Do not rise, my wife, my queen, it will avail thee

nothing. I will not go within till she hath danced. Dance, Salomé, dance for me.

HERODIAS: Do not dance, my daughter.

SALOMÉ: I am ready, Tetrarch. (SALOMÉ *dances the dance of the seven veils.*)[20]

HEROD: Ah! Wonderful! Wonderful! You see that she has danced for me, your daughter. Come near, Salomé, come near, that I may give you your reward. Ah! I pay the dancers well. I will pay thee royally. I will give thee whatsoever thy soul desireth. What wouldst thou have? Speak.

SALOMÉ (*kneeling*): I would that they presently bring me in a silver charger . . . [21]

HEROD (*laughing*): In a silver charger? Surely yes, in a silver charger. She is charming, is she not? What is it you would have in a silver charger, O sweet and fair Salomé, you who are fairer than all the daughters of Judæa? What would you have them bring thee in a silver charger? Tell me. Whatsoever it may be, they shall give it to you. My treasures belong to thee. What is it, Salomé?

SALOMÉ (*rising*): The head of Jokanaan.

HERODIAS: Ah! that is well said, my daughter.

HEROD: No, no!

HERODIAS: That is well said, my daughter.

HEROD: No, no, Salomé. You do not ask me that. Do not listen to your mother's voice. She is ever giving you evil counsel. Do not heed her.

SALOMÉ: I do not heed my mother. It is for mine own pleasure that I ask the head of Jokanaan in a silver charger. You have sworn, Herod. Forget not that you have sworn an oath.

HEROD: I know it. I have sworn by my gods. I know it well. But I pray you, Salomé, ask of me something else. Ask of me the half of my kingdom, and I will give it you. But ask not of me what you have asked.

SALOMÉ: I ask of you the head of Jokanaan.

HEROD: No, no, I do not wish it.

SALOMÉ: You have sworn, Herod.

HERODIAS: Yes, you have sworn. Everybody heard you. You swore it before everybody.

HEROD: Be silent! It is not to you I speak.

HERODIAS: My daughter has done well to ask the head of Jokanaan. He has covered me with insults. He has said monstrous things against me. One can see that she loves her mother well. Do not yield, my daughter. He has sworn, he has sworn.

HEROD: Be silent, speak not to me . . . ! Come, Salomé, be reasonable. I have never been hard to you. I have ever loved you. . . . It may be that I have loved you too much. Therefore ask not this thing of me. This is a terrible thing, an awful thing to ask of me. Surely, I think you are jesting. The head of a man that is cut from his body is ill to look upon, is it not? It is not meet that the eyes of a virgin should look upon such a thing. What pleasure could you have in it? None. No, no, it is not what you desire. Hearken to me. I have an emerald, a great round emerald, which Cæsar's minion sent me. If you look through this emerald you can see things which happen at a great distance. Cæsar himself carries such an emerald when he goes to the circus. But my emerald is larger. I know well that it is larger. It is the largest emerald in the whole world. You would like that, would you not? Ask it of me and I will give it you.

SALOMÉ: I demand the head of Jokanaan.

HEROD: You are not listening. You are not listening. Suffer me to speak, Salomé.

SALOMÉ: The head of Jokanaan.

HEROD: No, no, you would not have that. You say that to trouble me, because I have looked at you all this evening. It is true, I have looked at you all evening. Your beauty troubled me. Your beauty has grievously troubled me, and I have looked at you too much. But I will look at you no more. Neither at things, nor at people should one look. Only in mirrors should one look, for mirrors do but show us masks. Oh! oh! bring wine! I thirst. . . . Salomé, Salomé, let us be friends. Come now . . . ! Ah! what would I say? What was't? Ah! I remember . . . ! Salomé—nay, but come nearer to me; I fear you will not hear me—Salomé, you know my white peacocks, my beautiful white peacocks, that walk in the garden between the myrtles and the tall cypress trees. Their beaks are gilded with gold, and the grains that they eat are gilded with gold also, and their feet are stained with purple. When they cry out the rain comes, and the moon shows herself in the heavens when they spread their tails. Two by two they walk between the cypress trees and the black myrtles, and each has a slave to tend it. Sometimes they fly across the trees and anon they crouch in the grass, and round the lake. There are not in all the world birds so wonderful. There is no king in all the world who possesses such wonderful birds. I am sure that Cæsar himself has no birds so fine as my birds. I will give you fifty of my peacocks. They will follow you whithersoever you go, and in the midst of them you will be like the moon in the midst of a great white cloud. . . . I will give them all to you. I have but a hundred, and in the whole world there is no king who has peacocks like unto my peacocks. But I will give them all to you. Only you must loose me from my oath, and must not ask of me that which you have asked of me.

He empties the cup of wine.

SALOMÉ: Give me the head of Jokanaan.

HERODIAS: Well said, my daughter! As for you, you are ridiculous with your peacocks.

HEROD: Be silent! You cry out always; you cry out like a beast of prey. You must not. Your voice wearies me. Be silent, I say. . . . Salomé, think of what you are doing. This man comes perchance from God. He is a holy man. The finger of God has touched him. God has put into his mouth terrible words. In the palace as in the desert God is always with him. . . . At least it is possible. One does not know. It is possible that God is for him and with him. Furthermore, if he died some misfortune might happen to me. In any case, he said that the day he dies a misfortune will happen to some one. That could only be to me. Remember, I slipped in blood when I entered. Also, I heard a beating of wings in the air, a beating of mighty wings. These are very evil omens, and there were others. I am sure there were others, though I did not see them. Well, Salomé, you do not wish a misfortune to happen to me? You do not wish that. Listen to me, then.

SALOMÉ: Give me the head of Jokanaan.

HEROD: Ah! you are not listening to me. Be calm. I—I am calm. I am quite calm. Listen. I have jewels hidden in this place—jewels that your mother even has never seen; jewels that are marvellous. I have a collar of pearls, set in four rows. They are like unto moons chained with rays of silver. They are like fifty moons caught in a golden net. On the ivory of her breast a queen has worn it. Thou shalt be as fair as a queen when thou wearest it. I have amethysts of two kinds, one that is black like wine, and one that is red like wine which has been coloured with water. I have topazes, yellow as are the eyes of tigers, and topazes that are pink as the eyes of a wood-pigeon, and green topazes that are as the eyes of cats. I have opals that burn always with an ice-like flame, opals that make sad men's minds, and are fearful of the shadows. I have onyxes like the eyeballs of a dead woman. I have moon-stones that change when the moon changes, and are wan when they see the sun. I have sapphires big like eggs, and as blue as blue flowers. The sea wanders within them and the moon comes never to trouble the blue of their waves. I have chrysolites and beryls and chrysoprases and rubies. I have sardonyx and hyacinth stones, and stones of chalcedony, and I will give them all to you, all, and other things will I add to them. The King of the Indies has but even now sent me four fans fashioned from the feathers of parrots, and the King of Numidia a garment of ostrich feathers. I have a crystal, into which it is not lawful for a woman to look, nor may young men behold it until they have been beaten with rods. In a coffer of nacre I have three wondrous turquoises. He who wears them on his forehead can imagine things which are not, and he who carries them in his hand can make women sterile. These are great treasures above all price. They are treasures without price. But this is not all. In an ebony coffer I have two cups of amber, that are like apples of gold. If an enemy pour poison into these cups, they become like an apple of silver. In a coffer incrusted with amber I have sandals incrusted with glass. I have mantles that have been brought from the land of the Seres, and bracelets decked about with carbuncles and with jade that come from the city of Euphrates. . . . What desirest thou more than this, Salomé? Tell me the thing that thou desirest, and I will give it thee. All that thou askest I will give thee save one thing. I will give thee all that is mine, save one life. I will give thee the mantle of the high priest. I will give thee the veil of the sanctuary.

THE JEWS: Oh! Oh!

SALOMÉ: Give me the head of Jokanaan.

HEROD (*sinking back in his seat*): Let her be given what she asks! Of a truth she is her mother's child! (*The* FIRST SOLDIER *approaches.* HERODIAS *draws from the hand of*

the TETRARCH *the ring of death and gives it to the* SOL-
DIER, *who straightway bears it to the* EXECUTIONER.
The EXECUTIONER *looks scared.*) Who has taken my
ring? There was a ring on my right hand. Who has drunk
my wine? There was wine in my cup. It was full of wine.
Some one has drunk it? Oh! surely some evil will befall
some one. (*The* EXECUTIONER *goes down into the cistern.*) Ah! Wherefore did I give my oath? Kings ought
never to pledge their word. If they keep it not, it is terrible, and if they keep it, it is terrible also.

HERODIAS: My daughter has done well.

HEROD: I am sure that some misfortune will happen.

SALOMÉ (*she leans over the cistern and listens*): There is no
sound. I hear nothing. Why does he not cry out, this
man? Ah! if any man sought to kill me, I would cry out, I
would struggle, I would not suffer. . . . Strike, strike,
Naaman, strike, I tell you. . . . No, I hear nothing. There
is a silence, a terrible silence. Ah! something has fallen
upon the ground. I heard something fall. It is the sword
of the headsman. He is afraid, this slave. He has let his
sword fall. He dare not kill him. He is a coward, this
slave! Let soldiers be sent. (*She sees the* PAGE OF HERO-
DIAS *and addresses him.*) Come hither, thou wert the
friend of him who is dead, is it not so? Well, I tell thee,
there are not dead men enough. Go to the soldiers and
bid them go down and bring me the thing I ask, the thing
the Tetrarch has promised me, the thing that is mine.
(*The* PAGE *recoils. She turns to the* SOLDIERS.) Hither,
ye soldiers. Get ye down into this cistern and bring me
the head of this man. (*The* SOLDIERS *recoil.*) Tetrarch,
Tetrarch, command your soldiers that they bring me the
head of Jokanaan.

A huge black arm, the arm of the EXECUTIONER, *comes
forth from the cistern, bearing on a silver shield the head*

of JOKANAAN. SALOMÉ *seizes it.* HEROD *hides his face with his cloak.* HERODIAS *smiles and fans herself. The* NAZARENES *fall on their knees and begin to pray.*

SALOMÉ: Ah! thou wouldst not suffer me to kiss thy mouth, Jokanaan. Well! I will kiss it now. I will bite it with my teeth as one bites a ripe fruit. Yes, I will kiss thy mouth, Jokanaan. I said it. Did I not say it? I said it. Ah! I will kiss it now. . . . But wherefore dost thou not look at me, Jokanaan? Thine eyes that were so terrible, so full of rage and scorn, are shut now. Wherefore are they shut? Open thine eyes! Lift up thine eyelids, Jokanaan! Wherefore dost thou not look at me? Art thou afraid of me, Jokanaan, that thou wilt not look at me . . . ? And thy tongue, that was like a red snake darting poison, it moves no more, it says nothing now, Jokanaan, that scarlet viper that spat its venom upon me. It is strange, is it not? How is it that the red viper stirs no longer . . . ? Thou wouldst have none of me, Jokanaan. Thou didst reject me. Thou didst speak evil words against me. Thou didst treat me as a harlot, as a wanton, me, Salomé, daughter of Herodias, Princess of Judæa! Well, Jokanaan, I still live, but thou, thou art dead, and thy head belongs to me. I can do with it what I will. I can throw it to the dogs and to the birds of the air. That which the dogs leave, the birds of the air shall devour. . . . Ah, Jokanaan, Jokanaan, thou wert the only man that I have loved. All other men are hateful to me. But thou, thou wert beautiful! Thy body was a column of ivory set on a silver socket. It was a garden full of doves and of silver lilies. It was a tower of silver decked with shields of ivory. There was nothing in the world so white as thy body. There was nothing in the world so black as thy hair. In the whole world there was nothing so red as thy mouth. Thy voice was a censer that scattered strange perfumes, and when I looked on thee I heard a strange music. Ah! wherefore didst thou not look at me, Jokanaan? Behind thine hands and thy curses thou didst hide thy face. Thou didst put upon thine eyes the covering of him who would see his God. Well, thou hast seen thy God, Jokanaan, but me, me, thou didst never see. If thou hadst seen me thou wouldst have loved me. I, I saw thee, Jokanaan, and I loved thee. Oh, how I loved thee! I loved thee yet, Jokanaan, I love thee only. . . . I am athirst for thy beauty; I am hungry for thy body; and neither wine nor fruits can appease my desire. What shall I do now, Jokanaan? Neither the floods nor the great waters can quench my passion. I was a princess, and thou didst scorn me. I was a virgin, and thou didst take my virginity from me. I was chaste, and thou didst fill my veins with fire. . . . Ah! ah! wherefore didst thou not look at me, Jokanaan? If thou hadst looked at me thou hadst loved me. Well I know that thou wouldst have loved me, and the mystery of love is greater than the mystery of death. Love only should one consider.

HEROD: She is monstrous, thy daughter, she is altogether monstrous. In truth, what she has done is a great crime. I am sure that it was a crime against an unknown God.

HERODIAS: I approve of what my daughter has done. And I will stay here now.

HEROD (*rising*): Ah! There speaks the incestuous wife! Come! I will not stay here. Come, I tell thee. Surely some terrible thing will befall. Manasseth, Issachar, Ozias, put out the torches. I will not look at things, I will not suffer things to look at me. Put out the torches! Hide the moon! Hide the stars! Let us hide ourselves in our palace, Herodias. I begin to be afraid.

The slaves put out the torches. The stars disappear. The great black cloud crosses the moon and conceals it com-

pletely. The stage becomes very dark. The TETRARCH *begins to climb the staircase.*

THE VOICE OF SALOMÉ: Ah! I have kissed thy mouth, Jokanaan. I have kissed thy mouth. There was a bitter taste on thy lips. Was it the taste of blood . . . ? But perchance it is the taste of love. . . . They say that love hath a bitter taste. . . . But what of that? What of that? I have kissed thy mouth, Jokanaan.

A moonbeam falls on SALOMÉ, *covering her with light.*

HEROD (*turning round and seeing* SALOMÉ): Kill that woman!

The soldiers rush forward and crush beneath their shields SALOMÉ, *daughter of* HERODIAS, *Princess of Judea.*

Curtain

NOTES

THE IMPORTANCE OF BEING EARNEST

Act One

1. **Half-Moon Street:** Wilde's audiences would have recognized this as a fancy, fashionable address.
2. **Shropshire:** An idyllic inland county, still well known for its pastoral landscapes.
3. **Scotland Yard:** As any Sherlock Holmes fan knows, the central location of London's police detectives.
4. **Tunbridge Wells:** A very convenient location for an aunt. Officially known as Royal Tunbridge Wells, in Kent (southeastern England), the town was a fashionable nineteenth-century sea resort and spa.
5. **the Albany:** A neighborhood in London.
6. **the Savoy:** A fashionable hotel with an equally fine dining room.
7. **sent down:** It was the custom for guests to assemble in the drawing room before the meal. Men were then partnered with women whom they escorted to dinner.
8. **corrupt French Drama:** Likely a reference to the

"well-made plays" patterned after those of French dramatist Eugene Scribe. They dominated European and British theater for some time and often featured adultery or other scandalous themes, though always with a reassuringly conservative ending that punished transgressors.

9. **Wagnerian manner:** Richard Wagner (1813–1883), celebrated German composer best known for his "Ring Cycle" of operas, which featured sweeping chords and dramatic singing, here mocked for their thunderous Germanic style.

10. **ready money:** Cash instead of credit. A sly reference to Algy's financial state.

11. **the season:** The round of social parties and public engagements (such as theater and opera) presided over by nobility during which many of the gentry moved from their country homes to London residences. Young women were "debuted," and marriage proposals often were sought and made during this time.

12. **duties exacted:** Lady Bracknell refers to the newly enacted inheritance taxes of 1894, introduced by the Liberal Party.

13. **Belgrave Square:** Another fashionable address.

14. **Liberal Unionist:** Jack places himself safely in the middle of the political spectrum. Liberal Unionists were not quite Tories (conservatives), as Lady Bracknell indicates, but they had voted against the controversial movement for Irish Home Rule.

15. **Victoria Station:** A major train station, similar to New York City's Grand Central Station.

16. **the French Revolution:** The French Revolution (1789–1799) was marked by waves of violence and counterviolence during which thousands of people were summarily executed.

17. **Gorgon:** One of three mythical female monsters, of

whom Medusa was one, whose hair was made of live snakes and whose gaze, when met, turned men to stone.

18. **the Empire:** A famous music hall.

Act Two

1. **Schiller:** Friedrich von Schiller (1759–1805), German playwright and poet and author of *Wilhelm Tell* (1804), based on the Swiss legend of William Tell, who shot an apple off his son's head with a bow and arrow.

2. **three-volume novels that Mudie sends us:** Some of the best-selling novels of late Victorian England were long (therefore printed in three volumes), sensational stories, often written by women and printed in installments in weekly periodicals before being sold as novels. Mudie was a private chain of lending libraries that charged a small fee to its subscribers for borrowing books.

3. **Dr. Chasuble:** A chasuble is the overgarment worn by officiating priests.

4. **Fall of the Rupee:** Rupees were the currency of Britain's troublesome colony, India. They had been falling for several decades.

5. **Socialism . . . Rational Dress:** Socialism was associated, appropriately or not, with all manner of radical protest in the late Victorian age, including women's rights. The Rational Dress movement called for alterations in restrictive women's clothes, including the loosening or abolishment of corsets.

6. **1889 champagne:** As revealed later, this is a Perrier-Jouet Brut in one of its finest vintages and, reputedly, a favorite of Wilde's. Pâté de foie gras is a rich, expensive paste made from goose livers.

7. **Maréchal Niel:** A yellow country rose. In the Victo-

rian language of flowers, yellow roses signified jealousy and decreasing love.

8. **Primitive Church:** Early Christian.
9. **In Paris!:** Paris symbolized frivolity and moral laxity to the conservative British mind.
10. **Paedobaptist:** *Paedo* means "child."
11. **Nonconformist:** Belonging to no established church.
12. **portmanteaus:** Large suitcases. The amount of luggage Algy has brought suggests either a long stay or an extremely well-dressed one.
13. Jack's bill in pounds (762), shillings (14) and pence (2), units of British currency. The amount is fabulously large.
14. **the fly:** Light horse-drawn carriage.
15. **Wordsworth's:** William Wordsworth (1770–1850), American Romantic poet.
16. **Holloway:** A suburban prison.
17. **dog-cart:** Small horse-drawn cart.

Act Three

1. **Bimettalism:** A gold and silver standard. Britain's money was based on silver.
2. **volume form:** Another reference to the three-volume sensational novel.
3. **14th of February last:** St. Valentine's Day, also *Earnest's* opening night.

Act Four

1. **dreadful . . . British Opera:** Likely a dig at the popular operettas of Gilbert and Sullivan.
2. **temperance beverage:** A nonalcoholic drink, likely carbonated; hence the explosion.

3. **"The Green Carnation":** A sensational English novel celebrating aestheticism, decadence, and veiled male homosexuality. It was supposed by some (erroneously or not) to have been modeled after Wilde, who was famous for wearing a green carnation, a symbol of the Decadence movement and, in Paris, homosexuality, in his buttonhole. The puns on exotic cultures here are multiple.

LADY WINDERMERE'S FAN

Act One

1. **Carlton House Terrace:** An expensive, well-respected neighborhood near St. James' Palace and within walking distance of government buildings and expensive clubs.
2. **at home this afternoon?:** The butler asks whether madam is available for social calls, usually held in the late afternoon. If her answer were negative, visitors would leave their cards and pass on.
3. **Selby:** The Windermeres' country home.
4. **of age to-day:** Twenty-one.
5. **Curzon Street:** In fashionable Hyde Park.
6. **Mayfair:** The most prestigious district among high society in London.
7. **£400:** These sums add up to a very large amount of money. The implication is that Lord Windermere must be paying Mrs. Erlynne's rent or some other significant expense.
8. **receive her at once:** Social status in the Windermere's circle is largely determined by where, and by whom, one is invited ("received"). As the giver of "small select" parties, Lady Windermere is in a position to lend

Mrs. Erlynne an aura of respectability and to open her way into other houses, but at risk to her own reputation.

Act Two

1. **Sydney:** Australia's largest and most cultured city. Nevertheless, to say London is less exclusive is quite telling, since Australia was founded as a penal colony and remains, to this day, famous for its earthy ways.
2. **wicked French novel:** Victorian England considered France and all its products scandalous and immoral. French novels were printed with yellow covers. Dumby suggests Mrs. Erlynne is wickedness in a good dress.
3. **Grosvenor Square:** A highly respectable address, much more so than Lady Bracknell suggests.
4. **a handsome settlement:** Dowry.

Act Three

1. **Wiesbaden:** A popular German spa.
2. **raise the wind for them:** To throw one's cap over the mill is to marry "up" socially. To "raise the wind" is to acquire wealth. Dumby suggests joining a social circle versus a purely individual greed.
3. **for dyed hair:** The expression should be "for grey (or white) hair" with obvious implications for Lord Augustus' hair.

Act Four

1. **Club Train:** A special, luxurious express train that will sweep Mrs. Erlynne away to her exile in Europe.

2. **pink shades:** Pink lampshades, which cast an especially flattering light.
3. **Shrewsbury and Talbot:** The taxi manufacturer's name.

AN IDEAL HUSBAND

Act One

1. *Triumph of Love—Watteau:* This passage, as with the descriptions that precede each character's entrance, is written from a deliberately Aestheticist point of view. Thus, clothes, paintings, and works of art take precedence, and people are compared to works of art. The description of the Chilterns' reception room suggests tremendous wealth and social status. Francois Boucher (1703–1770) was a French painter who designed many lavish tapestries and decorations during the "reign" of Madame Pompadour (mistress to Louis XV). Antoine Watteau (1684–1721), a delicate colorist, was his much-admired contemporary. The Louis Seize chair is from the Louis XVI period. "The Triumph of Love" refers to Boucher's *The Triumph of Venus*, in which Venus's beauty has overcome Mars, the god of war.

2. **portrait by Lawrence:** Sir Thomas Lawrence (1769–1830), the leading portrait painter of his time. The Order of the Garter is the oldest of the chivalric orders. A Whig was a moderate Liberal, the party in power at the time Wilde's play was produced.

3. **Tanagra statuette:** A classical Greek statue. Note the contrast between Mabel's type of beauty and that of the Watteau women and (below) the very European Mrs. Cheveley.

4. **at home on Wednesday:** Society ladies traditionally welcomed visitors at least one afternoon a week.

5. **my wife's milliner:** Lord Caversham comments unfavorably on the rising middle class.

6. **Venetian red . . . too many schools:** Venetian red is a scarlet paint color made from native Venetian ochre. Heliotrope is a highly scented flower, deep blue-violet in color. Like the other characters, Mrs. Cheveley is a work of art but with too many interests, pasts, and influences—fascinating but a tad overdone.

7. **Vandyck:** Sir Arthur Vandyck (1599–1641), a Flemish painter of the Baroque era specializing in portraiture.

8. **Vienna:** The center of European politics.

9. **blue spectacles:** Dark glasses, like sunglasses.

10. **psychological novelists:** A reference to the burgeoning literary movement of Realism, as would come to be typified by Americans Henry James and Edith Wharton.

11. **Corots:** Works by French painter Jean Baptiste Camille Corot (1796–1875), a pioneer in his time. More evidence of Chiltern's wealth and sophistication.

12. **the Old Greek:** A reference to Odysseus, the rascally Greek hero and traveler whose wife, Penelope, as Mrs. Cheveley notes in her next line, waited patiently at home for him for more than a decade.

13. **a flawless dandy:** In Wilde, dandyism goes beyond the usual definition of a man who seeks perfection in dress and style to encompass the agenda of Aestheticism, which prizes art (and sometimes artifice) above all else. Lord Goring's dandyism is part and parcel of his epigrammatic speech, his philosophical nature, and his morality.

14. **Stock Exchange swindle:** The swindle most likely would involve selling shares in the proposed project under falsely optimistic projections for its success.

When the project fails, stockholders must sell their shares at a loss, and the original seller absconds with the raised capital. If Mrs. Cheveley knows ahead of time that the project will be promoted, she can anticipate a rise in the price and sell at a profit before the project fails, even if she knows the scheme as a whole will fail. Insider information is also key to Chiltern's secret sin, below.

15. **a second Panama:** Before the United States successfully completed the canal, it had been the object of several fraudulent schemes.

16. **the House:** The House of Commons, in Parliament, in which Sir Chiltern holds a seat.

17. **Ladies' Gallery:** The separate section of Parliament to which women were relegated.

18. **Claridge's . . . leave a card:** A fashionable hotel. Mrs. Cheveley invited Lord Goring to call on her, saving him the possible embarrassment of having her arrive at his home.

19. *en règle:* Regular, i.e., polite and correct.

20. **the Royal Academy . . . novels in Scotch dialect:** The Royal Academy of Arts was, in Wilde's view, far too conservative. In the 1890s, several authors included Scotch dialect in their novels as part of the Scottish nationalist movement.

Act Two

1. *décolleté:* Usually, a cleavage-revealing neckline. Here, a metaphor for *risqué*.

2. **Woman's Liberal Association:** A women's political organization founded in 1886 that, among other "dull, useful, delightful things," as Lady Chiltern puts it, lobbied for the eight-hour working day and other labor reforms she mentions below. The fact that Lady Chiltern

is an active member marks her as one of the small but active and growing number of earnest progressive Victorian women involved in causes ranging from the prevention of cruelty to animals to education for women, as Lady Markby deplores below.

3. *The Morning Post* . . . **Lambeth Conference:** It was the custom for the private guest lists of high-society events to appear in the paper. County Council is the London County Council. Lambeth Conference is the Conference of Church of England Bishops, held at Lambeth Palace, home of the Archbishop of Canterbury, in London.

4. **bimetallist:** One who believed England's silver standard should be changed to include gold. One of Wilde's favorite examples of political absurdity.

5. **Bath . . . Pump Room:** Bath was a fashionable resort popular since Roman times for its hot springs. The Pump Room is a social gathering place.

6. **agricultural laborer . . . Welsh Church:** The acute depression of agriculture and the possible disestablishment of the Welsh Church were hot political topics.

7. **yellow covers:** Government reports were printed with blue covers. Risqué French novels were printed with yellow covers. Yellow covers were also a mark of the Decadence movement and its premier journal, *The Yellow Book*.

Act Three

1. **silk hat. . . . Seize cane:** The accoutrement of a dandy, and of Wilde himself. Top hat, large double-layered Scottish cape, and cane of the same Louis XVI period as the Chilterns' couch in Act One. A "buttonhole" is a flower in the lapel buttonhole of one's dress coat. Wilde was famous for his flamboyant buttonholes.

2. **Lamia-like:** Lamia is a female demon with the body of a serpent from the waist down. In the version of the story appearing John Keats's poem, Lamia has the ability to change herself into a beautiful young woman in order to seduce and destroy men.
3. **hock and seltzer:** White wine and seltzer.
4. *Voila tout:* That's all.

Act Four

1. **Canning:** George Canning (1770–1827), British statesman.

SALOMÉ

1. **Jokanaan:** Hebrew version of "John." Jokanaan is generally known as John the Baptist.
2. **Syrian . . . Cappadocian . . . Nubian:** Syria, as today, was a Middle Eastern kingdom. Cappadocia was a kingdom in what is now Turkey, held by the Roman Empire. Nubia was an ancient kingdom of northeastern Africa, where Ethiopia and Sudan are now. Along with the Jews and the Romans, these peoples represent the cosmopolitan world of the Roman Empire.

Act One

1. **Pharisees . . . Sudducees:** The Pharisees believed in a law-driven Judaism and were the mainstream party. The Sudducees were a political and religious sect who rejected the Pharisees' belief in resurrection and angels.
2. **Island of Samothrace . . . Caesar:** Samothrace is an island in the Aegean. Caesar is the emporer of Rome, here Tiberius (A.D. 14–37).

3. **Cyprus:** An island in the Aegean, not a town.
4. **After me shall come another . . . by their manes:**
   Christ. For sources of Jokanaan's prophecy, see Isaiah
   2:6–8 and 35:1.
5. **locusts and wild honey:** Matthew 3:4.
6. **centaurs . . . sirens:** From Greek mythology, centaurs are wise teachers and hunters with the head and
   torso of a man and the lower body of a horse. Sirens are
   fantastical temptresses with beautiful singing voices,
   sometimes pictured as half woman, half bird, who
   lured sailors to their death on the rocky island where
   they were imprisoned. Wilde's imagery deemphasizes
   the Greek myths and emphasizes instead the idea of
   pagan gods and creatures disappearing in the wake of
   Christ's arrival.
7. **Elias:** The Old Testament prophet Elijah. His return
   meant the restoration of Israel.
8. **basilisk:** Ancient king of the serpents whose gaze turns
   the living to stone. See also Isaiah 59:5.
9. **a little green flower:** One of Wilde's personal symbols and, as a green carnation, one of the symbols of
   French Decadence.
10. **ambassadors into Chaldea:** See Ezekiel 23.
11. **baldricks, incestuousness:** Baldricks are girdles.
    Herodias and the Tetrarch belong to the same very
    complicated family tree, and their marriage is incestu-
    ous on several levels. Herod the Tetrarch is the son of
    Herod the Great, who had ten wives. Herodias is
    Herod the Great's granddaughter and the Tetrarch's
    niece, daughter of his brother Aristobulus. In addition,
    she previously had been married to his half-brother
    Phillip, which was incest according to Old Testament
    laws. It was the report of the Tetrarch's incestuous
    marriage that first brought John the Baptist to his
    court. The theme of incest is further strengthened by

the Tetrarch's lust for Salomé, Herodias's daughter from a previous marriage to (according to some ancient historians) her stepbrother.

12. **Daughter of Sodom:** See Genesis 18 and 19. Sodom and Gomorrah were two cities destroyed by God for their immorality and faithlessness. The male citizens of Sodom were said to have raped a male angel sent by God, hence the term *sodomy*, referring to the "sin" of male homosexuality.

13. **vine trees of Edom ... Lebanon:** Neighboring kingdoms, as are Tyre and Moab, below. Salomé's descriptions of Jokanaan throughout resonate with the Song of Songs and a deliberate perversion of it.

14. **crown of thorns:** A prescient reference to Jesus's crucifixion.

15. **Stoics:** School of Greek and Roman philosophers. They were famous for their asceticism and strict moral fatalism.

16. **Messias:** The prophesied Messiah, here Christ. Contemporary Jews believe the Messiah is yet to come.

17. **water into wine ... two lepers:** John 2:1–10 and John 4:45–52. Luke 17:11–19 reports Jesus healing ten lepers. Matthew 20:30–34 tells of Jesus healing two blind men. Importantly, these acts linked him with Elijah, who also had healed the sick.

18. **Samaria:** The former capital of northern Israel, enemy territory for the Jews. While there, Jesus met a woman and, through her, converted the Samaritans. See John 4. Wilde's events either do not follow accepted biblical history or reflect the confused sense of rumor and future-present-past time shift in the presence of the prophet.

19. **restoration ... do they not?:** The Tetrarch's father, Herod the Great, had begun a great expansion of the second Temple, political and religious symbol and cen-

ter of the Jews. The Temple eventually would be destroyed by the Romans. The veil of the Sanctuary separates the holy inner sanctum from the inner temple.

20. **dance of the seven veils:** In most productions, the dance has been figured as a slow, sensuous strip tease, gaining in momentum to a frenzied climax as Salomé removes veil after veil.

21. **charger:** Platter.

Interpretive Notes

⚜

The Importance of Being Earnest

Plot

Two young men, the upright Jack and the hopeless dandy Algernon have improved their social lives with a few useful falsehoods, but as they fall in love, they quickly find themselves trapped in their own lies. The action moves from London to Jack's country house, where gentle mayhem and a send-up of romance and social conventions of all kinds ensue, ending in a surprising revelation about Jack's heritage.

Major Characters

Algernon (Algy) Moncrieff. A perfect dandy, Algernon is a beautiful, clever young bachelor brought up to be rich and useless but seemingly always lacking in money. He has an insatiable appetite and a wicked tongue.

John (Jack) Worthing, J.P. A wealthy bachelor trained in law with a country estate and an eighteen-year-old ward,

Cecily Cardew. While in town, he is a man of pleasure; while in the country, he is upstanding, even somewhat stiff.

Hon. Gwendolen Fairfax. Algy's cousin, a beautiful and clever young woman with an independent spirit and many firm, if curiously stated, views.

Cecily Cardew. Jack's ward. A beautiful, seemingly naive country girl, who is nevertheless fully capable of holding her own with Gwendolen. She possesses an active imagination and a rich fantasy life.

Lady Bracknell. Algy's aunt and Gwendolen's mother. A stern but fashionable woman with strong ideas about social propriety.

Miss Prism. Cecily's governess and author of a three-volume novel. Her stereotypical old-maid primness hides a romantic heart and a secret mistake.

Rev. Canon Chasuble, D.D. The amiable rector of Jack's country estate.

LADY WINDERMERE'S FAN

Plot

The moral conventions of the young Lady Windermere are challenged when she discovers her husband has been offering financial support to the mysterious and beautiful social adventuress Mrs. Erlynne. Feeling betrayed and tempted by the passionate avowals of another man, she nearly loses everything, only to be saved from the brink of ruin by her supposed enemy. Although her understanding of love and life is much improved, she never learns Mrs. Erlynne's poignant secret.

Major Characters

Lady Windermere. A young (twenty-one-year-old) new mother and wife, brought up to be just what she is—a gracious hostess and arbiter of taste and morals. She is well respected and careful of her reputation.

Lord Windermere. Lady Windermere's devoted husband, a man of wealth and taste, who is as upright as his wife but somewhat more experienced and forgiving.

Mrs. Erlynne. A woman of uncertain past who lives by her wits and charm. She looks, dresses, and only admits to being some ten years younger than her actual age.

Lord Darlington. One of a group of cynical dandies, men of wealth and leisure, he harbors a secret hopeless passion.

The Duchess of Berwick. Society personified. A gossipy, cynical matron all too ready to pass on her "wisdom" to Lady Windermere.

Lord Augustus Lorton. Dignified and wealthy, Lord Augustus is trusting and somewhat romantic. His cynical friends, especially Mr. Cecil Graham, make fun of him, but he ends up happy and in love.

An Ideal Husband

Plot

Lord and Lady Chiltern, a wealthy, well-respected couple of excellent taste and high morals, are thrown into crisis by the arrival of the beautiful, scheming Mrs. Cheveley from Vienna. Carrying a secret from Lord Chiltern's past, Mrs. Cheveley threatens to destroy the rising star of his political career with a terrible scandal. When Lord Chiltern reveals his secret to Lady Chiltern, she withdraws in horror. Meanwhile, the dandy philosopher Lord Goring, who has his own connections to Mrs. Cheveley, makes a series of sometimes successful efforts to prevent his friends from falling into tragedy. Just when everything seems as though it might be resolved, Mrs. Cheveley produces a fresh scheme to destroy the couple.

Major Characters

Sir Robert Chiltern. Handsome and young to hold his position as under-secretary for foreign affairs but headed toward the prime of his life, Sir Robert is morally upright but fiercely ambitious.

Lady Gertrude Chiltern. Beautiful and loving but severe and very English. She believes in her husband's moral exceptionality and works for progressive causes.

Mrs. Cheveley. Gorgeous in a thin, exotic, hothouse manner, Mrs. Cheveley is an expert in political matters and a world-class seductress. She loves money and power and is unafraid of scandal. She is, at this point in her life, more European than English.

Viscount Goring. Lord Goring is a devoted dandy who cultivates a false air of vacancy in order to maneuver better through his social scene. At heart, he is a philosopher, and a fairly conventional one at that.

Miss Mabel Chiltern. A vision of English roses beauty, Miss Mabel meets Lord Goring's witticisms with her own. She is Robert Chiltern's younger sister.

Earl of Caversham. Lord Goring's conservative, stereotypically old-English-gentleman father.

Lady Markby. An older woman, kindly and oblivious and therefore popular.

SALOMÉ

Plot

Drawn by the news of Herodias and Herod the Tetrarch's incestuous marriage, the prophet Jokanaan has come to admonish them for breaking Jewish law, and the Tetrarch has imprisoned him. On the night during which the play takes place, Herodias's virgin daughter, Salomé, deeply compelled by the prophet, is scorned and reprimanded by him, and a captain of the guard commits suicide on her behalf. While rumors of the Messiah and his miracles rush through the court, Salomé dances for her lustful stepfather, who has promised her anything she wants in exchange. She requests the head of the prophet on a platter.

Major Characters

Salomé. A beautiful virgin, nevertheless intensely sensual and passionately emotional. She is both an innocent and already corrupted by her birth and family lineage.

Herod. A powerful, lustful, sensual, cosmopolitan tyrant, Herod is nevertheless insecure and bows to both the Roman Empire and the holy power of Jokanaan, whom he imprisons but is afraid to kill. Son of Herod the Great.

Herodias. A cruel and beautiful princess who has shocked the Jewish kingdom with her several incestuous marriages. She keeps a sharp, manipulative eye on her husband. Granddaughter of Herod the Great.

Jokanaan. Prophet of Christ the Messiah and of doom for the Herod line. He is described as beautiful, gentle, terrible, and fascinating, and he speaks in lyric revelations.

The Four Plays: Themes and Symbols

The dandy, the adventuress, the aesthete, and their accoutrements

Frivolous buttonholes, silk hats and canes, rare fans, rich tapestries, heliotrope gowns, and fabulous (stolen) diamond brooches—Wilde's plays are filled with the exquisite objects of the aesthetic life, lived in celebration of beauty and sensation. The characters who wear, use, and steal these objects most successfully are themselves works of art, dandies and adventuresses dedicated to the power of what is beautiful and charming and to trading on that charm to survive and thrive in their high-society world. Wilde's dandies are those handsome, epigram-spouting spend-thrifts who seem to do nothing but who are crucial to the truth and action of his plots. Lord Goring—and, some claim, Mabel Chiltern—in *An Ideal Husband* and Algernon from *The Importance of Being Earnest* are classic dandies. Lord Darlington and his more cynical compatriots in *Lady Windermere's Fan* are another variant. His adventuresses are the series of "outsider women" who appear to trouble the domestic waters of his characters. They reach their apogee in Mrs. Cheveley, whose heart is not so evenly split between a desire for power and a desire for love, and who treats scandal as though it were another beautiful stolen brooch to wear. Mrs. Erlynne is another classic outsider, but one can see her in different forms. Gwendolen, for example, who travels to Jack's estate all alone without permission, and even the seemingly conformist Lady Chiltern, with her progressive political work, have the independence and strength of adventuresses.

The question of identity

False names, hidden secrets, masquerades, and fake or mistaken identities run throughout Wilde's plays. Turning the idea of a "true self" hidden within a "false self" inside out, Wilde insists on both the truth of posing and artifice. Thus, it is always the poseurs and the dandies who speak the truth in Wilde's play. Lord Goring's detachment and the fact that others constantly misunderstand him give him the room he needs to maneuver through the hypocrisies and doubleness of high society. Similarly, Algernon's insouciant nonsense places him slightly above and to the side of the events that cause Jack such distress and allow him just enough sangfroid to bear up under the revelation that he has been engaged to his true love (or so she tells him) for months before meeting her.

Wilde also insists on the deep links between the secret self and the public mask. In *The Importance of Being Earnest,* Jack's false identity turns out to be his true self, the one he didn't know about and would never have learned if he hadn't posed as Ernest in the first place. In *An Ideal Husband,* Sir Chiltern's secret sin of ambition is not the folly of his youth, as he initially claims, but merely the one facet of his fierce ambition of which society—and his wife, whose work in her progressive societies shows she has ambitions of her own—disapprove. (As he readily admits, Chiltern still believes in the gospel of power, even though he has used that power to the good.) In *Lady Windermere's Fan,* the hidden identity of Mrs. Erlynne remains hidden: her encounter with the selfless sacrifice of motherhood reveals to Mrs. Erlynne not that she was always meant to be a mother but that she cannot be one.

Morality, hypocrisy, and conformity

In spite—or perhaps because of—his devotion to beauty over truth, all of Wilde's plays, from the lighthearted shenanigans of *The Importance of Being Earnest* to the weird tragedy of *Salomé,* deal with the problem of morality. When is it all right to lie, and to whom? How does one get and maintain power? What is the importance of one's past and one's heritage? His characters ask us to question what constitutes a moral life, and especially to divine the differences between that life and social approval. Wilde's favorite target is the elaborate conventions of the upper classes, but he does not simply skewer them in favor of holding up the working class as the more noble and natural alternative (although Algernon does complain that his butler is not setting him a proper example). Instead, he stays within that glittering world, forcing his characters to face their hypocrisies and the price they pay to remain among their beautiful objects but allowing them to resolve their tensions in a series of audience-pleasing happy endings. For Wilde, it seems, the point is not to give up the world of society but to bend it to one's will.

Language, play, and truthful nonsense

Many of Wilde's most devoted readers have dismissed his plots as derivative and his characters as thin. Instead, they love his work for its "word music," or what Wilde's compatriot and critic Max Beerbohm called the "beautiful nonsense" spoken by his characters. In his plays, as in his life, it was the dizzying play of words that allowed Wilde to dwell in unresolved paradoxes, to be and mean more than one thing at a time, and to paint the world as it could be, rather than as it so dismally existed.

Some early reviewers complained of Wilde's epigram-encrusted dialogue, describing it as a kind of cheap trick, a fashion that, while currently popular, would soon annoy. Even some of the characters in Wilde's plays complain about the incessant cleverness of their dandies or, in *Salomé*, the relentlessness of the ornate language's high drama. Yet Wilde always comes down on the side of those who can turn a good phrase. In the comedies, his truth-telling characters are nearly always epigram-spouting dandies (like Wilde himself), who celebrate artifice but somehow manage to escape cynicism, often through falling in love. In *Salomé*, this role is taken on by the seemingly mad prophet, who speaks in lyric revelations.

CRITICAL EXCERPTS

⚜

Biographical Studies

Ellman, Richard. *Oscar Wilde*. New York: Alfred A. Knopf, 1988.

Ellman's Pulitzer-prize-winning biography is the result of more than twenty years of research. More exhaustive than the important but largely anecdotal 1946 biography by Hesketh Pearson and aided by the critically important 1962 publication of Wilde's letters (edited by Sir Rupert Hart-Davis), it is both scholarly and highly readable. Here, Ellman discusses Wilde's state of mind upon beginning work on *Salomé* in Paris.

Wilde seemed to obsess himself with his idea, and every day he talked of Salomé. The women on the streets seemed possible princesses of Israel to him. If he passed the rue de la Paix, he would examine the jewelry shops for proper adornment for her. One afternoon he asked, "Don't you think she would be better naked? Yes, totally naked, but draped with heavy and ringing necklaces made of jewels of every colour, warm with the fervor of her amber flesh . . ." He began to imagine Sarah Bernhardt dancing naked before the Teterarch.

Raby, Peter. *Oscar Wilde*. Cambridge: Cambridge University Press, 1988.

This is a compact (147 pages) introductory study of Wilde's life and works by a well-respected Wilde scholar. Part of the Cambridge University Press's introductory critical series on British and Irish authors.

The difficulty of placing the dandy satisfactorily within the dramatic context remained Wilde's most intractable aesthetic problem: it is the problem of "finding a world fit for the dandy to live in." . . . The dandy, like the Shakespearean fool . . . functions most effectively as commentator when unassimilated into, or at least distanced from, the action.

Early Reviews and Interpretations

Walkley, A. B. Review of *Lady Windermere's Fan*. Speaker, February 27, 1892.

Arthur Bingham Walkley was an admirer of Wilde's and a highly influential critic. His review, in which he disparages the play's plot and unity while celebrating its language and novelty, is typical of a strain of Wilde criticism that continues to the present day. Later, he was one of the few critics to recognize *The Importance of Being Earnest* as Wilde's best work.

It is by no means a good play: its plot is always thin, often stale; indeed it is full of faults—oh! dear, yes! glaring faults. . . . Yet, again, it *is* a good play, for it carries you along from start to finish without boring you for a single moment. While it is a-playing, it convinces you, in spite of yourself, that life is not monotonous. If we have had more sparkling dialogue on the stage in the present generation, I have not heard it. . . . The man or woman who does not chuckle with delight at the good things which abound in *Lady Windermere's Fan* should consult a physician at once: delay would be dangerous.

Douglas, Lord Alfred. Review of *Salomé. The Spirit Lamp*, May 1893.

Salomé was in production in 1892, with Sarah Bernhardt in the title role, when the play was shut down by England's Examiner of Plays, putatively for the heresy of portraying biblical characters on the stage. The play was published first in French and later in English translated by Douglas. In his review, Douglas defends the play against English notions of health and morality, as typified by the anonymous reviewer below.

I suppose the play is unhealthy, morbid, unwholesome and un-English, *ça va sans dire* [that goes without saying]. It is certainly un-English, because it is written in French, and therefore unwholesome to the average Englishman, who can't digest French. It is probably morbid and unhealthy, for there is no representation of quiet domestic life, nobody slaps anybody else on the back all through the play, and there is not a single reference to roast beef from one end of the dialogue to the other.

Unsigned review of *Salomé. The Times*, February 23, 1893.

The reviewer's summary of his repulsion typifies the anti-*Salomé* camp.

It is an arrangement in blood and ferocity, morbid, *bizarre*, repulsive, and very offensive in its adaptation of scriptural phraseology to situations the reverse of the sacred.

Archer, William. Review of *An Ideal Husband. Pall Mall Budget,* January 10, 1895.

Archer is, on the whole, delighted by the play, which, he writes, the audience "enjoyed very nearly as much as [Wilde] himself did," but he cannot resist pleading for fewer epigrams.

For Mr. Wilde's good things I have the keenest relish, but I wish he would imitate Beau Brummel in throwing aside his "failures," not exposing them to the public gaze. His peculiar twist of thought sometimes produces very quaint and pleasing results. To object to it as a mere trick would be quite unreasonable. Every writer of any individuality has, so to speak, his trademark; but there are times when the output of Mr. Wilde's epigram-factory threatens to become all trademark and no substance.

Shaw, George Bernard. Review of *The Importance of Being Earnest. Saturday Review,* February 23, 1895.

Shaw was, with Wilde, one of the great playwrights of his day. Although he was generally supportive of Wilde, he did not share Wilde's taste for artifice and paradox, believing instead that even comedies should deal seriously with political and social issues.

I cannot say that I greatly cared for *The Importance of Being Earnest.* It amused me of course; but unless comedy touches me as well as amuses me, it leaves me with a sense of having wasted my evening. I go to the theatre to be moved to laughter not to be tickled or bustled into it. . . . Now in *The Importance of Being Earnest* there is plenty of this rib-tickling. . . . These could only have been raised from the farcical plane by making them occur to characters who had, like Don Quixote, convinced us of their reality and obtained some hold on our sympathy.

Modern Critical Interpretations: 1940s–1960s

Bentley, Eric. *"The Importance of Being Earnest,"* in *The Playwright as Thinker.* New York: Reznal & Hitchcock, 1946.

Bentley's brief but trenchant analysis was one of the first to argue that Wilde's superficiality allowed him to make a pointed social critique.

Wilde is as much of a moralist as Bernard Shaw but . . . instead of presenting the problems of modern society directly, he flits around them, teasing them, declining to grapple with them. His wit is no searchlight into the darkness of modern life. It is a flickering, a coruscation, intermittently revealing the upper class of England in a harsh bizarre light. This upper class could feel about Shaw that at least he took them seriously, no one more so. But the outrageous Oscar (whom they took care to get rid of as they had got rid of Byron) refused to see the importance of being earnest.

Roditi, Edouard. *Oscar Wilde.* Norfolk, Conn.: New Directions Books, 1947.

Wilde's persona long overshadowed his work. Roditi's study, reprinted and enlarged in 1986, was an important step toward understanding his work's complexity. In "The Politics of the Dandy," Roditi considers Wilde's complex relationship to class and society and argues against previous charges of Wilde's escapism.

Algernon, in *The Importance of Being Earnest,* is clearly of no social use and prides himself on his irresponsibility; and when Bracknell remarks, in the same play, that if education produced any effect in England, which it fortunately does not, it would prove a serious danger to the upper classes, Wilde certainly does not intend to suggest that the proletariat should be kept ignorant, but rather that an educated upper class might develop an uneasy conscience instead of taking, as Lady Bracknell does, so many of its privileges for granted.

Auden, W. H. "An Improbable Life," *The New Yorker,* March 9, 1963.

Auden, an esteemed British critic and poet, wrote this essay in response to publication of Wilde's letters. In his remarks on Wilde's dramas, he argues that Wilde "was not a thinker" but "a verbal musician of the first order."

While "Salomé" could become a successful libretto, "Lady Windermere's Fan," "A Woman of No Importance," and "An Ideal Husband" could not, because their best and most original elements—the epigrams and comic nonsense—are not settable; at the same time, their melodramatic opera plots spoil them as spoken drama. But in "The Importance of Being Earnest," Wilde succeeded—almost, it would seem, by accident, for he never realized its infinite superiority to all his other plays—in writing what is perhaps the only pure verbal opera in English.

San Juan, Jr., Epifanio. "The Action of the Comedies," in *The Art of Oscar Wilde.* Princeton, N.J.: Princeton University Press, 1967.

In his remarks on Wilde's comedies, Epifanio argues that Wilde's genius lay in his ability to combine "the would-be serious subject, which often verges on sentimentality, with gay verbal with and paradox." In his extended readings of *Lady Windermere's Fan* and *An Ideal Husband*, he draws out some of Wilde's major themes.

Wilde presents the question of true identity in all his comedies. Who am I?—that is, how define the network of social relations that condition and ultimately determine my public image? How articulate the stream of consciousness, impulses, feelings, and intuitions whose center I am?

1970s–1980s

Shewan, Rodney. *Oscar Wilde: Art and Egotism.* London: Macmillan Press, 1977.

Shewan deliberately concentrates on Wilde's literary, rather than biographical, context. In "The Comedy of Manners: The Dandy's Progress," he traces Wilde's use of the dandy (which he considers both female and male) and the "adventuress" to turn his conventional forms into social and literary critique.

[The dandy] is he, or she, in whom intellect and emotion, "male" and "female" attitudes, ideal and real standards, individual and society are seen somehow, sometimes, to converge. The best of these agile spirits, who by "normal" standards are heartless, socially irresponsible, and self-centered, are by the terms of Wilde's comic characterization amused and enlightened skeptics, self-sufficient and healthily androgynous personalities. There is just a hint here, briefly expanded in *Earnest,* that "the real life" need not always be "the life we do not lead."

Gagnier, Regenia. *Idylls of the Marketplace: Oscar Wilde and the Victorian Public.* Stanford, Calif.: Stanford University Press, 1986.

Gagnier argues that Wilde's apparent contradictions can be understood only by understanding his Victorian audiences and that in this historical context, Wilde's aestheticism emerges as an engaged critique of "the middle-class drive to conform" and debates over "the place of art in a consumerist society."

To be commercially competitive and critical—or to marry and divorce art and life simultaneously—was the goal of Wilde's comedies. Wilde wanted freedom from authority for the imagination and human society to develop. With their glittering packaging, their pages and performances mirroring the spectator, their illustrations . . . Wilde's works give us both the images of advertising and the images of desire. In our analysis of art from the point of view of consumption, Wilde's works offer a site where the imagination—a romantic, indeed utopian, imagination—meets the marketplace that inevitably absorbs and transforms it.

Woodcock, George. *Oscar Wilde: The Double Image.* Montreal: Black Rose Books, 1989.

A reprint, with a new introduction, of Woodcock's pioneering 1949 study, *The Paradox of Oscar Wilde,* which examines Wilde's intellectual lineage and agendas. Its continued relevance points to the persistence with which critics have been baffled by Wilde's doubleness and his apparent contradictions.

Wilde, from whatever aspect we observe him, appears as a man of continual variety and contradiction. On the surface he is all movement and change, shifting fitfully from one mood to another, dispensing an iridescence so patently superficial that those who have never taken the trouble to penetrate below the surface dismiss him as an obvious charlatan. But beneath the glittering ripples there are depths of thought and feeling, stirred by conflicts rising from the same basic impulse towards personal realization. Thus it is that, among those who knew Wilde personally and also among those who have encountered him only in his writings and his legend, there seems an almost irreconcilable divergence of attitudes.

1990s and later

Coakley, Davis. *Oscar Wilde: The Importance of Being Irish.* Dublin: Town House and Country House, 1994.

Drawing on archival materials, Coakley assembles a narrative of Wilde's "Irish years" and argues for their formative influence on his later life and works.

Oscar's tutor at Trinity College, John Pentland Mahaffy, described wit in Irish society as a kind of social religion, with rules that demanded spontaneity, and anyone suspected of rehearsing beforehand would be ridiculed. "There is no doubt," wrote the novelist and academic

Walter Starkie, "that the brilliant epigrams in *Intentions*, *Lady Windermere's Fan*, and *The Importance of Being Earnest* sprang up naturally in the mind of one who was brought up in the atmosphere of Dublin in the days when Irish Society was unrivalled for its spontaneous wit. (Webb, D. A., ed., *Of One Company*. Dublin: Icarus, 1951.)

Varty, Anne. *A Preface to Oscar Wilde*. New York: Addison Wesley Longman, 1998.

This is a dense and insightful critical overview of Wilde's life, philosophy, and works. In her chapter "Salomé, *Salomé*, and Symbolist Theatre," Varty places Wilde's play in the context of the French Symbolist movement, in which objects and colors became links to "larger cosmic forces," and discusses its connection to his comedies and the scandals surrounding its attempted British production and subsequent publication with censored illustrations by Aubrey Beardsley.

Wilde's *fin de siècle* was an age when, as Pater's *Renaissance* and Ibsen's *Ghosts* proclaimed in their different ways, the dead would not stay dead. The *avant-garde* projected an age of artistic rebirth and rejuvenation, when everything from woman to journalism was "new," yet it was painfully aware of an inherited burden from the momentous century it concluded. The material of the Salomé legend therefore focuses on the moment of poise before the old sectarian confusions could be swept aside and the new century ushered in.

Beckson, Karl. "Oscar Wilde and the Importance of Not Being Earnest," in *Oscar Wilde: The Man, His Writings and His World*, Robert Keane ed. New York: AMS Press, 2003.

Written on the occasion of his keynote speech for a centenary celebration of Wilde's work, Beckson, a long-renowned Wilde expert, gives a pithy survey of Wilde's life and works, tracing the importance of paradox, artifice, and aestheticism to Wilde throughout.

When, within a month of the opening of *An Ideal Husband,* Wilde's most original achievement, *The Importance of Being Earnest,* reached the stage, one wonders whether Wilde deliberately chose the play's title to confound some drama critics who had complained of his lack of earnestness and sincerity. In *Dorian Gray* and in his critical essay, "The Critic as Artist," Wilde had written that insincerity was merely "a method by which we can multiply our personalities." Like Nietzsche and Emerson, Wilde believed that insincerity, by means of the mask, was essential to the creative artist. Hence, Wilde asserted: "Man is least himself when he talks in his own person. Give him a mask, and he will tell you the truth."

QUESTIONS FOR DISCUSSION

In *An Ideal Husband,* the dandy Lord Goring makes several earnest speeches about love that surprise the other characters in the play (Lady Chiltern remarks that she has never seen him be so serious, and Mabel seems alarmed at his attempt to make a serious romantic speech). Why do you think Wilde has Goring make these speeches? Can one be a dandy and still believe in committed love?

Many of Wilde's critics—including, at times, Wilde himself—have denigrated the plots and even the characters of his plays as flat, stale, or simply unoriginal. Instead, they argue, the plays exist simply to showcase Wilde's genius for sparkling, witty dialogue and its philosophical insights. Do you agree with this assessment? Is it more or less true of *The Importance of Being Earnest,* for example, than of *Lady Windermere's Fan* or *An Ideal Husband*?

In *The Importance of Being Earnest,* the plot turns on the discovery of Jack's heretofore unknown heritage. How does the question of knowing who one is come up in the rest of the play?

Wilde felt that the final act of *Lady Windermere's Fan,* in which Mrs. Erlynne claims that she cannot suddenly become a mother, was the most shocking psychological revelation in the play. How did you interpret Mrs. Erlynne's declaration? How are mothers portrayed in the play?

Many big-budget Hollywood-type films have been made of Wilde's plays, some quite recently. Why do you think studio heads might be willing to invest in Wilde's plays? What is their appeal to a contemporary audience?

Salomé is radically different from Wilde's social comedies. Do you see any links among their themes, characters, and language? Why might Wilde have wanted to write both kinds of plays?

Salomé was banned from the English stage for portraying biblical characters. How do you feel about the play as a Bible story? Is it religious or sacrilegious? How does it compare to more recent controversial portrayals of stories from the Bible, such as Mel Gibson's *The Passion of the Christ* or Martin Scorsese's *The Last Temptation of Christ*?

Wilde's flamboyant persona, his scandalous personal life, and the trials that led to his tragically early death often have overshadowed his work. Do you see any value in learning about Wilde's life as a way of understanding his plays? How does it add to or detract from your understanding of them?

SUGGESTIONS FOR THE INTERESTED READER

If you enjoyed *The Importance of Being Earnest and Other Plays*, you also might be interested in the following:

The Importance of Being Earnest (DVD, VHS). This classic 1952 film version of *Earnest* is justly famous for Dame Edith Evans's portrayal of Lady Bracknell alongside Michael Redgrave's Jack Worthing. A more recent version was released in 2002, directed by Oliver Parker with a distinctly Wildean Rupert Everett as Algy, Reese Witherspon as Cecily, and Judi Dench taking over the role of Lady Bracknell.

An Ideal Husband (DVD, VHS). This lively, glossy 1999 version of the play places Lord Goring (Rupert Everett) squarely at the center of the show. Cate Blanchett is Lady Chiltern, Julianne Moore is Mrs. Cheveley, and a sassy Minnie Driver is Mabel Chiltern.

A Handful of Dust and *Vile Bodies,* by Evelyn Waugh. These two novels of the 1930s were written by satiric and comedic master Evelyn Waugh, who is every bit as funny as Wilde. Waugh examines the lives of the smart, rich, young set of post-World War I London. *Vile Bodies* was adapted for film as *Bright Young Things* in 2004.

Life with Jeeves, by P. G. Wodehouse. A collection of three very funny works by Wodehouse, detailing the adventures of Bertie Wooster, a bumbling young English gentleman, and Jeeves, his wise and patient valet. A series of acclaimed television adaptations of Wodehouse's stories, starring Hugh Laurie as Wooster and Stephen Fry as Jeeves, was made in the 1990s.

Selected Poetry and Prose, by Stéphane Mallarmé. Nineteenth-century Symbolist poet Mallarmé was highly influential. His prose poem *Herodiade,* about Salomé and John the Baptist, clearly inspired Wilde's own *Salomé.*

FROM SIMON & SCHUSTER

**SIMON & SCHUSTER
PAPERBACKS**
A CBS COMPANY